FITTING THEM ALL IN

THE COMPLETE COLLECTION OF EXTREMELY EXPLICIT EROTIC HARDCORE TABOO SEX HOTTEST STORIES FOR ADULTS

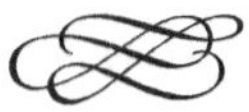

TINA HUDSON

CONTENTS

STRAY

I had just parked my truck, which sometimes can be not exactly an easy thing to do. It took me at least a half dozen trips around the parking lot looking for a space large enough.

That is because it is a huge Dodge crew cab, oversize duallies on the back that sort of stick out.

Yep, she needs a bit of room.

I opened the door and had just put my foot on the running board to step down, being careful to not let the door scrape the top of the little thing parked in the next lane.

If it had been a couple of inches shorter my door would have cleared the top of it, I swear.

It was at that moment that I heard a scream.

Looking over, about four rows down I could see a fairly large he was in some kind of a rage.

Scruffy short beard, stringy hair, I saw he had on a Levi vest over a dirty T-shirt, and he had one balled up fist drawn back.

Then he swung, that was when I realized he had his out stretched arm holding someone and was hitting the person with the other.

The next realization was that it was a small woman.

I am Dan, I am 62 years old so I don't go around getting into scuffles, but every once in a long time a scuffle comes my way.

"Hey!" I yelled, just as the guy drew back to belt her again. She was screaming loudly, a tangle of noises that were not any words I could understand. All I could see of her was the long dark hair as she was bent over, her arms flailing in a vain attempt to protect herself.

The guy didn't even look my way.

"HEY! Knock that shit off!" I yelled even louder.

He hit her again and it was not gentle at all. That pissed me off, the jerk was at least twice the woman's size.

I reached back into the cab, grabbed my little .22 caliber 9 shot Hi-standard pistol I carry everywhere I go. It is strapped to the front of my seat within easy reach, I have a permit for it in my wallet.

In all the years I carried that with me in my vehicles, not one time had I ever taken it out except out in the woods shooting at cans, or down at the gun range down the coast a few miles.

Cans don't stand a chance with me, I can pop one at 30 feet from the hip about 90% of the time.

That sounds easy, try it sometime. I buy ammo by the thousand round case, and probably have run 5-6 cases through the tool just practicing.

By the time my feet hit the ground the guy was flailing at the woman who by now had torn loose somehow and was trying to get away. But he had grabbed her by her blouse and was swinging at the back of her head as she tried to cover up. I saw he was missing her more than managing to connect, she was moving back and forth pretty good, and trying her best to swing back.

He didn't appear to notice me when I came around the rear of the parked car they were beside.

"I said knock that shit off!" I yelled again.

"Mind your own fucking business, pops!" He snarled, connecting that time and putting the woman on the ground.

I pointed the pistol at him.

He looked down, when that registered on him he came to a stop.

"What the fuck are you going to do, dickhead? Shoot me?" He snarled but his expression was changing.

"Yes." I said, cocking the pistol.

I don't have to cock the pistol to fire it since the tool has a double action, but there is a certain emphasis to a hammer coming back with a click that lends pause to people.

Now I never had actually pointed a gun at anyone before, but from what I hear that click makes most folks a bit more polite.

We looked at each other for a few seconds, I could see what he was thinking but I was a good six to eight feet away and I was going to get at least two hollow point rounds into him before he got to me.

Plus I might be 62 years old but I am a big man and in shape, and while I might not be able to handle any long dragged out fight, by God I was going to do one hell of a lot of damage in the perhaps sixty seconds I could manage.

"Fuck it! The bitch ain't worth it." He snarled, regaining some of his composure. I could tell that I had rattled him.

"Walk away." I said flatly.

He glared at me, trying for a bit of bravado, but he turned and walked to a nearby dirty green van and got in. I watched him all the way, he spun the tires as he left.

I uncocked the little pistol and stuck it in my belt, then turned to the woman. She was sitting on the pavement, her face in her hands.

"Are you OK?" I asked her. She tipped her head up and looked at me. Her face was red and puffy, her lip swollen and I could tell she was going to have one hell of a black eye.

Her blouse was ripped open, she had on a simple white bra. Looking down, she saw that and pulled the torn material back together.

"Come on, I have a first aid kit in my truck." I told her, reaching for her hand. She looked at my hand for a moment, then took it and I helped her to her feet.

Back at my truck, I used the alcohol swabs on the abrasions, she winced a bit but didn't protest. I didn't see any real cuts anywhere but the guy had landed several pretty hard blows from the looks of things.

"I better get you to a hospital, get you checked out, miss." I said.

"No! The last time Duke did this we both ended up in jail." She wailed.

"Maybe you had best stay away from that guy?" I offered.

"I was trying to, but he just keeps coming after me. I don't know what to do!" She wailed, then the tears came.

Suddenly she grabbed me and hugged me so tightly I almost couldn't breathe. That I didn't expect, finally she let go.

"I'm sorry, I didn't mean…I just…" Her face flushed.

I opened the door to my truck, pulled the pistol out of my belt, flipped out the chamber and spun the cylinder around so the hammer rested on an empty one. I dropped it back into my holster by the front seat.

"Can I take you somewhere?" I asked her.

"I don't have any place to go, I was staying with my sister but she got fed up with Duke coming by all the time and she has kids so I guess it was a hassle and besides she was afraid of him so I had to leave and then as I was coming here to maybe get something to eat Duke showed up and...."

That poured out of her in a jumble of words.

"Whoa! Slow down!" I managed barely to not laugh, she was beginning to relax.

"Parents, friends, maybe a relative here I could take you to?"

"Just my sister. I have an aunt but she lives in Chicago. Mom passed away last year and I don't have a dad."

"Do you have any money? Maybe get a motel room or something?" I asked her.

"I have six dollars. My brother Joe lives in Chicago too."

Chicago was one hell of a long ways from the Oregon coast.

Then I made a decision.

"Come on, I will take you to my place, you can clean up and I have some clothes there that I think will fit you OK."

"Oh, thank you. Can I maybe stop and get some food? I haven't had anything since last night." She asked.

"Sure, no problem. I have food at home, I can whip up something." I opened the door on the passenger side. She looked at the running boards and up at the seat with hesitation, then climbed up and into my rig.

"Wow, this is big!" She said, looking around.

"Yea, if anybody ever runs into me I still get to go home." I made the wisecrack I had perhaps made several dozen times to others that commented on my truck.

"Dang, Dan, yer supporting Soudy Araby all by yerself!" I bet I have heard that or similar a hundred times down at the tavern I go to.

That's a great bunch of guys down there, most of them old coots getting long in the tooth like me.

They tease me about my tires, too. I have 18″ split rims with 8 ply tires on her, I hate flats.

And sure, it uses a lot of Diesel but I only drive it maybe 150 miles a month and it's paid for, what the hell. I never was able to get comfortable in any normal vehicle, not with my 6'2″ and 240 pound frame.

I had some lunch meat and bread at the house, so I made a sandwich for her. She ate it in about 5 bites, I could tell she was very hungry. I found my last can of Pepsi and handed it to her, she drank half of it without stopping.

"Thank you sir, I really appreciate this. You saved me, you are a hero." She actually smiled for the first time.

"I am no hero. By the way, my name is Dan."

"You are to me! My name is Melinda but everyone calls me Billie." She stuck out her hand.

"Well, pleased to meet you, I wish it was under better circumstances." I told her.

Then I went in and got some wash cloths, and a small bandage and ointment, she had one scrape on the side of her neck I hadn't noticed.

She sat there in a chair holding her torn blouse together as I quickly tended to the wound. As I finished, I glanced at her and her eyes were closing, then she had dozed off.

I went and got a blanket, slipped it over her as she lay back in my easy chair and slept.

I took the moment to look her over. Billie was on the skinny side, I had noticed that. Her dark hair was long and straight, she had a rather pretty face. I would guess her to be perhaps in her mid to late twenties, no more than that.

I figured I would just let her rest. I went into the kitchen and put away the cake batter I had been making when I ran out of eggs. That was why I was at the store in the first place, I just wanted a dozen eggs. Maybe some milk and I was thinking of getting one of those five quart tubs of ice cream. With the fuss, I didn't even get the eggs.

Then I went out to my truck, unlocked it and retrieved my pistol, took it inside and locked it up in my gun case with my old model 1894 Winchester and my nice LC Smith 16 gauge hammer less shotgun. I also keep my Marlin and my little .22 caliber auto loader in there, it has a hundred round canister on it, wicked looking thing.

I am always very careful with firearms, I like them but never leave them laying around. Even leaving my pistol in my truck for about a half hour is way out of character for me.

In my bedroom, I found a plain white blouse that my wife Marie had. I came back out with it just as Billie opened her eyes.

"Oh, thank you!" She took the blouse and looked at me. I understood that, so I turned my back. There was a rustle of clothing.

Turning around, I could see my guess was right, Billie was about the same size are Marie was.

"So where is your wife?" She asked me.

"Gone. I lost her about 4 years ago."

"Oh, I am sorry." She looked slightly uncomfortable.

"Me, too. Marie was a fine woman."

The uncomfortable moment passed quickly and I was wondering what I was going to do with this woman. Sure, I had lots of room, my house has three bedrooms but Billie was a total stranger to me.

"May I take a shower?" She asked me, breaking my thoughts.

"Sure, go ahead." I told her. Billie went into the bathroom, I went into my living room and clicked on the TV. It wasn't five minutes and I heard the door crack open.

"Sir?" She asked.

"Something I can get you?"

"I have a bruise. It's on my leg. Can you please take a look?" The expression on her face told me instantly that something had her upset.

"Sure." I got up and went in, she had one of my big bath towels wrapped around herself. She reached down and lifted the bottom of the towel, I looked down.

She had a bruise that was the size of a football, it was so swollen and filled with blood that it was actually frightening.

"Good lord!" I said.

"I didn't even notice it until I got undressed, now it tingles and hurts."

The swollen mass hung down almost like a sack.

"No choice now Billie, we need to get you to a hospital." I told her.

I stepped out as she got dressed, then I helped her to my truck. She now had an obvious limp.

The wait at the emergency room was about an hour, I was fuming by the time they took her inside. I am not sure why, concerned for her I guess.

Finally a man came out and told me what they had found, and he explained that she would need full bed rest for several days. He mentioned some bruises on her back also, I didn't know about those.

"We gave her some medication to help prevent any blood clots, that injury is very bad. It might be best if we keep her here overnight." Then he handed me some paperwork.

"I only met the lady today, I am just trying to help her, we aren't related." I told him, handing the forms back. I could see the exasperated expression on his face and understood as he retrieved the paperwork.

No way did Billie have insurance, which meant they probably were not going to get paid.

He left, in a few minutes he came back and told me they were going to release her to me.

Great. Now I not only had a stranger to deal with, but an injured one at that.

They wheeled her out, I helped her to the truck, reaching down to actually lift her up and in.

I was back to the driver's side when I sensed something and leaned sideways just as a fist went by my head.

It was Duke.

My pistol was safely locked up in the gun case at home, in my haste to get Billie checked out I had left it there.

Then he was on me. The guy was strong, I have to give him that, but he must have thought he was going to mess up an old man with ease.

It didn't work out quite that way, I jammed my fingers into his face, catching both eyes and his nose with the flat of my palm. That tipped his head right back, just as it came forward again my elbow hit him in the throat. At the same time I brought up a knee, got him dead square.

I still remembered a few things I had learned in my Navy days.

I don't think he even knew what had happened, he went down like a stone.

Mad as hell now, I reached down and dragged him across the parking lot by his hair, up the short handicap ramp and inside the doors, dropping him in a heap on the floor.

A nurse looked at me in surprise.

"Here is another one for you." I told her, then I turned and walked back to my truck.

Billie's eyes were as big as silver dollars, I didn't say a single word all the way to my house and she didn't either.

For the next several days I cared for her, telling her she had to stay in bed. I had no real idea how I ended up with what was basically like a stray puppy dog showing up on my doorstep but that is what had happened.

The good part was that she healed very quickly, since she did have youth on her side. The huge blood bruise got smaller, her leg turned to a dark purple color, then that faded to pink.

Checking that was mildly intimate, I noticed the underwear she had on was getting a little bit over used and she had absolutely nothing else.

One of my T-shirts made a pretty good sack dress and I gave her a few more of Marie's tops which fit her nicely.

At one point I went down to a clothing store after carefully locking my door and taking my pistol with me.

I had to ask the saleslady for some simple white panties, she smiled as she selected and sold me a half dozen pair of them.

That was the first time in my life I ever purchased any woman's undergarments and I hope I never have to again.

Billie got used to me, so seeing her in her panties while I checked her injury was nothing. She could walk so at least I didn't need to help her in and out of the shower.

By the end of the second week she was up and around. One thing I did notice, she began to clean things, and let's face it. I am a male, and normally live alone. This means everything has it's place, which is where it happens to be at the moment.

After 43 years of living with one woman a man gets used to them doing what they do while we do what we do.

Suddenly I had a maid, and also a cook. We had some great fun cooking together though.

I came in from the garage one day to find her sorting out clothes, the washing machine running.

I guess I got used to having Billie there.

The other good part was there was no sign of that Duke guy at all, and I had no idea what happened to him. I really didn't care, plus I figured he had no idea of where I lived anyway.

Maybe he just got the message? I never did figure out how he found us in the hospital parking lot unless he just realized I might take her there.

Yea. I found I got used to Billie living there, and I guess I have to admit I liked it.

So it came as a shock when she told me she was all healed up and it was time for her to go. I was at the point where I didn't really want her to leave.

What was I supposed to say? Hell, 62 years old, what does an old man have to offer a 26 year old on the pretty side young woman, anyway?

The truth?

Nothing. Nothing at all, it's just the way of life.

Money, comfort perhaps? Yea, I had a dab of capital, enough but I was far from rich. Sex, maybe? The other truth is that never once crossed my mind, Billie became a friend if that makes sense.

I still had an interest, but the females I saw that might be someone I would enjoy all looked at me like I was grandpa. That is just the way things are, most men like young women, women seem to like young virile men.

So there were no naked breasts, Billie always had a bra on. I did see her in her white cotton panties but that was just to check her leg, the Doctor had explained what to watch for. There was never any sign of any problems, though, she healed up normally and very quickly.

There was one thing that happened, I picked up my razor to shave and realized she had borrowed it. Now I am not completely sure just what she shaved with it but I rinsed it out and changed the blade.

Yea, I got a bit of a laugh to myself about that one but I never mentioned it.

Another time I heard some quiet noises in the bathroom, and I knew what she was doing. I just went into the living room and turned on the TV.

"Well. I understand, but I have to say I do enjoy having you around." I answered when she told me she was ready to move on.

"Really? I figured I was just in the way, I really do appreciate you helping me and being so nice to me." She smiled. I had come to like that smile, a pretty and happy face sure can light up an old man's life.

"So where will you go?" I asked her.

"My brother in Chicago, he said I could live there with him until I get a job and get back on my feet. We get along good, and I can help him with the expenses once I find something."

"OK. That sounds like it might work OK."

"I have never been to Chicago, it seems so far away." Billie got a sad expression on her face.

"As soon as I make some money I will pay you back, too." She said.

"Billie, you don't owe me anything, you have been fun to have around."

She hugged me, her eyes got damp so she turned her face away.

I had a spare suitcase, and lots of Marie's clothes. No point in keeping them around, I had had plans on gathering them up and taking them to Goodwill anyway.

Down at the bus station, I sat with her until it arrived.

Billie turned to me and hugged me again, then she tipped her head up for a kiss. I leaned down and gave her one, that was nice. It had been a long time since I had kissed a woman, she felt pretty good in my arms.

"You should have done that earlier." She grinned at me, then there was a hiss of air as the driver impatiently worked the brakes, so she got on. I watched until she was gone out of sight.

My house seemed empty, by late afternoon I couldn't stand it so I walked down to the tavern. I hadn't been there the entire time Billie had stayed with me.

Several of my friends were there like always, they were asking where I had been. One of them popped up with the idea I had probably been shacked up with some broad, plus the usual wisecracks about my truck.

I shot some pool, had a few drinks, flirted mercilessly with Jenny, the barmaid who of course could give as good as she got. I had actually given her a couple of my best shots but she was all bluff and tease. She showed a lot of cleavage to the guys but never did anything with any of them, me included. It all felt rather normal and later I went home and went to bed.

A few weeks went by, then my phone bill arrived. There was one long distance call on there I didn't recognize, so I turned on my computer that mostly sat gathering dust against the wall.

I Googled the number, it came up as Chicago.

"Oh! Billie's brother, of course." I said out loud to myself.

What the hell. I reached for the phone, punched in the number.

A man's voice answered, I asked to speak to Billie.

"Who's calling?" The man asked. I told him who I was.

"OK. You are the guy she talks about all the time. Just making sure you aren't her asshole boyfriend. Billie is at work, I will tell her you called, OK?"

"OK, thanks." I hung up. At least I knew she was all right, and apparently she had found a job.

I dozed off in my chair that evening, it seemed I did that quite a bit the last few years, although oddly I never did while Billie was staying with me.

I woke up with a start, my phone was ringing.

"Danny! How are you? Joe told me you called, I am glad."

"I'm fine, I just wanted to know how you were doing." I glanced at my watch, it was 12:45 in the morning? What time was it in Chicago, two hours, three later? I wasn't sure about that.

"So where are you working?" I asked her. The line was quiet for a little bit.

"I...I am dancing, it's all I could find." She admitted.

"Dancing? I didn't know you were a dancer." I said. That didn't register on me, I was thinking in some show or chorus line.

"I worked some of the clubs before I met you, it's easy work to get." She said.

I got it then. That meant she was up there...naked.

"Oh. I don't think I want you to be doing that." I blurted out without thinking as it hit me what kind of dancing she meant. Somehow I just could not picture her up on a stage nude in front of strange men.

"I had to, things are expensive here. I need to pay Joe $900 a month for half the rent, and there are things I need."

I sighed, not liking that one bit but it was none of my business. We chatted for awhile easily like it had been when she was here.

"Hopefully one of these days you will meet some nice guy and settle down." I told her.

"I would like that, if I could find one like you!" She laughed.

"Like me? I am an old man, you need someone your own age." I said.

"Yea sure. So far all I find is guys that are drunk all the time or chasing after some other woman the instant I am out of sight, you are the only real man I ever met."

I guess I have to say that made me feel pretty good, and a couple of ideas popped into my old head. Hell, Billie had been right here, in my house. Right there in the other room, perhaps all I would have needed to do….?

"You are like the Daddy I never had!" She added, then she sounded like she was crying.

That stopped the silly fantasy that had slipped into my mind, though. We finished the conversation and finally hung up.

I did some of that tossing and turning that night.

Phone calls became a regular event after that, at least once a week we talked, sometimes even more.

That became something I really looked forward to, it filled one of the holes in my life.

Then when she called one day a few months later, she was excited. She told me all about a man she had met, and how good he was to her. His name was Ray and he ran a company, they had only had a few dates but I could tell that she was thinking seriously about him.

The conversations after that were mostly about Ray did this and Ray wanted that. She sounded happy which made me feel good. I knew the end of our odd relationship was coming, but since she sounded like everything was going well, I was happy for her.

When I came in from one of my regular trips to the local tavern and saw my message machine light flashing, I knew it was from Billie. I had just finished playing the message when the phone rang.

"Yes, I would love to." I told her when she asked me to be the one to walk her down the aisle.

* * *

That is how I found myself getting off an airplane in Chicago. I spotted Billie right off, she squealed and piled into my arms. She had put on some weight, filled out. She looked so beautiful it almost brought tears to my eyes.

Then she introduced me to Ray, a tall good looking young man.

I had planned on staying at a local hotel but he would not hear of that, instead I found myself being put up at what was a rather large condo.

The place was very large, and Ray actually had two middle aged women working for him as housekeeping staff, another that ran the kitchen.

I wasn't real sure exactly what he did but it was obvious he was doing well.

We did find time to talk quite a bit, I couldn't help but like the man. He was relaxed and easy to talk to, and it was clear that he was hopelessly in love with Billie. Plus Billie was happy, happier than I had ever seen her.

Her brother Joe stopped by, he was a quiet rather studious acting guy. I was thinking from looking at the two of them that some genes got crossed up in there somewhere, they were nothing alike.

But there wasn't much time to visit, dwell on anything.

Big weddings are mayhem, things were going on all over the place so I did my very best to stay out of the way. I was sitting in the main living room killing time watching TV when a woman in her fifties walked in.

She was absolutely beautiful.

"You must be Dan, I sure have heard a lot about you." She said as she walked up to me. I got up.

"I'm Carol, I am Ray's mother." She told me as we shook hands.

"Billie told me you were a pretty good looking guy, I see she was right." She grinned at me, making me blush slightly. Then she sat down in a chair and we talked quite a bit.

It was one of those cases where meeting someone and clicking with them instantly occurs. I don't know the why of it but I think everyone has it happen once in awhile.

I told her a bit about my life, she told me some of hers. Her husband had passed away, her son had taken over the company and it was doing well.

I found myself liking Carol very much, there was something about her that was real, she put on no airs at all which belied her rather expensive looking appearance.

The next day I walked down an aisle to give away a young lady that was not my daughter but felt like one somehow. That by itself was amazing, I never had a daughter of my own but it sure felt like I did now.

At one point I glanced over at Carol to find her looking at me, she smiled and one hand came up to brush at her hair, then she turned back to the ceremony.

Later at the reception, I sat by her as everyone had a good time. I asked her to dance, even though my feet can barely manage to do it, she felt like a feather.

Hell, I didn't even step on her, not once.

Carol was right beside me as we laughingly threw rice, Billie I noticed had kept looking our way at the party. She had grinned at me and raised an eyebrow, I grinned right back.

I did notice that as they prepared to leave, Carol reached down and took my hand. I gave it a little squeeze, getting a smile for my reward from her.

Then Billie and Ray were in a big car, and it was over. Carol turned to me, stood on tiptoe and gave me a quick peck on the lips. Then she let go of my hand. We looked at each other for a few long seconds, I felt a familiar stirring at that.

I had a feeling that I would be calling her from time to time, Carol was a very nice looking and interesting woman.

* * *

I had a flight scheduled out the next day so I got my bag packed, ready to go. There was only Carol and I, and the three people on staff left at the condo.

Carol came in and sat down, she looked completely different than I had seen her before. Dressed in a T-shirt and blue jeans, she no longer looked like the expensive type woman she had appeared to be before. Her face had a fresh scrubbed look, she wore no makeup at all.

"You know, Dan? I never expected my son to fall for a woman like Billie, but I have to say I am sure glad he did."

"Yes, I am happy for her, Ray really seems to love her and it is obvious that she loves him."

"You two seem very close. Billie talks about you all the time." She said.

"That was one of those accidents of life." I told her. Then I explained how we had met, leaving out nothing. I got the feeling that she had heard it all already.

"Did you two ever..you know..make love?" She asked, bluntly.

"No. I guess it never really crossed my mind."

Carol laughed at that.

"I didn't think so, but from the way Billie talks I know she loves you. Anyway. So my son was hanging out in a strip club, and he picks up one that he ended up keeping." She grinned.

"Well, I guess so." I said. Carol didn't really sound upset but I wondered what she was getting at.

"She is very pretty, and in today's world I guess he got to check out the goods before hand." She giggled.

I had to laugh at that one.

"When I met my late husband Jim, you will never guess where?" She smiled.

I just looked at her.

"All I had on was a tiny little G-string and some pasties."

I broke up laughing again, it certainly explained why she wasn't too upset at her son's choice of a woman.

"When I was a young girl I could shake them pretty good!" She let out a giggle, looking at me sideways for a reaction.

Damn was this one right up front female.

"I have to admit that brings quite a vision into my mind." I smiled at her, chuckling.

"I certainly hope so." She was looking right at me.

We sat there looking at each other for what seemed like several minutes but was probably only a few seconds. Then her hand slid over slowly and covered the back of my hand.

Sometimes there are no need for words, it was one of those moments. She slid over and we kissed, when we finally broke for air, I looked around.

The staff had all vanished.

"Would you like to come to my room?" She asked quietly.

"I would like to very much." I told her.

"It's been over four years, so if I seem a little hesitant…?" She said.

"About the same for me here." I answered. Carol so far had not seemed to be the least bit hesitant.

"Come on!" She reached out and tugged on my hand.

* * *

I sat on the edge of her bed and watched as she tugged the T-shirt over her head. Then she unfastened the jeans and slid them off, standing there in just a semi sheer sports bra and small white panties. Her belly was flat, her hips flared out nicely. Carol was full in the bust with just a hint of a sag, her dark nipples showed clearly through the thin bra. It was clear she did not shave from the bulge of pubic hair I could discern through her panties.

Then she shook her upper body, causing her breasts to jiggle delightfully. She rotated her hips in what was almost an obscene manner.

I felt my lower body flush with blood at that.

"Well?" She asked with a grin, almost posing.

"I can see how you caught your husband." I laughed.

"Stand up!" She told me, suddenly serious, so I did as she dropped to her knees. Her hands went to the catch in my slacks, she undid them and slid them down my legs. She lifted first one leg, then the other, removing my shoes which she flipped over her shoulder. The way she did that was hilarious. My socks came off next, then my pants.

As her hands went to my briefs, she had a small struggle getting them off because by then I was fully erect.

"Damn!" She exclaimed, both hands coming up to cradle my groin. She was looking at my 8″ erection with fascination, then her fingers wrapped around it and she was holding me by the shaft.

Her hands slid upwards, she squeezed slightly, sending shivers through me as she tugged, causing my foreskin to roll back.

"There it is!" She exclaimed, nearly causing me to explode right then.

I reached out and picked her up, sat her on the bed. I tripped her bra, watching as her breasts swung free. Then I slid her panties off as she lifted first one hip, then the other to help me.

My hands slipped up to her breasts, they felt silky smooth and were obviously real. Her nipples puckered up as I tickled first one, then the other with my fingertips.

I felt her hand reach down to fondle me as I slid my own between her legs. Carol opened them easily, allowing me full access. She was already flooded with moisture in anticipation.

Everything became a blur after that, our bodies slid together like they had been made for each other.

At one point she was on top of me, her hands pressing on my shoulders as she thrust at me with her eyes closed.

"God it's been so long!" Escaped her lips as her body shook in climax.

"Now that was one hell of a lot of fun!" She told me later as we lay there in each others arms.

"You just seduced me!" I accused her.

"Damn right I did. Billie spent so much time telling me what a hunk you were that I wanted to before I even met you!" She giggled.

"Me? A hunk? Hell, if I had known she thought that….?" I teased.

"Don't you even think about it." She growled, reaching down and grasping my cock again.

"This is all mine!" She said.

* * *

It was just over two weeks later when we heard some noises out in the main living room. Carol got up, tugged on a robe to go see what was going on.

We had sort of been interrupted so Carol looked like…well…like she had just been fucked.

I could not hear all of the conversation, but I quickly realized that Ray and Billie had just gotten back.

I was thinking that this just might be interesting, so I reached for another robe and pulled it on, going out there.

"Danny?" Billie looked at me in surprise.

"Mom? What's going on? What is Dan doing still here?" Ray looked at me and then back at his Mother in shock.

I would think the situation should have been reasonably clear.

Billie started laughing. Then she piled into me, damn near knocking me over.

"I got me a Daddy for real now!" She squealed.

"My God, Mom! Are you two….? Ray began. He still looked a little shaken, his eyes were huge.

"Oh, shut up, Ray. There is going to be another wedding!" Carol told him.

We had already decided on that.

STUCK

Sometimes in life we become so lonely that we are willing to do most anything to fill the void. Frequently we do things that are risky and foolish. Often our high risk actions come with unexpected consequences.

Clair Davis woke late that Saturday morning. As she sat up she looked at the digital clock sitting on her nightstand.

The red numbers displayed ten thirty.

"Richard?" She called out.

There was no response.

Clair remembered that her husband of fifteen years had left the evening before to play golf with his buddies.

Richard and his friends had been planning the weekend getaway for weeks. He wouldn't be back until late the following evening.

Clair threw the covers off. She was wearing a green, mid thigh length night gown. The material was almost see-through. The gown displayed her amazing curves. Her matching panties clung to her hips, and butt. The gusset of her panties outlined her thick pussy lips.

At thirty seven Clair was an amazing woman to behold. Her face was lovely, and her thick, curly, blond hair was shoulder length. She was voluptuous, with D cup breasts, and a round, full bubble butt that just begged to be fondled. Her legs were long and shapely. Her thighs well developed.

Clair was a woman that most any man would want to take to his bed.

Unfortunately after fifteen years of marriage, Richard, Clair's husband, had grown tired of his lovely wife. He'd grown as bored with the sex as he had with their time together. He was always working late. On weekends he would leave shortly after Clair woke up to hang out with his friends at the golf course. He usually came home about an hour before bedtime. Richard had time for everyone in his life but Clair.

They'd never had children.

Clair had always wanted kids, but Richard didn't.

He always insisted on wearing a condom during sexual intercourse. In the last two years he hadn't even bothered with sex. He would just come home, climb in bed, roll over, and go to sleep.

On that fateful Saturday morning Clair stood and went into the bathroom to relieve herself. She peed, and emptied her bowels. After cleaning herself, Clair flushed the toilet, pulled her panties up, and then headed downstairs to the kitchen.

The coffeemaker had been preset to brew a fresh pot earlier that morning.

Clair grabbed a cup off the counter and poured herself a badly needed cup of coffee. She sat down at the breakfast nook and took a sip of the hot liquid. "I hate my life," she muttered in disdain. She sat there drinking her coffee for fifteen minutes, as she tried to decide how to spend her day.

She gazed out the window at the pool. She didn't really feel like taking her usual morning swim, but she was a creature of habit. Besides, Rory would miss his Morning peep show if she didn't swim. "What the hell," she muttered. "The boy needs his daily fix."

Clair rose, rinsed out her coffee cup, and then set it on the counter next to the coffeemaker. She turned off the machine, stripped off her nightgown, and panties, and then headed out the back door, leaving it open as usual.

The door had a tendency to stick if it was closed too hard, so she always left it open to keep from getting trapped outside with no clothes.

Clair knew the only person who could see their backyard was Rory Jennings, her neighbors' nineteen year old son.

His second story bedroom window faced her backyard. Rory was the reason Clair had started swimming in the nude to begin with.

Clair had noticed the young man spying on her as she swam. Every Saturday and Sunday morning, as well as when he didn't have college classes, Rory would wait for her to come out in one of her sexy bikinis and watch her swim.

Clair took great pleasure in the knowledge that a young man enjoyed watching her swim. She knew she'd never do anything inappropriate with the boy, but she did enjoy the fact that he was turned on by her body.

Then few weeks ago, on a Saturday Morning, she found herself feeling extra neglected by her Husband. She decided to give the young man a treat. She spotted him watching her from his bedroom window. She peeled off her top and threw it on the deck, and resumed swimming topless.

Rory was stunned. He watched his sexy neighbor as she swam her usual fifty laps. His cock was rock hard. He took his dick out of his shorts, and started masturbating. He watched the gorgeous woman swim back and forth, as he stroked his thick meat.

Every once in a while, Clair would stand up, and run her hands through her hair, giving the young man a good look at her ample breasts. Clair began to get excited by her little display. She was becoming turned on because of the show she was giving the boy.

Rory desperately wanted to cum, but he held off as long as he could.

Then with fifteen laps to go, Clair became more emboldened. She pulled off her bikini bottoms and threw them onto the deck next to her top.

Rory lost it. He shot a load of sperm onto his bedroom window.

A sly smile appeared on Clair's lips when she saw the boy's cum splashing against his bedroom window. That day an exhibitionist was born in the middle aged woman.

After completing her swim, Clair went up to her room and masturbated. Not daring to fantasize about her teenage neighbor, she pictured Richard standing at the window watching her nude display instead.

The next day she repeated her little performance. By the time Rory's college classes had let out for the summer, Clair didn't even bother putting on a bikini. She would wait until Richard left, strip out of her night gown in the kitchen, and then head for the pool.

Afterward she would bring herself to orgasm while picturing her husband watching her from Rory's bedroom window. She was tempted to imagine Rory watching her, but somehow she resisted the temptation.

That morning Clair glanced up to Rory's window before diving into the warm water.

There he was peeking from one side of his bedroom window. He was already holding his hardened dick in his hand.

"Rory," his Dad called out from downstairs. "Come downstairs please. Your Mother and I need to talk to you."

The sound of his dad's voice caused Rory to lose his erection. The young man tucked his flaccid penis back into his shorts, and ran downstairs. He was feeling frustrated that he'd miss out on his morning show.

Rory's parents were standing near the front door.

"Son," his dad said. "Your mom and I are going antiquing and we will be gone until dinner time. There's money on the kitchen counter for lunch."

"Dad, I've got money."

"No, you need that money for gas, and lunch during the week. You will be starting your internship Monday morning at my office."

Rory's face lit up. "You got me an internship with your company?"

"It will look good on your resume once you've finished college. Who knows, maybe I can get you a job there once you graduate. Anyway, there's twenty bucks in the kitchen."

"Have a good time," Rory said as his parents left.

He immediately bolted back upstairs to his room.

Clair had already swum ten laps by the time he got back to his usual hiding spot.

Rory pulled his cock out of his sleeping shorts, and began massaging it back to its full length.

A few moments later Clair's home phone began to ring.

She climbed out of the pool and trudged back inside.

"Shit," Rory exclaimed. He stood there for five minutes, hoping she would come back out. His erection slowly went limp as he waited.

Clair sat at the breakfast nook listening in shock as Richard gave her the bad news.

"Clair, I don't know how to tell you this, so I guess the best way is to get it over with. I'm divorcing you. I've grown tired of our marriage, and I'm moving out when I get back from the golf tournament. I'm sorry, but it's just not working for us anymore." Richard hung up the phone, leaving his wife speechless.

A burning rage rose up in the distraught woman. She slammed the phone down, and cursed. "That fucking piece of shit," she exclaimed. "He didn't even have the decency to tell me in person. He calls me over the phone to tell me that fifteen years of my life has just been flushed down the toilet."

Clair stood up and began pacing back and forth. The more she paced, the madder she got. "Well fuck him," she growled. "He's not the only one who is tired of this dead marriage."

Clair needed to cool off, and she knew there was only one way to do it. She headed back out to the pool for a swim, having completely forgotten about her peeping Tom. As she strode through the back door, she slammed it hard.

At that moment Clair remembered the sticking door. She tried the knob, and sure enough the door was stuck. "Damn it," she growled.

Rory watched the woman from his window. He could tell that she was angry. He watched his lovely neighbor fight to get the back door opened. The young man wanted to help her, but to do so would be admitting that he'd been spying on her during her morning swims.

Clair shook the door for several minutes but it wouldn't budge. As she stood there not knowing what to do, she spotted the pet door.

They didn't own a dog; however the door was there when they bought the place ten years earlier. The rubber cover had been removed years earlier, and the door had been secured with a hook and eye from the inside.

Clair looked around and spotted a small, flat stick lying on the ground. She picked the stick up, and knelt next to the door.

Rory stared hard at Clair's sexy ass. His dick began to harden once again.

Working the stick into the narrow gap, she wiggled the slender piece of wood back and forth until the hook popped out of the eye, unlocking the small door.

"I'm having this door replaced first thing Monday," she declared as she poked her head through the small doorway. Clair turned her body sideways, and stuck her arms through the dog sized hole. She then forced her upper torso through the opening. Her breasts were a little too large to go through comfortably, but she managed to squeeze her D cup melons through the hole. "Damn it," she exclaimed as her nipples were painfully scraped across the wooden frame of the pet door.

Rory watched as his neighbor's upper torso disappeared through the hole. He watched her force her upper body through the hole until her sexy hips and buttocks came to rest against the wooden frame.

Clair pushed with all her might, but she couldn't get her hips and buttocks to go through the hole. "Fuck," she exclaimed. "I can't get my big ass through the doorway."

Clair tried to back out of the hole, but her breasts wouldn't go back through. She quickly realized that what goes in doesn't always come back out. "Shit, I'm stuck. Now what the hell am I going to do?"

The pretty blond broke down and started crying.

Rory knew Mrs. Davis was stuck. He quickly bolted out of his room and ran downstairs. He ran out the back door, across the lawn, and bolted through Mrs. Davis side gate. He then sprinted to her back door. The young man knelt next to Clair's shapely thighs, and looked through the small space between her waist, and the door frame. "Mrs. Davis, are you ok?"

"No I'm not ok. My back door is wedged shut. I'm stuck in this damned pet door, and I can't get in or out."

"Don't worry; I'll call the fire department.

"No," Clair screeched. "I don't want anyone seeing me like this. Hell, I'm naked and stuck in a doggy door. This would be humiliating. It's bad enough that you're seeing me like this. I don't want the fire department and all our neighbors gawking at me."

"What do you want me to do?"

"I need something to make my body slick so I can ease back out of the hole. Does your mom have any water based oils?"

Rory thought about the skin cream his mom was always rubbing on her arms. "Yeah, she keeps a tube of skin cream on her nightstand."

"Go get it. But whatever you do, don't tell your parents about this, ok?"

"They are gone for the day. I'll be right back."

Rory took a quick look at Clair's sexy legs and ass, and then headed for his house.

Clair half lay, half reclined on her side. She was both physically, and emotionally uncomfortable. "Richard, this is your fault."

Rory returned a few minutes later with a large bottle of lube. "Mom seems to be out of skin cream. The only thing I could find is a bottle of lube. I think my parents use it for sex. I hope that's ok?"

"Honey, I'll buy them a new bottle. Just get me out of this hole."

"What do I do with it?"

"Shove it through the hole between my waist and the doorframe."

Rory looked at the bottle. "I don't think it'll fit. It's a big bottle."

Clair groaned in frustration. "It would be. Then I guess you have no choice but to apply the lube to my skin."

Rory's cock lurched. He never thought in his wildest dreams that he'd get to touch Mrs. Davis' sexy body. "Where do I apply it?" He asked half stammering.

Clair sighed. "If I can get my breasts through the hole, I'll be free. I can't believe I'm about to say this, but rub the lube on my breasts."

Rory's cock stiffened to full length. With trembling hands he managed to open the lid. He applied a generous amount of lube to his right hand. Setting the bottle on the ground, he squeezed his lubed up hand through the opening.

Clair could feel the young man's lube covered hand caress her waist as Rory moved toward her ample breasts. She watched his hand appear through the hole.

"Don't rub the lube off until you reach my breasts."

Rory moved his hand away and kept moving forward. He was forced to place his left hand on Clair's hip to maintain his balance.

"Rory, what are you doing?"

"Sorry, I didn't want to fall."

Clair understood. "It's alright. Don't worry about being a gentleman right now. Just get me out of here."

Rory slid his arm through the hole until he was next to Clair's breasts. He grasped her left breast and rubbed a liberal amount onto her large tit.

Clair felt embarrassed by the fact that her teenage neighbor was massaging oil onto her breast.

Rory then withdrew his arm and applied more lube. He slid his arm through the hole again and lubed the sexy woman's other breast. His dick was ready to rip a hole in his shorts.

"Alright, that should be enough," Clair said.

Rory reluctantly withdrew his arm back through the hole. He was thoroughly enjoying feeling his neighbor up.

Clair then tried to push her upper body back through the hole. Unfortunately her breasts were just too large to fit. "Fuck," she exclaimed after several tries. "This isn't going to work. My tits will bend down but getting them to bend up is a different story."

"Have you tried pushing them flatter?"

"I need my hands to push myself through the doorframe."

"What if I pushed them flat?"

Clair felt her temples begin to throb. It was bad enough that she had to let a teenager massage lube onto her breasts. Now she would be forced to allow him to push them flat so she could squeeze through the opening in the door. "It can't hurt to try. Hell, you've already touched them once." Clair braced herself for another try. "Alright, push on my breasts, as I try to get back through."

Rory eased his trembling hands through the hole and mashed on Clair's breasts.

Clair's embarrassment increased. The feel of her breasts being mashed by a teenager was mortifying.

Clair took a deep breath, and then slowly let it out.

The feel of Mrs. Davis breasts was exciting Rory even more.

Clair forced her body to move backward. She felt the wood drag across her side as she eased her flattened bosom towards the exit.

Rory felt the back of his hands jamming against the wood. "Wait," he said.

"What?" Clair asked in disgust.

"You'll break my knuckles if I keep holding on. I can get my wrists to bend to the sides, but my hands are between your breasts and the wood."

"Great," Clair exclaimed as she slid her upper body back inside. "Now what do we do?"

Rory reluctantly released Clair's breasts, and withdrew his hands. "If I lubed your hips, could you squeeze into the house?"

Clair sighed again. Her humiliation was about to become even more intense. "Hell, it's worth a try. But you're going to have to lube my pelvis and butt as well."

Rory poured a generous amount of lube over Clair's hip, letting the lube pour down her lower body. He set the bottle down and began rubbing the lube into her butt, hips, and pelvis. He ran his hands through her neatly trimmed pubic hair. His middle finger caressed her clit several times as he massaged the oil into her skin.

The thirty seven year old woman involuntarily jerked each time Rory's finger touched her clit. "He's touching my clit," Clair whispered in frustration. "Can this day get any worse?"

Some of the lube ran into Clair's butt crack, and along her pussy lips.

Rory's dick was screaming for attention. The young man wanted to spread his sexy neighbor's legs wide and shove his cock into her lubed up pussy.

"Are you finished lubing me?" Clair asked impatiently.

"Yeah, I'm finished."

"Alright, I'm going to try to squeeze inside. You're going to have to push on my butt."

Rory laid his hands on Clair's ample bottom. "I'm ready," he croaked.

Clair pushed against the doorframe, trying to force her body through the hole.

Rory pushed against his middle aged neighbor's sexy behind.

Clair's hips, and bottom, pressed against the opening, and immediately stopped moving.

Rory was pushing so hard that his slippery right hand slid inward, and his thumb sank into Clair's lubed up pussy.

The pretty blond was shocked by the lubricated digit sinking into her hole. Her body involuntarily shook. "Fuck," she gasped.

"I'm sorry about that Mrs. Davis," the young man sheepishly said. "My hand slipped."

Clair sighed in resignation. "It's not your fault. I'm the one who slammed the door and locked myself out. You're just trying to help me."

Rory knew he should remove his thumb, but the woman's cunt felt too damn good.

Clair noticed that her teenage neighbor still had his thumb buried in her vagina. "Rory," she quietly declared. "Your thumb is still in me. Please remove it."

"Sorry," the young man replied as he slid his thumb out of Clair's cunt. He quickly raised the pussy juice soaked digit to his nose and inhaled.

Clair's pussy juices mixed with the fruity aroma of the lube, smelled wonderful to the young man.

Rory couldn't resist tasting the woman's vaginal juices. He quickly stuck his thumb into his mouth.

The lube as it turned out was grape flavored.

But Rory could still taste Mrs. Davis' juices on his thumb.

Clair shook her head. "I don't know what to do now. I guess you'll have to call the fire department."

Rory didn't want the fire department to be called. He was enjoying his lovely neighbor's nude body too much to bring in firemen. He thought hard, desperate to come up with another idea. "I know how to get you free," he exclaimed. "The pet door has a small frame built into it. What if I take a pry bar and pry the frame off?"

Clair was instantly relieved that the firemen wouldn't see her like this. "That just might work. Do you have a pry bar?"

"My dad has one in the garage. I'll be right back."

"Make sure you wash the lube off your hands before you handle the pry bar."

"I will," the young man replied.

As Rory headed back to his house, Clair half lay, half reclined in the hole, feeling like a complete idiot.

As she waited for her young neighbor to return, her thoughts drifted to the thumb he'd accidentally shoved into her cunt. She couldn't believe that her nineteen year old neighbor's thumb had been inside her pussy.

Of course Rory hadn't done it on purpose, but still it did happen.

Clair had felt the young man's hands on every personal part of her body over the last twenty or so minutes. She silently cursed for playing that stupid game of sexually exciting the boy over the last several weeks. If she hadn't been so damned lonely, she wouldn't be in this mess right now.

Then the realization that their intimate contact over the last twenty minutes was probably driving the young man wild with sexual desire, seeped into Clair's mind.

"Rory's dick is probably as hard as granite by now," Clair muttered.

She was glad that it was Rory who had come to her rescue.

A lecherous man would have taken advantage of her predicament, and shoved his cock in her exposed pussy by now.

Clair had no doubt that her young neighbor would be using the memory of this morning for future masturbation sessions. But she didn't blame Rory. This was her fault after all.

As she waited for Rory to return, her side began to ache from having the frame digging into her flesh. Clair slowly eased her body over until she was on her hands and knees. She could still feel the sides of the doorframe pressing against her waist, but at least she wasn't lying on her side anymore.

Rory returned a few minutes later. He was carrying a small pry bar.

The sight of Mrs. Davis on her knees with her voluptuous ass sticking up in the air was too much for the young man. His dick once again became rock hard. He wanted to kneel behind her, rip his shorts down, and shove his cock into her waiting pussy. Instead he squatted behind her, and announced his presence. "I'm back." He continued to take in the sight of Clair's sexy ass.

"Give me a minute to turn back over, and then you can break the frame loose."

"Wait," Rory said almost too quickly. "Let me pop the top board off first. That way I won't jab you with the pry bar."

"That's a good idea. Now take it slow. I don't want to get stabbed."

"I'll work slowly, I promise."

"Did you wash the lube off your hands?"

"Yes I did Mrs. Davis."

"Rory, I think we're past the point where you can start calling me Clair. After all you've touched me in places that no other man but my soon to be ex husband has touched me."

"You're getting a divorce?"

"It was his decision, not mine."

"Your husband is an idiot. If I had a woman as beautiful as you, I'd never let her go."

Clair smiled. "Thank you Rory. I appreciate the compliment."

"Mrs. Davis, I mean Clair; I'm going to have to get really personal with you again."

Clair smiled in spite of her condition. She was glad that a considerate young man like Rory had found her instead of some lecherous asshole. "It's alright Rory. Get as personal as you need to. Just get me out of this damn hole."

"I need you to move your knees closer to the door so I can kneel directly behind you."

Clair obediently moved her knees forward until they touched the bottom of the wood beneath the pet door. She was glad the back walk was made of wood instead of concrete, or her knees would be trashed by the time she got out of this mess.

Rory eased his legs on either side of Clair's legs. He scooted forward until his rigid cock was pressed against her butt crack. He then leaned over the nude woman's body and pushed the tip of the pry bar into the edge of the frame. He then slowly leaned forward, applying gentle pressure to the metal bar.

Clair could feel the underside of the young man's hard cock pushing against her butt crack. Her eyes grew wide.

Rory was indeed sexually excited. His erect cock was pressing against her butt crack as he worked.

Clair could only hope that the young man would resist the temptation to take advantage of her. The last thing she needed was to be fucked by a horny teenager while her butt was sticking out of the pet door to her house.

Rory leaned forward, applying more pressure to the frame. His granite hard dick felt like it was going to explode. He couldn't believe he was dry fucking Mrs. Davis.

Furthermore, she wasn't objecting. She had to know that his dick was rubbing against her butt.

Rory began to suspect that perhaps she wanted him to fuck her.

She could be as horny as he was at that moment.

The young man struggled to keep his mind on his work. But the thought of burying his dick in her hot cunt kept getting in the way.

Every time Rory pushed the pry bar upward the underside of his dick was rubbed against Clair's butt cheeks. His desire to fuck his sexy neighbor grew stronger with each thrust.

Clair's embarrassment increased as well. She was being dry humped by her teenage neighbor like a dog and there was nothing she could do about it. Her only hope was he would free her quickly before he exploded in his pants.

The thought of having Rory cum with his dick wedged against her butt crack would be too much for the woman to bear.

She would never be able to look the boy in the eye again.

As Rory worked an idea hit him. He knew it might not work, but he had to try. Rory purposely slipped as he dug the pry bar into the wood. He fell slightly forward, wedging his dick tighter between Clair's naked butt cheeks.

Clair groaned with embarrassment. She'd never felt so humiliated in her life.

"Sorry about that."

"Just keep working," Clair replied.

"Mrs. Davis," Rory said without remembering to call her Clair. "This isn't going to work like this. I can't get enough leverage. Could you spread your legs so I can kneel between them?"

Clair clenched her eyes shut.

The young man wanted to kneel between her spread legs.

Her cunt would definitely be exposed to Rory. "Are you sure it's necessary?" She asked.

Rory was desperate to press his dick against the woman's cunt. "I can't get any leverage with my legs spread. I need to kneel between your legs."

"Why can't you just stand over me?"

"In a standing position, I could slip and impale you with the pry bar."

"Don't do that," she screeched. "Then we'll need a fire truck, and an ambulance." Clair shook her head. "Move back for a moment and I'll spread my legs. Just be careful."

Rory quickly stood and watched his sexy neighbor spread her legs wide enough for him to kneel between them.

Clair's rosebud and pussy lips instantly entered the young man's view.

Rory knew that he had to touch his bare cock against her cunt. Looking down, he saw the perfect excuse. His shirt and shorts were covered with lube. He pulled off his shirt, and dropped it on the ground. He then eased his shorts down around his knees before kneeling between Clair's spread legs. The underside of his dick was lined up with her rosebud and cunt. His body shook as he scooted forward until his bare skin was pressed against her naked butt cheeks. Rory's cock nestled against Clair's cunt lips and asshole.

Clair gasped as Rory's bare cock came to rest against her exposed holes. "Rory, where are your clothes?"

"I had to remove them. The lube on your butt was beginning to soak into them. Just relax. I'll have you out of that door in no time."

Getting out of the pet door wasn't what she was worried about. Clair was more concerned with what Rory might put in her. She could tell that her next door neighbor was definitely well endowed. For the first time, the lovely woman was genuinely afraid that Rory might shove his thick cock in her and fuck her.

"Rory, I don't think you should be pressing your naked penis against my bottom."

"My mom does my laundry. I really don't want to explain how I got sex lube all over my shorts and shirt."

Clair knew that was one conversation she didn't want Rory having with his mother. "Alright, but be careful. The last thing I need is to have something else stuck in me."

Rory grinned as he slipped the pry bar into the groove of the door frame. "I'll be careful. I promise. I'm really sorry about my erection. But my equipment sort of has a mind of its own."

"I understand completely. It's not your fault," Clair replied. "I'm the one who got into this mess. You're just being a good neighbor. Just be careful with that thing. The last thing I need right now is to have your cock shoved in me."

"I'll be careful, I promise." Rory had no intention of being careful. But he wasn't going to tell Clair that. He was going to have as much fun with this opportunity as he could. Once again he began digging at the wood. With each thrust of the pry bar, the length of his bare cock rubbed Clair's clit, cunt lips, and rosebud.

Clair buried her face in her hands. She hated herself for teasing this young man all these weeks. Her little game had meant to be a way of relieving her loneliness without it going too far.

Now it was obvious that the game had gotten out of hand, and Rory was obviously working up the courage to fuck her.

Clair knew that before she was free from this trap she'd gotten herself into, she'd end up having her nineteen year old neighbor's cock buried in her cunt. "Me and my stupid games," she softly whispered.

Rory kept prying at the top section of the frame. His heart was pounding with excitement. He was dry fucking his neighbor's butt crack and pussy with his bare cock, and she wasn't objecting. Well, she wasn't objecting much.

Clair could feel the length of Rory's cock slide along her exposed clit, pussy, and rosebud with each upward thrust of the pry bar. Although she was mortified, her long unused cunt began to moisten with each gentle push.

Rory dug the pry bar deeper into the wood.

A small piece of the frame broke off.

Rory lurched forward, shoving the underside of his shaft against Clair's sex. His thick shaft spread Clair's cunt lips.

Clair felt the piece of wood fall on her butt as well as the young man's shaft forcing itself between her pussy lips. "Fuck," she silently groaned. "He's going to fuck me, I just know it," she whispered so he wouldn't hear. "That boy is going to stick his cock in me and fuck me."

"Are you ok?" Rory asked. He could hear her speaking, but her words were muffled by the door.

Clair sighed, knowing she wasn't going to get out of this without getting her cunt filled with Rory's cock. But, she had started this, so she had no one to blame but herself. She had teased and tormented the young man for weeks. Now she was going to get what she had coming to her. She resigned herself to the fact that she was going to be fucked whether she wanted it or not. Clair decided to get it over with so Rory could concentrate on freeing her. "Rory, we both know where this is heading. I can feel your hard shaft jammed between my pussy lips. I know you desperately want to fuck me. I also know you aren't going to be able to concentrate on freeing me until you do. So you might as well get it over with. Just get me out of here afterwards, ok?"

Rory's dick jerked involuntarily. "Are you sure it's ok?" He carefully asked.

Clair was sure it was anything but ok. The last thing she wanted was to have her nineteen year old neighbor's thick pecker buried in her pussy. But she couldn't see any other way of getting Rory's mind off fucking her, so he could concentrate on freeing her from this hell she was in. "Yes Rory, I'm sure. You won't be able to concentrate on freeing me until you've shot your cum in me. So go ahead and fuck me. But you've got to get me out of this damn door after you've finished."

"I will, I promise." Rory immediately laid the pry bar down. He leaned back several inches and lined his cock up with her cunt.

Clair closed her eyes and clenched her teeth as she waited for her teenage neighbor to shove his dick in her. "This can't be happening to me," she quietly groaned.

Grasping his cock with his right hand, and her lube covered left butt cheek with the other; Rory eased forward until the head of his dick slipped between her cunt lips.

Clair trembled as the head of the young man's cock penetrated her cunt lips. She was about to be fucked, and there was nothing she could do about it. Her only other option was to let Rory call the fire department.

That meant having her neighbors gathering around for a free show.

Clair was not ready to have her neighbors gawking at her nude body.

They would whisper behind her back for years to come.

Rory pressed the tip of his cock against the entrance to Clair's pussy.

Between the lube, and Clair's natural juices, his cock slid into her without too much difficulty.

Clair trembled as the young man's dick sank deep into her body.

His thick cock spread her vaginal walls wide as he slowly sank his dick into her pussy.

Clair was shocked at how big the boy's dick was. Even though she'd felt the shaft against her sex, she had no idea the boy's dick would open her pussy up this much.

Rory had already gone deeper than Richard ever had, and he was still sinking into her depths.

"Fuck, just how big are you?" Clair asked in disbelief. She couldn't believe this young man's dick was filling her like this.

Rory smiled as he continued to push his dick into his neighbor's tight pussy.

Clair felt like she was being stuffed with a sausage. Her cunt continued to expand as Rory sank deeper into her semi willing body. "Rory, how much more of your cock is left?" She asked.

The young man grabbed her other butt cheek, gave her flesh a tight squeeze, and then slowly eased the remainder of his cock into her body.

Clair grunted when the tip of his cock pressed against her cervix. She could feel his balls resting against her clit. "Shit, I've never been stretched like this before. I'm glad you took your time, or I'd be in serious pain right now."

"Clair, the last thing I want to do is hurt you," the young man replied.

"Thank you for being gentle. Another man wouldn't care if I was comfortable or not."

Rory moved his hands to his helpless neighbor's hips. Taking a firm grip, he began to withdraw his cock until only the tip was inside her. He wanted to shove it back in, but he knew if he did, Clair might get hurt. Instead he eased his cock back into her with a slow gentle stroke.

Clair involuntarily trembled as the hardened pole slid back into her. "I can't believe I'm being fucked by a teenager," she quietly exclaimed.

Rory's cock sank into her until once again the tip came to rest against the entrance to her womb. He noticed the pry bar lying on the ground next to him. A sly smile crossed his lips. He grabbed his nearby shirt, and wiped the lube off his hands. He then dropped the shirt. Picking up the pry bar, Rory pushed the edge into the wooden frame.

Clair began to wonder what the young man was up to.

He slipped his cock half way out of her cunt. Then he pried upward as he shoved his cock back into Clair's depths.

The trapped woman grunted when his cock head slammed into her cervix. She expected pain. But all she felt was pleasure.

Rory began to pound his cock into his sexy neighbor as he worked on freeing her from the pet door. With each inward thrust he would dig into the wood.

Slowly the top of the frame began to loosen.

Halfway inside the house, Clair's body was beginning to respond to being fucked. Her pussy muscles contracted with each inward thrust of Rory's impressive cock. She laid her forehead on the tile floor. She began to groan with lust. Clair couldn't understand why, but being fucked by this teenage boy was turning her on. She began to tug on her sensitive nipples. "Fuck, it's been too long," she groaned.

Rory worked harder at freeing his neighbor from the small doorway. He also worked harder at pounding the bottom of her cunt out.

Clair's body was beginning to thrum with excitement. She craved the feel of this nineteen year old cock pounding out her thirty seven year old pussy. "Fuck, don't stop," she groaned.

Rory began to thrust even harder into her willing cunt. He continued prying on the top section of the frame.

Suddenly the strip of wood popped free. It fell on Clair's ample bottom.

Rory grabbed the wood and tossed it aside. He then dropped the pry bar, grabbed Clair's hips, and began to pound her mercilessly.

Clair felt her pussy began to contract around Rory's hard shaft. She knew her orgasm was near. She couldn't believe it, but she was going to cum as a teenager pounded her cunt with his dangerous weapon.

Clair was being fucked by a boy who was young enough to be her son, and she was enjoying it. "This is so fucking insane," she groaned.

Rory continued to ram his cock into Clair's cunt. His balls began to churn with the need to cum.

Clair's vaginal walls continued to contract around Rory's cock. She began to shake as her impending orgasm began. "I'm cumming," she whimpered. "Fuck I know it's wrong, but I'm cumming." She clamped her pussy muscles down on Rory's thrusting cock.

Rory felt his cock lurch inside Clair. His dick expanded as his own orgasm began. He shoved his cock head against the entrance to her fertile womb, and released his baby makers into her body. The young man's churning balls fired load after load of baby making sperm against the entrance to Clair's unprotected womb.

Clair felt her young neighbor explode inside her. Her orgasm intensified. She clawed at the tile floor as her body shook with unimaginable pleasure.

"He's cumming in me," she whimpered. "He's filling me with his sperm." As Clair came it never occurred to the trapped woman that this was not a good time of the month for a virile young man to unload a million sperm cells into her cunt. At that moment all she cared about was her much needed orgasm. She shook and rocked against Rory's cock as she rode out the most intense orgasm of her life.

Rory slumped against Clair's butt as his spent and softening member slipped out of her sperm saturated cunt.

Clair's body continued to shake as her orgasm continued. She trembled with lust. Her body couldn't stop shaking.

Rory knelt over his lover for a few minutes until his strength returned. He then picked up the pry bar and began working on the right side piece of framework.

By the time Clair's orgasm had diminished, Rory had already pried off the second strip of wood.

The young man then pried off the other piece. "You should be able to get out now," he told Clair.

Barely hearing Rory's words, she turned on her side and attempted to slide out.

Unfortunately Rory had failed to consider that the framework was built on the inside of the door as well.

Clair's heavy breasts were stopped when she slid against the inner frame. "Shit," she exclaimed.

"What's wrong?" Rory asked.

"There's framing on this side too."

"I can't get at the inside. You'll have to pry it off from in there."

"How the hell do I do that?"

Rory slid the pry bar through the gap in the frame. "Here, take it."

Clair took the pry bar from the young man who had just fucked her. She turned onto her back and started working on the top section. She quickly realized that she'd never pry the wood loose without help. "I can't hold my weight up without help. The wood is digging into my spine. You'll have to support my lower back." She lifted her hips so that she was half sitting, half lying on her back.

Rory, still on his knees, nestled up against her pelvis, and slid his hands under the small of Clair's back. He gently lifted her hips so she was no longer resting her weight against her spine. His limp cock was lying against her clit.

Clair began to work on the top piece of framework. With each push against the frame her cunt rubbed against Rory's cock.

Within minutes the young man's dick began to harden and grow.

Clair was so intent on breaking the wooden strip free that she didn't notice Rory's hardening member.

Rory slipped his right hand free from under Clair's lower back. He grasped his cock and slid it between her pussy lips.

Clair was too caught up in her work to notice.

Rory lined his cock up with Clair's fuck hole and began to push the thick shaft back into her body.

Clair gasped as the thick shaft once again began to sink into her depths. "Oh hell, I'd forgotten how horny a young man can be," she exclaimed as the thick meat continued to sink into her body. "Damn, I haven't even got a kiss yet."

Rory grinned as he pushed his cock into Clair's cunt until the head came to rest against her clit. "I'll give you lots of kisses once you're free."

A smile appeared on Clair's pretty face. "I'm never going to get free if you keep fucking me, young man."

Rory began fucking his sexy neighbor once again. "Just keep working on the frame."

Using her left hand to hold her weight up, Clair resumed prying on the strip of wood. "This is one sexual encounter I'm never going to forget, that's for sure."

Rory supported Clair's lower body with his hands as he once again began to fuck the older woman.

Clair tried to pry the frame from the door, but she soon found out that being fucked while trying to get free was most distracting. Within several minutes she gave up trying to pry the wood from the door. She laid the pry bar aside, braced both hands on the floor, and then wrapped her long legs around Rory's hips. "To hell with it, I'll pry the wood loose after you fuck me. But this has to be the last time until after I'm out of this damn pet door."

Rory's laughter poured through the small space between her waist and the doggy door. "I don't know. I'm pretty horny. I might have to fuck you at least once more before you're free."

Clair sighed. "Great, I'm stuck in a dog door, and my neighbor can't stop fucking me long enough to let me pry off the wood."

"You know you love it."

"Yes, damn you, I love it. I haven't been this thoroughly fucked in years. If I'm going to be stuck like this with your cock in me, I might as well enjoy it. Go ahead stud. Pound my pussy until I can't take it anymore. Make me cum until I beg you to stop."

"Who says I'm going to stop?"

"Fuck, I'm going to be a quivering mass of flesh by the time you're through with me." Clair knew she was in for the fuck of her life.

Richard had never fucked her like this.

Rory rammed his hard cock into Clair's well used pussy repeatedly.

Clair began to squirm as her teenage neighbor used her to satisfy his sexual hunger. She clenched her legs tightly around his young hips and hung on.

Rory thrust into her cunt again and again. He fucked her so hard, and for so long that she was beginning to feel uncomfortable

The wooden frame beneath her back had begun to rub her flesh raw. "Wait," she exclaimed. "I've got to turn over before this damn pet door rips the hide off my back."

Rory stopped fucking his sexy neighbor. He withdrew his long, hard cock and waited for her to twist around so she was once again face down.

Clair settled onto her elbows and knees. "Alright stud," she said playfully. "Fill my hungry pussy with your wonderful cock."

Rory grasped Clair's hips. He then lined his cock up with her stretched out cunt. He was about to penetrate her when he once again noticed the bottle of lube sitting on the ground next to him. A devious idea ran through Rory's young mind.

Clair couldn't understand why Rory hadn't stuffed her pussy with his monster yet. "Come on Baby. What are you waiting for?"

Rory picked up the bottle. He poured a generous amount of lube down the crack of Clair's ass.

"Hey," Clair said in protest. "What the hell is that?"

"It's just a little lube," Rory replied as he poured more liquid onto his thick shaft.

"Why are you lubing my ass?" Clair's heart skipped a beat as the realization of what her neighbor intended to do. "Rory, you can't fuck my ass. Your dick is too thick. You'll split me wide open."

Rory gripped Clair's left hip with his left hand. He then grasped his shaft with his right.

"Rory, no," Clair exclaimed fearfully. "Your dick is too big."

The nineteen year old man pressed the head of his cock against Clair's anal entrance.

"Please, it'll hurt like hell." Clair tried to pull her round hips through the door, but she was stuck with nowhere to go.

Rory gently pushed the tip of his cock against her asshole.

Clair gritted her teeth, knowing she was helpless to stop him from having his way with her. She knelt there and fearfully waited for her young lover to ram the length of his cock into the depths of her bowels.

Rory however took his time. He gently pushed his cock head against the entrance to her rectum. He kept applying slow, gentle pressure until her asshole began to open up. The tip of his cock sank a fraction of an inch into her body.

Clair groaned as her sphincter began to open up. "I can't believe you're going to do this to me."

Rory kept quiet. He continued to slowly work his cock head into her body a fraction of an inch at a time.

Suddenly her anus opened up.

The head of Rory's cock slid into Clair's anal opening.

"Shit," the trapped woman hissed.

"Don't shit on me," Rory teased playfully.

"I would if I hadn't taken a dump before I got into this mess."

Rory slowly worked his cock head back and forth in Clair's rectum. The lube helped to keep his dick from rubbing her inner walls too much. With each small inward stroke his dick slowly sank deeper into the middle aged woman's rectum.

Clair had been expecting unimaginable pain. She was amazed to discover that being stretched by Rory's cock was not nearly as uncomfortable as she'd imagined.

Rory slowly worked his shaft deeper into her bowels. With each inward stroke his dick sank a little deeper into her rectum. "How does it feel?" He asked through the hole in the doorway.

Clair shook her head in disbelief. "It doesn't feel nearly as bad as I thought it would. I expected to be in agony by now. To be honest with you it's starting to feel good."

"I thought you might like it. The secret is lots of lube and patience." Rory pressed his dick deeper into Clair's colon.

The pretty blond moaned as nearly half of her young lover's dick sank into her depths. "Fuck, I can't believe I'm starting to enjoy this."

Rory sank a few more inches of his cock into Clair's stretched out bottom.

Clair mewed in pleasure.

"Would you like me to go deeper?" Rory asked through the space in the door.

"You know damn well I want you to go deeper. I want you to stuff as much of that sausage into my ass as you can. Just be careful, and keep going slow."

Rory kept working his dick deeper and deeper until his balls finally came to rest against Clair's pussy lips and clit.

Clair felt like she had a giant turd stuck in her ass. Yet for some reason that she couldn't explain, having Rory's dick buried in her colon felt pleasing to her. "I can't believe this is turning me on," she muttered.

Rory gently gripped Clair's hips. He slowly withdrew his cock until only the head was still inside her. He then grabbed the lube bottle and poured more lube onto his shaft, and down her butt crack.

Clair felt the clear liquid running down her butt crack. A satisfied smile crossed her lips. She'd found a lover who knew how to be gentle while taking care of her needs.

Rory set the bottle down. He grasped her hips again and began sinking back into Clair's body. He fucked his lover slowly at first. Each inward thrust was gentle. Each withdraw was agonizingly slow.

Clair slid her right hand through the small space between her tummy and the doorframe. She began to manipulate her clit. She could feel Rory's nut sack touching the back of her fingers with each inward stroke.

"Are you ready for me to go faster?" Rory asked.

"Hell yes. Fuck the shit out of me."

"I thought you'd already taken a dump this morning?" Rory asked playfully.

"Just fuck me," Clair demanded.

Rory rammed his long, hard cock into Clair's bowels.

Clair gasped as his nut sack banged against the back of her fingers.

He began to thrust harder into her body. Each inward thrust rammed her hips tighter against the inner frame.

Clair groaned loudly as she rubbed her clit furiously. She was close to cumming yet again. "Harder," she screamed. "Fuck me harder."

Rory began to pound his middle aged lover's ass mercilessly. He thrust his shaft into her repeatedly. His pelvis practically bounced off her ass cheeks. His ball sack was striking her fingers to the point that it was almost causing the young man pain. But he had no intention of slowing down.

Clair's body tensed up as her next orgasm began to erupt from her loins. The thirty seven year old woman rubbed her clit harder. She screamed in ecstasy as her body shook from orgasmic bliss.

Rory's own orgasm hit him just as he slammed his dick deep into Clair's body.

The final jolt of his inward thrust caused the inner framework to pop free. The entire frame hung around Clair's waist like a strange looking belt."

Clair whimpered as wave after wave of sexual pleasure shot through her loins.

Rory hung on tightly to Clair's hips as he emptied another load of sperm into her body.

The pair shook and moaned as they rode out their mutual orgasms.

After what seemed like a lifetime, Rory withdrew his cock from Clair's asshole.

Clair slumped forward so her forehead was resting on the floor.

The framework slid down her body. It came to rest against the underside of her ample breasts.

Clair realized that she was finally free. She rested for a minute, then turned her body sideways, and slid into her kitchen. She lay there for a few minutes before standing.

Rory grabbed his clothes and slid through the doorway after her. He stood up and took his lover in his arms. He kissed her deeply.

Clair moaned into Rory's mouth. Breaking the kiss she gazed into his eyes. "That was one hell of a way to get me out of that pet door."

Rory noticed the frame hanging around Clair's waist. He grasped the wood and started to lead her through the kitchen.

"And just where are you taking me?" Clair asked in mock disapproval.

"Well, I've fucked you in the doorway long enough. I think it's time I fuck you in your bed."

"We wash that dick before you stick it back in my pussy. We need to take a nice long bath before we go to bed."

Rory's eyes gleamed with a burning desire to fuck Clair all day long. "A bath sounds like a good idea." He leaned over and gently kissed her lips. "Afterward we can continue having fun together. Come to think of it, I've already used two of your holes. There is one hole that needs to be filled."

Clair softly laughed. "I take it you intend to shove that sausage into my mouth."

"I'm also going to lick your pussy until you beg me to stop." Rory replied.

"Something tells me I'm in for one hell of a day."

Clair and Rory fucked throughout the day and into the night.

The middle aged woman's body ached from the repeated times she'd cum. She had lost count of the times Rory had cum in her mouth and pussy.

The last time he fucked her; he laid her on her stomach, and shoved his cock into her asshole.

Clair came so many times that she lost track.

As Rory lay on his side, sleeping soundly with his semi erect dick still buried in Clair's bowels; the middle aged woman reveled in the sexual pleasure the young man had given her.

She knew they could never be lovers out in the open.

Rory's parents would never approve.

However, Rory could slip over to her house any time he wanted. He could fill her stomach, pussy, and ass with as much sperm as he wanted.

Clair had begun to drift off to sleep when a thought popped into her mind.

Rory had repeatedly cum in her unprotected pussy.

Her pussy was filled to overflowing with his rich young baby makers. Clair knew it was the absolute worst time to be letting a potent young man cum in her unprotecte4d cunt.

Rory's sperm cells would soon be working their way towards her fertile womb and the egg that lay waiting.

"Oh hell," Clair groaned. "Rory has filled my pussy with enough sperm to knock ten women up. I'm going to end up pregnant for sure."

Clair did indeed end up pregnant. She thought about having an abortion, but she decided she still wanted a baby.

Richard had never wanted kids.

But with Rory, she could finally have the child she had always wanted.

When Rory found out he was going to be a father, he immediately told his parents. He then moved in with Clair.

His parents were furious with the couple at first. Eventually, however, they decided they loved their son too much to stay mad at him and his lover.

Clair divorced Richard. She got the house, and half of everything he owned. She wasn't rich, but she had enough money to help Rory's parents put him through college, and live until he joined the working world.

Rory and Clair got married the week before he returned to his sophomore class.

Clair was already beginning to show when they said I do.

Two and a half years later Rory graduated college, and then got a job at his dad's company, where he still works to this day.

After two years, Clair is pregnant with her second child. Even at thirty nine her womb is very fertile.

It seems Rory hates condoms with a passion, and he refuses to allow his wife to use birth control.

The middle aged woman loves the way her swollen belly moves when Rory fucks her. She has no idea when her womb will dry up. But Clair knows she will continue to let her husband fill her womb with babies as long as she is fertile.

Oh, and in case you are wondering what happened to the inner pet door frame?

Clair managed to get it off that fateful day. She mounted it to the wall above their bed as a reminder of how she ended up getting the best lover of her life.

WENDY TAKES IN HER BOARDER

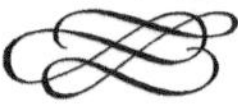

Wendy awoke just past 5 a.m. Kenneth lay spooned behind her an arm around her so that a hand cupped one breast. Wendy wore nothing and luxuriated in the warm expanse of Kenneth's body pressed against her.

Reluctantly she pulled herself away and padded into the bathroom. She sat and peed. There was slight irritation of the extremely tender walls of her vagina. No surprise. He had made love to her into the night, first visiting each of her erogenous zones including ones she didn't know she had and maybe had not had previously.

He lingered at each spot as he patiently ministered to Wendy's body. He used his hands and feet, his very stiff penis, his mouth, his lips and his tongue, even his chest; setting off repeated orgasms, toe-gasms, ear-gasms, nipple-gasms, my God, an armpit-gasm, before he at long last put his mouth on her swollen and yearning pussy, then plunged his tongue into her vagina withdrew and set upon her shiny wet, warm and pulsing clitoris, lip-nibbling and licking around it. When he sucked the distended little nubbin she entered into a state of delirious ecstasy, squirming and thrusting on his relentless mouth as a crescendo of orgasms overwhelmed her, finally gasping a plea to stop as she could stand no more of the agonizing pleasure. But straightway that he did she implored him, begged him to take her.

"I want you in me," reaching and grasping his prancing cock, rubbing the glans, feeling a slick droplet expressed out of the slot as she fondled him. She felt wild; out of control, her pussy dictating in this moment, more than ready , desperate for union yet once again.

He commanded her onto her knees. She knew what to do. He had shown her how he wanted her positioned when he fucked her; trained her, rejuvenated her pussy and made it , long un-penetrated, accommodate his wonderful muscle and welcome it. Never mind the ache in her hip. He wanted her head down, broad ass up; inflamed vulva waiting between her open thighs; dripping coital fluid and lubricant, out of her mind, "fuck me now" excited as he positioned himself; Wendy on the verge of orgasm yet again, waiting for the indescribable bliss of that first thrust as he impaled her, slamming up against the broad bolster of her ass with strong hands pulling her hips back onto himself. She reveled in his vigor as he stallioned in and out and she had rolling orgasms that made the walls of her vagina squeeze his shaft over and over with remarkable strength. Occasionally he withdrew and massaged her clit with the slick head of his beautiful dick making her groan with intense pleasure, coming yet again. Then the bliss as he again drove himself into her. Both sweaty now, his thighs made a slapping sound as he slammed into her. Her soaking pussy squished as his shaft slid in and out. Throughout she moaned, groaned, cried out at the crescendos and urged him on, "yes, oh yesssss. Oh Kenny you beautiful lover, fuck me," fuck me, give me your cum; cum for Wendy and "aaaaahhh, ahhhh, oooooh, yesssssss," as she came with him; Kenneth straining against her as his own orgasm overtook him, reaching under to grasp her fleshy belly and simultaneously boost her and squeeze her tightly as he strained to probe the last millimeter of vagina just there at her cervix. She could feel his hot dick pulse with each ejaculation and her vagina clamped and re-clamped the spurting organ.

* * *

She wiped and flushed. At the vanity she retrieved a hand mirror; then sat on the toilet again and used the mirror to look at her pussy while she spread the lips with the fingers of one hand. Well and truly fucked she thought. Her vulva was crimson and her full inner labia swollen so they protruded between the long full pistolettes of her proud outer labia. She felt as horny as ever she had been in years past, even now at 75. No sex had been as good as Kenneth gave her, preceded by tender albeit sometimes vigorous, loving and extended foreplay until she was consumed with lust. But her body and her sex in particular could not sustain the sort of rampant fucking they had torn from each other earlier; not like she could fuck in her younger days. She took as much hormone therapy as she could convince her gynecologist to prescribe, risks be damned, and supplemented the juices her pussy secreted with good quality lubricant. The Bible said threescore and ten years was the allotted time of man. Well, she was beyond that by half a decade. So as far as she was concerned she was playing with the house's money.

But just now it was good he would make the long seven hour trip home to his wife, at 37, three years younger than Kenneth. The four days he was away home would give her pussy a respite. She would need to awaken him and get him going. The horny beast, she thought, smiling inwardly. He will wake up with that hard on and be wanting sex before he leaves. What would you call that, she wondered, warming up for the main event? The old mare getting the stallion hot for the thoroughbred (bed?) filly? It didn't matter, she and Donna had a unique understanding; the key that had unlocked the way into his heavenly embrace and body. Well, she would give him a blow job, a quickie to sustain him until got home to the mother of his three children and Donna could get from him the sex she missed so much in the days and weeks he was away on the construction project. The man was amazingly virile. Despite making love until she could go no more and his multiple ejaculations, she knew there was no doubt that he would be able to service Donna vigorously. She pushed away the unwelcome thought that this arrangement that made him her lover would end when he finished his work and moved on to the next job somewhere else.

Standing now in the bathroom doorway she looked at her 40 year-old lover, naked and asleep. Her heart did a somersault. He was so beautiful, possessed of a hard body, with little fat, kept fit by the strenuous work he did as a foreman on the massive university hospital project that had flooded her town with construction hands. Mayor Monica Hawkins had appealed to residents with spare bedrooms to accommodate workers if they could. Wendy had two unused bedrooms and no one else living in the house for the past 10 years after Frank's death. So she put her name on a list and the first person who showed up was Kenneth.

He was in hardhat, boot cut jeans and a flannel shirt, wearing pull-on steel toed work boots. He was about 6 feet tall; dark hair with some gray showing, nice eyes, a dazzling smile and an unaffected charm. Never mind also a very cute tush that she checked out as they climbed the stairs to look at the two available bedrooms and decide which, if either, he would choose. She noted that he smelled good too; some sort of men's cologne and warm male smell, the two mixed in an odor that made her center warm as she sniffed it in his wake. Wendy chastised herself for thinking about him that way. But she crossed her fingers and anxiously waited for him to decide.

"If you want I can provide some meals as well, she said. And you can use the living room, dining room, kitchen if you want to do some cooking. Your bathroom will be the one at the end of the hall. This will be your room unless you like the other one better. This one is a little bigger."

"Yes, Miss," he said as they entered. "May I just try the bed for a second?"

"Oh, well, of course," Wendy replied. "Make yourself at home."

He stretched out on the bed, face up, letting his feet dangle off the edge.

Wendy could see the swell in his jeans where his "package" made an inviting bulge.

"I like this bed better than the other one," Kenneth said. "How much?"

"$250 a month $350.00 if you want board as well as room"

"Deal," he said with an endearing smile that made him look like he was a teenager again.

So Kenneth moved in. That was two months ago. Wendy was very happy to have his company and they fell into a pattern where he would return from work, shower, have a beer and watch some news then dine on whatever Wendy prepared. Although he had to be up very early she made it a point to get up and fix him something for breakfast. She took to arranging her hair and putting on her makeup before joining him in the kitchen, well covered by her long terry cloth robe and "birth control" flannel pajamas beneath. Initially he objected to her rising and serving up breakfast but Wendy brushed it aside and continued. She loved being with him like a wife each morning before he left for the construction site. Every day he called his real wife in the evening .

He worked seven days a week. Once each 45 days he had six days off and made the 700 mile flight home to see his wife, Donna, and the children, a son and daughter; pictures of all of them on the dresser in his room at Wendy's house. Wendy imagined the passionate lovemaking that must take place when this virile man was once more in his hot wife's arms.

Wendy and Kenneth had their first sex together, (although it might have come about otherwise in any event), as an outgrowth of Wendy overhearing his end of a telephone conversation with Donna, Kenneth's wife, and a subsequent, quite remarkable phone call from Donna to Wendy. Wendy had gone to the laundry room and Kenneth was sitting out on the deck. Apparently he thought Wendy was in the front of the house in the living room and out of earshot. He did not know the laundry room window was open to let in a breeze. He spoke quietly and intimately. Wendy, feeling a bit chagrinned, nevertheless eavesdropped. (What follows is Kenneth's end of the conversation that Wendy could hear. The reader will have to use her imagination to complete Donna's end of the conversation.)

"Oh baby, I miss you too."

"It is hard not being able to fuck whenever and as much as we want."

"Don't be silly. I could never do that. Anyway I've no time to play around even if I wanted to."

"What? You say some outrageous things Donna. She's old enough to be my mother. I don't know, maybe in her sixties or more, I can't really tell."

"Yes, I like her. She's a loving and generous person and feeds me too. Got some extra padding but looks pretty good for her age. But that's not something to start thinking about."

"She has been fixing her hair and makeup before she comes down to make my breakfast. Well, yeah she makes my breakfast . No she didn't start to fix herself up like that until after I moved in, I'm pretty sure. OK, let's say she does, that doesn't mean I'd do anything about it."

"You are a piece of work, you know that? I haven't talked about her as much as you say. Yes. She has all the parts that a woman has as much as I've seen any. I don't know. How would I know? She'd have to be naked for me to know that. They're nice, sure. Yes, bigger than yours but she's put on a few extra pounds over the years. No I haven't seen them. Christ Donna, she's a nice older lady who is happy to have a guy around, nothing more."

That's what you think, buster, Wendy thought.

"Honey, if you can take it so can I. I do go solo when the need builds up and I think about you. Look, it's not a matter of you not being jealous. I'm your guy. Besides I can't ask her something like that," she'd have me out on my ear."

"For God sakes, I'm only so strong. OK, yes if I thought you'd understand and not be hurt and she walked into my bedroom naked I might, you know; aw this is ridiculous."

"Huh? Now Donna don't you dare do that. You'll get me thrown out and I might not be able to find another place. This town has filled up with construction workers. So you just behave. Hell, she might have me arrested if … for something like you're suggesting."

Wendy felt the color rise in her cheeks . She drew the only reasonable inference she could in overhearing just Kenneth's end of the phone conversation. Clearly Kenneth's wife had suggested that he seek intimacy with her, with Wendy. Perhaps the man's wife have been teasing him, albeit in an odd way. But that didn't really fit as an adequate explanation. She went to bed later and had a good deal of difficulty getting to sleep, turning over in her mind the half-conversation she had overheard. She could not stop thinking of Kenneth a few steps away in his bedroom. She could not stop thinking of his remark, if "she walked in my bedroom naked, I might…" Sometimes the punishment for bad behavior comes right along with the behavior she thought. I'm being silly but I'm horny and that's a fact; doesn't matter how old I am. And he's horny so… She sighed and put her hand on her vulva and soon lost herself in masturbation; rubbing her clit vigorously until she had a wracking orgasm. Then, satiated for the moment, she finally slept.

The next morning she thought he looked at her differently than ever before. More the way a man's gaze gets when he is sizing up a woman as a sexual partner. She felt the color rise in her cheeks. He kissed her warmly on the cheek and lingered there for several beats before he left.

"Thanks for everything, Wendy. One thing, if my wife calls just keep in mind that she can have a very weird sense of humor sometimes. I hope you'll just overlook anything silly that she may say. I love her dearly but I can't always control her."

"Don't worry Kenneth. It will be fine if she calls." When Kenneth was gone, Wendy slumped at the kitchen table and fanned herself. She was in a turmoil. "Fine" she thought, hah! Consciously she didn't know how she would react, what she would say if Donna laid it all out on the table. God knows she wanted sex. Chronological age be damned. She had wandered in a sexual desert since Frank's death. Almost ten years without a man. The possibility of being a surrogate for Kenneth's wife pulled at her body like a magnet. Would Donna actually, not only agree to such an arrangement, but also sanction and promote it? More fundamentally, was she, Wendy, up to it?

She went to the supermarket. Came home and put the groceries up. Made herself a sandwich, watched the news and managed to take a catnap. Shortly after 2 p.m., the phone rang.

"Mrs. J, hi this is Donna, Kenneth's wife."

"Why, hello Donna, Kenneth speaks of you quite often, " Wendy said. "But I'm afraid he's not here now."

"Oh, that's alright. I'll talk to him when he calls tonight. I called because I want to chat with you; girl talk, just the two of us. Is that okay?"

"Well, I will be happy to chat with you Donna, although I am more 'old gal' than girl anymore." Wendy had a pretty good idea already of what Donna wanted to talk about. Nevertheless, she wanted to let Donna bring out what she wished to discuss so she said, "What sort of girl talk did you have in mind?"

Donna giggled. "We could talk about Kenneth, Wendy. I love him so much and, from all I've heard from him, I think you are quite taken with him."

"He is a wonderful man. I was a bit concerned when I decided to rent to the construction workers. I was so lucky that Kenneth chose my home. I've enjoyed having a man in the house and Kenneth is certainly all man, isn't he?"

"Oh, he is VERY much a man, Wendy, may I call you Wendy?"

"Of course you may, my dear. And I know what you mean by very manly. It must be very difficult for you to be without him for such long periods."

"I am glad that you mentioned that Wendy. It is hard for me. I think about him when I go to bed and it is often very difficult to get to sleep unless I, well you know...."

"I understand Donna. I am old but I know what it is for a woman to need a man, her man. I haven't had a man in my bed for years. Sometimes you just have to relieve the tension."

"Exactly. You know it is very, very hard for Kenneth, too. I try to give him as much loving as I can when he gets home and I know I satisfy him. But then when he's gone without for four days, then five and six, then weeks, it gets hard for him. Solo just seems to make him need it more, you know what I mean? And Wendy, I get worried that he will just get to needing a woman so bad that he'll be out running around. And there would be plenty of horny women out there who'd love to get him in bed. I'm afraid I'll lose him. We need this job and the money is really good but we need each other. Not having each other is harder for both of us than we thought it would be when he took the job. I just don't know."

"This is difficult for you isn't it Donna? But this is not my first rodeo, as Frank, that's my late husband, as he used to say. You won't offend me. Go ahead and tell me now what is on your mind."

"You're right Wendy, this isn't easy. But, well since you are right there with him could you, you know, like help him when he needs it so bad? It would be doing me a huge favor, because if he could come to you, then he won't be looking for someone out on the streets and in bars.

Oh Wendy it would really be ok with me and from what Kenneth tells me, I think you would enjoy him. Lots of older women your age are still in the game. He does excite you some. Isn't that so?"

"If I stood in his doorway naked," Wendy said, "do you think he would take me into his bed?"

"Oh my God, Wendy! Did you overhear Kenneth talking to me yesterday? Oh you must think I am terrible."

"Of course not, Donna. But yes, I had a moment of weakness and I listened to Kenneth's end of your conversation with him. I was very surprised as you can imagine. But what I heard excited me a lot. Kenneth is a gorgeous man."

Wendy continued, "But let's put that aside for the sake of discussion. Have you thought this through? Why do you think it will be different for you if Kenneth has intimate relations with me rather than someone young or more his and your ages? I am still another woman having what is supposed to be yours. Is it the fact that I am elderly that leads you to think you can accept Kenneth having relations with me? And one other thing, Donna, "What about me; my emotions? If I give myself to your husband I am inevitably going to become emotionally involved; the more love-making we do, instead of just getting sex from each other the more I am going to want him, even though I can't have him, other than temporarily."

There was silence from Donna and Wendy waited. Finally Donna spoke, "Oh Wendy, I am so sorry. I did think if he got satisfaction with you he would not fall in love... that he would see; that you both would see this could only be temporary, that your age difference would keep him from leaving me where if he took up with someone his age he might decide to leave me for her especially if she was better in bed than I am. I guess my thinking is that you would be a surrogate for me rather than a rival."

"And Wendy, Kenneth could not just have sex with you; he is acutely anxious to make sure his partner is satisfied. He doesn't just want intercourse, 'wham, bam, thank-you ma'am.' He makes slow love and takes a lot of his pleasure from pleasing his partner. So I suppose it could be hard on you emotionally when the job finishes up and he comes home. You're right Wendy, I didn't think about your feelings. I am truly sorry I've upset you."

"Donna, you've been very honest in your answers and I admire you for it and appreciate your candor. I'm not upset. The truth is, you've opened a door for me to turn a fantasy into reality. Why don't you and Kenneth have your evening chat and discuss this again? We'll put off any decision for 24 hours to give us a little more time. Once Kenneth and I are intimate, that is if we are, it will change all of our relationships and we will not be able to return to the status quo. Would you like to call again tomorrow evening and tell me what the two of you have decided and then you can find out what my decision is as well."

Donna agreed and they rang off. It worked out but not quite as they envisioned.

That evening when Kenneth returned from work they had dinner and talked about nothing important. What was left unspoken weighed in their minds and occupied their thoughts far more than their somewhat strained table talk. After dinner Kenneth helped clean up the kitchen then excused himself to call Donna. It was just as well because Wendy needed some time to herself.

I am 75 years old and I still want sex, Wendy thought. She knew from surfing the Internet that she was not alone. There were other women her vintage and more who still wanted to be held and cuddled and stimulated to lust by a willing, capable and considerate partner. A tall order, she reflected, given the general mortality rate of men who do not live on average as long as women. How many women her age would have the opportunity to have what was being offered to her; not by the aggressive come-on of the husband but by the anxious appeal of the distant wife? A Latin phrase she once heard swam up into her consciousness. Carpe diem, she thought. Seize the day. When you're playing with the house's money it is no time to deny yourself an opportunity offered. What had the Welsh poet Dylan Thomas written? "Do not go gentle into that goodnight." She made up her mind. She would give herself to Kenneth if he wanted her. She knew instinctively that Donna would not change her mind. Wendy would deal with the corollaries of her choice, known and unknown, as they presented themselves.

Her mind made up, she went to bed and slept peacefully.

The next afternoon Donna called once more. She and Kenneth had discussed the arrangement thoroughly and he had agreed, admitting that the thought stimulated him and his excitement in turn arousing Donna.

"Don't get so turned on," Donna cautioned, that you have to give yourself a relief cum. Save it for Wendy."

Breakfast was a bit strained as each of them thought about "the arrangement" not yet consummated. Kenneth took his lunch pail and at the door he hugged Wendy and kissed her cheek warmly.

"We'll talk when I get home," he said.

"Yes, we should," Wendy said. She watched him climb into his pickup and only when he had driven off down the street did she close the front door.

Donna called again in the afternoon.

Wendy told her, "I am willing to accept that I cannot have him permanently no matter how much I might come to care for him. So... If I am convinced that it you truly endorse and want this; that it really would not harm your relationship with him, I would love to give myself to Kenneth. But he has to be comfortable with your acceptance and with himself. And, Donna I can only do this if Kenneth asks me. Donna, I'm no prize. There's a big age difference. My body looks nothing like yours. Kenneth's shown me pictures. It's been so long I'm not sure how good I can perform. I might not be able to satisfy him."

"If he asks, will you try Wendy? Please? And Wendy you might be surprised but if you'll be a little flirty I think it will make him want to ask. He won't be able to help himself because he's so horny."

Before dinner Wendy put on a button front spaghetti strap sun dress with a scooped neckline that showed a generous amount of cleavage. Her bra lifted her full breasts and her panties, on impulse were left in her dresser drawer. It made her feel wanton and warmed her groin. When Kenneth sat down to eat that evening (Wendy fixed breaded pork chops, pan fried potatoes, peas and a lettuce, tomato and cucumber salad with balsamic vinegar dressing and served up still oven warm chocolate cake for dessert.) Wendy served him, leaning over and lingering to let him get a good look down her dress. He did not disappoint. She felt the color rise in her neck and moved away to sit opposite him, her straining nipples now clearly apparent where they pushed up her bra and bodice. It pleased her that he greedily drank in the view of breasts and bra, probably her bare skin to the waist too. She poured each of them a glass of the cabernet she had been saving. He immediately drank half and she refilled his wine stem.

Kenneth said, "Wendy you look right fetching in that dress. I don't recall seeing you in it before and I'm sure I would remember if I had. You know, I'm surprised you don't have any men trying to win over a fine looking widow lady like you."

"Thank you, Kenneth. I love a compliment about my looks, even if I'm old and overweight. You've made me blush." Wendy leaned forward, ostensibly reaching for the salt shaker so that he could get another good peek down her front. They looked at each other and he tried not to but he broke eye contact and looked down the front of her dress. Wendy again felt the pleasant warmth in her groin.

Kenneth cleared his throat and asked, "Did Donna call you today?"

"She did, yes."

He drank half his glass of wine. "So what did you talk about.? I'll bet she had some crazy notions." Wendy was bemused with Kenneth. She had not seen him as tentative and uneasy as he was just in that moment.

Wendy smiled, "It was not 'what' we talked about it was 'who'."

There seemed to be a little charade that Kenneth needed to play out. Wendy readily accepted his need to approach her in his own way. She too was tense with anticipation.

Kenneth put his fork down and wiped his mouth with the cloth napkin Wendy always set out.

He knew she meant him. "Darn," he said. "Donna has a mind of her own. She gets a notion and won't let go. I hope she didn't say anything foolish or that might have been out of line. I sure don't want you to tell me to pack up and get out."

"Goodness," Wendy said. "I wouldn't put you out Kenneth. Why would you think that? Over something you think Wendy might have said that would offend me? I like your company very much Kenneth. It is a pleasure to have a nice handsome man in my house. What do you think she might have said?"

Wendy was toying with him, knowing very well what Donna had proposed was something Kenneth had talked to her about and he was edging towards it. She took a long drink of her wine. She felt more pleasant warmth in her groin and knew her sex was moistening.

Kenneth drew a deep breath and let it out slowly as he spoke, "She probably said something about my needing it a lot and being hard to keep from looking for a woman. She probably said she was afraid she'd lose me to another woman being apart so much. And I'll just bet she asked you if you'd help keep me satisfied, while I'm here on me job. She told you it would meet with her approval and that it would be good for both of us. Is that about right?"

He abandoned the gloss that Donna's call was just her quirky way of joshing. He stood and ran his hand through his thick hair and rubbed his face. He had put on shorts and a tee after showering when he got home. He emptied his wine and refilled his glass. Wendy could see by the bulge in his shorts that the discussion had aroused him. She longed to caress that bulge, to hold it and rub it, to take it in her mouth.

"Yes, that's about right," Wendy said simply. She could feel moisture in her armpits and on her upper lip dew began to gather. She almost trembled with the excitement that grew in her eager body. Memory of sexual gratification, of being taken by a man soaked with lust in anticipation of having her, sprang into her consciousness with urgency.

Kenneth leaned on the table with both hands flat palms down. "What is your answer, Wendy?"

"I, well, what I said was I would, if you would have me, old as I am and not so much to look at anymore." The words tumbled out of her. She rushed on, "I told Wendy that I had to know she was really okay with us having sex. I told her I did want you but I didn't know if I could satisfy you. And I said that you would have to ask me first."

Wendy blushed from her chest to her hairline. She had gotten it out; said what she needed to say. Would he respond as she hoped?

"This has got me feeling pretty randy," Kenneth said. "I have thought about you , about coming on to you, what it would be like to get it on with you. I'm so horny and I do want you. "

Wendy opened her arms wide to him in response. He stepped over to her and put his hand on her cheek and she clutched his hand with her own, moved it so she could press her lips to it and smell his smell.

"I think you're the sexiest landlady I've ever had," he said smiling.

"That could be flattering Mr. construction foreman, if I knew how many landladies you've had.

"Only one," he said with a grin.

"I might surprise you with this old body. Kiss me, Kenneth."

Wendy turned her face up to his, already descending. They kissed lightly several times, then he kissed her neck and her cheeks, and her ears. His breath smelled of the wine they had drunk. Then with unspoken agreement they both opened their mouths and French kissed, invading each other with phallic tongues. It made Wendy's pussy throb. Finally they stopped out of breath.

"Wendy, you are a damned fine kisser." Kenneth's voice was thick with lust.

Wendy was still seated. She put her arms around Kenneth's hips as he stood by her chair. She hugged him close and could feel his straining erection confined in his underwear.

"Oh, Kenneth I've wanted to hold you, be held by you from the moment you appeared at my door. " She rubbed her cheek against his groin, pushing against the engorged protrusion. She put her mouth on the bulge and exhaled ho t breath that sank through his shorts to flow around his cock.

He gave a long sigh. "Wendy, that feels good. Do you suck cock Wendy? I'd like it if you would suck mine."

"I haven't done that to a man for years, Kenneth. But I'd love to suck you. Shall I do it now?"

Kenneth dropped his shorts and underwear and Wendy got her first look at his proud penis. It made her vagina spasm. She watched enthralled as it continued to stretch and stiffen, now untrammeled by clothing. Am I dreaming, Wendy thought? But the penis at that moment oozed a drop of viscous pre-ejaculation fluid. Instinctively she grasped it and stroked the shaft as she leaned in and kissed, licked and finally took the head into her mouth, swirling her tongue around the and sucking vigorously.

So they had their first sex in that tender, rather comically lurid vignette there in the dining area of Wendy's country kitchen. Kenneth naked from the waist down, caressing Wendy's head as she sat at the front of her chair, knees wide apart taking his stalwart erection in her mouth. The only sound in the room came from Kenneth's "ahhhs" and "mmmms" and the slurping sounds made by Wendy's mouth as she sucked and kissed and licked his cock and balls. Where her tongue was not she fondled and petted with her free hand while, with the other, holding and rubbing the part of his shaft not in her mouth at the moment.

"That's good, Wendy. That's real good. You're doing just fi… fi… fine," he said. His hips had begun to undulate instinctively as the bliss intensified, adding the lubricated friction of his glans and shaft rubbing the hot wet flesh of her mouth and tongue to enhance the waves of keen pleasure rolling out through his body.

Wendy reveled in the feel and texture of his cock on her lips and tongue and in her mouth. There seemed to be a pleasure circuit of nerves leading directly from her mouth to her pussy where excited tissue began to swell and ooze preparatory coital fluid. The warm glow in her sex increased in pleasure as he communicated the increasing intensity of pleasure radiating from his own sex.

She took his cock out of her mouth and smiled as she looked up at him. "Am I doing good, Kenneth? Do you like me sucking and licking your big beautiful cock? Want more? Want to spurt your stuff in my mouth?"

"Yes, yes, yes to everything. Put me back in your mouth and make me cum. I need it bad."

She took him in again and resumed. Thereafter he soon cried out, "Ah, ahhhh We… Wen….Wendeeeeeee! I'm cumming!" which he did straightaway, spurting into her mouth, She clutched his buttocks. He held her head. His hips jerked as he came. A frisson caused Wendy's vagina to spasm with sympathetic pleasure as Kenneth ejaculated into her mouth. She swallowed his load and licked away the semen clinging to his cock. When he withdrew from her mouth his penis had begun to soften but the tissue looked puffy from the distended rigidity; thrilled to be receiving a fabulous blow job from this remarkably wanton elderly lady.

"Wendy that was fantastic. You give great head."

Looking up at him, Wendy said, "Kenneth look at what I have for you. " Wine brave and brazenly she pulled her dress up to her hips thereby revealing that she wore no panties and, with her knees wide her sex was completely revealed to him.

He drank in the sight of that entrance to her body; that place of blissful transport; long thick swollen outer labia slack now like plush curtains lifted aside to reveal the hot wet flesh within. Her inner labia too were engorged, succulent and protruding flutes of delicate deep pink. The entrance to her vagina was a dime sized flexing opening into the sweet darkness of her anxious sheath. She spread herself with two fingers and lifted the folds, with her knees spread wide so that her swollen clit came into view, a glistening, throbbing finger tip nubbin of blush red flesh.

"Aw, Wendy," he said, "that is just about the nicest pussy I have seen for an age. It sure looks like it needs a lot more attention. When you extend an invitation like this I couldn't refuse if I wanted to. " HIs moist cock twitched as he spoke.

Wendy watched mesmerized as he brought his hand towards her then looked up into his eyes. When the tip of thumb touched her clit she jerked and gripped his flaccid cock. She could hear sounds and realized it was she making them, grunts and moans of pleasure as he massaged her cunt and worked not only her clit but her vagina with two, then three and finally four fingers in her, fucking her with his adroit hand . It brought Wendy to the edge of the chair, clinging to him, humping his wonderful hand, taking her to a crescendo.

"OH, OH, OH, OH. AAAAHHHH. Oh my god! Oh fuck! AAAAAGH!. EEEEEEAAAHHH, WHOOOOOO, AUGHHH, UGHHH, UNHHH," Wendy screeched and groaned in ecstasy. The intensity of that orgasm flashed through her like a lightning bolt. Wendy bucked so hard against the invading hand that she lifted off the chair. Kenneth held her so she didn't collapse to the floor until he could get her backside onto the chair again. As the rapture suffused her body she squirted pee and coital juices hotly over his hand , some dribbling onto the floor.

Wendy gasped and giggled at the mess she made. Her thighs clamped together and she sucked in her breath, threw her head back and groaned as the blissful waves continued to pulse through her; jerking and squeezing; making little sounds of pleasure,

Kenneth was blown away by Wendy's fierce orgasm. He extracted his hand finally when the orgasmic spasm had diminished to the point Wendy could open her thighs and release him. He stared at her in amazement.

"By God," he marveled, "that was a hell of a cum, Are you okay?"

"What," Wendy asked? She opened her eyes and Kenneth's question slowly registered with her. "Mmmmm," she sighed deeply. "Oh, I am so okay. Oh yes darling. Oh my! I thought for a minute I was going to pass out. I did not have any idea that I had that in me at my age. Goodness! Just let me rest a minute Kenneth. Whew! I need to recover a bit. That was a shock. I didn't expect to cum and certainly not so hard. My clitoris is still throbbing ."

The blow job and now Wendy's intense orgasm inflamed Kenneth so that he was overcome with desire for this incredibly hot elderly woman; and now he desperately wanted to get his needful cock up inside her and fuck her thoroughly.

"Wendy, doggone it, I should have been fucking you since you took me in. I wish I'd known how much you like, hell how much you need some good fucking. We could have been taking care of each other. We got to make up for what we missed. Let's get on up to your bedroom. Can you do some more tonight? We can take our time now. I going to love you like you should have been getting loved all these years since you husband passed. I will give you slow loving' and taste your pussy until you can't stand it for another minute That's when I'm going to fuck that fine pussy I'm looking at so pretty right here."

He helped Wendy stand and she clung to him for a couple of minutes. There was a blooming wet spot on the back of her dress where juices had drooled out of her and run down her crotch.

Although still aroused and needing much more from him, Wendy's practical side asserted itself. "Oh dear I made a mess on the floor. I'm going to clean that up. You ought to call Donna like you always do. She will especially want to hear from you now. When you're done with your call come to my room if you still want more of me . You've wrung me out but I still want more of you."

She cupped his cheek with one hand and kissed him on the lips. She left him and went to her bedroom, hoping he would still come to her after talking to Donna; that his wife would not have changed her mind. She wanted and needed Kenneth now that the barriers of convention had been swept aside, but the last thing she wanted to happen was to be instrumental in causing them to become estranged.

When Kenneth called, Donna picked up immediately.

"Hey, sweetheart, it's me."

She knew as quickly as she heard the timbre of his voice that Wendy had agreed to do as Donna had requested and that Wendy and Kenneth had sex of some sort.

"Well," she said, "You horny guy, tell me all about it. I want details. I know you guys did something together."

"Donna," Kenneth said, "Are you sure you're okay with this? I mean, I feel just now as though I've strayed on you tonight."

"Oh baby, don't feel that way. If you were having sex with Wendy behind my back then you would be straying. But when we've all agreed with each other that's not cheating honey. That's me being selfish and asking Wendy to be my surrogate so you don't run off with some young slut. Now give it up. What did you two do?"

"She gave me a blow job. It was mighty fine."

"Oh, you randy man. Did you come in her mouth?"

"Yes, she wouldn't have it otherwise."

"Donna, I ouched her clit and finger fucked her briefly and she had a cum you wouldn't believe. She's up in her bedroom now and wants me to come and do her good. I'm feeling' so horny right now, even with the blow job I'd fuck your brains out if you were here. "

Learning that she had told him after the blow job that he should come to her if he wanted more, Donna told him to, "go on, get off the phone and go take care of that woman and yourself. Wendy is my surrogate and she's going to keep you out of the hands of some hussy trying' to take my man. Just know that I am going to want to hear all the juicy details. I love you so much sweetie. I can't wait to get you in my pussy "
.

"You going to use your toys?"

"Baby, I got one doing me right now. Want me to put the phone down by my pussy so you can hear it?" Without waiting for his response Donna put the earpiece close to her very wet sex that made squishy sounds as she massaged herself with it.

"Like that honey?"

"Oh yeah. That's hot. Wish it was my tongue doing that instead of a dildo. I'll be thinking about you while I love up Wendy. Man, this is going to take some getting used to."

"OK baby, you go ahead on to her now. I love you and give Wendy a big hug and a kiss from me."

"You know I do not deserve you, Donna. I will talk to you tomorrow. Love you darling.'"

* * *

When Wendy reached her bedroom she went into the adjoining bathroom and rinsed her mouth, peed and washed her crotch to remove the dribbles of coital fluids that had wet her thighs. Then she gave herself a quick flavored douche. Back in the bedroom she removed her dress and bra allowing her ample breasts to sag. Although gravity had taken its toll on her DD sized pair they did not droop like two pendulous sock saps. They retained their globular shape despite becoming somewhat elongated . Her large erect nipples signaled readiness for attention.

Added weight now amplified the size of the generous mound of Venus that formed an inviting soft portico above the apex of the cleft in her pussy. When she masturbated, rapidly diddling her clit made the plump flesh of her mound quiver and shake. When not aroused her vulva was guarded by two large labia like soft French pistolettes . When she wore snug crops her camel toe was erotically outlined by the fabric. More than once she had startled and pleasured strangers in the mall food court with a flash of her prominent labia tightly covered by fabric that followed ever dip and curve of the oasis hidden beneath.

On an impulse she got out her black unmentionables. These included a suspender (garter) belt, black fish net stockings and lacey black boy cut cheeky panties. Experience told her that she would present a far more stimulating vision in the seductive ensemble than if she were completely naked when he came to her.

She had just finished checking her hair, and applying a touch up of her makeup and lipstick when he knocked on the door to her bedroom although the door was wide open. That charmed Wendy; that he would not enter without her permission. But at the same time once they got going at lovemaking she needed him to assert control. Doing whatever, well almost whatever he wanted was such an exciting prospect that she experienced a nice spasm in her vagina.

Wendy did not need to look at his penis, swelling erect again even as he stood in the doorway, now completely naked, to know that he was thoroughly consumed by lust. She knew the look on a man's face, in his eye when he is fiercely aroused.

He smiled broadly and said, "Look at you now Wendy. That is a very, very sexy looking outfit. This arrangement between you and Donna is just looking better and better. "

Wendy slowly turned her back to him so that he could see the expanse of cheeks showing below the lacey panties. The sight made Kenneth flex his hands itching to hold those pillows of soft flesh, caress and fondle them.

"Honey," Wendy said, "I really like you in that birthday suit you're wearing too."

"Now Wendy, as horny as I am and as good as you're looking', I know you're not as young as you used to be. If doing some more tonight is going to be too much for you, we can just cuddle if you want."

"Let's lie down together here in my bed and see what happens," she answered.

"Okay, but don't take off any of the things you're wearing. You look sexy as hell."

He took her in his arms by the bed and she sighed with content at the feel of his sinewy arms and firm muscles around her. His erection pressed between them and firmly against her round belly. He wanted to kiss her and lifted her chin.

"I need to lie down Kenneth. "

She sat on the bed and rolled in, stretching out on her back and he lay down beside her on his side so that his stiff cock pressed against her thigh. He kissed her lips, just several light brushes of his lips on hers.

He put his hand on her just below her breasts. She sighed with contentment at the feel off his hard fingers and calloused palm. He kissed her then repeatedly beginning with her forehead, her eyes, then her cheeks, on to her ears, leaning over her prostrate body to reach the opposite side. When he did his cock slid up her thigh and his chest pressed her breasts. Wendy loved the feel of him poking into her and his weight across her. She reached for his cock but when she clutched it he asked her not to yet. She reluctantly let go.

"Just let me do everything for you and to you right now Wendy. "

"You're stoking up a fire in my pussy with your kissing. I'm getting all moist and squishy again."

He reached down and ran a finger up her cleft, pressing panty fabric into the fissure that now separated her outer lips. That made her tremble and spread her legs. He brought the finger up and looked at it. She watched him sniff the finger then put in his mouth. That too made her squirm and she wanted badly to put her own fingers to work in her pussy but he told her no, not to do that.

Wendy began to wonder if he gave oral sex. She wanted his mouth, his lips, his tongue; all feasting on her with his face buried between her ample thighs. She almost asked him if he would do that but decided to go with his program. It was hardly difficult in one sense because he was making her feel oh so good and very relaxed.

He returned to kissing her moving down from her soft shoulders to her arms, probing her armpit with his tongue which made her squeal and giggle because he had found her most ticklish place. He kissed down her side and onto her midriff then down, pausing on her belly button before stopping at the waistline of her panties just short of where her mound began.

Moving on he kissed the outside of her thigh below her panties on the bare patch before coming to the top of her stockings. Then he moved to her other side and repeated a trail of kisses until he was once again at her forehead.

"Now I want you to roll over on your belly."

She complied and he blazed another path of busses that ranged over her back and half exposed cheeks and naked backs of her thighs between stockings and panties.

Wendy ground her mound against the mattress. She could not recall ever enjoying such extended foreplay; being tantalized to a plateau of arousal that made her shiver with excitement. Her anxious pussy throbbed. Was he ever going to tend to her tits and nipples? Was he ever going to eat her pussy? She liked fucking, no question, but she loved oral sex and desperately wanted him to please go down on her. Momentarily that she had these reflections he spoke softly.

"OK time for some attention to those beautiful tits. Those nipples must be mighty anxious; feeling' like they were going to be left out maybe."

Kenneth unfastened Wendy's bra and told her to turn over.

She did, holding the bra so that the cups stayed in place, sort of; except they slipped down a bit and showed a plump crescent of each and Kenneth leaned in to kiss each of them. He tugged at the material of one side and Wendy coquettishly very lightly restrained but did not prevent the fabric from slipping slowly down. First a carmine arc of areola emerged followed by a nipple that popped deliciously into Kenneth's view. It was a DD sized nipple to go with the DD sized breast that it served.

":Ah, Wendy that's a fine, fine looking tit and that nipple surely needs some sucking."

Kenneth ran his hands over the exposed breast, caressing and kneading it.

Wendy sighed happily. "Be gentle with them. They're not as firm as they used to be. But you can play with the nipple and I love to have them sucked."

Kenneth let a dollop of saliva drop directly onto the nipple and it made Wendy shudder. Straightaway he lowered his face and took her nipple into his mouth and set about giving it the wonderful oral attention Wendy craved; each variant, nibble, tongue spears and sweeps, gentle labio-dental tugs and hearty sucking, sent pulses to her whole pussy making it too throb with pleasure. It also caused her sheath to lubricate and relax in anticipation of a hot slick welcome to the anxious flesh shaft sensed nearby so stiff and eager.

While Kenneth sucked this one his hand groped across her and he slid it under the cup of her other and attended it as well with caresses , then rubbing, rolling, and gently squeezing and twisting the marvelously erect nipple. This continued for some minutes during which Kenneth alternated his oral attention from one to the other. Wendy groaned and sighed and kissed his head, ran her hands through his hair and encouraged him.

"That's it darling. Oh, that is so good. Don't stop, please! Yes, pull on it, ahhh. Pull them; lift my tits. Just like tha…. thAT!"

It had been so long since a man had tended her generous breasts. God almighty she wondered if it had ever felt as good as Kenneth's mouth and hands worked her over. Several times she approached orgasm or had little "zippers" as she called them. Not a full cum but a nice little flare would periodically pulse out of her sex and warm her groin. The housekeeper's voice within faintly called to her attention, although she was now beyond caring, that the pad she intended to use on the bed was forgotten in their preoccupation with the sexual urgency that washed over them. She could feel that the crotch of her panties was soaked. She needed him to go down on her.

"Kenneth, she said hoarsely. "Baby my pussy, eat my pussy pleASE."

Kenneth relinquished her breasts and remarked, "And I am going to take care of that right now."

He positioned himself between her knees.

"Aren't you going to take my panties off," she asked?

"Oh yes. But first I want to do this." Kenneth pulled a pillow over.

"Lift your butt up," he instructed.

When she did so he slipped the pillow under her. Then he had her draw up her knees and spread her legs wide. When she did her pudenda was manifest through the damp fabric that clung to her and by the large wet spot that had flowered in the crotch. He gripped behind her knees.

"I want to push your knees back further so that it will bring your pussy up further. Think you can handle that position for me? Otherwise you could kneel over my face."

"I can do this position for awhile," Wendy said. "If I get uncomfortable or catch a cramp we'll change position. I am so hot for you now. Just do what you want down there."

What he wanted and what he did was put his mouth on her pudenda smelling the redolent mixture of scented douche and the pungency of a female in heat. He sucked on her wet panties and pressed and jabbed his fabric restrained tongue into her slack cleft. He breathed hot breath that washed over her pussy. He licked the crevice at the margin of her bare thighs and moist panties. There was something terrifically erotic for Wendy having her pussy mouthed through her panties and she began the suffusing throbbing that presaged another orgasm. She pushed and ground herself eagerly against his face.

Kenneth sensed that she was on the cusp of cumming. He sat up smiling at her through the damp sheen on his face.

"Now let's get those panties off."

Wendy lifted her hips and he worked the wet garment down over her hips and out of her crotch. Once more he pushed her knees high and let her thighs rest on his forearms with her feet crossed behind his neck. Wendy gasped and cried out with delight when his open mouth touched her vulva.

"Oh geeezzzzzzz," she cried, "I love it. Love it. Love IT! Oooh Kenny my cunt is all yours. That's it. That's IT! Lick that spot. Thaaaat's my cliiiittt! Yes, yes, yes. Do that more baby. Do THAT!! "

Kenneth happily did that. He did other things as well so that Wendy commenced humping his burrowing face . She grunted with each thrust. She played with her tits with one hand and pressed his head against her pussy with the other. They lost track of time. Kenneth did not seem to tire of the roundel of kisses, slurps, lip nibbles and darting tongue applied with enthusiasm and received by Wendy with visceral lust.

Kenneth struggled against her hand making it clear he wished to back off. She reluctantly let go of his head. Was he going to fuck her now, she wondered? But no, he stayed at her crotch and then she felt his fingers at her entrance. He stretched the plump flesh in the apex of her vulva until her pulsing clit emerged erect. It was filmed with coital fluid. He plunged his face onto her sex once more and immediately began vigorously working her clit causing Wendy to cry out.

GAAAAD Kenny, you darling fucKER!!! YaaaaHHHHHH! Make me cum baby, make Wendy cum, make meeeeeeeee. Yes, fuck FUCK! I AM CUMMMMMMING. Oh God, Oh God. Oh God." She twisted about and strained upward against his face trying to wring out the last quiver of bliss with which he had infused her. Her pussy spasmed; her clit pulsed in the delicate grip of his thumb and forefinger.

"My clit is too sensitive," she gasped pushing on his hand, "let it go before...it... get's painful if I cum as hard as, oooooh ahhhhh, Jesus another one...., as I am now, still cu....mmmm cum......cumming now!"

He crawled up her torso and smeared his pussy wet face on her belly and all the way to her head as he stretched out and lowered his weight on her.

"Oh Kenneth, how good you feel, I haven't had a man's weight on me for yea... mmmf!"

He cut off her remark when he clamped his mouth on her. She tasted her juices and smelled the odor of her sex fully aroused as they kissed.

When he lifted from her lips, much as she liked the feel of his muscular chest mashing her tits she could not get deep enough breaths and he raised up on his elbow when she asked. His erection lay between her nether lips and the shaft touched her clit. That maleness in intimate contact but not penetrating felt wonderful. She worked it with her full outer lips clutching the shaft.

"Like that," she asked?

"Oh yeah. Nice."

"Want to put that big dick of yours in me?

"Oh yeah. That would be nice."

Wendy smacked an ass cheek. "Just nice huh?"

"Well I can't judge until I've stuck it up inside you. Are you up for some more? You came so hard."

"Start slow and gentle because I haven't had a man in me for years."

He knelt up and positioned himself. Sweat cooled on both of them. Wendy's pussy was leaking. Kenny eased his hips forward into the lava pool of her vulva the head of his penis slipping into her. He slowly eased through the musculature until just the head of his penis was in her vagina.

"Ah, damn he breathed. That feels so fucking good."

He did it several times prompting Wendy to exclaim, "Kenny that is soooo good. Keep pushing in slowly."

He eased his cock all the way into her causing Wendy to sigh and she squeezed the welcome invader tightly with her vagina.

They fucked slowly, at first she rolled her hips slightly causing just enough friction to ripple out little frissons of orgasmic promise.

"That is so darned nice," Kenny murmured, looking down into her face while holding himself up over her. "You've got some moves I'm going to have to show Donna."

"Mmmm," Wendy said, "You do that. Tell her your old landlady fucked you in ways you hadn't been fucked before."

She upped the ante for the game then by introducing vagina squeezes tightly clutching his cock.

"Ahhh, shiiit," he moaned. "You're going to make me go off like a kid if you keep that up too."

"I'm ready now if you want to step it up. Go ahead and fuck me good now. Fuck my cunt, Kenny. Go for it."

He drew out of her and jammed into her. Then again and again and once more. Then they caught a rhythm as Wendy rolled her hips to meet him on each stroke, huffing and puffing and groaning. Kenneth marveled at the turn of events that led him to now be stroking vigorously in and out of Wendy's pussy. There was nothing special about her appearance that would hint at the sexual appetite hidden inside her; nothing to hint at the superb quality of her pussy and her fucking. There was nothing to hint at the unprecedented gratification she gave him first in the exquisite blow job; then the excitement of her hungry response as he turned her entire body into a shuddering sex organ with his all over kisses and eating her pussy. Now he was on the cusp of an orgasm he could feel building with exceptional urgency and intensity. He had intended to have her doggy fashion before cumming but what was happening to him washed over any such notion. He did think very briefly about pulling out of her to stave off cumming but he could not pull out; the pleasure building and radiating from his penis was too intense, too good . He could not will himself out of her.

A few more plunges then it crashed upon him, "AWWWW ARRRRGH," he roared. "OOOOOH UUUGH, UUGH," Kenneth strained against the bolster of Wendy's broad thighs. I…AH AH AM CU…CU…CUUUMMMING!!!!" Kenneth cried out. He ejaculated, seminal fluid streaming out of him in one, two, three, four jets and a final small squirt; each paroxysm causing his penis to flex within her so that she knew he was filling her vagina.

She had a nice vaginal orgasm with him, not of the intensity that he induced with his mouth but any orgasm was a good one Wendy felt. Just the feel of his cock filling her was wonderful. And she loved to watch his face contort as he blew his load; the strong strain of his thighs against her as he spurted his load into her She felt like an empress bringing a virile man in his prime to such a shattering orgasm; sapping and draining him entirely.

"Don't pull out Kenneth. Leave it in me for awhile. Mmmmm, so nice"

Kenneth collapsed on her, holding off his full weight by resting on his elbows. He was breathing heavily. He put his chin on her shoulder and she hugged it against her own cheek and ran her other hand up and down his back and buttocks feeling the sheen of sweat on his skin.

"I think you liked that," she murmured into his ear. "Was I any good?"

"Good? Good? No it wasn't good. It was one of the best, maybe the best fuck I've ever had. "

She squeezed him tightly, "Aw that is such a nice thing to say to an old lady," Wendy said.

Epilogue

Wendy and Kenneth happily fucked each other and he continued to not just fuck Wendy but also made patient and meticulous love to her and his foreplay brewed a steaming stew of lust in her that made her almost unhinged. Inevitably a few of her closest chums could hardly avoid noticing the vivacious changes in her demeanor. Once they noted the effect it took them little time to ken the cause. (But therein lies another story.) Donna, the remarkably pragmatic wife, continued to give her blessing to the role she and Wendy had agreed upon. Kenneth, that sturdy cocksman, served Donna on his days off with even more vigor than before Wendy. As an upshot, Donna became pregnant and gave birth to a beautiful little girl whom they named Wendy. When the hospital project ended Kenneth was offered and accepted a position as maintenance superintendent for the new complex. A twist of fate that must have had the gods chuckling brought the commodious old craftsman bungalow next door to Wendy's on the market and Kenneth snapped it up. That set the stage for development of a rather unusual tripartite sexual arrangement in which the two women not only shared Kenneth but did so in a threesome recorded in some very torrid home videos. As it turned out the ménage brought Wendy and Donna together whereby they discovered and traveled down a thick subterranean current of lesbian sex that both amused and excited Kenneth; not that they relinquished one centimeter of his sturdy cock but only added each other to their rich sexual stew.

This development was accommodated with Kenneth lying on his back and the two women astride him, one plunged upon his dick and the other facing her sexual sister with her pussy mashed against Kenneth's dispatcher to heaven mouth. In this position they brought each other to the gates of paradise with deep kisses , sucking and rubbing of breasts and clitoral massages enhancing the ministry of Kenneth's adroit tongue and eager cock. Cum spattered, sweaty, sticky and redolent with the odors of sex; that is the way we leave the happy and satiated trio, as we withdraw discreetly the sounds and images of their sex runs through our minds in a looping amateur video clip.

THE HOOKER AND THE MARINE

Another hot one, 3 in a row, it was an official summer heat wave, after just having had one last week and the week before. Judging by the extended weather forecast, next week didn't offer much relief from the 90 plus degree, high humidity weather. The kind of day that Frank could fry an egg on the sidewalk, he'd be too hot to eat it.

He was looking forward to seeing snow; it had been a while since he saw any. Yet, he should have a problem. He was alive, when so many of his best buddies were dead. Compared to what he endured during his 4 tours of desert duty in Afghanistan and Iraq and before that, during the Gulf War, in Kuwait, and special op missions in between, this weather was a relief.

Now that he was finally home, the chow he had here was better than eating baby food, mushy ready-to-eat meals, MRE's. Still coughing up and spitting out sand, he was looking forward to grilling out later. A linguist with an expert ear for dialects, fluent in 10 languages, he could curse in Pashto, Dari, Arabic, Kurdish, Urdu, French, Italian, Spanish, German, and English. Even at his age, with his skills, he was still highly regarded by the CIA and a dozen private, mercenary outfits, that pay by body count, dead or alive. They all enticed him with money to return to active duty.

This hot summer weather was nothing like the deadly weather Frank endured, when wearing a vest and a helmet, carrying a weapon, and shouldering a full backpack of gear when in country, all while watching his ass and protecting the backs of his buddies. Relaxing, but never fully relaxed, always on edge, he remained vigilant. Continually on and never off, he couldn't help himself, that's how he was trained to be.

With his back to the wall, much in the way how Wild Bill Hickok sat when playing poker in the saloon, so that no one could surprise him from behind and shoot him in the back, he sat on his stoop having a beer in his shorts and tee shirt, while wearing his ever present unlaced combat boots. Sitting in this way from his perch on the top step, with a commanding view of the street, his back was one side he didn't have to watch. Normal men hate it when their backs are up against the wall but Frank preferred it. Besides, there was nothing normal about Frank. He was a trained killer, an assassin.

Already in a foul mood, he hated how his old neighborhood had deteriorated in his absence. Hoping to improve his mood, he listened to his favorite team lose a ballgame on the radio. His team losing another game, when in a pennant race, always put him in a lousy mood. Bored and antsy, bouncing off the wall, he was thinking about re-upping. He rubbed the sweat from his crew cut and spat his indecision on the sidewalk.

"Marine Corps! OORAH!"

Programmed to die for his country and for his buddies, removing him from combat was akin to bringing a cage fighter to a formal dance. Out of his element, he didn't belong here. He more belonged in the desert with his buddies, the guys who understood what they needed to do and did it to survive. The conscience that never came into play then, reared its ugly head now. He was having the headaches and the bad dreams again. He couldn't sleep.

He took a good look at his street. Foreclosures had taken their toll and every other house on the street was boarded up or had a for sale sign in front. With transients replacing familiar faces, now a stranger in his own neighborhood, he didn't recognize anyone. Not hard to find, the gutter collected needles and spent condoms; there was litter everywhere. The trees that lined his street were dead or dying. Pit bulls walked wanna-be tough guys and, in a four-on-one confrontation, he convinced the gang members that sold drugs on his street to find another corner in a different neighborhood to do their dirty business. With him home now and on duty 24/7, the Marine has landed, this neighborhood was on its way to being secured.

He grew up here and this used to be a beautiful street with kids playing and families gathering. Now, look at it. Symbolic of the state of the economy and the empty political rhetoric on the war on drugs and on gun control, his old neighborhood was no different than any other slum anywhere in America. A war zone and an unsafe place where residents had to watch their backs, this street could have been a street in Bagdad. What happened to his country?

Frank watched a woman walking on the other side of the street. He didn't recognize her and even though he never saw her before, he knew what she was. She was a young, pretty thing, petite but with big tits. She was a prostitute. He's been with enough of them all over the world to recognize their gait and their stare. They all had the same walk and look about them, especially when approaching a potential customer.

"Hi ya, baby," she said with a wave and a smile, as she neared. "Wanna date?"

There was always a man behind the woman and when he woke up from his drunkenness and put his pants and shoes on to leave, he felt bad about taking advantage of these women. Impossible to overcome what they had endured, he felt bad about leaving them behind to fend for themselves. Yet, if he let his guard down, they'd slit his throat. Had he been somewhere else, anywhere else, he'd take care of their man and set them free. Yet, where would they go and what would they do? Akin to indentured servitude, some women were born into that lifestyle and it was the only life they knew.

Suddenly, his mind morphed into a stew of naked body parts, tits, asses, and pussies. When not on duty, when not in combat, drunk out of his mind, he just wanted to forget and how better to chill than to be with a woman. Faceless women, as foreign to him as he was to them, they all looked alike. Yet, when with him, they all had one thing in common. No matter what language they spoke, he taught them all to say God bless America.

"Say it now, say it. Say God bless America," he'd tell them, just before he was about to cum.

"God bless America."

Some said it better than others, but it was the sentiment that counted. Most times, most women, didn't even understand what they were saying. Repeating his words phonetically, they smiled their cooperation for the money he gave them.

"Louder. Say it louder."

"God bless America!"

Appropriately, his way of indelibly stamping their brains with those words, after he fucked their bodies, maybe they'd make the connection in their minds. Certainly, if they repeated those words to the wrong person, they'd be targets themselves. He fucked them, just as his country fucked him with non-existent help from the Veterans' Administration for the emotional wreck that he was now. How could some Army doctor, who had never been in combat and who had never taken a life, help him? He was too far gone. Keeping him out there too long, his country fucked him up real good.

"God bless America," he said softly.

Needing to chill not to lose his mind, needing some sense of comfort from someone, he had been with so many women in so many countries, he lost count. More dangerous for the women than it was for him, in the part of the world where he was, stoning was the sentence for adultery and worse for prostitution. Yet, no matter, where he went, there were always women willing to do anything for money and anything to survive.

"Don't tell me your name. I don't want to know," he'd say to them. Not knowing their names was his way of staying disconnected from them and from the real world. Caring for someone other than himself and his buddies' backs would slow his reactions. He didn't have time to think and knowing their names would clutter his mind with all the women he's fucked and with emotions he couldn't afford to have. "I'll call you Robin."

His favorite bird, he called every woman of the street Robin and no matter if they understood him or not, they'd just smile. Then, when he was done with them, in his mind's eye, he'd watched them fly away.

"Fly. Fly. Fly away little birdie, my beautiful robin. You're free. Bye, bye."

Unfocused thinking, fantasizing about pumping her pussy or her sucking his cock, daydreaming about some woman, while pumping rounds in the enemy, would get him killed. He needed to stay focused. He needed to stay in the zone, the war zone.

He was the sweeper, the cleaner, and they called him in as a last resort. He cleaned up the political messes that the Generals made. There was no place for love in the Hell where he was stationed and where he was going, when he died. He only had room for hate.

He had the instincts of a veteran street cop, but one without the attitude, the backup, and the badge. He didn't have time for attitude.

When in country, it's that cockiness that will get you killed. Besides, already the best of the best, better than all the rest, he was a Marine.

"Oorah," he mumbled under his breath, now that he wasn't alone and now that he had an audience of one watching him.

Wrapped too tight, he was having difficulty loosening up without unraveling. He's seen some stuff, too much stuff, and he's done some stuff he's not proud of doing. Yet, when it was him against the enemy, either he did what he had to do to survive or die trying.

He watched her walk closer and it was obvious that she was inexperienced. He wondered if this was her first time and if he was her first, potential customer. She looked that raw. She had to start somewhere, why not with him?

He could tell from her body language that she was nervous. Was she wondering if he was a cop? He certainly looked like one. All he needed was the uniform and patrol car. Too dumb to know any better or maybe she was too desperate to care, he knew she was going to solicit him anyway.

His neighborhood had gone to shit, since he left. After an IED nearly killed him, he was home for good or so he thought. Even after he got his hearing back, he still had the headaches. Tortured with physical pain and mental anguish, even when he didn't have the headaches, the bad dreams kept him awake.

After he was released from the hospital and home for only a couple of months, his Colonel called him wanting to know if he'd accept a special op mission, going deep undercover, and kidnapping a bad guy from Pakistan. It was suicide, but it sounded like fun. It sounded like something he'd do and had done, so many times before. Suddenly, pumped with adrenaline and feeling like Rambo again, he slept like a baby.

"Oorah!"

Now with a mission on the horizon and real purpose to his life again, he felt alive. He felt needed. A key player, he was part of a team.

"God bless America."

Just like Rambo, his motto was they drew first blood, not me. The same as Rambo, that was always his justification to kill, not that he needed any. Pulling the trigger was easy. It was the consequences of his decision to kill or to set his adversary free that he had to live with later. The judge, the jury, and the executioner, he was God when out there. He was okay with those roles, that is, until he was home alone with his bad self and all those he killed returned as ghosts to haunt him.

Assembling a team of the best of the best, he was first on the list. Only, if they were captured in Pakistan, they'd be on their own; the United States couldn't help them. He didn't even have to think about it; he said yes. After just two months home, with nothing to hold him here, he was already stir crazy and ready to re-enlist.

"Semper Fidelis."

Trying to make herself appear sexy, he watched her walk her walk. Strutting her stuff, she was laughable. He's had plenty pay-as-you go pussy the world over and she had much to learn. Yet, there was something about her that he liked, a veiled innocence that made him feel protective of her, as a father would lookout for his innocent daughter, only he could see that she wasn't so innocent.

"Either you have money in the bank or you're crazy," she said crossing the street and walking closer. "You talk to yourself more than I ever talked to my dog," she said with a laugh.

"You have a dog?"

"I did, but he died."

"I don't have any money in the bank," he said with a laugh.

She was so young, younger than his youngest daughter. She was just a kid. Figuring she was older, guessing she was in her early twenties, she looked 18-years-old. He wondered how life could get so bad so quickly for someone so young? Two of a kind, a paradox and a quagmire with both selling themselves short, the parallel of her selling herself for money and him selling himself for his country wasn't lost on him.

Judging by her complexion and her hair, she looked like a natural blonde and after spending so much time with women who had dark hair, dark skin, and brown eyes, he was attracted to her blue eyes. Nearly as tall as he was, she wasn't a bad looking woman. With a bit of makeup, her hair done, and some nice clothes, she'd be pretty.

He had been with worse, only, even when he was in Bangkok and offered supposed Thai virgins, he had never been with anyone as young as he imagined she was. Maybe he felt bad for them, but he preferred the older whores to the younger ones, and he always chose the ones that the others didn't want. They were the ones more appreciated of him selecting them and they always showed him a better time.

It had been a while, since he had been with a woman, one who could speak English, that is, and he was already thinking about accepting her proposition, before she even asked. How old was she, he wondered? Eighteen? Nineteen? He'd be surprised to learn, later, that she was twenty-five.

"Twenty bucks for a blowjob, Mister," she said stopping in front of him.

She had a lot to learn. If he was a cop, he could have arrested her. Maybe he was underestimating her. Maybe she knew he wasn't a cop. Maybe she didn't care, if he was.

For some reason, he could see his cock in her mouth, while fondling her enormous tits. It's been a while, since he's seen, felt, and sucked a rack like hers. Feeling a bit tense, he could use a blowjob right about now. She looked hot and tired and he thought about inviting her upstairs to his air conditioned apartment for a cool drink and some hot sex. Yet, if he was going to make the effort to take the time to be with her, he'd want more than a blowjob.

Tired of paying for sex, he wanted a commitment. He needed a girl-friend, someone to love him for who he was. If he had a girlfriend, a woman to come home to, he wouldn't even think about re-upping. Suddenly, he felt as tired as he was old. His mind wasn't right. A suicide mission, he knew if he went back in county this time, he wouldn't return.

"That's pretty cheap," he said giving her the look over.

"It's a tough economy and I go with the flow to make a living," she said.

"Are you any good at sucking cock?"

"I've sucked my share without complaints. Put it this way, no one has asked for a refund," she said with a laugh that made him laugh with her.

She was cute and he liked her. Only, instead of feeling excited to have his cock sucked by her, he felt sad. She made him feel bad. This is America, the land of the free and the home of the brave. It saddened him that his buddies, better men than even him, better men than she'd ever meet, died for her right to walk the street to solicit him.

With three daughters of his own, he wished he could help her. As his way of continuing to give back in hopes of fixing all that is so wrong with his country and his neighborhood, he had a sudden need to help her. His ex, after she remarried, wanting to get as far away from him, as she could, took his daughters and moved to California, when they were still young.

Perhaps, his need to help her was a manifestation of a need he had to still be in the lives of his daughters. Out of control with Post Traumatic Stress, something he didn't even know he had, until he was diagnosed with it and given therapy for it, his ex-wife, his daughters, and their marriage were all victims of his rage.

Now, when he wasn't filled with adrenaline with the thoughts of re-upping for the sake of a mission, he had nothing but headaches, heartaches, and bad dreams. It hurt his head and pained his heart to think of all that he sacrificed for his country for the likes of this streetwalker and everyone else who now plagued his neighborhood. Forsaking ballgames, barbeques, and long drives through the country on a nice sunny day, ever since 9/11 and Pappa Bush before that, he hasn't been around much. Always gone and landing on some makeshift runway in a God forsaken place, there was always some fire, somewhere in the world, that needed to be extinguished. He hadn't been much of a Dad, and he wondered if his daughters even remembered who he was, but he loved his girls.

With all the death and misery he saw and had an active role in creating, he had a difficult time trying to live a normal life and feel real emotions. Standing on a tightrope of indecision, if he felt anything, if he waivered while walking the line of his call to duty to God and to his country, he'd die. If he needed to feel, then he needed to stay home. If he could still sever his emotions, then he was fit for duty and could return.

With his head turned around by all that he's been through, he had a hard time severing his feelings. Returning home and returning to everything familiar made him feel and made him realize all he had done in the name of his country. When he was 6,000 miles from home, in a foreign land so far from home that it was surreal, he didn't have time to feel. He didn't have time to think. He only had time to react or die. Now he needed to make a choice. Either he was a Marine or a civilian.

"Oorah."

Everything he felt was gag reflex. He didn't even have to think about his next move. He was trained not to think, just to do. With a flick of his hand, a kick of his boot, or a butt of his head, he just reacted. He was trained to get his opponents down on the ground, where he could control them and put real hurt to them. Don't let them get up, never give them an inch. No mercy. Stand tall. Be brave. You're a Marine.

He wasn't a regular Marine. Most times, when working for the CIA, he didn't even wear a uniform. Able to mingle with the locals, he was invisible. He was a ghost. He was a specialist. He was a killer. He was the one they called when they needed someone to be found or someone to disappear. The only fear he felt was failing his mission. He couldn't die. They couldn't kill him. He was dead already.

"No, I don't think so, but thank you anyway for offering to blow me," he said with a little laugh, while giving her a smile and studying her. She walked away looking rejected, as if just having interviewed for a job she didn't get, and he felt bad.

She had a nice ass and he'd do her, just to spend some quality time with those big melons. Maybe some alone time with a woman was just what he needed to quell his headaches and stop the bad dreams. For sure, he'd never call her Robin and with that, he wondered what her name was.

He had the urge to give her the twenty bucks. She looked like she could use it. Except for her big tits, she was so gangly thin. She looked like she could use some grub and he suddenly had the need to feed her, to take her under his wing, and to take care of her. Maybe he was reading her all wrong, but she looked just as broken, as he was.

Whether putting his adversaries at ease with conversation and a kind word or beating them senseless in hand-to-hand combat, he always engaged the enemy. It's funny how he perceived her as much an enemy to his neighborhood, as was her pimp and as were those drug dealers he relocated. He loved to meet up with that guy. Just as he did with those four gang members selling drugs at the corner, he'd make it so that he'd never run another hooker on his street again.

"Can I ask you a question?"

"Sure," she said stopping in her tracks, a few feet past him, "for five bucks you can," she said with a smile. "It doesn't mean I'll answer it, though. I'll just allow you to ask it."

He loved the repartee of teasing and he imagined she'd be fun in bed. She turned back around and walked to him. Blonde hair, blue eyes, white teeth, and big tits, if she lived in Texas, they'd make her a beauty queen but here in New York, she was a hooker. Go figure. He reached in his wallet, pulled out a five, and handed it to her.

"What's your name?"

"Robin," she said.

He laughed wondering if that was really her name. Robin was too pretty of a name for a woman in her profession, yet it served him right that would be her name; that's what he called them all. He imagined her proud parents when they named her that. For sure, she was prettier when she smiled. She looked so sad otherwise. She was pathetic, but there was something about her that made him want to know, protect, and shelter this little, wounded bird.

He had slit the throats and shot better women than her, women who believed in something and women who were willing to die for their beliefs. Stopping them from blowing themselves up and everyone else around them, he facilitated their departure from this life to the next with his razor sharp knife or a few rounds from his gun. It was his job to make sure that they got to their promise land without taking him and any of his buddies with them.

That was a funny way to put it, he thought. He was a facilitator. Now he had something to write on his resume. His government spent a lot of money to train him and thousands of men, just like him, to be the Grim Reaper, the harbinger of death. A highly trained killing machine, he had lost count of how many bodies he had left to rot in the desert heat. For sure, with his bullets flying on errant pathways and ricocheting off walls, he had killed more than he even knew he had. It wouldn't surprise him, when in the rage of war, if he was responsible for accidentally killing one of his buddies.

Serves them right for attacking us on our own land. Serves them right for bringing down the Twin Towers and killing all those people. Serves them right for starting the downward avalanche of our economy. If he could kill them all again, he would.

"Oorah. Once a Marine, always a Marine."

"What? Did you say something?"

"Sorry, I have this uncontrollable urge to blurt out my thoughts sometimes. It's a way for me to get things off my mind and to release stress."

"Like that Tourettes Syndrome?"

"I guess you could say that, only in my case it would more be called, Marine Corps Syndrome."

"Yeah, I figured either you were a cop or a soldier. I was hoping you were the later rather than the former."

Yet, suddenly feeling as if he was a reverend on a mission to save a soul, he thought he could save her. As soon as he thought that, he felt foolish. He felt like every other John. After they fuck her, use her, and abuse her, they all want to save her. Only, this woman was different. There was something about her that made his bones ache and his heart melt.

He didn't know what it was, it was something indefinable and indescribable that made him unable to let her go. For some inexplicable reason, he had an instant connection with her. He liked her and would like to get to know her better, if the hooker thing could be put to rest for a while. He wasn't the jealous type and, as far as he was concerned, especially since he had so much of it, what's in the past is history, but having a girlfriend as a hooker was an extreme case of unfaithfulness. Once he committed to someone, he was too possessive to have his woman be with another man.

Certainly, he was more than twice her age. Other than for money, why would someone like her be interested in someone like him? Suddenly, he felt like a dirty old man about to take advantage of a woman young enough to be his daughter.

"Why do you do this? Are you on drugs? Do you have a pimp? Do you have kids to feed? What is it that makes you have sex for money?" He fired off his questions in the way that he fired his M60 machine gun, in a controlled spray leveling anything that moved.

"You already asked your question, Mister, and I answered you."

"I did?"

"You asked my name. Your five dollars already bought you my one answer, Mister. Then, you asked me five more questions."

"Frank. My name is Frank."

"For another five bucks, Frank, do you want me to pick which one of those five questions not to answer or do you want to chose?"

She was funny. He liked her sense of humor. Just like any normal couple, with his arm around her and his hand fondling her big tits, he could picture her sitting next to him on the couch and making out, while watching a movie. He yearned to have a normal life with a normal woman. Only how can a killer expect to live normally with a hooker?

"You're not a bad looking woman. You could interest a nice, young man, get married, have a couple of kids, and live a normal life," he said looking at her. "Why do you do this?"

He looked at her more closely. She had a pretty face, but her massive tits controlled where he looked, as well as his horniness. Definitely, she was a D cup. Yet, because she was so thin, her tits looked even bigger on her slim frame and, because of that, it wouldn't surprise him, if she was only a C cup. Only a C cup. She still had big tits and he was enamored with her huge breasts.

"Why? Duh? For the money. What do you think? I have no education. I have no skills. The only job I can get is at some fast food joint standing on my feet to make $50, after taxes, when I can make more than that on my back or on my knees."

Her confession made him realize that they had much in common. They were much alike in that regard. With him a killing machine, what kind of job could he get, after being discharged from the military? They'd have to debrief him and after years of psychotherapy, maybe he could live a somewhat normal life, but doing what? He could always become an instructor. An instructor for what, on how to kill? Only, never having to think about it, he was better at doing than teaching.

She had plenty of attitude, but he could tell she was all bark and no bite. He could tell she was scared. Someone had put the fear of God in her for her to do what she so obviously hated doing. He could see that in her eyes. He's killed enough people to know the good from the bad and deep down inside, she was a good woman.

Just by looking at her, he could see she wasn't happy. Just by looking at her, he could tell she was a survivor. She was miserable having sex for money and, if she survived this low point in her life, with a bit of tender, loving care, she'd make someone a good woman, a good wife, and a good mother. Someone was forcing her to do this, but who? He didn't have to wait long for an answer, when a new Caddy rounded the corner and screeched to a stop.

"Shit!"

"Who's that?"

"Desmond. My pimp. Pretend you agreed to date me," she said looking from him and back to her pimp. Now she really looked scared. "Okay? Okay, Frank? Please?"

Frank watched it play out, before giving her his answer. A tall, muscular, black man got out of the car and walked towards her. Stereotypical in the car he drove, the clothes he wore, and the swagger he had. He looked like a real asshole.

"You got my money, bitch," he said walking up to her face and talking to her as if she was less than human, when he was dog crap that he'd wipe from his shoe, if he had the pleasure of stepping on him.

"I'm still working on it. I haven't had a lot of takers. There's been cops, but this guy," she said looking over at him and pointing, "he–"

Nearly knocking her down, he slapped her hard enough across the face to blowback her hair and leave a handprint on her pretty cheek. The expression on her face went from shock to anger to submission. It was then that Frank knew she had been beaten before, probably as a little girl because in an instant, she was somewhere else. Disappearing within her sad self, her pimp could do anything to her and she'd never feel it. He had seen enough of this show to know he'd intercede and help her.

"You don't give me excuses, bitch. You just give me my money," he said grabbing her purse and taking what little money she had, before tossing it back at her.

He grabbed and pulled open the front of her blouse and stuck his hand down her bra.

"All you whores hide my money on me."

"All I have is what you took. I'm not hiding any money. I swear. That's all there is. You took my last dollar, I have no more," she said palming the five dollars that Frank had given her.

"Hell you ain't," he said reaching up to hit her again.

"Don't do that," said Frank.

"Say what?" The pimp looked over at him, before turning back to Robin and slapping her again, this time even harder. He turned towards Frank and, with a nod of his head, gave him a hard look. "You a cop?"

"Nope," said Frank standing.

"Unless you're buying, best you get your white ass off my street, old man."

"I told you not to do that and you did," said Frank stepping down from the top step and squaring up on the sidewalk in front of him. Slowly, he shook his head, as if he was tired of having to correct the bad behavior of others by teaching them a lesson they'd never forget.

Able to sever his emotions, a man you'd never see coming, Frank had a relaxed, calm, matter of fact manner about him. A waste of energy that interfered with what he had to do, it served no purpose to get angry. He had the dead-eyed stare that Javier Bardhem had in No Country For Old Men, when he played Anton Chigurh, the man with the cattle gun, who fired compressed air to kill his victims. A walking, talking, breathing weapon, Frank didn't need a cattle gun to kill someone.

Sensitive about his age, he didn't like being called old man. The last man who called him old is no longer breathing. Admittedly nearer to sixty than he was to forty, he could do anything a man half his age could do without breaking a sweat.

The pimp moved his shirt aside to show Frank the butt of a handgun. Unless this guy was a quick draw, the gun was useless where it was. The sight of the handgun was all Frank needed to go into automatic mode, kill or be killed. As if a fast forward movie played across his mind, he saw all the faceless dead men and women, who made the fatal mistake of pulling a weapon on him.

He wasn't a cop. He was a Marine in a war zone and in war to save his neighborhood. He didn't have to warn his victim first, before launching his attack, a preemptive strike, that left little doubt in the mind of the victim, who had just been attacked by Frank, that he was lucky to have survived and still be alive.

Usually a fatal mistake anywhere else outside the United States, Desmond made a mistake in showing Frank his gun, a telltale sign that he was too much of a coward to use it. Much like Arnold Schwarzenegger, when he played Julius Benedict in Twins, against the Klane brothers, this man had no respect for logic. Defenseless even when possessing a handgun, this poor excuse of a man wasn't even trained in life and death, hand-to-hand combat to give him the time to draw it and the opportunity to use it.

"You don't tell me what to do with my woman, asshole," said the pimp walking up to Frank and shouting. "And you don't tell me what to do on my street and in my neighborhood," he said jabbing a stiff index finger in Frank's chest, leaving it there and turning it, as if it was a corkscrew. "You dig?"

Suddenly, the neighborhood was alive with people watching. Frank didn't have to look away from his intended target to know there were eyes staring to see what would happen. He could feel them. An innate level of awareness, as if walking in a hamlet or a village with little or no cover, as if having eyes behind his head, he had the benefit of a sixth sense, when confronted with danger in a life and death situation. Like rats hiding in a hole, not only did he know they were there but also he knew where they all were.

Looking nowhere else but in the man's eyes, Frank could see all he needed to see with his peripheral vision. With Desmond already showing Frank his violent intention, the fight was over before it began. Even though the man towered over him by a good six inches, had him by more than 50 pounds, and was half his age, in one fluid motion, as if performing a choreographed dance, faster than a blink of an eye, Frank snapped the man's finger's, bent him forward with a sidekick that crushed his kneecap, broke his nose with a head butt, and busted out both his eardrums with a two handed, cupped clap to his ears.

If he felt threatened, if he had wanted to kill him, he would have given him a fatal chop to his neck or a deadly palm to his chest. Allowing him to live, instead, he took his gun away from him for good measure, before reaching in his pockets and taking his money, too.

"This isn't your street, shithead. I live here. This is my street and my neighborhood, and my name isn't asshole, it's Captain Frank Parker," he said nearly lifting the man off the ground with a one handed choke hold to his neck.

"You lied to me. You're a cop," he said with blood gushing from his nose and his ears.

"I told you I'm not a cop. I'm a Marine and if I see you on my street again, now that I have your gun, I'll kill you with your own weapon. You dig? Who are the police going to believe a decorated war hero or you, a lowlife pimp, who hits women?"

He tossed the man sideways across the sidewalk. Desmond crawled back in his car and left faster than he came.

"Why'd you do that?"

"Why? I just saved your skinny ass," he said handing her the money and when she wouldn't take it, he grabbed her wrist and stuffed it in her hand.

Her face was red and swollen from where Desmond slapped her. She could use some ice to reduce the swelling and lessen the pain.

"My skinny ass didn't need saving, Frank," she said with tears welling up in her eyes and putting the money in her purse. "Now I have no one to protect me. I can't make any money. And I have no place to stay."

"Stay? You were staying with him?"

"Yeah, a bunch of us girls live together in an apartment he rents. We have nowhere else to go. He takes all our money in exchange for a place to live and food to eat."

"I have a spare room," said Frank. "You can stay with me."

That was the start of their co-dependent relationship. The one thing that Frank needed that was missing from his life was a woman. Both a work in progress, they helped one another. Frank even turned down his Colonel to go to Pakistan to stay home with Robin.

Instead, she was his mission and he accompanied her to get her things. Fortunately for Desmond, he wasn't there to receive another beating. After she was cleaned up and ate regularly, she filled out and turned out to be a very pretty woman. Prettier even than his ex-wife, she was the prettiest woman that Frank ever had.

Not wanting to be like the rest of the men in her life, he gave her some space and respected her privacy. That first night, the gentleman that he is, he gave her his bed and he took the couch. With her sleeping in the next room, if he had trouble sleeping before, he was definitely having trouble sleeping now.

He wondered what she wore to bed. He wondered if she was naked. He wondered if she was thinking about him, in the way that he was thinking about her. He couldn't stop thinking about her. Now that she's here, now what? Thinking with his cock, instead of his brain, what was he thinking to get involved with her?

Will she just stay the night and leave in the morning? Where will she go? Who will she go with? Will she continue being a prostitute, working out of his apartment and taking guys home with her, whenever he wasn't there? Will she use him, in the way that so many men have used her?

Still, even though he knew it was wrong, even though she was younger than his youngest daughter, he was horny for her. There was something that he really liked about her. Her voice, the way she moved, and how she looked excited him. Horny just thinking about her pretty face and big tits, he should have taken her up on her offer of a blowjob. He could use a release right now.

He was so horny for her that he'd pay to have sex with her but that would make him no better than her pimp. He wished he could have more than that with her, a real relationship, something he thought he had with his ex-wife. Because of his job, with him being away so much and because of his rage, when he was home, finally, he was unable to have a loving relationship with a woman before. Thinking about not re-upping, retiring from the military instead, and not going back to active duty, he could have a relationship with her now.

Yet, what in the Hell would a young, good looking woman want with an old, broken down man like him? Why would Robin want him? It wasn't bad enough that he had anger issues from the effects of Post Traumatic Stress, he was a trained killer.

Thinking about her sucking him, while he fondled her big boobs, he started fingering his cock through his underwear. Not needing much sleep, anyway, accustomed to sleeping with one eye and both ears open, Frank was a light sleeper. Tired from thinking too much about re-upping or retiring, he finally closed his eyes and slept for a few minutes. When he opened his eyes, she was standing at the end of the couch in her nightgown watching him sleep.

"I can't sleep," she said with a sad smile.

As if she was naked, the moonlight from the window behind her revealed every contour of her slim but curvaceous body through her sheer nightgown.

"Why not?"

Accustomed to seeing in dim light, he couldn't help but stare at the mountainous impressions her huge breasts made in her nightgown. With her nipples pushing against the shear fabric of the material, he wondered if she was cold or excited.

"I never slept in a bed before."

The irony of a hooker, who had never slept in a bed before didn't escape him and he thought it funny.

"Seriously? You never slept in a bed before? Where'd you sleep?"

He imagined her a vampire and sleeping upside down in a closet or in a closed coffin.

"When I lived with my Mom, I always slept on the sofa or the floor. She always had company, if you know what I mean. Then, I was homeless for a while, lived on the street, until Desmond found me sleeping on a bench in the bus terminal and offered me a place to stay. Not a real bed, all he had were mattresses on the floor."

He imagined a half dozen mattresses side by side with two prostitutes to a mattress, pick-a-dilly.

"So, what's wrong with my bed?"

"It's too hard. Besides beds are only for fucking and I'm horny," she said with a sexy smile.

Good God, she's horny. Frank thought of all the things he'd do to her to help her through her horniness, while satisfying his sexual desire for her.

"Robin, I–"

"Can you sleep with me? Please? I'll make it worth your while... Frank," she said pausing before saying his name.

One never at a loss for words, he was too excited with the thoughts of sleeping with her to think of what to say now. It almost didn't matter to him, if she really wanted him or was using him. Seeing her standing in the moonlight in her nearly transparent nightgown was a vision come true.

"I don't think–"

"Don't worry," she said. "You don't have to pay me."

It bothered him that she played the prostitute card. He didn't see her as a hooker. He saw her more as a desirable, young woman, someone who he was interested in developing a serious relationship and for her to mention money soured his desire for her.

"I don't intend to pay you for something you should learn how to give to a special guy for free."

She looked at him and smiled and he felt his cock twinge for her. She was so damn pretty, when she smiled.

"Will you be my special guy?"

Imagining having her in his life, as her special guy and her his special gal, he softened with her words, that is, until reality kicked him hard in the nuts.

"I'm too old for you," he said looking away from her tits to look at her face. She was so damn pretty that he didn't know where to look. "I'm old enough to be your father."

He wished he had met her twenty years ago, when he was 35-years-old, but then she'd only be 5-years-old. This won't work. This will never work. What's wrong with him to even think she'd be interested in him.

"I've been with older men, before, some of my mother's boyfriends had their way with me."

"I'm sorry. That's terrible."

"It's just the way it was, back then," she said so matter of fact, as if not expecting any more out of life. "Her Johns would beat me, if I didn't give them what they wanted and when my mother found out that I was giving it away for free, taking away her business, she threw me out."

He knew she was a survivor. He recognized it in her eyes. She was the type who'd do whatever she had to survive. He had been right about that with her. Yet, is that what she's doing now? Is she playing him for a place to live and for food to eat? When she sat on the edge of the couch, he scooted over to make more room for her and when he rested his hand on her exposed thigh, when he felt her warm, soft skin, he didn't care if she was using him or not.

She reached out her hand and fondled his cock through his underwear. He watched her toying with his cock, before looking up at her face. Immediately he became hard with the touch of her hand and when they made eye contact, he wanted to kiss her. He had never kissed a prostitute before. Just as he called them all Robin, so as not to get emotionally attached, they didn't want to be kissed for the same reason. Only, even though she was a hooker, he didn't see her as that.

"Robin, I'm not in a good place right now."

"I can make you forget your problems," she said fingering his cock with her fingertips, before tracing the length of his penis with her fingers, and cupping his balls with her hand.

"I'm too vulnerable and I–"

"Shut up, Frank," she said.

She reached her hand in the pee hole of his boxers and removed his cock from his underwear. She held his cock in her hand looking at it, fingering it, and fondling it, before stroking it. Then, she leaned down and took him in her mouth.

He reached out his hand and felt her body from her shoulder, down her back, to her round ass. Soft, yet firm, a ripe piece of fruit, she felt so young, unlike so many of the foreign, prostitute women he had been with. He reached down and around to fondle her breast and finger her nipple through her nightgown. She had such big tits and her nipples were so hard. He couldn't wait to see them. He couldn't wait to suck them.

He moved her hair out of the way, so that he could see his cock in her mouth and when he did, she looked up at him and smiled. With all the hookers he hired over the years, even though he found that so erotically exciting, not one has looked up at him with his cock in her mouth and smiled. None of them teased him in that way and looked like they enjoyed what they were doing. A total unexpected contrast with Robin, he was pleasantly amazed at how lustfully she sucked his cock. He loved seeing her pretty face, while he stroked her long, blonde hair and fucked her warm, wet mouth.

Unaccustomed to having a woman actively participate in his lovemaking, she actually appeared to enjoy blowing him. He's had a lot of blowjobs over the years, but this blowjob from Robin, was the best, by far. He put a hand to the back of her head and ran his fingers through her lush, blonde hair. Then, lifting her up to him, he kissed her. She was the first woman he had kissed, since his ex-wife, and he could taste himself on her lips.

Unable to remember the last time he French kissed a woman, he couldn't get enough of her soft, full lips and her warm, wet tongue. She totally blanked his mind with her kisses. With every kiss and with every touch of her oh, so young body, he had reached an excitement he had never felt before.

At first he was uncomfortable because she was so young, younger than his youngest daughter, but now that he was with her and she was such a willing and giving sexual partner, he could get used to having her in his life. She made him feel younger. She made his cock the hardest it's ever been and he liked the feeling of protecting her, comforting her, and having her in his life. In one fluid motion, she removed her nightgown and took him by the hand to bed.

From that first night that she took him to bed, they had sex every night after that. The best sex he ever had, it was more than the sex. It was the connection. It was the relationship. It was love. Definitely, she was the best kisser and never had he experienced a woman with breasts so big.

A warm and generous lover, when he was on top of her and inside of her, kissing her with her big breasts flattened against his muscular chest, he'd reach down and cup her sweet ass with both hands. Pulling her up and closer, he was able to go so deep inside her pussy that he felt he was one with her. Including his ex-wife, never had he been with a woman who had an orgasm from intercourse and she had one nearly every time they were together.

"Oh, Frank! Oh, Frank! Oh, yeah, that's it, baby, don't stop. Fuck me, baby, fuck me."

Between her kisses, her good looks, her big tits, and her screaming his name every time she had an orgasm, she made him feel special. He loved it when she rolled him over and got on top of him. Sitting upright on his cock, he loved watching her big tits bouncing, before he reached up to corral them with his big hands. Then, while still sitting on his cock, with his prick deep inside of her, he loved it when she leaned down to kiss him. He loved the feel of her long, blonde hair on his chest, before she lowered herself further and, as if being electrified, touched his chest with her big boobs.

"I love you, Frank," she said looking in his eyes and he knew she did.

"I love you, Robin," he said looking in her eyes and meaning it.

Since his ex-wife left him, able to sever his emotions to be with every hooker he called Robin, never did he ever think he'd say he loved a woman again. She wasn't kidding about her cock sucking skills, either. Never has he had his cock sucked like that. Sex is one thing but love is another dimension and never has he had anyone make love to him in the way that Robin made love to him.

No matter the difference in their ages, they had made a real love connection. After spending a season of summer lovin', they were married and bought a house in a better neighborhood. A year later, she was pregnant. Finally Frank was home for good and Robin had a home with a bed.

EXTRA CREDIT

This story takes place about six years ago when I was in high school. I was a senior and very much ready to get the hell out of school. But one thing I did regret was that I would not be able to see Mrs. Shannon again. She was my physical science teacher and one of the most beautiful women I've ever seen.

I'll describe her to you the way she looked the very first time I saw her. On the first day of my senior year word was going around campus that there was a new teacher and that she was fine as hell. Luck being on my side my first class was with this new teacher. I walked in the room and nearly passed out. There was Mrs. Shannon sitting on her desk, legs crossed, and leaning back on her hands. She was a tall for a teacher, about 5'10, and wearing a black knee length dress with two really thin straps to hold it up. She looked very young, probably no more than 28 with a killer body. Her ass was nice and round with great long dark legs. Her tits were definitely D cups but not those nasty sagging water balloon tits, they were tight and round and barely being held back by her dress. Too top things off, her face was beautiful, framed by long slightly curly brown hair.

Anyway back to the present. I had about a month left in school and was enjoying everyday watching Mrs. Shannon bending over to pick up chalk or a paper she would occasionally drop. Since it was getting close to summer I was dreading my usual summer job of pool cleaning. The endless wars with horse flies, and watching fat ass old people sun bathing while telling me how to do my job. My mind quickly snapped back with the sound of the bell ringing. On my way out Mrs. Shannon grabbed my hand and said,

"James, please stay for a minute I need to talk to you."

"Sure Mrs. Shannon" I said.

After everyone left she walked over to me and said that she had just gotten a new pool put in and that she would need me to fill it up and add the chemicals. While she was talking I was inhaling her scent, she was driving me crazy. I began to feel my dick getting hard and with her looking right at me I was sure she was going to notice. Luckily she turned around to write down her address and I quickly arranged myself.

"Can you be there at 5pm?" she said.

"Sure I'll be over at 5pm sharp today."

With that I turned and walked out the door clicking my heels at the thought of maybe seeing Mrs. Shannon in a bathing suit before summers end.

After school I gathered up my gear and headed over to Mrs. Shannon's house. I had never been to any teacher's house before and it was a little weird. I made my way to the front door and knocked. The door opened and so did my eyes. There in the doorway was Mrs. Shannon in a bathing suit top and low cut blue jean shorts.

"Glad you could make it." she said.

"Just doing my job." I said grinning.

"Well come on in, the pools out back. You can start whenever you're ready."

I made my way to her back yard and started the water filling the pool. I was sitting with my feet hanging over the side of the pool when I heard the back door open. I turned around to look and there was Mrs. Shannon carrying a lawn chair and a bag of something. She sat the chair down and unfolded it and said,

"No need in wasting all this sunshine."

"Yeah, it is a beautiful day." I said.

I grabbed my net and started getting all the leaves and crap out of the pool. I looked up for a second and nearly shot my load. Mrs. Shannon was facing away from me pulling down her shorts. She shook her ass from side to side sliding her shorts down those long smooth legs of hers. The site of my hot teacher in a black two-piece nearly gave me a heart attack, especially her round ass in a thong! Before she turned back around I slid my shades on and turned away but just enough where I could still see her without her knowing.

I continued watching her out of the corner of my eye while she put sun tan lotion on her shoulders and legs. She laid back and pulled out one of those tanning mirrors and put it under her chin. Once I was sure she couldn't see me I took the time to soak her up. I traced her long legs with my eyes all the way to her ass. Then her tight stomach, up to her gorgeous tits. I watched in awe of them going up and down with her breathing. After rubbing myself for a moment I went back to my work.

A few minutes later I saw her turn over.

"James, can you do me a favor?' she said. "Sure, what do you need." I said.

"Could you please rub some lotion on my back and legs? I can't reach them and I don't want to get burned"

"Sure thing Mrs. Shannon." I said. But I was thinking, " You bet your sweet fucking ass I will"

I kneeled beside her and put some lotion on my hands. But before I could do anything she said,

"Just do my whole backside, I want to get a really good tan this year."

And just when I thought it couldn't get any better she reached up and untied her top.

"I hate tan lines. "she said.

She was on her stomach so I couldn't see her tits but I could see the sides of them and they were spectacular. I started with her shoulders rubbing in the lotion real good and even throwing in what little I knew of massaging.

"Ummm… that feels great." she said . "Got too get the lotion on good, don't want you to burn." I said.

Down over her entire back and sides. As I was going I was massaging her skin to the best of my abilities. My fingers grazed the sides of her tits more than once but she said nothing so I continued. Once I got to her ass I didn't know if I should stop or just rub lotion all over that fine piece of meat. But my conservative side kicked in and I just went straight for her legs, not wanting to push my luck.

I'm a leg and ass man and my god these were some great legs. Not a trace of stubble. On the legs I stated doing circular motions with my hands squeezing her entire leg. On her feet I gave her tender caresses with my thumbs. I paid good attention to her arches and in between her toes.

"My god, I've always heard about foot massages but I didn't know they felt this good' she said.

"Just remember this when your writing out your check for my bill." I said laughing. "Well that just about does it." I said when I finished her feet. By this time my cock was bulging my pants into a huge tent and I knew I couldn't take much more. It's a good thing she had a towel over her eyes or she would've gotten a big surprise.

"Not so fast." She said. "Don't forget about my rear."

"Oh yeah, can't forget that can we." I said. As I put more lotion on my hands I tried to think of sports and other things to calm down my cock because I was about to explode. I started at the top of her ass and as I made my way down I thought what the hell and grabbed a cheek in each hand and pushed up spreading her ass with my thumbs. I could've sworn I heard a gasp from her lips but she said nothing. I repeated two more times but I had gone to far. Not with her but with me because I was now soaking my pants with a huge load of cum.

I sat there a minute convulsing before she said, "Are you all done?"

"All done I said standing up. I went back to cleaning around the pool for about a half hour. Mrs. Shannon turned back over on her back being careful not to let her tits escape. Damn, I thought to myself. She put her mirror back under her chin. By this time I was getting uncomfortable with all that cum in my pants.

"Mind if I use your water hose to cool down, it's hot as fire out here." I said.

"Go right ahead" she said.

I went over to the hose and turned it one and started to wet my self down. I made sure her she was looking away from me and I pulled down my shorts a little and my cum-covered cock sprang out. I quickly washed it off and put it back in my shorts.

About this time Mrs. Shannon got up and said, "Well that's about enough sun for one day, I'm gonna go shower. Make your self at home while the pool fills up and I'll make us some snacks when I get out."

"Sounds great" I said.

On the way in I took the opportunity to admire her body. Her ass when she walked was enough to get me rock hard again.

"I'll be done in a minute," she said as she disappeared up the steps into her room.

I was horny as hell and thought I deserved a peek at Mrs. Shannon. Once I heard the water start I waited a few minutes then tip toed up stairs and into her room. Her bathing suit was on the floor in a wad. I was kind of shaking buy now but I picked up the thong bottom and I'll be damned, there was a wet spot. I smelled the spot and walked over to the door to her bathroom. The smell of her pussy excited me almost to the point of losing it again, gut I contained myself. The door was cracked a little but I couldn't make out shit on the steamy mirror across from her shower. Disappointed I took one last sniff of her bikini bottom and went down stairs.

In the shower Mrs. Shannon soaped herself up, rubbing her tits together and soaping her ass. She couldn't help but be a little turned on after her foot massage and her hand slowly found its way to her pussy lips. She stuck one finger in her hot pussy and rubbed her clit with the palm of her hand.

"Damn, that boy's got me rubbing myself" she said to herself.

"You're a married woman Shannon, snap out of it."

After drying off Mrs. Shannon took moment to admire herself in the mirror. "Can't blame the boy I guess, he's so young and with him rubbing oil all over me I'm lucky he didn't blow his load all over my back," Mrs. Shannon giggled to herself. "I wish John wasn't gone all the damn time because I would fuck his brains out. Oh well, between my vibrator and James' massages I guess I can make it until my hubby comes home tomorrow."

When Mrs. Shannon came downstairs I told her that it would take a about a day for her pool to fill completely and that I would just come back tomorrow and add the chemicals.

"Do you think it will be ready for swimming by this weekend, my husband is coming home tomorrow and he's the one who loves to swim," she said.

"Most definitely, probably by Friday at the latest," I said.

As I headed out the door Mrs. Shannon said "See you tomorrow in class."

"I wouldn't miss it for the world," I said. That night I must have jacked off about 5 times thinking of Mrs. Shannon. Finally drained I drifted off.

The next day at school my friends and me were walking into class when Mrs. Shannon put her hand on my shoulder and said "Hey James," with a smile.

One of my friends whispered to me "Damn man I been here all year too and she ain't said hi to me."

"I got a way with the ladies," I said with a laugh.

"Sure you do buddy," my friend said.

After class Mrs. Shannon grabbed me again, "Are you coming over today as planned James?"

"Sure am, same time as yesterday," I said.

"Great, you can meet my husband John," she said.

"Sounds good," I said while thinking "Oh joy, I get to meet the lucky fucker that gets to pound Mrs. Shannon's ass."

Later that day once I got to Mrs. Shannon's house I started adding the chemicals to her pool. I kept looking up hoping to see her coming out to sun again. After a while I thought "Damn, no show today." After a couple hours I walked into the kitchen and poured myself a glass of water. The next thing I saw made me choke on my water. Mrs. Shannon coming down the stairs in a strapless, tight as hell, black dress with high heels to match

"Think my husband will like it," she said.

"Like what," I said trying to catch my breath.

"My new dress silly," she said.

"I don't see how he wouldn't like it with you in it. You look gorgeous," I said with water still dripping off my chin.

"Thank you very much for the compliment James, coming from a handsome young man like you makes me feel all sexy," she said.

"It's the truth," I said. "What's the special occasion," I asked?

"My husband John is coming home today, he works three weeks out of the month so I only get to see him for one week each month."

"That's got to be hard," I said. "Yeah it is, but anyway with my new dress you like so much and the new pool I plan on making the most of this week," she said. "Tonight I have a special dinner planned that I worked all afternoon on. Then maybe some dancing and a romantic night snuggling on the couch with a good movie."

"Sounds like tonight will be fun, well I'm gonna grab me a seat in the living room while the chemicals sit," I said.

"Help yourself, I'm just gonna put the finishing touches on the dinner."

After about an hour I heard the phone ring. I heard Mrs. Shannon pick up. "Hello?" Normally I'm not that nosey of a person but curiosity got the better of me so I quietly picked up the phone in the living room and did a little eavesdropping.

"Shannon, this is John, what cha doin?"

"John… where are you?" I always thought her last name was Shannon, oh well noted for future use.

"Baby I was gonna call you this morning but I got sidetracked. I'm still in Detroit, something came up and I'll be a few days late coming home."

"Detroit… but you said you'd be home today… I had a whole evening planned and even a surprise for you."

"I'm sorry baby but I can't help it, it's only a few days."

"Only a few days? You haven't been home in a month. I miss you and I'm getting real lonely."

"Sorry baby, but we've been through this before… ..well I gotta go. See you in a few days. Love you bye."

I quietly put the phone back on the hook and sat back down. Damn this guy must be stupid to leave such a fine girl sitting at home while he works. I felt kinda bad for Mrs. Shannon but I didn't know what to do. I got up and walked into the kitchen. Mrs. Shannon was sitting at the table with her head in one hand and the other hand tightly clinched in a fist. The table was all set and the food smelled wonderful. I walked up beside her and asked her if she was ok.

"Yeah, I'm fine James. Thanks for asking," she said. I played dumb.

"When's your husband getting here," I said.

"Hell if I know, he just called and said in a few days, but who knows with him. I don't know why I put up with him? After all the trouble I went through… all for nothing."

I did feel bad for her on one hand, but on the other I was glad it was just the two of us. I looked around a minute then I decided to take matters into my own hands. I walked up behind her and put my hands on her shoulders and started giving her a massage.

"Your so nice James, thank you very much," she said.

"No problem," I said. I continued massaging her shoulders for a while then I glanced down and noticed I had the perfect view of her tits. Immediately my dick started to stir. I then noticed that my hands where inches from the top part of her tits. The dress she had on was pushing her tits upward just enough to where I could almost reach them. I thought maybe I could just touch the tops of her tits and she would think it was just part of the massage. I made my move ever so easily. Inch by inch I started making the movements of my hands go lower.

"James, you give the best massages… god they feel good," she said. I took that as so far so good and went back to trying to cop a feel. Finally my fingers made contact. I didn't here any objections so I went down a little further. Her tits were rising and falling with the movement of my hands. I dared not go any further. The parts of her tits I was touching were so warm and smooth. Even without knowing it she was giving me one hell of a hard on.

"Oh my god, he's trying to feel me up." Mrs. Shannon thought. "I wonder if I should say something?" "God this boy's got magic hands… ummmm..it feels so good" "I deserve to feel good after today. My useless husbands never home, and even when he is he never treats me this good." "James is such a nice boy anyway, and so handsome too. If I was a little younger I could see myself being attracted to him." "Ummm….shit this feels so good… "

What I didn't know was that my massage was turning Mrs. Shannon on even more than she knew.

"Oh my god… my pussy's getting wet," Mrs. Shannon thought. "Just a little longer and I'll have to stop him… but… god he's treating me so good." "But if I let him keep going I might get arrested for rape"

In the meantime I was floating in dream world with my hands all over my teachers shoulders and chest. But I was snapped back to reality…

"James, do you like steak?" she said.

"Uh, sure," I said.

"Well there's no need to waste all this food. Have a seat."

"Are you sure," I said. "You fixed all this for you and your husband."

"The way I feel right now James, I would much rather eat dinner with you than my husband."

I couldn't believe my ears. She would rather spend time with me that that loser of a husband. I sat down at the table and started to eat. I noticed a bottle of wine. Man if she likes me now I wonder how much she would loosen up with a few glasses of wine in her.

"Why don't you have a glass of wine," I said.

"I guess it wouldn't hurt," she said. Throughout the course of dinner I counted three glasses of wine she drank. I figured she should be feeling the effects by now. I noticed she was staring at me from across the table but I tried to act like I didn't notice.

"It must be the wine talking but James is hot," Mrs. Shannon thought to herself. "After that massage maybe I should return the favor and give the boy a little excitement of his own."

Just as I was about to finish up with dinner I felt Mrs. Shannon's leg brush up against mine. I acted as if nothing had happened. Then I noticed her foot rubbing my leg. The sensation was overwhelming and I fought the urge to say something.

"I wonder what he's thinking now?" "Maybe I should turn up the heat a little? Not too much but enough to make the night fun for him," Mrs. Shannon thought.

The next thing I noticed was that her foot was getting higher. Before long she was rubbing her foot against my inner thigh. I wondered what she was trying to do and if I should say or do anything myself. Her foot was inches away from my cock and I was about to soak myself again, but I wasn't going to stop her until the last minute.

"I bet he's about to blow his load," Mrs. Shannon giggled to herself. "Well I'd better stop my fun, I am his teacher after all."

By this time I was ready to blow and she was still rubbing my leg with her foot. I had to do something… "Would you like to dance?" I said.

"I would love to," she said. It's a good thing too because her foot was driving me crazy.

I stood up and pulled her chair out for her. "I'm not a good dancer, all I can do is slow dance," I said.

"Don't worry about it, that's my favorite way to dance," she said. She walked up to me and put my right hand on her hip and grabbed my other hand and off we went. She put her head on my shoulder as we danced. She seemed so comfortable but I on the other hand was almost shaking trying to keep from cumming all over myself. She was so close that I was worried she would feel my cock pressing against her stomach.

"Holy shit, he's got one hell of a hard on," Mrs. Shannon thought. "God it feels so good to have a man treat me like James does. This is wrong but if he doesn't have a problem with it then neither do I. Besides I won't let it get out of control. And what high school boy doesn't have a hard on."

"She's got to feel my cock pressing into her," I thought. "But she's not saying anything."

With her tits pressing against my chest and my cock in between us I knew I couldn't take much more.

"I bet he's about had enough for tonight," Mrs. Shannon thought. "Thank you for the dance James, but my feet are tired from all the walking and dancing I need to sit down."

Thank god I thought to myself. After she sat down on the couch she lied back and I couldn't help but notice how beautiful she was.

"I don't suppose you have another one of those foot massages in you?" she said.

"Just so happens I do." I said.

I sat down at the end of the couch and started taking off her heels. God this is great I thought to myself. I'm here alone with this fine woman and she wants me to rub her feet. I grabbed one leg and put it in my lap and lifted the other one up and started to work my magic. I just so happened to glace down and notice that I could see her panties while I had her leg up in the air. I didn't think much about it at first until I noticed that I could see a wet spot forming. Could I be causing my teacher to get turned on enough that her pussy is soaking her panties.

"Oh no… my pussy's getting wet again." "I know he's got to notice. What are you doing Shannon, this is your student and you're a married woman." "It's just the wine and the loneliness, get a grip on yourself.

"That's about all I can take James, thank you," she said.

"Your welcome," I said. Little did she know but that was about all I could take as well. "I guess I'll be heading home. The chemicals should be just about right after they sit over night."

"Let me see you out," she said. When we got to the door she opened it and leaned over and gave me a kiss on the cheek. All I could say was "See you tomorrow in class." You can still come by to finish the pool,' she said. And with that she closed the door. I just stood there for a moment to relish my day. I had felt her tits, well the top anyways. She rubbed my leg with her foot and to top it all off my massages were turning her on. After a minute or two I went home and jacked off till the sun came up.

After I had left Mrs. Shannon did some reflecting of her own. What a day she thought. My husband neglects me once again and the day looked ruined but James makes it turn out all right after all. Just a little harmless flirting between student and teacher. But when he gives me those massages I have to admit I do get excited. I wanted to just grab him and tear his clothes off more than once tonight. But I'm married and he's so much younger than me. Oh well as long as I keep it under control I don't see the harm in us helping each other feel good. When we were dancing I could feel his cock pressing against my stomach… I wonder what what it… oh never mind there's always tomorrow.

The next day at school in Mrs. Shannon's class I noticed her staring at me. She wore this little sundress and had her hair up in a pony tail.

Her legs were driving me crazy, she kept crossing them and uncrossing them as if she was teasing me.

"I think James likes my dress, either that or my legs," Mrs. Shannon giggled to herself. "He's so good to me the least I can do is give him a little show."

When the bell rang Mrs. Shannon asked me to stay for a minute. "James why don't I just give you a ride to my house?" she said.

"Sure, it would save me a trip," I said.

In the parking lot I kept starring at Mrs. Shannon's ass as she walked, she's so graceful. By this time I decided that I had a certain relationship with her. I was going to try my luck.

"You look hot today Mrs. Shannon," I said.

"Thank you James, I take it you like my dress?" she said.

"Well its not the dress, it's the woman in it." I said with a smile.

"James please... your going to make me blush." "So you like my body do you, well let me give you a little peek." She thought to herself.

After my attempt at a pick up line Mrs. Shannon dropped her keys on the ground. Before I could pick them up she bent over in front of me. She didn't bend her knees so her dress came up over her ass a little, I saw a lot. White thong panties that were barely there and her ass in all its glory. She stood back up and got into her car.

"I bet you liked that little show." Mrs. Shannon said under her breath.

I got in and off we went. In the car I kept seeing her dress going up her legs like she was trying to show off. If she was I was all for it.

"Have a look at these." Mrs. Shannon thought. "By the bulge in his pants I'd have to say he likes them, god how big is that thing? Bigger than John's that's for sure." "I bet he could last forever... I'd better get a hold of myself but he's making me so horny."

"God she's driving me crazy… if she doesn't stop I'm gonna rape her right here in this car."

Finally we pulled up to her house. I walked out back to look at the pool. It was perfect and ready for swimming. "Pool's ready." I hollered into the house.

"Great news, I've been wanting to try my new bikini out, you go ahead and get in." She said.

New bikini I thought, hell yeah. I took off my shirt and jumped in the pool. The water was just right. After a few minutes Mrs. Shannon came out wearing a towel. When she got to the pool she undid the towel and raised her arms in the air. "Well what do you think," she said.

I was speechless. It had to be the smallest bikini I had ever seen. The top barely held her tits back and the bottom came down so low that I now knew she shaved her pubic hair.

"My god," I said.

"My god it's hideous or my god you like it?" she said.

"My god I love it," I said.

With that she jumped into the pool. When she came up she swam over to me. She was so close that her tits where touching my chest and she was just staring at me.

"You know this is wrong, putting ideas into the boys head. Its just that you haven't seen your husband in weeks and you have needs." Mrs. Shannon thought to herself.

"The waters wonderful James, you did a very good job," she said.

"Thanks, all in a days work." I said.

"I love swimming, the water makes me feel all frisky," she said.

"Frisky huh?" I said.

I grabbed her by the waist and tossed her. "Hey no fair, I wasn't ready." She said. She came at me and pushed me. When she tried again I got behind her and held her by her waist. In this position her ass was right up against my crotch. I know she had to feel my cock but she didn't seem to notice.

"Whoa there tiger," Mrs. Shannon thought to herself. "All this wrestling seems to be getting to James, he's not the only one either. I have to admit that I haven't had this much fun with a man in ages."

Mrs. Shannon kept squirming but I held on tight, it was almost dry humping. "Give up?" I said.

"I surrender," she said. I loosened my grip enough where she could turn around. When she did it was heaven. Her tits were pressed tightly between us and my cock was poking at her belly. I didn't know what to do so I just stayed still for a minute relishing the moment.

"I know I shouldn't but a little kiss wouldn't hurt," Mrs. Shannon thought to herself. "God he's so hard… "

What happened next I'd remember until the day I die. Without saying a word she leaned forward and kissed me right on the lips. They were soft, smooth, and tasted wonderful. She pulled back for a second I guess to see if I reacted. Staying still got me this far so I continued. She leaned in and kissed me again. This time I felt her tongue trying to penetrate my mouth so I let her in. Our tongues coiled together like snakes. I let my hand slip down to her ass and I grabbed hold.

"Oh no… what should I do, I've let this go to far," Mrs. Shannon thought to herself. "But I want this… .but I'm married… .but god I want this soooooooo bad."

"James, I'm sorry but we have to stop. I shouldn't have done that." She said.

"No no Mrs. Shannon don't be sorry I liked it very much. I think your beautiful."

"That's so sweet James but I'm your teacher and I'm married."

"So what if you're my teacher and as far as being married, I see you more than your husband does." I said.

" I know James but it just isn't right." She said.

"Well if you don't want to I'm not going to force you. Just remember that I'm here for you." I said.

"Thank you so much James." She said.

She reached out and hugged me for about a minute. I was let down that it had stopped but I knew that I was the man she wanted, not that stupid ass husband.

"Well I've had enough swimming for one day," she said.

"Yeah, me too but it was fun." I said.

"Yeah from that tent you got there I'd say so," she giggled.

I didn't know what to say, for the first time she had acknowledged our situation. There was no sense in playing dumb anymore so I decided to talk more openly to her. "Well wrestling with a beautiful woman does it every time." I said.

"Well wrestling with a fine young man gets me all hot as well." She said getting out of the pool. I was excited to here that she thought I was hot. This day couldn't get any better.

"I'm going to rinse off James, you're welcome to stay for a while. I've got some movies we could watch or something." She said.

Normally I don't like to sit around and watch T.V. but anything to be with Mrs. Shannon for a while longer.

"Sure sounds great." I said.

While I made myself comfortable in the living room on the couch Mrs. Shannon was having a moment of soul searching. After her shower she was deciding what to wear. "Should I be naughty and have a little more fun or should I just play it safe?" she thought. "This is getting out of hand, I'm very attracted to James and I know he likes me but if I let it go on it'll end up with us having sex." "I'm his teacher but I'm also a woman and he's a man."

She was doing a good job of talking herself into taking her relationship with James to the next level but it just seemed so wrong to her.

"Well this t-shirt and these black panties should make the night more interesting," she thought. "If anything does happen I'm just going to let it."

Finally Mrs. Shannon had come to the realization that on this night she would fuck me. Downstairs I was watching T.V. thinking about how all I could think of lately was Mrs. Shannon. "I may be in love with her," I thought to myself. My thought was interrupted when I looked up to see Mrs. Shannon coming down the steps in a t-shirt and black panties.

"Not the usual teacher student attire," I said with a grin.

She sat down beside me and looked directly into my eyes. "James I don't know how to tell you this but I think I'm in love with you." I tried to say something but she wouldn't let me.

"I think about you all the time, and you treat me so good. Better than that no good husband of mine. He doesn't love me, he's never here. Every time I look at you I get turned on and up until now I've been hiding my feelings. When you give me massages I get all wet. If you don't feel the same way I'll understand, you can get up and leave and I'll never say another thing about it. But if you do feel the same way…"

"Mrs. Shannon I do feel the same, I think about you all the time. Every time I see you I get a hard on. I'm not going anywhere until you say so." I interrupted.

She crawled over to me on the couch and leaned her head over in front of mine.

"I think you'll be staying over tonight." She started to kiss me deeply. Her tongue found its way inside my mouth again but this time there was no holding back. She kissed me like no woman had ever kissed me.

"James I want you so bad. Make love to me," she said.

"I'm going to make you forget you ever had a husband." I said.

I grabbed the back of her head and again we kissed. Her hands were feeling the outline of my cock and I was exploring her body as well. I took off my shirt and did the same for her. To my delight she wasn't wearing a bra.

"God I love your tits," I said grabbing one in each hand. I began circling the nipple with my tongue and biting slightly.

"That's it, suck my tits," she said.

After a few minutes she got off the couch and bent down in front of me. She unzipped my pants and pulled them down freeing my cock.

"James I've been wanting to do this for a long time." She said.

She started licking my balls and stroking my cock with one hand. Then she started to kiss up the shaft. When she reached the top a shiny drop of precum was oozing out of the tip. She stuck her tongue out and lapped it up. Then she engulfed my cock. She took about half in her mouth and sucked back up the shaft. The next time though she went all the way. My cock was completely inside her throat and it felt wonderful.

"God you suck dick like a pro," I said. She came up for air and smiled and went back to sucking my cock. She would deepthroat my cock then on the way up stop when just the head of my dick was in her mouth and circle it with her tongue.

"I love your cock James. It tastes so good."

After about fifteen minutes I was about to loose it. "Mrs. Shannon I'm gonna cum, if you don't want to swallow you'd better stop." I said.

She didn't say a word she just looked in my eyes and opened her mouth and started sucking up and down on my cock really fast.

"Oh god... Mrs. Shannon... fuck... I'm gonna cummmmmm!!!"

With that my cock exploded. The first blast of cum gagged her a little but she didn't miss a drop. Shot by shot my cock emptied what seemed like a gallon of cum down her throat. After I had deposited the full load in her mouth she held my cock in her mouth gently circling the head with her tongue.

I broke the silence. "I don't know where you learned to that but god you suck dick like no other,' I said.

She finally let my limp cock plop from her lips with a wet smacking sound.

"God I've never sucked a dick before. Your cum tastes great, I could drink gallons of it," she said.

"You never given a blowjob before?" I asked.

"No never, John didn't like taboo things in bed. He was a strait up guy on top for fifteen minutes then its over kinda guy." "I've always wanted to try it, I'm glad I waited though."

She came up in front of my face and starred me in the eyes. "Your cock's bigger anyway." Then she kissed me. I could still taste the salty residue of cum on her lips. As we kissed I started to rub her pussy through her panties.

"Ummmmmmmm... ..rub my pussy... .god that feels good," she said. Her panties were soaking wet. I stood up and pulled her panties down with one motion. Then it hit me fully. There I was standing with my dick hanging out over my now naked teacher.

"It's your turn now," I grinned. I began kissing down her stomach.

Then I made little kisses on her inner thighs.

"Ummmm... gooooooodddddd... ..eat me James," she said biting her bottom lip.

With one hand I spread her pussy lips and began licking in circles.

"Oh... .Jesus Christ!!!" she said grabbing the back of my head and smothering me in her snatch. I start teasing her clit with my tongue. Then I eased one finger inside her pussy. God it was tight as hell. Her dumbass husband must not fuck her at all.

"Yeah, finger my pussy, god it feels so good James, your more of a man than my husband ever was... don't stop lick that pussy," she screamed.

"Your pussy tastes so good." I said in between licks.

"James I want you inside of me... now please... fuck me."

I stood up and slid her down the couch and got between her legs. I bent over and kissed her so she could taste the pussy juice on my lips. She must have liked it because she sucked every bit off my lips.

"Your so dirty James, I had no idea," she said. "Your so fucking hot I'm turned on like I've never been before." I said.

"Enough talking, fuck me pleeeaaassseeeeee," she begged.

I grabbed my cock and started to ease it into her pussy inch by inch.

"Goddamn your pussy's tight," I said.

"That and your cock is so much bigger than John's. My pussy's not use to it yet." She said.

Inch by inch until I was all the way in. I leaned in and kissed her passionately then started to fuck her brains out.

"Shit... .oh god..yes yes... fuck me good James," she hissed.

I kept up the pace for about ten minutes then I started slow deep thrusts. "God your so tight, your fucking unbelievable," I said.

"I'm not going to last much longer, your pussy is so tight… god it feels good," I said.

"I'm not gonna last much longer either baby, god your fucking my brains out… I love your cock."

After five more minutes I felt my balls surging. "I'm gonna cum… can I cum on your tits," I begged. "Not on your life," she said.

She wrapped her legs around me so tightly I couldn't pull back if I wanted to.

She whispered in my ear,"I want to feel you cum inside me, don't worry I'm on the pill. Now fuck me." She said.

I started fucking her hard and fast I knew it wouldn't be long now. I felt her pussy grab my cock and she started to shake.

"Oh fuck… god..James… fuck me… .yes… ohhhhhh god I'M CUMMIIIIIIIINNNNNGGG!!!!"

Hearing her scream my name in pleasure pushed me over the top.

"Here it comes… fuckkkkkkkk yeeeeeaaaaahhhhhh!!!!!" I yelled.

I felt jet after jet of cum being deposited in her womb. I kept pumping and I kept cumming. I never came that much before in my life. After it was over I collapsed on top of her. We both lied there breathing hard for a while. Finally she leaned over and kissed me deeply.

"James that was… that was the best I've ever been fucked." "You were unbelievable." "I felt you cumming inside me. I loved the way it felt to have all that cum inside me. Cum from a man that I know now I'm in love with."

"Mrs. Shannon, or should I say Shannon now, you were great. You're the most beautiful woman I've ever seen and I love you too."

After that she fell asleep in my arms. I didn't know what the next day would hold and I didn't care. But one things for sure… it can only get better.

YOUNG TOM AND WIDOW RITA

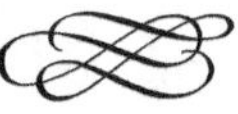

I'm Tom Davis, kid brother of Laura Hughes. I was a 30-year old high school social studies teacher and girls' basketball coach; after five years of coaching, thanks to two athletic sisters on the team, we won the district championship. Often, I saw the superintendent of the schools, Harry Bradley, and his wife, Rita, among the spectators at home games.

I saw Rita at a reception in the team's honor. She was about 5-ft 6-in, 125 lb, big boobs, green eyes, and shoulder-length, light brown hair; she had on a white turtle neck blouse, beige skirt, black stockings, and a navy blue blazer.

Often, after she congratulated me and my team, she visited with my wife, Ali, and our one-year old son, Tim. I thought she looked very elegant and sexy. Also, she always smelled of a light floral perfume. I saw her a few more times, usually at various school functions.

Ali was a petite, 5-ft, 2-in, 115 lb, 34B boobs, blonde with a round face, light blue eyes, and a bubbly personality. She attended most of the girls' basketball games. She listened to the girls and helped them with their problems. She was working hard to overcome the belief that her pussy and oral sex were dirty. Still, we had a great sex life, with lot of fucking outdoors.

Ali told me, "Rita also attended my state college and was a member of the same sorority. She is 16 years older than me but has the same birthday in the summer; she is also a distant cousin of my mom. She invited me to play tennis with her and join the club."

Ali and I were invited to a Christmas party at the home of Harry and Rita. Rita had on a long red, low-neck, dress that showed her cleavage prominently. Her cousin, Ellie, a widow, was the only unattached person at the party. There were three other couples, but they all left soon after dinner. Over coffee, while Harry and I talked, Ali, Ellie, and Rita seemed to be having a good conversation and laughed a lot in the living room. I agreed to help Harry remove an old deck and build a new one. Harry invited me to play golf with him; in fact, Harry, who was heavy-set, needed to exercise and loose about 70 lbs.

After using the toilet, as I came down the steps, I saw Rita at a large window looking at the falling snow.

She smiled at me and said, "It's beautiful outside."

I walked to where she was standing, stood next to her, and said, "You have a nice home, especially the backyard."

"It's quite private. Harry said he may consider building an in-ground pool."

Later, still standing next to Rita, I noticed her large boobs and that they nearly spilled out of her low-cut dress. Rita must have realized I was admiring her chest and blushed intensely. After Ali joined us, Rita showed a few photos of her daughter, Claire, who was coming on Christmas Eve with her fiancé; Claire was on the basketball team the first year I became the coach.

Sadly, after Tim's second birthday, Ali discovered a lump in her heft breast that was malignant. After surgery and chemotherapy, she seemed to have been cured, but the cancer returned a few months later. I took a leave of absence from my coaching job to take care of Ali. Several friends of Ali, especially Rita, helped with taking care of Tim and driving Ali to the cancer center. After a courageous struggle and considerable suffering, Ali passed away. It was a sad end to the life of a beautiful woman to whom I was married almost seven years. I received many cards of sympathy, including one from Rita, who urged me to be positive, take care of Tim, and live my life as best as I could.

Taking care of Tim became my highest priority. At the suggestion of my parents and in-laws, I found a teaching/coaching job in a town only 20 miles, instead of 60 miles, from them. I continued to maintain contacts with Harry and Rita; she baby sat for Tim when I was in town. Tim became fond of Rita and called her "Ta." Harry played golf with me when he had the time and, invariably, afterwards, Tim and I had dinner at his home. Harry and I worked on removing the old deck at the back of his home. But, he was too busy to work on the new deck and I ended up working alone. When Harry was not home, Rita talked to me either while I worked on the deck or afterwards. I managed to complete the deck and promised Rita that I would stain it at a later date. As I recovered from the loss of Ali, I began to notice Rita's sexy figure.

Rita noticed me stealing glances at her and explained, "Harry is the love of my life. He has been working hard on the budget; he is worried about saving jobs, especially of the teachers. He is under lot of stress. He is not eating healthy meals."

I said, "I'll get him to play golf; that should lower his stress. Is he doing any exercises other than playing golf?"

"No," and then blurted out, "Our love life has disappeared. He does not like oral sex either."

"I'm sorry to hear that."

I volunteered to grill salmon one evening, but when I arrived at Harry's home, he had not left his office yet. Rita, who was dressed in pink shorts and a light blue halter top, and I talked on the patio while drinking wine. I told her she was a beautiful woman. In turn, Rita flirted with me by rubbing my back and patting my butt couple of times.

Rita told me, "I was an only child of a strict couple in Maine, a high school cheerleader, a tennis player at a small college, and an office manager in a school board office. My older, second, cousin, Ellie, helped me through adolescence and through my college years. She understood that I didn't want to be controlled by my old-fashioned father. When Harry, a science teacher, asked me to marry him after dating about six months, I accepted his proposal. He was smart, worked hard, ambitious, and moved up the school administrators' ladder. I had a good life with lot of women friends, and time spent playing tennis and bridge. Sometimes I wonder what my life would have been had I married a not-so-ambitious amateur actor who was a wonderful lover.

"Ellie became my mentor. She married an older man, who died couple of years ago and left her well provided. She has been living with Brett, a man about 15 years younger than her. Ellie and I are close enough for her talk openly about her love life."

I realized Rita and I were lonely, but that nothing intimate would happen. That night, I masturbated imagining I was playing with Rita's big boobs and later licking her juicy pussy.

After playing golf on a Saturday, as I drove Harry to his home, he began to complain about chest and shoulder pain, and I took him straight to the hospital's emergency room. The medical staff began to attend on him right away and wheeled him inside the emergency room. I called Rita to inform her what had happened and asked her to come to the hospital. Soon after Rita came to the hospital with Tim, an emergency room physician informed us that Harry had passed away from a massive heart attack.

I took Rita home; I stayed with her as she wept and talked about her life with Harry. I called Claire; I told her about her dad and to come home. I went home about midnight, carrying Tim, who was asleep. For another week, I spent time helping Rita. Soon, got busy executing Harry's estate and planning Claire's wedding.

I kept in touch with Rita through regular text and email messages. She appreciated the funny pictures and cartoons I sent her. A few months later, she started to send me limericks that showed her bawdy sense of humor.

One day, she complained in a message, "My boobs are saggy."

"They are saggy only if the nipples are at your crotch. I recall your bra-covered boobs look magnificent. Can I see a photo of them bra-less?"

A few days later, much to my delight and surprise, she sent me a photo of her magnificent boobs, attached to the message, "For your eyes only."

"They are magnificent. I love them. I wish I could kiss them."

She replied with only a smiley face emoticon.

About a year after Harry died, Rita sent me a message, "I am working as an office manager; also taking yoga classes and resumed playing tennis."

A few days later I had to attend a conference for teachers at my old school and hoping to see her after my conference ended, I wrote to her that I would like to see her. She suggested I meet her at the local country club after she finished playing tennis. We met at the club bar.

I said, "You look gorgeous. You must be very popular."

Rita confided to me, "Thanks. I am still reluctant to be introduced to single men. Still, an acquaintance invited me and a 78-year old widower to lunch on a Sunday who was looking for someone to take care of him, a responsibility I am not ready to undertake. Also, I did not want to tie myself up with a much older man. I will not marry for money. Harry left me well provided."

To tease her, I said, "So you are a rich widow."

"Well, you are not doing that badly with the money Ali left you. Are you serious with anyone?"

"Not now; I was interested in a fellow teacher, but she moved away for a better-paying job. I met other women, but they all have too much baggage."

"I know what you mean."

After a long pause, I took a chance of getting turned down and asked her, "Please go with me to the basketball team's banquet; it's at the Lake-side Restaurant, Next week's Saturday."

I was delighted when she said, "Sure. I remember the banquets are fun. Harry and I had dinner several times at Lake-Side. I can get there by myself."

—-

That night, when Rita called Ellie, she was ecstatic that Tom, a younger man, asked her out. Then she whispered to Rita, "Brett's licking my pussy while I am talking on the phone. It feels good. Now, he wants to fuck me doggy-style. I'm lucky I found a young and considerate lover; his gentle love making is exactly what my old body needs."

—-

After Rita woke up on Saturday, as she drank coffee, she thought about seeing Tom and going to the banquet with him. She got excited knowing a younger man wanted to be with her and go out with her. She fretted over what to wear, but decided that first she would make herself alluring. She took a long shower, and shaved her legs and under arms. Carefully, she trimmed the hair at the edges of her pussy for the first time after Harry died. She sprayed on small amounts of her favorite perfume on her cleavage and just above her pubic hair. As she looked at herself in the mirror and applied an anti-wrinkle cream on her face, neck, and boobs, she was grateful that she had a head full of light brown hair, large green eyes, and a thin nose. Then she saw the slight bulge in her belly as an inevitable effect of aging. She raised her arms above her head, and noticed her slender arms and lovely, smooth, armpits; she also noticed her large boobs stretched up. She turned to see herself in profile; she saw her boobs were still standing proudly on her chest and that she had, firm, meaty, thighs. She realized that she was still an attractive woman. Gently, she inserted her right middle finger in her pussy and smiled after realizing she had gotten wet. She said to herself, "I'm a horny widow." She decided not to masturbate then. Instead, she decided that she would let Tom fuck her. She hoped that Tom would lick her pussy first and brings her to orgasm, an act Harry did only a few times during their marriage. She decided to entice him with the phrase. "Check out my new, sexy, panties."

Rita came to the banquet dressed in a crimson, short-sleeve, knee-length dress, that had a plunging neck line; she had on diamond ear rings and a gold chain with a heart-shaped pendant that rested on her cleavage. She put on fishnet thigh highs, red garter belt, and red, low-heel, shows. She carried a red shawl and a red ladies bag. After the banquet, we moved to the bar where a noisy crowd was watching a baseball game. I sat close enough to her to smell her intoxicating perfume.

After we sat in a corner and each had a glass of wine, I said to Rita, "You were the most beautiful woman at the banquet. By the way, they are not at all sagging."

Blushing, she said, "Thank you. While you were stealing glances at my boobs, I looked around and did not find any one I recognized."

"Is that good or bad?"

"It's good because I don't want people talking about my personal life. Being a school superintendent's wife I became a public figure; I'm glad the banquet was in another town. I want to live a free, normal, life; a life I would have had if I had not met Harry," and laid her right hand on my left thigh.

"Was it him or his stressful job?"

"He was very conservative and, on top of that, his job was stressful."

"What did you miss?"

Rita looked at me with a sly smile for several seconds, lowered her voice, and said, "I missed my pussy being licked," and giggled nervously.

I knew I was blushing, but I managed to say, "I'm sorry."

About that time there was a loud cheer and we saw on the TV replay that someone hit a home run.

After each of us had a second glass of wine, Rita said, "After I freshen up, let's walk in the park. It's a very nice night."

Later as we walked hand-in-hand, we saw several couples making out, and I said, "Let's sit on the bench over there and just look at the reflected lights in the water."

After we sat down, Rita sat in my lap, placed her hands around my neck, and French kissed me passionately. When she ended her kiss, I kissed her long neck and her lovely upper arms for several minutes.

After a while, I said, "Would you like to see my place?"

"Sure. Where's Tim?"

"He is with my parents for the weekend."

Soon after we entered my condo, I put my arm around her waist and nudged Rita towards me. She turned to face me and threw her arms around my neck. Appreciatively, I looked at her lovely cleavage, and then kissed it and her soft lips. She kissed me back passionately; she was a good kisser.

She asked, "I will ask again. Many women must have been after you after Ali passed away. How come you have not been dating young things?"

"Every one has baggage. I was not ready to begin a relationship with someone I do not know. You're the first person I thought of."

"Thanks. You're a handsome young man," and initiated another long kiss.

I kissed her long neck and inhaled her perfume on her cleavage, and gently grasped her covered boobs, and pleaded, "Just take off your dress," and, smiling, she obliged me.

She had on a lacy, red, bra that held up her large boobs. As I suckled her covered nipples, she looked gorgeous and vulnerable. When she grasped my cock lump, I removed my shorts and underwear; I opened my legs and she gently rubbed my balls.

She said, "I've not been with a man, especially a younger man, since Harry passed away. He was the first guy with whom I went all the way."

"I'm not that young. In you, I see a desirable, beautiful woman. I'm not looking for a one-night stand. I hope that's ok with you."

Standing in her red, low-heel, shoes, red bra, black fishnet stockings and garter belt, and red panties, she whispered, "Check out my new, sexy, panties."

When I slid to my knees and pushed my face in to her red, lacy, panties-covered crotch, she moaned, and pushed at the back of my head. After I licked her covered pussy a few times, she pulled her panties down, and leaned against the large sofa. Her vagina was puffy, and her labia were thick and slick; she had a heavy growth of mostly brown, with interspersed grey, pubic hair that she trimmed at the edges. Her love nectar was thick and tasty. I was delighted that Rita liked my oral work on her pussy, as she moaned softly. I was more delighted when her moans got louder and eventually her pussy convulsed uncontrollably on my mouth signaling an intense orgasm.

Rita thought, "He ate my pussy willingly to bring me an orgasm. Ali mentioned that Tom liked oral sex very much."

After a short time, Rita pulled me to stand, kissed my pussy juice-covered mouth, and said, "That was wonderful. It has been a very long time since anyone licked me there."

"I loved it."

She grasped my throbbing cock and, while admiring it, slowly pumped it, and said, "I got you all excited. Wow, it's leaking cum. Your first time with me will be too quick," and grabbed a wad of tissues.

Soon, I mumbled urgently, "Yesssss. I'm cumming. Cummming. Ahhh-hhh," as jets of my cum flew out of my cock in to the tissues and the carpeted floor.

I was embarrassed, but Rita giggled and said, "That's ok. I'm glad I could get you excited and all that cum came out."

After we freshened up, I gave her one of my shirts to wear, and pleaded, "Stay until day light, please."

"Ok. Show me your condo."

In my bedroom, as she stood in front of the closet-door mirror, I hugged her from behind, pressed my cock in to her naked buttocks, and fondled her large bra-coved boobs for several minutes. In the mirror, I saw her pussy was glistening and I wanted to lick it.

I whispered, "I want to lick."

"Lie on your back, Tom."

After I was on my back on the carpeted floor with my head near the mirror, Rita removed the shirt, stood above me with her hands on her hips, and, while looking at her and me, slowly lowered her crotch to my face. Instinctively, I began to lick and suck on her pussy lips and vaginal opening. I knew Rita wanted to fuck my face at her own pace and desires. She would raise her crotch just enough off my face to watch my tongue and lips work on her pussy, and then lower and push it firmly against my mouth. Eventually, her pussy convulsed uncontrollably, as she kept her pussy pressed against my mouth. With her meaty crotch flesh covering my ears, I could not hear the sounds she made during her orgasm.

She got off of my face, sat next to my prone body, kissed my pussy juice-soaked face, grasped my throbbing, stiff, cock, and said, "Baby that was my second orgasm tonight. I'm all fucked out. You have to fuck me, if you want to."

"I would love to. Right here," nudged her to lie on her back.

"Go slow. I have not had my pussy probed with a big cock for a while."

"I'm very excited. It will be another quickie."

With my weight on my hands and knees, I hovered over Rota's sexy body and kissed her neck, bra-covered boobs, and long arms. I placed my stiff cock at her vagina and pushed it in pausing often to hear a signal of discomfort from her. After I got all of my cock in to her, she smiled.

I said, "You're tight and juicy. Too sexy," and began to fuck her slowly.

I said, "Sorry, I did not wear any protection."

She said, "I can't get pregnant. I had my tubes tied after Claire was born."

I lasted longer than I expected before I had my climax while releasing several jets of cum deep in Rita's pussy. Both of us were tired and fell asleep on the bed wearing my shirts.

—-

Next morning, when I heard Rita taking a shower, I made coffee and fixed cold cereal and fruit for breakfast.

She put on her crimson dress, saw the breakfast, and said, "Thank you for the breakfast. I like you very much, but I like my job and I have a nice home. You like your job and your parents are a short distance from here. For a while anyway, we may be seeing each other only over the weekends."

"It's ok with me, as long as I get to love you."

"Working on the wedding is taking a lot out of me; after the wedding, we should go away for a while to my condo in Florida. Oh, I almost forgot, please stain the deck you built. I would like to talk about Claire's wedding next weekend. What about Tim?"

"My parents love Tim and they will be glad to take care of him over a weekend. Would you have dinner with me?"

"Sure."

—-

It was warm on Saturday. After doing household chores, showering, and shaving, I put on shorts and a tee shirt. It was mid-afternoon when I reached Rita's home. She was in white shorts that showed her strong legs and lower thighs, and a red, low-cut, tank top that showed the top of her lovely cleavage, and her hair seemed to be lighter than I remembered.

I said, "You look terrific; very sexy."

Blushing, she said, "I'm glad you think so. I still have a few chores to take care of while you stain. I'll be back in an hour."

After she returned, she called out, "How did it go."

"It's a small deck. I finished staining it."

Smiling, she said, "I suppose you want your reward."

"Yes," and, as I proceeded to remove her shorts and began to kiss her white panties-covered crotch, her phone rang.

I continued licking Rita's pussy as she talked on the phone. Couple of times she directed me to lick specific spots on her pussy.

She was still on the phone when her breathing became sharp and rapid, and she whimpered incoherently as an intense orgasm washed over her.

After her orgasm subsided, Rita mumbled, "That was Ellie on the phone. She was glad you were doing your job. I'll make it up to you after dinner."

Later, Rita and I went to an Italian restaurant. She looked beautiful in a knee-length, light pink, sleeve-less, sun dress, industrial fishnet stockings, and flat shoes; she wore costume jewelry: dangling ear rings, a necklace, and bangles on her forearms. During dinner, when she asked me how I met Ali, I told her that I first saw her in an English class, fell in love with her, and courted her in college.

As we finished our meals, Rita said, "I have a chocolate cake at home. I can make coffee."

We left the restaurant after freshening up. After I parked my car outside her garage at the back of her home, Rita and I went to the backyard. After checking the new deck, she showed me her flower garden. It was windy and the bugs did not bother us.

When a gust of wind blew her dress up, I got a glimpse of her fishnet stockings-clad sexy thighs and pink lacy panties, my cock stirred, and I said, "That's lovely. It deserves a kiss," and grasped her by the waist.

Blushing, Rita threw her hands around my neck, kissed me, and said, "I would like that. Let's go to the oak tree; no one can see us in the corner."

At the tree, I kissed her mouth passionately as I rubbed her covered buttocks, nudged her to lean against the tree, removed my tee shirt and placed it on the ground in front of her, and slid to my knees. I lifted her dress up and, willingly, Rita held it up and watched me as I rubbed her fishnet stockings -covered lower thighs first and then her bare thighs to her crotch. I kissed her lacy, pink, panties, especially the small wet spot that indicated her aroused state.

"I hope you like my panties; I bought them especially for you."

I mumbled, "I sure do. You look gorgeous," and resumed licking her covered pussy.

I pulled her panties down to her ankles and got a good look at her thick, brown-grey, bush. Her clit was engorged and glistening, and her thick, mature, labia were wet; both looked delectable and I used my tongue and lips to eat them, pausing often to slurp her love nectar.

Rita mumbled, "Suck my clit; I'm close to cumming," and she lifted her right leg and hooked it on my shoulder, held on to my head as I sucked her pleasure button, and moaned incoherently as her pussy convulsed on my mouth.

Afterwards, she hugged and kissed me, and whispered. "Thank you for a second orgasm. Let's go inside."

Inside her home, Rita said, "Take off your clothes and sit on the couch in the den."

I said, "Keep on your lacy bra and your fishnet stockings."

"I was going to. You were ogling me."

After I took off my clothes, my cock stood straight out and, as I walked to the den, swung in the air.

When Rita stood in front of me, I said, "You're a truly gorgeous woman."

After we both freshened up, Rita put on a pink silk robe, and said, "I'm not expecting any company. Here, put on this tank top; I love to see your firm body. Let's have a small snack. You will need the energy," and, giggling, gently grasped my cock.

Just as we finished our cake and coffee, her phone rang. Rita answered and mouthed: "It's Claire." I went to the den and turned the TV on to a sports channel. I chose a photo album on the shelf to look at the photos of Rita and Harry during their wedding and the year after their marriage. Rita was a beautiful bride. In a series of photos in a bikini, she looked hot. She looked even hotter dressed for Halloween as a cheerleader in a short red-black plaid skirt, a very low-neck tank top, white socks, and her hair in two side pigtails.

Rita came in to the den and said, "Claire called to talk about the florist and the caterer. What are you looking at?"

"Your wedding and other photos. You were a beautiful bride."

She knelt in front of me, grasped my stiff cock, and said, "Which photos turned you on?"

"You were hot in a bikini; I assume you were on your honeymoon. Also, you dressed as a cheerleader," and added, "I think you look more gorgeous now."

Blushing, she said, "I was naughty. Harry knocked me up that night," and grasped my semi rigid cock.

As my cock grew and became stiff in her grasp, I said, "I'm a bit tired; I can wait. Are you ok with it?"

"Yes. I guess even an insatiable young man has to rest. I'm sure I'll be sore with the vigorous activity we have had. I am consulting with my gynecologist next week. I'm glad you're comfortable going out with me. By the way, Ellie will be visiting me for about a week. I'll call you in a few days."

"I'll miss you."

—-

I did not see Rita for a week or so, but as promised, she called and said, "Ellie is still here, but she's leaving Friday. In case you are curious, my gynecologist was glad to know that I resumed love making. I told her I was dating a younger guy; she said I should have no problem making love often, but we should enjoy long foreplay sessions. She also recommended I use a lubricating gel, when necessary. I bought more sexy lingerie to encourage fore play."

"I can't wait to see you dressed in sexy clothes."

"I'm sure you would do more than just see."

"I'll show my appreciation of your lovely body and beautiful face. I think we should try sex toys."

Softly, she asked, "What do you have in mind?"

"I can't tell you now. I'll buy something after checking the Internet catalogs. By the way, we should celebrate your birthday on Saturday."

Smiling, she said, "I'm glad you remembered that Ali and I share the same birthday."

—-

RITA'S BIRTHDAY

After I arranged for Tim to be with his grandparents, I invited Rita to lunch on Saturday to celebrate her 48th birthday. It was a warm day and she had on a black flowers on white, spaghetti-strap, short, sleeve-less, dress; high-heel sandals, and costume jewelry. She also had on her favorite floral perfume.

When I kissed her mouth passionately, she giggled, and said, "We will be late for lunch," and gently pushed me away.

At the restaurant, after we ate our salads, I gave her the present I bought, and told her, "It's a remote-controlled bullet; open it in private."

Rita whispered, "I missed you for a whole week. I would like to try it," and left for the ladies room.

A short time later, Rita returned, and with a big smile on her face, whispered, "I'm using it right now. It's awesome."

"Where's the control unit?"

"It's in my bag. Would you like to have it?"

"When you want me to."

"I don't think anyone can hear the buzzing sound, but, to avoid embarrassment, I'll turn it down to low," and reached in to her bag.

We managed to carry a conversation as best as we could, but I could see that Rita was sexually aroused by the vibrating bullet in her pussy and I was aroused knowing that my lover's pussy was juicy by that time.

Later, as I pulled in to her driveway, she giggled happily, and said, "Thank you for the present, lover. It's awesome."

I said, "I need to check out the situation."

As soon as we entered her kitchen, I closed the door, grasped her by her waist, and, as I kissed her mouth passionately, I placed my right hand on her panties-covered pussy; it was very wet and slick with a thicker fluid than I recalled. Then I felt the string for pulling out the bullet and I wanted to see it. Immediately, I slid to my knees.

She said, "If you think it will get in your way, I can take it out."

"Leave it in. Is it on?"

"Yes, it's on the lowest frequency."

After I pulled Rita's sopping panties down and placed my tongue on her engorged clit, I did feel the vibrating bullet. I licked her sopping clit eagerly. With the bullet vibrating inside her pussy and me licking her clit, Rita had an intense orgasm.

Shyly, Rita said, "Let's go to my bedroom. I want to wear my baby doll lingerie for you. I feel naughty," and walked towards her bedroom upstairs.

—-

Her bedroom was painted white with one large window, a large dresser with mirrors, and a king-size bed. I watched her change in to a red baby doll, a red lacy demi bra; red panties and red fishnet thigh thighs; she applied crimson lipstick, and, after combing her hair, pointed to a cushioned, arm-less, chair. After I sat on the chair, I noticed a mirror on the wall to my right. After Rita slowly pirouetted in front of me proudly, she slid to her knees, and watched in the mirror her red lipstick-coated lips wrap around my cock.

After sucking my cock for a minute or so, she whispered, "It tastes great. It's hard and throbbing. I want it in me," and, holding my stiff cock in her small hand, slowly straddled my thighs and impaled herself on my cock.

I held her tightly and looking at our reflection in the mirror, I said, "You're a gorgeous and elegant woman. Thank you for wearing the red fish nets."

Smiling, she said, "I'm glad you think so. Fill me up. You can seed me, but I can't get pregnant," and tightened her vaginal walls around my engorged cock.

"Let's go to bed. I'll carry you; just hang on to my neck with your arms and my waist with your long legs. Ok?"

"Ok."

After I lifted Rita up and held her up with my hands on her buttocks, and coupled, she looked at us intimately coupled in the mirror, and said, "Wow, my boobs are crushed against your chest; your cock is poking my cervix."

Slowly, as Rita kissed my face, neck, and shoulders, I walked slowly carrying her. Suddenly, I realized I was close to my climax.

I set her down on the dresser and said, "Baby, I'm close to cumming. Hold on to me with your arms and legs."

With urgency, I fucked her pussy in long, fast, thrusts, and, as I came deep inside her vagina, I thrust hard one more time making her grunt involuntarily.

"I'm sorry I got carried away towards the end of my climax."

Smiling, Rita, said, "You were an animal. I loved it. Lucky me, your cock is still stiff," and whispered, "Looks like you want to fuck me again. Let's freshen up and have a snack; you need to eat to be strong," and giggled.

—-

I went to the kitchen and was having a glass of water when Rita walked in. She smelled of freshly applied perfume; still had on the baby doll, fish net thigh highs, garter belt, and high-heel sandals. She put on stud-diamond ear rings. As she was putting together a tray of cheese and crackers, I kissed her neck and, while grasping her bra-encased boobs, pressed my cock in to her buttocks. She walked to her den, and I followed her watching her sexy buttocks undulate, and carrying a bottle of red wine, and two glasses.

In the den, as we sipped wine and snacked, she said, "Let's watch a movie."

I said, "How about Sexy Grandmas? I also bought another CD, Horny Mothers."

"Let's see grandmas. I hope the women are old enough to be grannys."

The first scene was of a very attractive 60+, blonde, lady, dressed provocatively and a young guy. The scene begins with the lady being courted by the young guy in a bar. After they go to her apartment, it didn't take long for the woman to show her large, slightly sagging, boobs.

Rita said, "Her buttocks droop a bit and are wrinkly; she must be about 65."

I said, "She looks very attractive. I think the young guy is lucky. She's very fuckable."

Blushing, Rita said, "I'm glad you think so," and added, "Oh, I forgot my love bullet. Let me go get it."

I grasped her hand, placed it on my partially aroused cock, and said, "We can also use my pistol."

Blushing, she asked, "You plan to use it while we watch the movie?"

"I would love to."

After Rita returned with her bullet in hand, I pulled her to sit in my lap and slowly snaked my growing cock in to her juicy pussy, removed her baby doll, and grasped her demi bra-covered boobs. I rubbed her back and meaty buttocks. I made her lean forward to see first her puckered pink ass hole and then my fat cock in her bushy cunt.

As the young guy began to lick the grandma's hairy pussy, my cock grew some more, and a small amount of cum flowed out of it. Soon, he was fucking her vigorously.

Rita said, "It turns me on to see a woman much older than me fucking a young man."

I pulled her to lean against my chest, opened her thighs a bit more, began to use the bullet on her clit, and said, "There's more to a woman than how old she is. Some women can fuck well in to their later years."

"I'm impressed the woman is to take the pounding for a long time. I'm sure I would be sore if I did that."

To tease her, I said, "You want me to have a quick trigger."

"All I am saying is I'm happy you bring me orgasms, but I don't want a sore pussy from excessive pounding."

I noticed Rita was breathing heavily and squirming. In the movie, at the urging of the young guy, the grandma agreed to fuck him while he was seated on a sofa. As she French kissed him passionately, she squatted over his crotch and, after he stuffed his big sausage-size cock in to her old pussy, she repeatedly pounded her crotch against his until she had an orgasm.

After a while, I had Rita lie on her back. She looked sexy in just her lacy, demi bra. Her pussy was slick and its walls grasped my cock tightly. I inserted my stiff cock deep in to her slick pussy, for several minutes I kissed her neck, lips, and cleavage. I fucked her in slow, long, strokes, for a minute and paused to squeeze her demi bra-covered boobs. I savored the contact between my crotch and her meaty crotch. I was too excited and had my climax deep in Rita's love channel.

Afterwards, as we rested, she said, "I'm glad you had another climax."

"You're a sexy woman. I'm loving being with you."

—-

Later, as Rita freshened up, she said, "It's a nice day. I would like to go the state fair and then to a movie."

"I'll go with you. Do you want me to grill burgers for our dinner?"

"Let's see what we can find at the fair."

Rita dressed in a white, sleeve-less, blouse, a beige skirt, sandals, sunglasses, costume jewelry, and a white cotton hat.

As we walked to my car, she said, "I'm going bra-less. The pockets are covering my nipples."

I said, "You look very elegant and sexy."

My rigid cock stiffened more every time I saw Rita's boobs jiggle. She noticed the tent formed in my pants by my stiffy and just smiled.

After I bought her cotton candy, she said, "I want to go on the water ride."

"Ok, but we will get wet."

"That's the idea on a warm day."

During the ride, we screamed as loudly as we could. Initially, I had my arms around Rita's waist; later, I had them around her chest and they kept her boobs from getting wet.

When she saw a taco stand, she said, "Let's eat tacos for dinner. You can grill burgers another time."

Later, I sat across from Rita at a picnic table and my cock stiffened just seeing her distended nipples; we let our clothes dry as we ate tacos and drank beer in the sun.

We ate our tacos and an ice cream cone I bought her at a picnic table. Rita made sure I saw her licking the cone lovingly, as if it was my cock.

—-

We went to see movie set in France at the turn of the century in a small theater that was half full. Rita chose the movie because it starred Michelle Pfeiffer and was billed as an older woman/younger man romance. After we sat in the last row, another couple, an attractive, well-dressed, older woman about 40 years old and a handsome younger man, about 25 years old, sat two rows ahead of us. The woman had a scarf around her head, as if she didn't want to be recognized.

I said, "That lady is old enough to be his mom."

Rita nudged me a short time later when the young man was kissing the woman passionately on her mouth and said, "That's not a mother-son kiss."

Soon after the lights were dimmed, I undid the top buttons of Rita's blouse and grasped her shiny right boob, leaned towards her, and French kissed her passionately.

Gently Rita pushed my hand off of her boob and whispered, "Don't you want to watch the movie?"

"I want to love you. You look gorgeous."

A short time later, Rita nudged me to look at the couple in front of us: it seemed that the young man had exposed the older woman's large boobs and was suckling them; later, he was trying to bury his face in her crotch. The couple quickly covered themselves with their clothes when an attendant led two late comers to the seats in the font.

Rita did not object when I began to suckle her right nipple. Wanting to taste her pussy nectar, I turned to my left, placed my right hand on her left thigh, and slowly moved it towards her crotch. I saw Rita was intently watching the screen. When my hand came in contact with her panties, she opened her legs enough to let me snake two fingers past the edge of her panties to her hairy mound. I stopped for a moment and then inserted my two middle fingers in to her pussy. For several minutes, I slowly moved my fingers back and forth, and rotated them. I stopped to let her enjoy being stimulated.

After a while, Rita whispered, "Play with my clit," and I grasped her clit, slick with her love nectar, and began to squeeze it between my fingers and thumb; her breathing quickened and she spread her thighs more.

Rita grasped my left arm and whispered, "Don't stop. I'm close," and, as I continued to squeeze her clit, her pussy convulsed uncontrollably around my fingers.

I noticed the young man was also leaning towards his older lover; presumably, he was also fingering her cunt. A short time later, I saw the older woman bend her face towards the young man's crotch. I do not know if the woman sucked off her young man because the movie ended a short time later.

Rita went to freshen up. In the lobby of the theater, as I waited for her, I saw the older woman walk out of the theater alone and go to the ladies room. The younger man walked out of the theater well behind her.

After Rita freshened up, as I drove, she said, "Thank you for bringing me off. Are you ok?"

"I enjoyed getting you off. I can wait till we reach home. Did you enjoy watching the older woman-younger man make out in front of us?"

"Yes. As I expected, the young guy was aggressive. I was really impressed how uninhibited the older woman was. She let her lover do what ever he wanted."

"I saw her walk out alone; later, the young man walked out alone too. May be she is married to another man."

After we were at her home, Rita said, "I know that mature woman. She's Daisy Miller, a history teacher at the high school. Her lover, Ron, graduated from high school a few years ago. When Harry was the Superintendent, there were rumors that Daisy was having an affair with one of her students. But, no one could produce evidence of her affair. She divorced her husband, who was older than her, for abandoning her for golf and having affairs with waitresses. Earlier, in the ladies room, she told me that her daughter and her two kids were visiting her. That explains why she and Ron were so amorous in the theater."

"How do you know Daisy?"

"She invited me to a meeting of a local support group for recently divorced or widowed women, known by the abbreviation RDWW," and, giggling, added, "I stopped going to that group's meetings after you seduced me. After a RDWW meeting, she told me in great detail her relationship with young Ron and told me that it's ok for me to let you love me."

"I'm curious."

"Ok, I'll summarize what Daisy told me. Ron was one of the seniors in her history class a few years back. He was a well-mannered young man, about 6-ft, 170 lb, and a full head of brown hair. He always addressed her as Mrs. Miller. He lived a couple of blocks away from her home with his divorced mom, who worked as a waitress and was not home much. After high school, he studied landscape design and maintenance at a nearby community college, and started his own business. Daisy kept hearing rumors about her husband having affairs, including with Ron's mom. She did not understand how her husband did not find her, a 5-ft 4-in, 115 lb, blonde with a 36C bust, attractive. But, she did not have an affair with one of her students.

"One evening, Ron, now 22 years old, came to Daisy's home and apologized to her for his mom's behavior. After that visit, they began to talk regularly, often for several hours in the evenings at her home. He also listened to her when she would get upset with her husband's affairs. In fact, Ron suggested that an attractive woman like her should have no trouble finding a man better than her husband, and that men younger than her would treat her better than her much older husband. He offered to mow her large yard after she divorced her husband. In return, she fed him after he mowed her yard and, on warm evenings, she allowed him to shower in the guest bathroom. As far as Daisy and her neighbors were concerned, she was a surrogate mom to a young man.

"Ron liked action movies and she appreciated him for taking her to a movie once a month and giving her presents on her birthday. She confessed that she was attracted to Ron, but when she went to movies with him she dressed to look old and dowdy to see if Ron would still be attracted to her. Daisy was delighted when Ron kissed her mouth passionately after he took her home from a movie; he told her she was a gorgeous woman. She invited Ron to go with her to a Halloween party at her friend's home; she dressed as a cheerleader and he as a football player. During that party, Daisy saw that Ron was stealing glances at her hair arranged in two pigtails, her bosom in a tight-fitting tank top, and her shapely stockings-covered thighs under a very short plaid skirt. After the party, she was happy to go trick or treating with a young man dressed as a football player. Later, Ron thanked her for taking him to a Halloween party, told her that she looked very sexy in the cheerleader costume and smelled nice, and kissed her pouty mouth passionately.

"A part of Daisy's mind said she should not socialize with Ron, but another part said she should because he was no longer a student at the school, she longed for a hard, young, cock in her pussy, and her ex-husband was running around with young waitresses. When Daisy found out that Ron would be home alone on Christmas day, she invited him for a ham dinner in the afternoon. On Christmas day, she finished decorating her home. Then she dressed up in a red, short-sleeve, low-neck, dress, and sprayed perfume on her cleavage. Ron put on dress slacks and a dress shirt. She thought he looked very handsome and told him he looks good. He told her she looked very attractive and thanked her for celebrating Christmas with him. She brought out her camera and took pictures of the dinner table and Ron. They shared a bottle of Cabernet Sauvignon, her favorite red wine, he brought. He thanked her when she gave him a nice dress shirt. She felt happy and, when she flirted with him, he caught her under the mistletoe, and kissed her first on her cheeks and then her mouth until she slipped out of his arms. When she saw snow showers outside, she wanted to go out after changing her clothes; Ron pleaded with her to put on the cheerleader costume; he promised that when she got cold, they would come inside. So they went to the backyard, which had a high fence, where they played a game of chasing each other and whoever got caught kissed the other, so that he kissed her several times. Daisy felt young; her pussy tingled being chased by Ron who also groped her boobs and buttocks every time he caught her.

"After they went in, Ron took photos of Daisy in the cheerleader costume. He then watched her make ham sandwiches and open a bottle of Chardonnay she had in the refrigerator. After they each had a glass of Chardonnay and a sandwich, Ron pulled Daisy to sit in his lap, played with her pigtails, and kissed her neck. He told Daisy that she was a great kisser and suggested they play, "spin the bottle." She said, "We did plenty of kissing outside." He said, "How about playing for removing clothing." She said, "Ok, boy. I'll beat your pants off," and they both sat on the living room floor and spun an empty bottle; after a while, Ron had no clothes on and Daisy still had her bra, panties, and plaid skirt on. When Daisy stood up to declare her victory, her panties-covered crotch was at the same height as Ron's face. Impulsively, he grasped her around her thighs, pushed his head under her skirt, and kissed her crotch. Daisy squealed in surprise and ran to the dining room. When Ron followed her with his stiff cock jutting out of his crotch, Daisy stood still mesmerized by the sight of Ron's massive cock, and muttered, "That's an impressive tool." Ron mumbled, "You're gorgeous," grasped her bra-covered boobs from behind, lifted up her short skirt and, while kissing her neck, pushed his stiff cock in to her soft covered buttocks. Being very excited, he had a climax and his cock spewed out jets of cum on to her covered buttocks. Ron was embarrassed and said, "I'm very sorry." Daisy said, "It's ok. You're young and got excited," and led him to the bathroom and cleaned his cock with a warm wash cloth. When Ron's cock stiffened some more, smiling, she said, "Put that thing away, stud. Go get dressed." In turn, Ron mumbled, "I want to lick. I have dreamt of eating your pussy for a long time, Mrs. M," and, after removing her panties soiled at her crotch, he nudged her to stand against the vanity, pushed his face in to her crotch, searched for her pussy in her hairy crotch with his lips, and licked her juicy pussy and slick, engorged, clit. Being already very excited due to being groped and kissed for couple of hours, Daisy had an intense orgasm as her pussy convulsed uncontrollably against Ron's mouth. She realized that Ron, unlike her ex-husband, loved to eat her pussy.

"Later she grasped his stiff, cum-leaking cock, and told him she's afraid of catching a disease and she would arrange for both to take blood tests. When she said she would love to play with his cock and balls, he agreed eagerly and mumbled it would make him happy to be loved by his beautiful girlfriend. After she freshened up, she led him to a chair; after he sat in it, she knelt between his splayed legs, grasped his 7-in-long cock, and licked along its length and took just the bulbous head in to her mouth. Ron held on to her pig tails, as he felt his cum dribble when she sucked his cock head. He leaned forward and grasped her bra-covered boobs. Daisy removed her bra, leaned forward, and wrapped her soft boobs around Ron's cock; after a short while, she massaged his cock with her boobs. They both watched in fascination as multiple jets of his cum blew out of his piss hole, hitting her neck and chin. Daisy kept Ron's cock wrapped by her boobs until it softened slightly.

"Daisy reminded him to go to the clinic for the blood test and that he is her date to a new year's dinner and dance at her country club. When Daisy suggested that they would not have much time to get together for several days, Ron pleaded with her to let him see her next day; softly, he told her that making oral love was not risky. Blushing, she agreed to see him. Next day evening, Ron arrived at Daisy's home with a bouquet of a dozen roses. He was delighted to see her in the cheer leader costume. As he hugged her, he realized that his mature lover was not wearing a bra; immediately, he lifted her blouse and suckled her nipples. After she sat in front of him in the living room, he saw she was not wearing panties. He did not know what Daisy had planned, until she told him to take off his clothes and lay on his back on the couch. She straddled his chest and slowly slithered to bring her aroused pussy to his face. She kept her pussy at just enough distance so that he could lick or suck it. After a while, her oozed out love nectar coated his chin, mouth, and nose, and she had a long, intense, orgasm.

"Quickly, Daisy turned around and began to suck on his cum-leaking cock. She knew Ron was examining her buttocks, ass hole, and wet pussy, and she felt very loved. Soon, Ron's cock let loose several jets of his sperm-laden cum in to her mouth. A few days later, Ron sent Daisy a text message that he was clean; she replied that she was too. Ron sent another message saying that he is growing a beard and sent a photo; Daisy thought he looked handsome and a bit mature.

"For the dinner and dance, Daisy had her hair done, put on diamond stud ear rings and a necklace with a diamond pendant, a form-fitting, black, spaghetti strap, open-back, mini dress, and a matching black jacket; black, silk, thigh highs, garter belt; black, silk, panties, and black patent 4-in pump shoes. She sprayed small amounts of her favorite perfume on her neck, cleavage, and top of her crotch. Ron put on a navy blue suit and a red tie. When Ron first saw her at her home, he told her that she looked very sexy. His cock became stiff and stayed that way most of that evening. They sat with an older couple, acquaintances of Daisy, who spent most of the night visiting with other friends. They had buffet dinner with wine. Ron danced well, but preferred the slow dances when he could hold his beautiful girlfriend close. At midnight, after a toast for a Happy New Year with champagne, a very happy Daisy kissed Ron passionately. Daisy saw her husband with a young woman and decided to go home soon after midnight.

"At her home, Daisy let Ron remove her dress until she was only in the thigh highs, garter belt, and panties. In turn, she removed all of Ron's clothes and hugged his hard, naked, body. With Ron standing behind her, she placed his hands on her magnificent boobs, grasped his stiff cock, and led him to her bedroom. She got on her bed, stretched out on her back, lifter her legs, and let Ron eat her juicy pussy until she had an intense orgasm. She then guided his stiff cock in to her pussy. Being a caring young man, Ron fucked Daisy with love and passion until he had a climax. Ron's cock was still stiff. He wanted to remain coupled in Daisy's arms, and his mature lover obliged him happily. In fact, Daisy and Ron remained in bed most of the next day."

—-

I said, "What a horny, love, story. Now, I'm turned on."

At the bottom of the stairs, I pleaded with Rita, "Take off your clothes."

After she took off her clothes, I slid to my knees in front of her and licked her still wet pussy until it became very juicy. Wanting to fuck, I turned her around to take her from behind, but she escaped from me, and quickly walked up the stairs to the bedroom.

I ran up behind her, caught her in front of the dresser, and muttered, "I want to fuck beautiful woman," and began to hump her naked buttocks.

By chance, my stiff cock slipped in to Rita's juicy pussy, and she said,

"Fuck me, stud," and bent over the dresser. I was too aroused and it did not take long for me to have a very satisfying climax.

We were having a snack, when she said, "Here is an album of private photos Harry took," and together we looked at pictures taken over several years.

She looked sexy in all of them. Most of the photos revealed her sexy boobs, but a few were of her totally nude; I noted she had a heavy growth of pubic hair even when she was young.

I said, "Baby, you're still gorgeous. Were you a beauty queen?"

Shyly, she said, "Yes, I was elected "Miss Dairy" of the county."

I nudged her to sit in my lap and, while holding her boobs underneath her robe, I kissed her mouth, and said, "You're still a beauty queen."

Rita said, "You're a horny young man, but you're also gentle with me. By the way, I will be busy with Claire's wedding."

"You mean I can't see you for a whole week?"

She said, "Yes."

—-

Several weeks before Claire's wedding, Rita asked me, "Please, be my escort at the wedding."

"Yes. I would be honored to be your escort."

I did not see Rita for a whole week before the wedding as she was busy helping Claire. I saw Rita looking gorgeous and sexy at the wedding in a beige, long-sleeve, full-length, low-cut dress, a pearl necklace, and pearl ear rings. Later, at the reception and during the dinner, I stayed close to her, and could smell her perfume and see her sexy figure. When the band started playing, she danced with me, while pressing her boobs in to me and occasionally groping my crotch.

As Claire and her husband, and their friends continued to party, Rita said, "I need fresh air," and walked out to the garden.

I followed her and we sat on a bench overlooking a lake. When I put my right arm around her shoulders, she leaned to wards me and French kissed me.

She then placed my right hand on her covered boob and whispered, "This puppy needs loving. They missed you."

I said, "I missed both puppies and you too. You look gorgeous."

When we heard some members of the bridal party nearby, she gave me a door key, and whispered, "Join me in my room. I want this night to be a special one," and left.

After I freshened up in a hotel's restroom, I went to Rita's room, and opened the door. I saw Rita standing in a short, pink, see-through, baby doll, a pearl necklace, and pearl ear rings. My cock got stiffer just looking at her. Quickly, I removed my clothes to my underwear.

When I hugged her passionately, she whispered, "I feel like a new bride," and pushing her buttocks against my hard on, added, "I guess you like me."

"Yes. You're gorgeous."

I stood behind her, inserted my hands underneath her robe, and grasped her unfettered, large, soft, boobs and gently pinched her nipples. I turned her to face me and, as I French kissed her for a long time, her grasp on my cock got tighter; in turn, my cock grew bigger and stiffer. I nudged her to sit on a sofa and quickly slid to my knees on the carpeted floor. I lifted her right leg and kissed it up from her ankles to her strong thighs. After I licked her left leg, I found my nose was close to her hairy crotch and I inhaled her aroused-state aromas.

When I licked her pussy, I found it was wet and slick with her love nectar, she started whimpering, and said, "I missed your tongue. Lick me. Lick meeeeee. Lick meeeeeee," and had an intense orgasm.

I lowered my underwear and quickly snaked my leaking cock in to her juicy pussy. I was deep in Rita's pussy. Immediately, my cock started to leak streams of cum in to her love channel. I heard my phone ringing.

Reluctantly, I picked it up, and a woman's voice said, "I'm Lilly. Laura Hughes is my daughter-in-law. Are you Tom Davis?"

"Yes."

"Your sister delivered a baby girl. Baby and mom are doing fine. Ok?"

I said, "Thank you for calling. I will visit my sister and niece soon."

Just coming out of the shower and looking into the door mirror, I grin a little bit thinking of an earlier conversation I had with my business partners. Half of the morning they were discussing shaving their junk to make them look bigger. I remember being a little annoyed, but then I shrugged it off thinking 'Whatever helps them sleep at night'. But it got me thinking, so I just tried it.

"Looks kinda cool," I said to no one, "Doesn't matter though, I've got it."

I kept thinking as I put my boxers on that it really didn't look that bad. At 35, I'm supposed to beyond that kind of personal grooming, but I would give it a try for a while. I knew that it wouldn't really change the skill set at all, but it might get some good attention. At the time I didn't know the personal attention I would get would be so soon.

It seems that sometimes a shower fixes all. I got a call from my son beforehand and had to speak to his mother afterward.

After bitching, and carrying on about one out of her encyclopedia of issues, I wasn't in the best mood. But that's ok. I was in a better mood after cleaning up. I guess it cleans the mind too. I went down to the kitchen to grab some juice. I was going to kick back and watch the late show. I don't get into those windbags very often, but there was something about that night's show I wanted to see. As I was pouring my juice I heard a noise in the yard space between my house and the neighbor. It was a bit of rustling and what sounded like someone trying to get a door open. I like my neighbors and I wanted to check it out. After turning the kitchen light off, I went over to my back screen door and looked out. Sure enough there was someone trying to break in to my neighbor's back door. I treaded lightly across the floor and went to my main door on the other side of the house. I was planning on coming around the other side, to outflank them.

When I came around the house I saw the shadowed figure. I didn't think it would be much of a struggle, since the person looked about eight inches shorter than me. I knew with my special forces training, I could take them. Then they would have to just be carried out of here when the police came. Slowly I crept up to the intruder who was heavily involved with trying to get the door open with what seemed like a coat hanger. Talk about low brow. My heart raced as I came within a meter, then just a bit closer.

"Come here fucker!" I exclaimed as I grabbed the person from behind.

Quickly I used a head lock with my other hand in front of their mouth and pulled them away from the door. They lost their footing and I had to pull them back. With this body next to me, I couldn't help noticing that this intruder was not a guy. I know the curves of a woman well. Not to mention the smell. But I didn't know what kind of danger this person posed, so it did not change my intent. I flung her around and pressed my hands around her arms. But there was enough light from my house in this backyard area between houses to see who the intruder was.

"Jan?" I asked with surprised as I let go of her.

"What the fuck are you doing?!" she exclaimed.

"I thought you were someone breaking in" I said with a lowered tone. "You are breaking in, why?"

"It's me," she panted as she adjusted her clothes, "I live here remember?"

"Yeah I remember," I said, "But what the hell are you doing breaking in to your own house?"

"Um…I forgot my key," Jan said.

"Why not just knock on the door?" I asked as I put my hands out to my side.

"Well," Jan started, "No one is home."

"Oh yeah," I said, "Your parents are gone this weekend."

"Yeah and I can't find my key," she said with a smile.

"Come to think of it, Jan, you are supposed to be in by midnight," I said folding my arms.

"I'm eighteen and three fourths or so," Jan said with sarcasm, "I shouldn't have to."

"Wrong, missy," I smiled, "You are still living in your parent house. If they said eight, it would be eight. If they said never, you'd stay home. Their house, their rules even if you're fifty."

"Whatever," Jan said, "You got a key, just let me in already."

I couldn't help looking at her. Even in the dim light I could see her plainly. Her curly brown hair that went below the shoulders of her medium frame seemed just a bit out of place. She wore a form fitting one piece black dress that came off her shoulders. It barely went halfway to her knees. I don't see how she could actually sit down and maintain any dignity. She might have well been wearing nothing at all. Her attire left very little to the imagination. After calming down a bit I remembered how tight she felt, up against me as I first pulled her away from the door. But I knew I was supposed to have a little dignity too. However, I'm not over the hill yet.

"You know you don't have much respect for your parents do you?" I asked.

"Yeah, but I should be able to do what I want," Jan said, "I'm old enough to do what I want."

"Yeah ok," I said as I looked her over again, "You can vote, own property, and everything else…you can't do as a minor."

"Yeah that's not all, opens up some possibilities huh?" Jan smiled.

"Your parents should know about this," I said as I put my hands to my side and headed back to my house, "I'll get my key."

"No wait!" Jan said as she pulled my arm.

"Why?" I said as I turned around, "You were actually on your way out, weren't you?"

"No," Jan defended.

"And you forgot something. So you were already out dressed like that," I said as she backed off a bit.

Now closer to the light of my own house she was more visible. It was even harder to keep my eyes off of her. I was never really in to a girl that dresses like a tramp, but for some reason I couldn't help thinking about it. I knew I had to get it out of my mind.

"Speaking of being underdressed," Jan said, "Do you always go running around outside in your underwear?"

"I wasn't planning to but I couldn't exactly go and find clothes when I thought someone was breaking in to your house, now could I?" I asked.

"Well I guess not, but why? Wait, um," she hesitated, then opened her mouth wide, "Your getting aroused aren't you?"

"What?" I said defensively.

"Looking at me…you're…just…it's right there," she said pointing to the front of my boxers.

"What?" I asked looking down at myself.

"The blood flow is going south, ya know," Jan said as she pointed.

"Grow up," I said defensively, "Don't tell me…don't even tell me you never saw a guy in boxers before. You are not exactly a choir girl."

"Yeah so I have more than a mental image so what," Jan said, "So I'm wearing this dress. It's tight, and…there isn't much of it, but come on, you're like forty five or something. Aren't you supposed to have some control over it?"

"Thirty five smart ass. I am not aroused," I said, with frustration,

"Don't try to turn this around on me."

"I was kidding, you look young," Jan grinned.

"Well we'll just discuss it with your parents later," I said.

"Ah just wait, sorry," Jan said quickly.

I noticed her for sure. Who in their right mind wouldn't? I saw her form and looked her over carefully. But I was far from arousal. At this point I thought that she was just trying to get me to back off and forget about it. I thought that she wanted to try to turn things around so that I would stay quiet. In my experience this is a rather common tactic when backed into a corner.

"Nothing unusual here," I said, "Why don't you focus on something else."

"You're full of crap neighbor," Jan said waving her hand in front of her face, "No way. You have to have it on the brain to get like that."

"Get like what?" I asked, "Wait, stop turning this around. "

"I'm not stupid is why," she said as she pointed toward me again.

"You know just a little too much for your age," I said as I looked at myself again, "What are you looking at your dad's fishing buddy for anyway? Who is really the weirdo here?"

I started to walk toward the house to try to hide my annoyance. I get plenty of attention and I don't mind. I have even played into it quite often. Sometimes I would walk away wondering what kind of thoughts they would have after my looks, posture, and behavior. But this was ridiculous. Plus it was a bit too close to home.

"There's a sock, or pepperoni or something in there right?" Jan smiled.

"Compensation."

"You should really quit while you're behind," I exclaimed.

"Ahem," Jan panted with a smile, "Guess I have something to shoot for."

"What's that supposed to mean?" I asked.

"I mean," she said nervously, "Gotta find one of those sometime."

"Enough of this," I said with a sigh, "You're going to go into your house and stay there."

"You know you could let me see it," Jan smiled, "Then I'd probably keep quiet about it."

"Keep dreaming," I said, annoyed, "This isn't show and tell."

"Oh I am dreaming," Jan said.

I was somewhat flattered. As I mentioned, I still get attention, but not as often as I use to. I still tried my best to maintain control of my thoughts. Inwardly I was smiling at her fascination. But it was testing even my cavalier attitude toward the subject.

"Think what you want," I said after a pause, then walked toward my house.

"Fine, an exchange of information then," I heard her say from behind me.

"What?" I said as I turned.

"I mean it's a fair exchange," she smiled, "I'm really curious to see if you are faking it. I can pay the price of admission."

"You're out of your mind," I said with annoyance.

I have always been weak to this. I have always been just a little bit concerned that someone might point out a weakness of mine. This is not a weakness but I couldn't help feeling challenged. I think it got the better of me, and put my judgment in check.

"Look little miss, I don't need to fake it", I defended.

"Prove it," she said folding her arms.

I looked at her expression and there was a definite determination. She looked at me and stood there as if she had made up her mind and there was no going back. I sensed that she was not going to back down. I wanted to end this. It was uncomfortable. I just wanted to get away from her before I did have a reaction to her presence.

"I don't need to, not to you," I said, annoyed.

I didn't care anymore. I was trying to walk a fine line and get out of this without much trouble, but it got too difficult. So I got a little rude. Call it a wakeup call to someone who should have had more control when she was growing up. Great parents don't always mean you're getting a kid who can behave themselves. I walked into the house without looking back and could hear her following me.

"Ok tough guy," Jan said as she quickly yanked down my boxers and grabbed my appendage from around my waist, "Holy!"

"Holy...what the hell?" I exclaimed as I jerked away and pulled my boxers up.

"Ok sorry, too curious I guess," Jan said nervously as I turned.

"You know that's assault," I said as I pointed at her.

"Like you really mind," Jan smiled as she walked into the kitchen, "What are you going to do about it, put me over your knee or something?"

"Where did that come from?" I said.

"Well I know one thing you could punish me with," she smiled as she took a cup out of the dish drainer and filled it with water.

"Keep dreaming," I said as I folded m arms. "That grope is all you are getting. Keep your hormones in check."

"Dream about rubbing it against my still tight, shaved pussy, making me wet, ok sure," she said with a slight whisper.

"Shut up already," I said quickly.

I knew what she was trying to do. She was giving me a mental image of her physical self to see if I was curious. She was baiting me. Young, way too curious, and horny, she was on some sort of mission. Obviously I could have her easy, but it wasn't right, and would probably have consequences.

"Look, sorry I'm just playing around," she said as she set the cup down.

"Get out of here and go to bed," I said as I turned my back and walked off into the family room.

"I was hoping you'd ask," Jan grinned. "An all night thing huh? My place? Wow."

"Go away, ok?" I shot back.

I was annoyed, but only mildly. I have certainly never been bothered too much when a girl grabs my stuff, but this was way out there. I went into the family room and planted myself in front of the TV. I became even more annoyed when I realized that I had missed half of the show I wanted to watch. But as soon as I turned the TV on, there was a knock on the open doorway. I ignored the first one, but the second was much louder. This girl just doesn't give up. But no more free shows tonight.

"What Jan?" I asked with a sigh.

"Well I still can't get into my house," she said.

"Oh yeah," I grinned and took my keys off of the side table, "Best to let you in so you won't go off and do something stupid."

"Yeah perish the thought", Jan said as she watched me walk past her.

I brushed past the girl, and got a whiff of the gallon of perfume she had on and shook my head. Quickly I walked over to her back door and put the key in. It didn't open. I wiggled it around then pulled it out to look at it to make sure it was the right one.

"Oh yeah," Jan said from behind me, "I was supposed to give you the new key today."

"Would have been a good idea," I said as I glared at her.

"Look, I'll just call my parents on your phone, then go to a friend's house," Jan said.

"Oh so you can go out and get in more trouble," I snapped, "No, get your ass in my house. You can crash on the couch for now."

"Yes sir," Jan snapped sarcastically and followed me in, "You want my ass in your house."

"Is that another?" I started but was interrupted.

"Never tried that so be gentle ok?" she smiled.

"You are just unbelievable," I said as I walked into the house.

"Thanks handsome, you're kinda hot too," Jan smiled.

I waited until she had stepped in the door, then I closed and locked it behind her. I looked her over a moment as she walked past me. Her demeanor had changed a bit. I think she knew she messed up. But I wasn't done yet.

"If you're going to be here, you can go take a shower," I said as I sat back down on the couch.

"Awesome, we get to start that way huh?" Jan said with an excited tone.

"I know what I want to lather up first."

"By yourself," I shot back.

"Why do I stink or something?" Jan asked.

"Yes," I said, not holding back, "Perfume, like a Louisiana cathouse."

"Fine," she said with a low shallow voice.

"There's some sweat pants and shirt clean on the dryer over by the bathroom. Get a bag and put those clothes in them if they have perfume on them," I barked.

"Fine," Jan said with a defeated expression.

"Sorry," I said, "Didn't mean anything really, just makes me sneeze. Don't feel bad."

"Sorry I was so strong with my ideas. It's no secret I've always been attracted to you," she said.

"I'm just a guy Jan," I said, "I make mistakes too."

"You forget, even though I was really young, I saw how you felt when you lost your wife. Underneath all that macho, you're kind and caring," she said as she walked off.

I spent the next few minutes trying to figure it out how she could be so raunchy one moment, and so level headed the next. I had forgotten that she was in her parent's family room when they were consoling me about my wife. It's funny what people remember about you. I have always been close with her parents and I had to bail her out of trouble a few other times too. I never wanted to upset her parents so I kept it quiet. Perhaps that wasn't the best approach. Maybe it's time they know that their daughter is not an angel. It might do her some good.

I couldn't get what she said out of my head. She couldn't possibly have feelings for me. Not with all the adventures she has had. Underneath all of it she does have good qualities. She was a straight A student from first grade on. Other than her own shenanigans, she is mostly responsible. She is also attractive of course, but way too young.

With all this going on, I didn't even get to watch my show. It was all done, and Jan was out of the shower. I felt bad asking her to do that, but it was a little rough. I heard her rustling around in the kitchen, presumably for a bag to put her clothes in. But when she came into the family room I did a double take.

"Shower was good actually," Jan said as she stood a few feet away from the TV and in front of me.

She looked at the TV and it was probably a good thing. She would have caught me staring. All she had on was one of my sweatshirts. Well at least I assumed that was all. It seemed as if she ignored the sweat pants. I knew it would be baggy on her, but it was all I had. The sweatshirt was big in her and was low enough to just barely cover her secrets. Her hair was wet, and brushed back, no doubt with my brush. She lifted both of her arms back to pull some hair back. When she did, the sweatshirt rode even further up to where I could just see a little that this was all she had decided to put on.

"Couldn't find the sweatpants in case you are wondering," she said as she stared at the TV.

"Ok," I tried to cover, "But yeah I'll find something else."

"No it's ok," she said, "This works. I can't sleep in sweats anyway."

"Well you can take them off when you sleep," I said with mild annoyance.

"No don't trouble yourself," Jan smiled as she looked at me.

"But Jan," I started because I couldn't shake the image of her wearing a single item of my clothing.

"Yeah I know what you are going to say, but I wasn't wearing any under my skirt," she said to me.

It was at that point that I realized that I still had just my boxers on. With all the irritation I completely spaced it. I should have put something else on. I realize that she already had a look, and a tug, but as much as I really would not like to care, I should probably have sweats on. Perhaps I should go find those ones she conveniently overlooked. My eyes kept wandering. It's true it's been a while since I've had anything, but that's no excuse. She just stood there looking at the TV. It was almost like a tease of some kind. How could she not know she would show if she lifted her arms.

"Oh my God, I want boobs like that!" she said, watching a commercial.

"Why?" I asked, looking at the TV.

"I'd be hot. Sporting those around, making every guy turn their head," she said as she bounced a bit, and then walked over to the chair diagonal to me.

I watched her sit down. Her torso faced away from me a bit. She lifted her leg a bit to examine nail polish or something on her toe. I really didn't pay much attention to that since even from a side view, she nearly showed all the way up to that ass with her leg raised. Suddenly I got to wondering what the rest looked like. I imagined a bit, and then stopped to scold myself. Don't get me wrong. If this was not my next door neighbor's daughter, I would have made a suggestion already. I broke with my daydream before it went any further, and of course covered for it in my own way.

"Not everyone is into a big rack but I'm sure you get attention," I said dryly.

"I really look ok?" She asked.

"You're fine the way you are," I said quickly, knowing I was getting baited again.

"Thanks for saying so," she smiled, "You can look this way if you want, don't be embarrassed."

"Watching TV," I said, as I looked away from her.

"I noticed that the shower was jus used before me. Is that when you did it?" Jan asked.

"Did what?" I asked.

"Shaved your goods," Jan smiled, "I didn't get much time, but it was very smooth."

"That's really more than you should know," I said.

"But I know," she smiled as she turned a bit in her seat, "Not bad for the first time."

"How would you know that?" I asked with annoyance.

"You missed a little on the base of your shaft on the top part," she smiled.

"Nobody's perfect," I sighed.

"I can help," Jan smiled.

"Ah, let's change the subject," I said.

"It's probably easier for me than for you," she said glancing at the TV.

"I can handle it," I said.

"No I mean it's probably easier for a girl to shave down than a guy," she smiled at me and put her leg down, "Less corners and curves."

"Ah yeah I suppose," I said dryly, "Let's talk about something else."

"Ok, how often do you handle it?" Jan grinned as she turned a bit.

"Huh?" I asked.

"You said you handle it, and you do live alone. So how often?" she grinned.

"You mean?" I scoffed, "You know that's not any business of yours."

"Nothing to be embarrassed about," Jan smiled as she turned a bit more toward me, "I'm no stranger to it. It's part of life, at least part of mine anyway."

"You know I shouldn't be hearing this," I sighed as I tried to look at the TV.

"I guess you probably don't want to hear about mutual masturbation between my friend Cindy and I then either," Jan grinned as she turned to almost face me completely.

"Really?" I asked without thinking, "Ah, never mind, forget it."

"Oh yeah, not often though, "she said seemingly ignoring most of what I said. "She has really soft fingers."

"Ah let's change the subject," I said nervously.

"Ok fine," Jan grinned, "Let me turn the channel to see if one of those late night, as you might call them, 'titty flicks' is on. I can get myself off before I sleep, and you can do, whatever."

"That's not what I meant," I sighed.

"You know the mutual thing doesn't have to be girl on girl," Jan said as she set her legs on the floor.

"You know you have a one track mind," I sighed.

"At the moment yeah," she smiled as she faced me with her legs close together, "But damn, I've been a straight A student since first grade. I'm going to Berkeley in the fall. A little craze in the brain about one thing isn't going to make me fall off the horse."

"Now I know why you're going to Berkeley," I grinned, "That whole girl on girl mutual thing."

"Oh why the hell does everyone think Berkeley is full of lesbians?" Jan shot back, "Just because, arg!"

"Struck a nerve finally," I laughed.

"If you weren't so hot I'd smack you," Jan grinned.

"Not gonna give me an inch are you?" I sighed.

"No, not at all," she said as she placed her hands between her knees,

"But I'd take whatever inches you have."

"Direct and to the point this time," I shot back.

"Great, your bedroom, or right here making me drool on the carpet?" Jan grinned as she bent her left leg and put it up on the seat chair.

"No, and no," I said, "Make yourself drool. But just wait a bit first."

I was trying the best I could. But her attitude was starting to affect me. I was feeling the loss of control start to happen. I kept thinking that I just should get away from this. But all this talk had created some flashes in my mind. This dirty talk coming from a girl that probably shouldn't be talking this way was making me start to think that way. Everyone that knows me knows I am a nasty 'ole' bastard. These words are nothing new to me. That's why at that moment I couldn't figure out why it was affecting me. Watching and listening to her raunchy talk made it so I could not possibly stand up without attracting the wrong

attention.

I watched as she seemed to be checking the smoothness of her skin. She looked her legs over as if studying them. I think she realized that I was studying them too. Then she fumbled a bit with the bottom of the sweatshirt and seemed to be thinking about something. Then she started right in again.

"You know, I'm not as bad as I sound." Jan sighed as she ran her fingers along the skin on her leg.

"If you say so," I said.

"I talk like I'm a walking mattress. But I've been with one guy." She said.

"Good for you," I said with a bit or sarcasm.

"I mean penetration-wise." She said, "A few hand jobs don't really count do they?"

"You aren't going to give up are you?" I asked.

"I guess I have to sometime," she sighed as she turned around and faced the TV.

When her attention was on the TV, I quickly stood and went for the kitchen. I needed some water and to get the tent I was pitching out of there. As I had my drink, I breathed deeply to try to relieve some of the pressure I was feeling. It wasn't just from her. I had to admit that she got to me. But I could not admit it to her. I grit my teeth thinking how much I just wanted to pick her up and head upstairs. I would show her how it's really done, and create a template for which she could judge everyone else that came after.

I was tired of this play on words. I have always prided myself on my own patience, even on the worst days. But inside I was frustrated. The feelings were aimed at both of us, especially to her for her open and obvious advances that as I had known in the past only the worst of whores had. I watched her grow up. It was that aspect of it and the fact that I knew her that it irritated me. I just wanted to grab her and tell her to have some damn pride in herself. Also these frustrations were aimed at myself, for being just a step away in my mind to just simply having her.

My plan of trying to calm myself physically and mentally had only made limited progress. I decided I had just better go upstairs and away from the situation. I set the glass down and walked out of the bathroom with the intention of heading quickly upstairs. But it didn't quite work out that way yet.

As I passed the entrance to the family room I had a double take and simply stopped and stared at what I saw. Jan had stood up and was facing the TV. She stood right in front of it. She had lifted the sweatshirt to just above her waist, fully exposing the lower half of her body. I stared and couldn't help it. Her well rounded curves just seemed to stare back at me. I watched as she reached around and placed her hands on her two cheeks. As she moved them around, she stretched her arms a little to each side. Perfect, young and fit, it did not help the feelings I had been fighting. But because of the anxiety, my physical reaction had slowed a bit. I still could not take my eyes off of her.

"Waiting for the judge's ruling," she said softly as she looked over her shoulder.

"Dammit," I said clearing my throat.

"What, does one cheek look better than the other?" She asked.

"I um, just was passing by on my way upstairs," I said as she let the sweatshirt fall to cover her.

"Oh is that all? Too bad." She smiled as she approached.

"What do you mean?" I asked.

"I was hoping you finally changed your mind," she said as she stood nearly toe to toe with me.

"I can't do that," I whispered as I looked into her eyes.

"Just tell me," she said panted with a slight moan as she quickly took y hands and placed them behind her on the skin, "Judge's ruling."

"Ten, congratulations, I need to go now." I whispered as I slowly removed my hands where she had placed them.

"I'm not a bad girl," She said as she put her arms around my shoulders, "In fact you're the only guy who has ever been straight with me."

"It's too bad," I whispered. "People should be more respectful."

"While they still think they have a chance to get me, I get the attention. But that's all most people want. I guess that's why I acted that way toward you." She said.

"As long as you respect yourself, you will always win," I said.

"I wish they all would, like you do," Jan whispered as she hugged me.

"Make them," I whispered, "Kick them to the curb if they don't."

"But I loved to be looked at too, and love the physical feelings that can happen," she sighed.

"You can, but they can't have it until they respect you," I said.

"I guess that's why I like you so much. I'm not just an object to you," she said as she gave me a simple peck and walked back over to the chair,

"I'll be good now."

"I'm going to bed, but I just want to say one thing," I started, "You're beautiful and smart. Stay that way, and demand respect for it."

"Thank you for being so kind," she sighed as she stared at the TV, "I'll go to sleep soon."

I walked away and as I headed up the stairs I had mixed feelings. I realized that I did something good for her, and I was confident she had learned a lot. It might even save her life someday. But there was also that part of me that wondered where that younger, more action friendly persona of mine had gone. This was the first time I had realized that I had changed. It wasn't long before that, that I would have 'tapped that' then again in the morning. Maybe I grew up too. I started to wonder when that happened. I had actually called her beautiful and it was not just to get some action. I had meant it and I didn't feel like I had made a mistake.

Flopping quickly down on the bed, I rested on my back and slowly fell asleep with my thoughts. Although I sort of missed the action, I had to realize I was beyond that. If I was younger I might think that what I did, just cost me some hot ass. But I felt good. Even if something had happened, I felt like I would have deserved it for a change. I drifted off to sleep unaware that Jan had decided not to sleep yet.

A few hours later I woke, and had to use the bathroom. I had not slept well, and was for some reason hungry. Perhaps it was all the excitement of the evening, but I needed a snack. Rubbing my eyes, I went down over the stairs and headed for the kitchen. I didn't hear a sound from the family room so before I had looked I was thinking Jan had probably gone to sleep. But that was far from the truth.

As I passed the entry way, I looked and what I saw made me freeze in position. The TV was off, but Jan wasn't. I stared with my mouth wide open as I saw her in the same chair. But the setting had changed dramatically. Her leg was arched upward on the back of the chair and the other one on the floor. She was completely nude. One of her hands was between her legs, and the other cupping one of her breasts. As I listened to her soft moans I couldn't help noticing that she might be the most beautiful young woman I had ever seen. I was wrong for watching, but I couldn't help it. My physical reaction was instant. I listened to her panting as her hips moved more wildly.

"I will get respect," Jan moaned as her eyes remained closed, "And…oh my God, you won't get this until you do."

I smiled as I listened to her words. I had made an impact on her. It's not exactly what I expected, but I had just figured that this is her way of learning it. She was roll playing a situation and her own reward. She had truly given it some thought. I wanted her right at that moment. Her breathtaking beauty captured me. I could respect her.

"Respect me, ah!" Jan panted as her his moved sharply up and down and I watched the end result of her self satisfaction.

Her head flopped backward as a smile formed on her face. It was like I had become intoxicated. My heart raced and I was excited. But oddly I was in complete control. The new discovery of my own personality had started to have this odd control over me. I knew if I moved in now I would still respect her in the morning, instead of just offering cab fare. I decided I couldn't take it anymore and see if I was worthy of such beauty.

"Ah holy shit," Jan said as she tried to cover herself, "I'm sorry."

"I heard what you said and I'm proud of you. You're dealing with this, in your own special way." I said as I watched her relax and just sit there.

"It's how I cope with a major epiphany," Jan said. "Things are going to be different."

"Good," I smiled, "But I have something to tell you."

"Oh sure," Jan said as she took the sweatshirt from the back of the chair and draped it over herself.

"You know I would still respect you afterward," I smiled.

"Are you saying what I think your saying?" Jan asked as she stood.

"Yeah," I said.

"I know you will," Jan smiled as she dropped the sweatshirt, "But there is one thing I can't promise you."

"What's that?" I asked as I pulled her close to me.

"That I won't fall in love with you." she said as she hugged me.

"One step at a time," I said as I started to kiss her.

"Wait, one more thing," Jan said as she pulled away a bit, "You will respect me. But I'm also going to work you harder than you've ever been worked. It's just how I am."

"Should I be scared?" I grinned.

"Answer that for yourself in the morning," Jan said as she yanked my boxers down.

Even though she was just two thirds my size, her strength and determination caught me off guard and in the start of things I was quickly down for the count. Grabbing my arm, she turned me around and thrust me down onto the couch so hard I could feel the cushions bottom out on the frame. It had caught me off guard with my drawers causing me to slip. But I really wasn't complaining.

Lying on top of me, she kissed me passionately. Pressing her lips forcefully, her hands moved to my sides then down my legs. After I recovered from the brief shock of being body slammed, I was determined to get into this as well. I remembered the beautiful lower rear half I had seen earlier and that's where I wanted my first moves to go. As I let my hands explore her soft, smooth skin, Jan reacted by pressing her advances harder.

Jan started kissing my neck. All of her moves had given me the reaction I was happy to have and would use to the best of my ability. Slowly, she trained her kisses lower and lower and eventually met what I was referring to. As her knees hit the floor and she knelt near the good stuff, her eyes widened.

"Fuck," she gasped as she grasped me with both hands.

"Let's gets some fun in a while before that dear," I smiled down at her as I watched her fingers dance around me.

"I mean look," she said as she placed her arm next to it. "Almost like from my elbow to my wrist. Cripes."

"Well if you think it's too much for you," I started.

"Oh no. Whatever you've got I can take" she smiled. "Eventually."

I looked into her eyes at the brief moment that we made eye contact. It wasn't long before her attention focused back onto what she really seemed to want. There was a slight smile that stretched her lips a little as she lowered her head. Softly she kissed the head several times as if she was politely introducing herself. Then she did the same up and down the shaft. This simple and gentle touch was highly erotic. I couldn't wait to see how her obvious sensuality would translate into love making.

Jan's mixed nature amazed me. I believed her when she told me she didn't have as much experience as she was implying earlier with her antics. She had become way too passionate and controlled not to be. Of course I started to wonder why the hell I was analyzing this so much.

"Oh sweetheart," I gasped as her tongue and lips slowly ascended from the base to the top, and back down again.

"I love this," Jan said as she worked her tongue and lips while gently rubbing her hand underneath.

Her fingers explored and very slowly one of them managed to make it between my cheeks. She giggled as she tickled my puckered hole. It was an odd sensation I had never experienced before. Just when I thought she was going to try to take that action a bit further, her fingers cupped my scrotum.

"You're amazing," I whispered.

"Is there nothing small on you?" she smiled as she cupped me.

But before I had a chance to react, her lips opened and she pressed them over my length. Closing her eyes, she moved her head up and down, with a slight moan. I couldn't help notice that she seemed to enjoy it as much as I did. But in an instant she changed her moves once again.

"Ack!" she coughed and gagged after attempting to get me to tickle her throat.

"Hey it's ok, take it easy dear." I whispered.

"Just trying to make you feel the best I can," Jan coughed.

"You already impress me more than you know," I smiled. "Just be yourself."

I know she was trying to impress me, thinking she wasn't doing enough and wanted me to be happy. But if she is going to learn anything tonight that will be to be herself and just relax. Respect comes full circle when you know your own limitations. However I was becoming more concerned about my own so called thoughts. I was examining everything. I was becoming fond of Jan, or else I was now tame. I had one last question: When did this happen?

Because of the tickling of her fingers just about everywhere, and her soft gaze as her lips surrounded me, I didn't take long to get back to what was really happening. There was a strange gaze as she looked at me. It was almost as if she really did have some budding feelings for me.

"Oh wow," I gasped as she opened her mouth and wrapped her long tongue around my shaft, moving it up and down.

"So soft, but so much power in this, I love it," Jan slurped. "It makes me crazy."

"You want crazy?" I smiled as I quickly got up from under her.

"I want whatever you've got," Jan smiled, "How wild can you fu... Ahhhh!"

Before she had a chance to finish her sentence, I reached down and grabbed her by the waist. Picking her up, I flipped her over upside down and held on tight. Her legs flopped on each side of my face. The quick move had smeared her wetness all over me. The sensation fired me up even more. I listened to her giggle even when my length hit the side of her face as I turned her into position. Holding on tight, I kissed her wet folds, and licked her entire opening. I found just the right spot and bathed her with attention. As soon as she got her bearings, she started in on me. I was amazed we were able to hold this position. But it was only a few moments before she bucked her hips and I had to let her down easy to avoid dropping her.

Gently I lowered her to the floor, and continued. Slowly and with careful attention I pleasured her like never before. I say that because later on she told me no one had done that for her before. Because of that I made it a point to do it often. Of course that statement gives hint to how this story really ends. But it seemed that me doing this was her weakness. One that she never knew she had. I would later wake in the morning to find her making breakfast, cleaning the kitchen and then mentioning several times how it gave her tears.

"I want you," I whispered as I sat up from the floor a moment.

"Any way, every way, any time, and for as long as you want sweetheart," she panted.

I had run up over the stairs to find some protection. But had not realized she had followed me right up there. I had come out of my bathroom only to turn around and see her lying on her back on my bed. I stopped at the edge of the bed and looked down at her. She touched one of her nipples gently as she softly licked a finger on her other hand. I had never in my life seen someone with such sensuality. Scooting over to the edge of the bed, she put her feet on the floor with her legs on each side of my body. Giving me my appendage the soft kisses she did earlier, she reached out and took the protection out of my hand. As she pulled away, she applied it with care, then scooted back on the bed again.

"All yours," Jan moaned as she gently rubbed between her legs.

I knew I had to take it easy for a while. Crawling onto the bed I pressed my weight onto her. She embraced me, and spread her legs as we kissed. Looking into her eyes, I slowly went home. I watched as her mouth opened got wider, and then smiled. I was very slow at first because I had noticed how tightly she had grabbed me. It was obvious that her experience had been limited. But as I kissed her medium sized breast I remembered her comment about working me hard. That would probably not happen this time. As I heard her soft and sensual moans, I felt so strongly that I was exactly where I needed to be. It was a strange sensation I was feeling. Where it had been just sex in all my encounters over the past several years, or even as I had felt drunk as hell one night, a major plowing, this was different. For Jan, we would make love. It was then that I felt her tighten, over and over, rhythmic and slow.

"So wonderful," Jan sighed with her eyes closed.

Her hands grasped me from behind, and pushed inward on me, seemingly faster than I was going. As I moved faster, she pressed faster again until her moans were as fast and as steady as a machine gun. I didn't want to just blurt out the comment to her, but it had been a long time since I had felt such tightness around me. She grabbed me, and not just with her hands. As she clenched her nails into me, it only made me more determined to pleasure her. Before I could kiss her, she wailed and bucked wildly underneath me. Her sensuality had turned briefly primal. I thought she might want to stop until she pushed me into her again. I looked into her eyes and she latched onto me with her lips. I explored her soft skin with my hands.

I was excited and it seemed like I never wanted this to end. It was as if I could not possibly get enough. I began kissing her all over. From her neck to her breast, down to her abdomen, and even her hands I reveled in the beauty named Jan. I buried my tongue in her young womanhood until she nearly screamed with joy. I loved every spec of her soft, young, and sensual body. I had even acted a little hungry. It may have seemed a little too aggressive, but it made Jan turn and make good on her statement from earlier.

Just as I had come up for a breather, Jan quickly moved to the side, panting heavily. She shook her head from side to side with her eyes half closed. Looking into my eyes, her gaze was primal. For a moment I actually felt a little timid.

"Lay down," she said as she got up on her knees and pushed me to the bed.

"Oh fu…oh my God!" I gasped as she devoured me just for a moment.

Pressing my back into the bed, Jan climbed on top of me and grabbed my length, rubbing it on her wet warmth, just as she had mentioned earlier. Letting out a small giggle, she positioned me the right way and began to sit down. As I saw her mouth open wide as she was parted, I smiled widely. Slowly at first her hips moved around me. Because I had been so excited I had a difficult time holding on and needed to concentrate. I wanted to make this feeling last. It had been so long. Even when she moved faster I held. I wanted so much for her to have her time and moments. I felt young again when I looked into her eyes, even when they would roll back in her head over and over. However I was straining to hold on. She saw my struggle.

"Cum on me," she panted as she flipped around and rested on her back.

I looked her over as I turned around and approached her on my knees. Her legs spread wide, I positioned between them. But quickly she reached down and pulled the protection off. Her soft fingers surrounded me as her fingers worked. I looked at her with amazement because she seemed to want this as much as anything else we had done.

"Are you sure?" I asked.

"All over me," she panted.

Jan barely had time to finish what she said. It was more powerful than I had experienced in a long time. I suppose that's why I grunted so loudly that I thought it startled her a bit. As I first exploded from her soft hand I felt more than just a release. I felt liberated. She had changed something in me. If this was her goal she had won. But I had also changed her. I heard her giggle as I finished what seemed to take forever, though I wasn't complaining.

"Oh my God," Jan giggled wildly, wiping her face.

I looked down at her and she was a mess. She laughed as she wiped her lips off with her fingers. I looked down to see that from her abdomen to her face there was strong evidence that I had really enjoyed that. I had not meant for it to be that expansive.

"Sorry," I said softly as I crashed back on the bed.

"That was awesome," Jan giggled as she looked at the end of her finger and gave it a little taste. "We need to work on your salt intake though."

I turned to the side and looked at her still smiling and simply relaxing on her back as if she was trying her best to remember the moment. Or perhaps she was simply tired. Obviously we were both satisfied, but there was something more. I knew I would want her again, but there was a new feeling within that thought of looking for the next time. I really wanted to spend time with her. I wondered at that moment if it was even possible, and thought that there was a good chance this was a onetime event.

But something inside me became hopeful of a continuance more than just physical. I smiled as I thought of the possibilities. However as it turned out, she was either reading my mind or thinking the same thing anyway. We talked a while because she didn't have any immediate interest in cleaning up. We discussed a little about the fun we had, and she even thanked me for all of my kind words and being straight with her. She had told me it meant a great deal to her and she understood now that she was a real person with many possibilities.

"Seems we have good conversations," I smiled.

"I like talking to you too," she smiled. "A lot. I feel like I could talk to you about anything. It's so strange really."

"Kinda natural," I said, "It is weird. Let's have dinner tomorrow, and maybe do something fun."

"Not before I make you breakfast, low salt of course," she smiled.

"Sounds great," I smiled, "Come take a shower? Let me help clean the damage."

"Ok but I can't promise I'll behave in there," she smiled.

"Me either," I smiled.

"Thank you," Jan smiled as she stood up, "For everything."

"Thank you dear," I smiled.

I turned to go into the bathroom and heard her following me. As I turned the water on I felt her soft fingers on my back. Her head rested on me as I waited for the water. I smiled widely knowing that I was starting to develop feelings for her. But my thoughtful bliss was interrupted again, with skill only she could possess.

"Am I going to be able to make you my boyfriend or what?" Jan said, "Exclusive and all that?"

"Depends," I grinned.

"On what?" Jan asked.

"On how good your breakfast is" I laughed.

"You are an ass, you know that," Jan laughed as she pinched mine.

"Kidding dear ", I said. "Sorry."

"It's ok," Jan said, "You can service me after breakfast."

"Depends on how good it is," I laughed, "I might not have the energy."

"You're going to pay for that, believe me." Jan said.

"Probably, but it was worth it," I laughed.

I did pay for it, and gladly. But I suppose that's another story…

MY FAVORITE NURSE

What a difference two days can make. When I woke up the day before yesterday, I was lying in a hospital bed with more cables attached to me than a substation feeding New York City. At least that's the way it seemed.

I really don't remember how I got there, but they tell me that I was rushed to the hospital after passing out at the mall.

Here I am two days later and all of the monitoring equipment has been removed and I in a private room waiting to hear if I'm being released.

The good news is that all the blood work, heart assessment and routine tests have returned normal. Anxiety attack, that's what they're telling me. That's pretty easy to understand. As a salesman who hasn't seen any improvement in the local market, the everyday pressures of "making that sale" must have finally taken their toll. This economy stinks, no denying it.

Being in the hospital is new to me, as I have been relatively healthy for nearly 56 years. I don't know what I would have done in this situation had it not been for the wonderful, caring attention that I received from the medical staff here at the hospital.

In particular, I have to tell you about Kim, a very special nurse say…….enjoyable.

When I first awoke, she was standing beside my bed jotting down notes and checking all my vital numbers on the monitoring equipment. She sensed my horror as I looked around at all the wires and equipment wondering "what the hell is going on?"

She stopped her writing, took my hand in hers and softly said "You are in the hospital because you had a spell of some sort and passed out. You are going to be okay. Your wife is here, she has been all day."

I looked to the other side of the room, immediately relieved to see my wife standing there moving toward the bed. "Hi, sunshine." She said. I smiled and said "Hi."

Even though I was now talking to my wife I couldn't help realizing that Kim was still holding my hand and gently squeezing it in the most reassuring way.

She must have decided that I seemed good enough to leave alone for a while as she patted the top of my hand and said "I'll leave you two alone to catch up and chat for a while."

As she turned to leave my room, I watched as she walked out the door. Nice nurse's dress, white, crisp and clinging so nicely to every voluptuous curve. Shear white stockings….H-m-m-m, I was feeling better already.

The next hour or so was spent learning about what happened, where it happened, and all the efforts made to get me "under control", so to speak. It was obvious that my wife was exhausted from being with me from the time I arrived until now. I told her and get some much needed sleep. No argument there, she gathered up her belongings, kissed me goodnight and walked to the doorway turning into the hall.

Nice jeans, snug and clinging to every voluptuous curve…..H-m-m-m, I really was feeling better already.

You know how they say you can get your days and nights mixed up when you've been "out of it" for a while? That's where I was. It was nearly 1:30 in the morning and I was wide awake fidgeting from being bored.

I noticed a friendly face walking down the hall. "Hey!" I called out the door. Kim stopped, turned around and stuck here head in the door. "You need something hun?"

"Not really, but I wanted to ask you a question"

"What's that?"

"How far would you have been if I wouldn't have called you?"

She stood there, thought for a moment, smiled and said "Aren't we the funny one!"

"I'll be back in a few minutes to check your stats. But first I have to go put my stethoscope into the freezer so it will feel good on your chest." She smiled almost giggling out loud as she turned to walk away. Damn she looked good in her nurse's dress.

I hoped she wouldn't take to long to come back. It would be nice to have someone to talk to for a little while this late at night.

It must have been maybe ten minutes before she reappeared at my doorway. She walked to my bedside and said "Okay Mr. funny guy, let's check you out"

"O good, does that mean I'll have to take my clothes off?"

"No, it doesn't, besides you seem to eager." She said trying to hold back her grin.

"I was just thinking maybe you'd make an old guy's day."

"If checking your blood pressure and temperature along with checking your pulse makes your day, you've got it made." She answered.

By now, I was bit taken with this young nurse that had a killer smile, captivating blue eyes and dark copper red hair that was pulled up in the back and held there by a large hair clip. I could tell that if she were to let it down it would probably drop to the middle of her back and be full of curls. Being an older guy, I now just look at these sweet young girls and think, "Jeez, if only I were just a few years younger."

Well, she'd been kidding, the stethoscope wasn't cold as she reached in under my hospital gown to listen to my heart. Now….. why in the world having someone listen to your heart would cause a stirring in your loins is beyond me. But, there it was a cute little tent starting to take shape in the bed sheet.

Not wanting to call any attention to my dilemma, I said "every thing sound okay?"

"Sounds just fine" Kim answered.

I decided to change the subject and maybe get my mind on something else.

"So, how long have you been a nurse?"

"A little over twelve years."

"That means you must have started when you were 15?"

"Oh aren't you the charmer? I'm 36, but thanks for the compliment. It was supposed to be a compliment right?'

"Of course! I really wouldn't have figured you for 36. I thought you were probably in your mid twenties at the oldest. That seems to be my problem any more. Even older women seem young to me, not that 36 is older….. you know what I mean."

Kim giggled out loud and said "You shouldn't talk about yourself as if

you are old. You actually look in great shape for.......how old are you?"
Now she was chuckling.

"You know how old I am, you have my chart. Do the math, I'm almost twenty years older than you."

"Fifty five is not old, besides, I sorta think you're cute for your age"

"Now who's trying to be the charmer?" I asked.

"I'm serious, do you know how many people I see come through this unit that are younger than you and look like they're barely able to get by?"

"You know, I think I'm starting to like you... you and your doll face. Tell me, would it be alright if I called you Doll face?" I asked

Eyes twinkling, cheeks blushing to match the color of her hair, she replied "Yeh.... I think I'd like that."

We spent the next hour just talking about why she decided to be a nurse, that she was married and all about her children. We talked about her hobbies and how she liked to read books, mostly romance novels. She found out that I liked golf and fishing. We talked about our jobs and how they are different, but how some things are a lot alike.

I was enjoying her company and just talking. At one point I asked her if it was okay for her to be with a patient for such a long time. She told me that is why she liked working the night shift because other than an occasional code call, most of the patients actually slept through the night or were actually kept sedated so that they could get the rest they really needed.

She then mentioned to me how much she enjoyed just sitting and talking. She told me I was easy to talk to. I felt the same connection. We talked for just a few more minutes and she said that there were reports to be written before the shift ended.

I asked if she was on duty tomorrow night and she said yes, that would be her last night for the week as she usually works three twelve hour shifts and then is off until the next week.

"Good! Maybe you'll consider visiting with me again if I can't sleep." I was hoping she would.

"Maybe I'll just come in here and keep pestering you so that you don't sleep" she teased.

"Let me check your lungs and heart one more time before I go" as she slipped the stethoscope under my gown. It seemed like she was being deliberate in her listening, moving the pad of the scope around ever so slowly. She gently brushed up against my left nipple but didn't let on that she knew what she was doing. Looking back, I think she knew exactly what she was doing.

As she was listening, her eyes were locked on mine. She stood there poised with what I would call a seductive smile. I felt as if I was melting under her touch. Well, not everything was melting. I felt the sheet straining to hold down my growing manhood and had no way of hiding it without calling attention to it. If I were to reach down or shift from one side or another, surely she would look. All I could do is hope that when she was done listening to my chest that she would just wrap the stethoscope around her neck, over her shoulders and leave the room.

What luck, she did just that. She turned to leave the room and I started to breathe a sigh of relief. To soon..... she stopped at the doorway, turned around looked directly at the tent in my sheet, smiled and said "I like..... goodnight." Just like that she was gone.

I spent the next half hour trying to think down my erection, knowing I had no way to relieve myself without someone noticing. Finally, after a while longer, the erection left and sleep arrived.

* * *

It was late morning when I felt someone softly stroking my arm. I opened my eyes and saw my wife standing at the side of the bed smiling. "Good morning sleepy head." She said. "Were you up all night with one of your nurses?" she joked.

"Who told you?" I jeered back. "I'd have been okay if it would have only been two, but the third one did me in."

"Well honey, they must be dripping Viagra out of that bag then because if you went three times last night, you shouldn't be as stiff as you are right now."

I couldn't believe it, there I was lying on my back sporting morning wood as if I were a teenager. My wife is standing there laughing at my dilemma, knowing how embarrassed I'd be if someone were to walk into my room.

"You know, you could be a sweetheart and help relieve this situation."

She reached down, rolled her fingers and the sheet around my erection and gave a long gripping squeeze....."I can't do that, I think someone's coming"

"I wish it was me" I said.

Just the thought of someone coming down the hall and entering the room was enough to scare down the big guy, but it didn't stop the funny comments from beside the bed.

Breakfast arrived, later lunch, a little later the doctor visited. The doctor explained that if I made it through the rest of the day and that night without any kind of incident, I would be able to go home the next day.

It wasn't long before the supper tray arrived.....hospital food.....e-r-r-r-r. Evening was approaching and so was the shift change for the nurse's station.

Sometime after 7:00, in walked a familiar face from late last night. "So, how are we feeling today?" Kim asked.

"Just fine." I said. "I'm ready for just about anything.'

"Anything?" she giggled……

Looking across the room, she said to my wife, "Looks like you'll have to put up with him when you get him home tomorrow" They both laughed knowing I would most likely be discharged in the morning.

"How much of a problem was he last night?" my wife queried.

"Actually, he was no problem at all. He was a good boy." She smiled.

Moving to the side of the bed, she held my wrist as she checked my pulse. She proceeded to check temperature and record my blood pressure. Next came the stethoscope, only this time, quick touch here, there, over there. Deep breathe…..done.

"Okay, everything looks good. If you need anything, just hit your button. I'll check on you later" Off, she was gone.

Wow, that was short and sweet, I thought to myself. At least the stethoscope didn't trigger the type of reaction it did last night.

It had been another long day for my wife so it took little to convince her that she should go home and get some sleep.

* * *

Opening the door to my room, Kim peaked in and saw me typing away on my lap top.

"Hey, honey! I hear you get walking papers tomorrow," she said, walking in to the side of my bed.

"Yeah, but I am thinking about putting you in my hospital courtesy bag and taking you home with me." I joked.

"Uh, huh! I bet. You are such a tease once your wife leaves. I'm beginning to think you are a dirty old man"

"Busted," I grinned.

"Besides, just what would you do with me if you took me home?"

"Good question" I said, "I'd have to give that some thought."

"While you're giving it some thought, let's check your vitals...you know the drill. Lean back, so I can listen to your ticker," she told me.

As she was putting her stethoscope into her ears my mind jolted into high gear as I started thinking about the previous evening.

"My favorite part! Be gentle with this old body of mine, you never know what might come up" I said, winking at her.

She laughed. Leaning down over me, she lifted my tee shirt to listen to my heart with her stethoscope. She seemed to be looking me over with more interest than before. I was loving the assessment. I am glad I've been able to stay in decent shape. I still wear the same size slacks as I did when I was 21. Although I have a slight middle aged spread, it's not all that bad. She was definitely taking her time being much slower about it than when the wife was here.

With her gloveless hand, she started checking for any swellings or lumps, so she said.... but I think she was using that excuse to run her hands over my body. She sensed just how much I was beginning to enjoy it.

As Kim ran her hands over my chest, I could see her eyeing the bulge under the covers. Gently she ran her fingertips across my left nipple. I have sensitive nipples, I guess some guys do. It's like they're wired to my penis because every time she brushed across the tip, my dick would twitch under the covers. Taking my nipple between her fingers she looked deeply into my eyes and gave it a firm pinch and slight twist. I was thinking I could shoot my load right then and there.

"You shouldn't start things you can't finish" I told her as I nodded to the tent in the bed linens. "You can take a look if you'd like." I taunted

"Maybe later hun. I really shouldn't though. I might not be able to control myself." She leaned over close to my ear and whispered "I couldn't even come close to your room last night after I saw your little tent as I left the room."

She continued whispering, "When I left your room, my panties were drenched. There is something about you that turns me on. I just get hot all over. I don't know what it is, but after I leave your room, I want to go to the bathroom and rub my throbbing clit, until I cum. In fact, when I got off work, I went home and finger frigged myself to a crushing orgasm…….thinking about you." She breathed a hot breathe into my ear, stood up winked at me and turned to leave.

"I need to do a more thorough assessment, but I have some other folks to look at right now. I will be back. Holler at me, if you need me," she told me, in a husky voice.

My dick was so hard it hurt. Kim had managed to get me quite hot and bothered. I think she knew exactly what she was doing. But why? I was so much older than her. Did she have a thing for older guys, I could only hope.

I laid there in my bed pondering what it was that I was about to do. I was consumed with this young vixen who seemed to be infatuated with me the "mature" guy. What would I do if she turned me down? My raging hard on convinced me to throw caution to the wind.

About 1:30 am, I pressed the call button. Kim was sitting at the desk with another RN, reading a journal. Looking over at her, she told her that she would be back. The other nurse smiled and told Kim to take her time, as nothing was going on. She knew that last night, during the slow time, Kim spent better than an hour with me talking, because I couldn't sleep.

She walked down the hall and knocked on my door. Upon hearing her, I told her to come in. She opened the door to come in

"Hey, Hon! What ya need?" she asked.

I had gone into the bathroom.

"Could you come in here for a min, Doll face?" I called.

She opened the door to the bathroom and peeked in. I was sitting on the toilet, fully dressed, grinning at her look of curiosity.

"I need some help getting all this tape off me. You busy?" I asked.

She took a deep breath, donned a huge smile as her tender skin began to blush, again.

"Sure! Be right back," she told me.

Kim called out to her partner and told her that she would be assisting "her favorite" patient with a bath. She was silent for a moment, then started giggling most likely because of the encouragement coming from down the hall. I am sure that Kim would give her all the saucy details when she returned to the desk. I wanted to give her something really good to talk about.

I heard a click as she locked the door to my room as I was taking off all my clothes except for my boxers which were barely keeping my growing erection from poking out through the fly.

When she returned to the bathroom, I noticed that the zipper on the front of Kim's nurse's dress had been lowered just enough that it exposed the top cleavage of her breasts. What an amazing sight that was.

She came back to the bathroom with a wash rag and some towels. Then she stepped into the bathroom and turned on the hot water. Fog filled the bathroom making it humid and steamy.

I caught her taking a quick look at my crotch as she pretended not to notice my aroused state. As she was preparing to bathe me, I was calculating what I really wanted her to do.

She bent over me, 'accidentally' pressing her breasts into my face. At that close proximity, I could see and feel her pebble hard nipples. I inhaled her fragrance a rather alluring perfume that I hadn't noticed before. It was most likely because I hadn't been this close to her before. My mind began to spin as I continued to breathe in all of her beauty; her smell, her soft cameo colored skin, her alluring smile, her perfect breasts which were now heaving right in front of my face. Our eyes met and I was lost.

Lathering up the washrag, she rubbed it up and down my back. She worked the muscles in my back, slow and steady. It was like electricity jumping across the surface of my skin. Oh how I enjoyed the delicate touch of this sweet, young beauty. My lips were close to her nipples, I was breathing erratically, my breathe bathing across her breast. She had to feel it. I could tell she too was labored in her breathing. I was thinking, now what? It was time to test the waters.

"Time to rinse your back," She told me.

I could see droplets of perspiration gathering on her chest as she rinsed and dried my back.

"Wow! It's warm in here," she remarked.

"It's just you and me, Doll face. I won't tell, if you slip that dress off. It would be a shame if it was to get wet and wrinkled," I told her hoping she would want to.

Looking down at me to see if I was joking, I looked deeply into her precious blue eyes. She knew...... She knew that there'd be no turning back if she did. Looking down at the raging erection I was sporting, she slowly, teasingly unzipped her dress and slipped it off her curvy body.

Standing there in front of me, she was only wearing a white, lacy bra and matching bikini panties, with a white garter belt and stockings. My dick lurched in the confines of my boxers. I felt my eyes soaking in the sight of this wonderful specimen of a woman. Looking down, her smile acknowledged the effect she was having on me. She could tell I was getting harder, if possible.

"Like?" she asked. I think she was feeling a little self-conscious. I don't think she'd ever done anything like this before......I hadn't.

"Turn around," I whispered.

Kim turned around, showing me a rear view. "I like very much."

"Bend over," I said, "I want to see your ass."

As she bent over, I decided it was time to find out just how far she'd let me go. I lifted my hands making contact with her my ass cheeks, gently cupping and squeezing them. They were soft, but so shapely. Lingering around the waist band of her dainty panties, I hooked my fingers under the top and pulled her panties down, slightly. An audible gasp escaped her from deep down in her throat. Slowly tracing my fingertips up and down the outside of her legs, I leaned closer toward her gathering in the aroma of her arousal. I now realized she must have been anticipating this as much as me. Goodness, she was aroused!

I was so horny I just had to explore the soft, subtle contours of her lovely body. I brought my tongue into contact with her waist band, concentrating at the very top of her crack. Moaning, she pushed her ass back toward me. That was the all encouragement I needed, the guy who loves to orally ignite a woman's passion. I continued to lap and nip her crack, obviously driving her crazy.

I stood up, turned Kim around toward me. I looked into her sparkling eyes, gathered her face into my hands and brought her lips to mine. It was electric, the soft inviting lips that pursed against mine. I dropped my arms around her and pulled her closer to me as our lips pressed harder together. I could feel the firmness of her stunning breasts pressing into my chest as she clung to me, our kiss intensifying. I offered the tip of my tongue, she accepted. The soft warmth of her tongue darting against mine was one of the most sensual kisses I could remember.

Reaching behind her I deftly unhooked her bra, removing it exposing her firm round breasts, proudly boasting stiff extended nipples.

Breaking our kiss, I whispered into her ear, "I want to taste you."

I dropped to my knees as she leaned forward and grabbed the hand rails, bracing herself. I lifted her leg and braced it on the shower seat. Her legs opened up, I could see the very wet crotch of her silky panties. I used my fingers to move her panties to the side, revealing her hairless, pink pussy lips.

"I'd never seen a shaved pussy in person. I'd seen pictures before. I'd never felt one. This was amazing." I couldn't wait to explore it with my tongue.

With a sharp intake of breath, I opened Kim's slit with 2 fingers and rubbed her hole gently. She was so wet. I could feel her juices welling up at the entrance of her hot pussy. I worked one finger inside, coating it with her nectar. Pulling it out, I raised it to my lips then stuck my tongue out to taste her juices………."Mmmm…..yummy"

"Mmm…God!" she groaned, working her hips. She began urging me to work my finger in deeper.

I held my finger right there at the entrance of her pussy, such a tease. Kim kept gyrating her hips attempting to get my finger further into her. I lowered her leg to slide her panties down and let her step out of them. I kept my finger playing with her pussy, while removing her panties. Having her completely exposed in front of my face bending her over slightly, I slowly began my tongue exploration beginning with circular tracings on the globes of her ass then moving to the top of her crack. I continued down her crack slowly lapping my way toward the waiting lips of her pussy.

I could hear her gasping as she tried to keep her composure. I probed my finger further into her pussy with more defined strokes as I drug my tongue across her rosebud about to take the place of my finger in her moist pussy. I could sense she was starting to get close to what I hoped would be a number of orgasms. I noticed how she was struggling to keep her balance, so I stood her up and led her to my hospital bed.

I lowered the bottom of the bed as she sat at the side. Gently I lowered her to laying on her back. I lifted her legs into the bed and the raised the side rails at the base of the bed. Her eyes were focused on what I was doing as I softly caressed first her left leg, then her right. I started at her foot and gently massaged my way up to where I was nearly touching her labia, then I repeated the action with the other leg. She seemed transfixed as her breathing became more labored and her breasts heaving up and down.

I lifted first her left leg and placed it over the bed rail, then did the same with her right leg opening her wide in a spread-eagled position. I leaned down to run the tip of my tongue across her left nipple while I slowly trailed my hand down across her abdomen until I reached the spread lips of her pussy. As I licked and nibbled on her breast, I probed her wetness with two of my fingers.

She was so soft, so delectable. I kissed a trail from her breast up to her neck and brought my lips up to meet hers. Our tongues were already out searching for each other as our lips met. The warm moist contact of our kiss was charged with unbridled lust.

I slowly pulled away…. our eyes hypnotized with each other. I moved to the base of the bed looking at the center of her spread apart legs. All I could do was stare at the pink lips that were puffed out in sexual wantonness. I could see the moist droplets of her arousal collecting on her labia. I inhaled her womanly perfume. Like a starving man, I leaned downward and drove my tongue into her wet pussy, sucking and slurping all over, partaking of her sweet taste.

I just had to explore every inch, every crevice of this lovely specimen. Her young body was moving to meet my every touch. I moved the tip of my tongue with slow, deliberate circles, passionately exploring every facet of her womanhood.

I love eating pussy. I went from tongue fucking her pussy hole and slurping her juices as they came out to flicking the tip of my tongue over and around her extended super hard clit. I loved the results of my oral escapades and watching as she arched her back up from the bed.

It was obvious that she was intent on cumming all over my face. Her hands cupped the sides of my head as she caressed the white whiskers of my beard. I love being able to arouse a woman to such a point with just my tongue.

"My clit, lick my clit!" Kim uttered. It was, actually, poking out from its protective hood, wanting to be pleasured. I wanted to show her just how much she could enjoy the benefits of an older man's experience. She was gasping, moaning, trying her best to hump my face. I would occasionally just stop moving …holding my tongue straight out allowing her to rotate her hips and rub her clit across the tip of it. I wanted her to enjoy every moment, even masturbating against my tongue.

Slowly, so slowly I took my time eating her pussy. I knew she had to be enjoying it. "So good, so-o-o-o good……eat me, eat my pussy…….Oh, make me cum….I'm so close" Kim hissed through her clenched teeth. I worked my fingers in and out of her hot cunt, and at one point had 3 fingers all the way past my knuckles.

I continued my assault on her love box with my fingers. I would open and close them in a scissor fashion, cross them together making them rub over her sweet spot, and wiggle them in a 'come here' fashion. I had little problem zeroing in on her G spot and began caressing it with my finger tip. All of my concentrated efforts on her clit, her G spot, the insides of her thighs, the swirling of my tongue around the walls of her love canal finally triggered a massive vaginal orgasm.

Kim's hips lifted completely off of the mattress as I felt the rush of her climax soak my face and beard. Now…. I had her where I wanted her. I continued to eat her pussy and bring her to one orgasm after another, stopping just long enough for Kim to catch her breath then I'd dive right back in. I don't keep count of how many orgasms I solicit when I'm eating pussy. I concentrate on trying to bring on one after another until I'm asked to stop, sometimes begged to stop.

I was sensing she couldn't take much more as her legs were clamped around my head like a vice. I was beginning to think I'd have to stay in the hospital for possible head trauma as I felt the trembling of her thighs as she was coming down from her last orgasm. "O-o-o-o-h, no more……no more…" she coo'd. Kim opened her legs and looked down toward her satisfied pussy as I looked up at Her and smiled. "Enough?"

"Oh yes……thank you!" "I don't know if I've ever cum that hard or that much."

I was happy that Kim was so receptive to letting me orally partake of her sweet spot. I knelt up on my knees looking down on the shiny wet pussy, then scanning up to the pert nipples on her marvelous tits and finally moving my gaze up to her sparkling eyes. Pretty eyes, happy eyes……satisfied eyes.

I slowly lowered myself down until I was lying on top of her, our lips locking into a hungry passionate kiss. Our tongues exploring each other, Kim moaning into my mouth as she tasted her presence on my tongue and lips.

Our legs were inter-twined as we laid together in a warm embrace. My erection was sandwiched between me and her pelvis. Kim hooked her leg around my lower back in an effort to position the opening of her love tunnel with the tip of my penis. I wiggled out of her grip and gave her a big smile as I turned around on the bed bringing my manhood just inches from her face. She took the hint as I

nudged her lips with my rock hard cock and eagerly opened her mouth, allowing my sweet meat to invade her starving mouth. Pulling gently on my ball sac, she began to suck me hard and slow.

I felt her relax her throat allowing me deeper access to her wet, moist throat. The more I flexed my hips the more she engulfed my stiff rod. She was amazing, her mouth was amazing…. I loved having her suck me. I purposely stroked my cock in and out s-l-o-w-l-y as I fucked her mouth.

She was doing magical things to my love stick as I positioned my face back in the opening of her pussy. I opened her legs wider with my hands as my tongue came in contact with her still erect clit.

I was barely touching her love button with the tip of my tongue as I slid my hand down the back side of her leg finding its way with my middle finger parting the warm, moist lips of her love hole. As I inserted my finger deeper and deeper into her wanton cunt, I gathered up some of the arousal juices seeping from her opening onto my other finger lubricating it just enough that it easily penetrated her sensitive rose bud.

As I applied a little more pressure with my tongue and fingers as they pumped in and out, I knew that Kim was loving it as she was grabbing both cheeks of my ass lifting her head up and down off the pillow as she devoured my dick.

We stayed in this position, just sucking and slurping each other in an ultimate 69 until we could not take it anymore. Desperate to experience as much as possible with this charming young woman, I pulled out of her tantalizing mouth, turned back around and positioned myself over her. I lowered the tip of my penis to her moist opening then pushed my fuck rod into her hot pussy. As I bottomed out she arched her back off the bed uttering a low guttural moan.

I stopped. I just froze in that position as my breath escaped me. The feel of this young woman impaled on my dick literally took my breath away. She was so tight, so wet, so hot, s-o-o-o-o passionate.

We tried to be quiet, as other patients were sleeping down the hall. Not to mention the nurse's station wasn't all that far away. Kim's co-worker only had a suspicion as to what was going on.

We soon fell into a rhythm with me slowly moving my engorged projectile in and out of her sopping wet cum tunnel. We continued humping, as I would push to enter her again and again, she would raise her hips thrusting her cunt up to meet me. She was so wet you could hear the slopping of her juices around my dick as it rammed in and out.

Without saying a word or giving any warning, I pull out of her and slid back down on the bed bending down to lick her pussy. "What are you doing?" she gasped out of breath. "Sh—h-h-sh….. I've gotta make you cum again"

I love doing this, it works every time. Pulling out and leaving that vacant feeling only to replace it with my tongue usually triggers an awesome climax. I wasn't wrong, the tip of my tongue barely touched her incredibly stiff clit and she raised up off of the bed, her back arched upward. Instantly, she was in the throws of a powerful, consuming cum attack. Kim's entire body shook, trembled, quivered……it was capable of registering on the Richter scale.

"Oh-h-h-h-h F-u-u-u-u-u-u-c-c-c-c-k……." she growled through her clinched teeth as she came, her juices gushing into my mouth and over my face.

I raised up looking down at her pink slit that was so wet that I could see her juices running down over her ass. I grabbed her legs and hooked one over my arm and the other up on my shoulder. Getting up on my knees, I re-entered her battered hot pussy. Reaching down with one hand, I started flicking and pinching her clit, rougher now. Jacking her clit, I worked my dick in and out of Kim's pussy, like a piston.

Breathing like a freight train, I knew I couldn't hold back any longer.

"Doll face, I am going to cum all over your hot, little pussy!" I growled.

"Oh! Fuck! Steve, make me cum," she gasped.

I thumbed her clit vigorously, and she came……. hard. Spasms and waves traveled her whole body with the epicenter right at her clit. Kim was cupping both of her breasts in her hands as she was trying to catch her breath. It was a delightful sight, her soft tender hands barely covering the prominently large tits, overflowing her palms.

I could feel the boiling of my eruption beginning, as I pulled out of her wet cunt, aware of a burst of her juice squirting out of her pussy and onto the bed below.

I wrapped my hand around my cock and jacked it with hard, short strokes. I watched, as 3 or 4 ropes of white, hot cum erupted from my dick and landed on Kim's bare pussy streaming up across her abdomen. I kept stroking it slowly, as if to milk every drop out.

The sultry look in Kim's eyes as we locked glances was one of pure satisfaction. Her hand drifted from the breast she was caressing down to her pelvis as she rubbed her fingers through the warm puddle I had made.

Bringing her fingers to her lips, she sucked my milky juice from her fingers. I reached for her hand and brought it to my lips sticking my tongue out to take a taste.

I gripped my cock and rubbed the head of it through the left over puddle of cum, and then jostled it over Kim's clit, sending small after shock waves through her.

Looking down at her, I said, "Do you think I would qualify for home therapy? Would you like a private nurse job?"

"Well, I have just the right qualifications for the 'head' nurse position, if you got one!" she laughed.

We both laughed, quietly.

"I better get a positive remark from you on your evaluation form! You have received phenomenal one on one nursing care!" she said to me with a make believe frown.

Laughing out loud, I hugged her to me. I spent the next few minutes helping her get dressed, putting her bra on and hooking it for her, holding her nurse's dress as she put her arms in. I inserted one side of the zipper into the other and gently pulled up leaving some cleavage showing. Reaching toward her chest I cupped both of her tits in the palms of my hands for one last feel. Her eyes sparkled as she smiled at me.

I leaned down our lips touching in one last soft, warm, appreciative kiss.

She turned to leave my room panty-less. In my hand, damp as they were, I kept them for myself.

* * *

The next morning I woke up as the morning shift nurse was moving about my room gathering my belongings. She informed me I was being released to go home.

A few minutes later my wife arrived to pick me up and take me home.

"So, are you tired from being up all night satisfying all the nurses?"

"Naw, not all of them……" I smiled. I felt a warm rush………

"Let's go home lover boy, maybe we can work on your therapy…." She winked.

H-m-m-m, I was feeling better already.

COVERED BY A STALLION

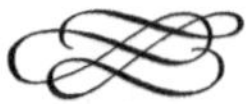

Jake Hughes, the owner of Blue Sky Horse Farm, sat at his kitchen table sipping coffee as he stared out the window at what could only be described as a gloomy Saturday morning. Overnight rains had left the farm drenched and a heavy fog had set in, obscuring his view of the mountains that encircled the pastures where his horses grazed. The house was quiet and dark and it was times like this that he was most lonely.

At age 52, Jake was a widower. He had lost Ramona, his wife of 17 years, in an automobile accident just over a year ago. The only thing had had preserved his sanity was that his step-daughter Steph, a high-spirited 19 year-old was still living in the house.

Both Jake and Steph were devastated by the loss of Ramona, and both grieved mightily, yet as time passed, they gathered themselves and began to move on.

Naturally, moving on was easier for Steph than Jake…A high school senior, her life lay ahead of her and she was attacking it with a vengeance. She had plans for college and although she missed her mom, she filled each day with a stunning variety of social and school activities. It seemed to Jake that she was always arriving or departing and never really home very much.

Jake, on the other hand, was not fairing as well and it was mornings like this that he missed Ramona the most. Had she still been with him, they would most likely still be in bed and most likely Jake would be mounting Ramona's upturned ass for their second fuck of the morning.

As corny as it sounds, Ramona and Jake met in the local grocery in the small town where they both lived. She was a successful trial attorney, dressed in a dark suit, stockings and heels, and he was in dirty jeans, muddy boots and an old shirt. His scarred hand brushed her neatly manicured one as they both reached for a can of black beans in the canned goods aisle and the connection was instant.

They had a couple of formal "dates" and then easily drifted into a comfortable relationship…About three weeks into the relationship, Jake took Ramona into his bedroom and it was there she discovered that her horse farmer boyfriend was a stallion in his own right. Jake would never forget Ramona's gasp of surprise and the wide-eyed look on her face when she first reached under the sheets and grasped the nine inches of thick, erect penis laying on his belly.

"Oh my!" she whispered as she pulled back the sheet. "You're a big boy!"

From that point on, sex was a constant in their life and Jake never tired of Ramona's gasps of, "Oh please go easy baby! You're so damned big!" as he pistoned his penis into her wide-stretched pussy.

Steph, two years old at the time, soon became part of his daily life as well and Ramona and Jake's wedding followed quickly. The three of them settled into a quiet lifestyle and lived happily for the next 17 years until the day the deputy drove into the drive with the news of Ramona's accident.

Unbeknown to Jake, Ramona had taken out a large insurance package which left him set for life and provided for both Steph's undergra-duate college education and graduate school should that be her choice. He was free to run his horse farm without financial concerns and both he and Steph were provided for, but he was a very lonely man.

He had made a couple of attempts to date, but it was much more difficult at age 52 than at 35 when he and Ramona had dated. The number of available women was much smaller now and he discovered that when you're a guy in your 50's, younger women don't even see you…You're completely invisible to any woman under the age of 45.

Additionally, he discovered that with age comes "issues" and between his issues and the collective issues of the older women who were available, a match was not in the making. After a few attempts, he gave up, rationalizing that he had experienced the one true love in his life and there was nothing left out there for him.

As Jake sipped his coffee and thought of Saturday mornings with Ramona, he shifted in his chair and rearranged his half-erect penis in his jeans. He had not had sex since the day of Ramona's death, resorting to the Internet, personal lubricant, and his right hand to relieve his frustrations and loneliness. Hours alone with only thoughts of Ramona squirming under him led to many nights of frustration followed by limited masturbation-induced relief.

After their marriage, Jake and Ramona had built a three bedroom house with the master suite on one end of the house and two smaller bedrooms and a connecting bath on the other. Steph had used one of the smaller bedrooms from the beginning, and when she started having friends over, Ramona just told her to "expand her domain" to both smaller bedrooms and the connecting bath. This, in effect, turned the Hughes' household into a small dormitory for young females. That had continued even after Ramona's death and this Saturday was no different than others.

There was a racket in the back of the house and Jake grinned as he heard feminine laughter and scurrying about coming from the vicinity of Steph's bedrooms. As was usual for a weekend, several of Steph's friends had spent the night at the house. Soon, the house was filled with the sound of the shower running, blow dryers whining, and girls giggling as they prepared for whatever the day would bring.

Jake busied himself with starting the day as well…Checking his email, making a couple of phone calls to arrange feed deliveries for the horses, and generally waiting for the weather to clear a little. Suddenly, the noise that had been contained in Steph's bedroom became significantly louder as four young women burst into the kitchen.

"Mornin' girls!" Jake grinned as Steph, Ann, Joy, and Amanda tumbled into the room, not unlike a small litter of puppies.

"Hey Dad," Steph replied as she wrapped him in a hug and kissed his cheek. The other girls all greeted him similarly, giving him a hug and kiss as well. He reveled in the sensation as their firm young bodies pressed against his and their arms went around his neck.

The girls had grown up together and he had known them since Steph's preschool years, so hugs were part of the routine for all of the girls. Typical of the custom in the area, they called him by his first name, reserving "Mr." and Ms." for teachers, employers and the like.

"Want some breakfast?" Jake asked, knowing the answer.

"Naah," Steph replied, "We're going down to the mall and will stop on the way and get something."

"How long you goin' to be gone" he asked.

"Probably most of the day," Steph replied. "We're going to see a movie while we're there."

"Oh, okay."

"Okay then, we're on our way!" Steph said as she bent to kiss his cheek one more time.

"Um, wait." Jake said. "Weren't there five of you when you came in last night?"

"Oh, yeah." Steph replied. "Billi's still in the bed. She's not going with us because she has something to do late this afternoon."

"Oh, okay."

With calls of "Bye Jake!" and "See you later!" the girls were out the door and walking toward Steph's SUV. Jake stood at the window and in an instant, his mood changed from sad to bitter. He watched the girls as their long legs carried their denim encased asses across the yard. Those asses, and the breast and pussies that came with them, had been a growing source of frustration for him over the last three months.

He knew what he was carrying between his legs and he knew that if it were on a twenty year old stud, those girls would be all over it, but once again, the phenomenon of the 52 year-old man that was invisible to young females had reared its ugly head. To them, he existed only as a dad, and an old one at that.....He was neither a threat nor desirable... He was invisible.

"How ironic is it," Jake thought bitterly, "that I would end up this horny when there is that much fine pussy just down the hall almost every night of the week?"

It wasn't that he was particularly interested in fucking these girls...He was simply horny beyond belief and had no relief in sight...And the girls were around him all the time.

He shook his head as if to clear it, turned and walked back into the kitchen. He paused in a brief moment of puzzlement as he heard a toilet flush in the back of the house.

"Oh yeah, Billi." he thought as he poured another cup of coffee and sat down at the table.

In a moment, he heard the bedroom door open and looked up with a grin as a tousled haired Billi walked into the room wearing an oversized tee shirt and little else.

"Hey Cowgirl!" he smiled at her, using a nickname he had given her years ago as a result of her insistence as a child to dress like a cowgirl, a preference she still maintained.

While Steph and her other buddies tended to follow fashion trends, Billi stuck with the classic cowgirl look of boot-cut jeans, boots, and western style shirts. Her only nod to fashion was a tendency to paint her nails bright colors. Today, as she walked across the room, Jake could not miss the vibrant hot pink flash of her fingernails and toenails.

"Hey Jake. " She grinned back.

"Coffee?"

"Ummm-Hmm."

"You know where the cups are."

As Billi shuffled by him she bent down and kissed his cheek. He closed his eyes as the scent of her body, still warm from bed, surrounded him.

Jake liked all of Steph's friends, but Billi was his favorite. She absolutely loved horses and unlike the other girls, was happy spending hours with Jake as he went about the business of running the farm. From the time she first started visiting Steph, if she went missing while visiting the farm, everyone knew that if they found Jake, they would find Billi.

Unlike the other tall leggy girls in Steph's group of friends, Billi was petite. Only five feet two inches tall, she had a very tight, athletic body. Her muscular calves and thighs blended into curvy hips with nice round asscheeks that protruded enticingly. Her hips were topped by a narrow waist and round firm breasts that stood proud, even when Billi chose not to wear a bra.

Jake had fantasized about all of Steph's friends at one time or another, but it was Billi that was the focus of most of his sexual attention. As a result, Jake often found himself gazing at her as she moved about the house. Today was no different.

As she stood on tiptoe to reach for a coffee cup, the muscles of her calves and thighs went tight and the hem of her tee slid up until the lower curvature of her panty-covered ass peeped into Jake's field of vision. He looked as long as he dared then took a sip of coffee.

Billi poured her coffee, took a sip and then set the cup down and stretched her arms above her head as she yawned and stretched. Again, the hem of the tee slid up, this time pulling tight over her nipples and revealing a taunt little belly and the waistband of her panties.

Jake surreptitiously glanced over at Billi's muscular little belly and the lacy waistband of her pink panties and his penis expanded at the sight of the dark shadow of her pubic hair under her panties. Without thinking he groaned aloud.

"You okay?" Billi asked, cocking her head in concern.

"M-m-m-m?" Jake responded distractedly, "Oh, yeah. I'm fine."

"So, you just groan out loud all the time?" Billi said as she sat down across the table from Jake.

"Yeah," Jake replied with a grin, "Old men groan more than you might think and for a variety of reasons."

"H-m-m-m-m…"

This was another thing Jake liked about Billi. Unlike the other girls, she didn't seem to mind, and usually seemed to enjoy, sitting and talking with Jake. More than once, the other girls had to goad Billi into leaving with them because she seemed more content talking with Jake than going with them to the mall or whereever. To Jake, Billi may have been a 19 year-old girl, but she had the soul of a mature woman.

They had been sitting at the table for a while, chatting about this and that when abruptly, the air was filled with a guttural, high pitched whinnying. Jake slapped his forehead and cursed.

"What?" Billi said.

"I forgot…I've got a mare in the barn that is in season and I was going to use Bolt to cover her. I thought it could wait until Monday when the hands are back and could help, but last night when I had her in the corral, she was breaking down in front of him and he was almost going over the fence to get to her."

"Bolt's young right? Has he ever covered a mare?" Billi asked as she sipped her coffee.

"No, this would be his first. That's why I wanted the hands here to help."

"Who's the mare?" she asked.

"Rain," he replied, "She's kind of laid back and I thought she would be a good first for Bolt."

"Yeah, you're probably right."

While this type of conversation may have seemed unusual or even bizarre to the casual observer, it was normal "horse talk" for Jake and Billi. It was inevitable that in their years of hanging around the farm, all of Steph's friends had, at some point, observed a stallion covering a mare.

As young children, their initial reaction to seeing horses breeding was the simple curiosity typical of youngsters. As they grew older they would giggle about the horses "making babies." Here lately, their reactions had evolved into casually ignoring the activity except for an occasional glance in awe at the massive erect penis on whatever stallion might be involved in the process.

Except for Billi…Her love for horses, combined with her natural curiosity, led to her involvement in all facets of running the farm. She had seen many mares covered by stallions over the years.

At first, Jake made every effort to try to keep her away from the process, but more often than not, she managed to end up hanging on the fence as he and the hands struggled with a reluctant mare or a timid stallion. He had never let her in the corral because he was concerned for her safety, but she knew the process very well.

She knew that when Jake said that Rain was "breaking down," he meant that the mare was squatting in front of the stallion and urinating, signaling that she was ready to be mounted and penetrated. She also knew that with Bolt being inexperienced it might be difficult to get him to cover the mare. Finally, she knew that this couldn't wait until another day. When a mare was ready, she was ready and there was no time to waste.

"Well," she said as she drained her coffee cup, "Let me get some jeans on and I'll come out and help you.

"Nope," said Jake as he stood up. "I don't want you in the corral with them. I'll do it by myself."

"Jake, you'll need some help. You just said you were hoping to be able to wait until Monday when the hands were here."

"Yeah, well, they're not here and this has to be done, so I'll do it by myself."

"Just let me get my jeans on and…"

"Billi," Jake growled, "You're not getting in the corral. I don't want you getting hurt."

"Fine!" she pouted as she pushed back from the table, "I'll just get dressed and go home!"

"Billi…" Jake said, exasperated…But she stomped from the room without another word.

Jake walked out to the barn, noticing as he passed the corral that the previous evening's rain had turned it to slop.

"Great!" he muttered to himself, "This is going to be nothing but a pain in the ass."

He opened the barn and walked to the stall where Rain danced impatiently. She was normally a fairly calm horse, but her need for a stallion had her nervous and jumpy. Jake led her to the corral, turned her out and then turned to get Bolt from a second corral across the barnyard.

Bolt, too, was nervous and jumpy, his ears pricked up, nostrils flaring and eyes walling as he was led to the corral where Rain waited. Rain immediately squatted and urinated when Bolt pranced into the corral and Jake watched with interest as Bolts penis immediately unsheathed itself and extended into full erection.

"All right!" Jake muttered, "This is going to be a piece of cake!"

But it wasn't. The mare was overly jumpy and Bolt just didn't know what to do. Three times he mounted her, but each time he didn't seem to know how to penetrate her. The more he tried, the more frantic both the young stallion and mare became.

Jake finally gave up on letting things happen "naturally" and stepped back into the corral. He thought if perhaps he secured Rain's reins to the fence to hold her still, Bolt would mount her and he could then help Bolt with the penetration by inserting the penis himself.

He grabbed Rain's bridle and tied it off on the fence. Then he gathered up Bolt and led him to the waiting mare. Bolt immediately raised up and mounted Rain, but just as Jake reached to grab Bolt's penis, Rain shifted violently to the side and knocked Jake against the wall of the barn and Bolt dismounted and trotted off around the corral.

"Shit!" Jake cursed as he rubbed his arm where it had been abraded by the rough barn wall.

Again he gathered the Bolt up and again, just as Bolt mounted, Rain danced sideways, knocking Jake off his feet.

"Fuck it!" Jake cursed as he stood and raked mud off his jeans and shirt.

Just as he turned to walk toward Bolt a third time, he saw a slim figure moving across the corral. It was Billi.

"Dammit Billi," Jake called, "I told you…"

"Shut up Jake!" Billi shot back, "You aren't doing so hot right now, so just shut up. Calm Rain down and let me see if I can get Bolt up on her."

"Billi…" Jake growled.

"Shut up Jake! I'm doin' this, so just shut up!"

"Dammit!" Jake spat as he walked to Rain and started trying to calm her.

Billi finally cornered Bolt and grabbed his reins. Talking softly and running her hands over his flank, she soothed him for a moment then led him to the mare.

"Now be careful…" Jake warned.

"Shut up Jake. I'm not the one who's been knocked down twice now am I?"

Just then Bolt raised up and mounted Rain. His engorged penis bobbed as he tried to thrust into the mare. He was close enough to her but simply couldn't hit the target. Rain was again getting antsy and began to dance. Billi looked in panic at Jake, understanding fully the danger of being trampled.

"You're going to have to help him" Jake said, trying to stay calm but the desperation in his voice obvious. "Just take hold of him and put him in her."

Billi nodded, turned and reaching forward, grasped the stallion's penis in her small hand. The engorged organ was thicker than her wrist and the contrast of her slim red-nailed fingers on the black flesh of the horse's penis was stark.

"Oh!" Billi whispered, almost to herself.

"What?" Jake asked, thinking something was wrong.

"His p-penis," she stuttered unthinkingly. "It so warm!"

Jake's head jerked around in surprise at her comment, but he said nothing.

Billi leaned down, biting her lower lip in concentration and after a couple of tries managed to insert the stallion into the mare. Then, it was as if a switch had been thrown in Bolt's brain and he settled down to the business of covering the mare. Rain, for her part, stood stoically and let Bolt have his way.

"Okay," Jake said as he exhaled heavily.

They both backed away from the horses and leaned against the barn. Jake turned to Billi to thank her, but stopped when he saw her face. She had not taken her eyes from the stallion's penis and she stood with her lips partially open, eyes slightly glazed.

"Hey," he said as he touched her arm. "You okay?"

"H-m-m-m-m?" she pulled her gaze from the horses and realizing she had been caught watching, blushed with embarrassment she mumbled, "Yeah, I'm okay."

At that moment Bolt's tail flagged, signaling that he had emptied his seed into Rain. He stood still, then dismounted after a moment.

"Well, so much for that" Jake intoned as he turned to walk from the corral. "Let's hope he took a lesson. I don't want to do that again anytime soon. C'mon, let's go into the barn and see if we can get some of this mud off."

Billi followed, walking along almost as if in a trance. As they entered the barn, Jake turned and walked toward the tack room.

"There's some towels back here we can use to wipe down with. That way we won't track mud into the house."

He stopped at the door to the tack room and removed his boots. Billi did the same and they walked into the warmth of the room. The tack room, filled with saddles, bridles and other gear, was one of Billi's favorite places. It was quiet and isolated and filled with the smell of leather and she was always soothed when she walked into the room.

After Ramona's death, Jake has enlarged the room into a "man cave," adding heat and AC, a bathroom with a shower, and furnishing it with easy chair, desk, and bed. He found the room to be a comfort when Steph wasn't home and often slept in the room when his house was empty and he was lonely.

Jake busied himself finding towels and when he turned to hand one to Billi he noticed that she still seemed distracted.

"You sure you're okay" he asked with concern.

Again, she jerked her head as if she had been brought back from another world. "Yeah, I'm fine."

"Well, take this towel see if you can get some of that mud off."

She wiped at her jeans for a minute and then she paused.

"Jake?"

"Yeah?"

"Um...Did she like it?'

"What?"

"Rain...Did she like it when Bolt went inside her?"

"Um...Why?"

"Well, I just wondered. I've, um, ya know, done it and it was fun but...."

"Billi! That's a little too much information!"

"No. Really Jake. I'm serious. Does the mare like it like humans do? Does it feel good to her?"

"Um, well," Jake stammered as he glanced in Billi's direction only to be met by her direct stare. "I'm not sure, but I think a mare's needs are more to, um, insure the survival of the species. Humans have sex for that reason too, but I'd say that sex is more fun for humans than animals...But I'm not sure. Rain's never told me."

"Very funny Jake." Billi replied sharply. "I'm serious."

"Sorry...I didn't mean to make fun."

"It just that he was so big and his, well, he was so firm and warm." Again she stared off.

Jake paused to look at Billi. He saw that her nipples were protruding against her damp tee shirt and she unconsciously had one hand cupped at the crotch of her jeans.

"Fuck me!" he thought as he continued to look at Billi, "She's so turned on she can't stand it."

Just then she caught him staring and she knew that he knew. She turned her eyes to the floor.

"Jake?"

"Yeah?"

"C-can you...Um...H-help me?" Her demeanor had suddenly become mild and submissive.

"Billi, baby..."

"Really Jake...I need it...Right now...Can I be you mare? C-can you cover me? Like Bolt? Please?"

Jake didn't know what to do…He knew what he wanted to do…

Billi, sensing his hesitation, upped the ante by reaching down to her sides, grasping the hem of her tee, and stripping it off over her head. She shook her hair out of her eyes and stood facing Jake nude from the waist up.

Tiny pink nipples stood rigid on the upturned surfaces of her perfectly round breasts, her need unmistakable. Jake stood frozen in place.

"Jake?"

Lust overrode reason and common sense. Jake unbuttoned his shirt, stripped it off and dropped it on the floor. Then he stepped around behind Billi.

Taking both her tiny wrists in one of his hands, he pulled her arms over her head until she stood with arms fully extended and she was standing on tiptoe. His other hand caressed her ribcage and moved around to cup her breasts, glossing over her nipples until she wriggled in need, then pinching them lightly as her hips began to slowly move back and forth.

"So, you want to know what it's like to be a mare? To be covered by a stallion?"

"y-y-e-s-s-s-s-s…" her response was a hiss of passion.

Still holding her arms high, he slipped his hand around to the button on the fly of her jeans, released it, slid the zipper down and slid his hand in to cup her pussy. Her panties were soaked through with her excitement.

"y-a-a-ah! Oh god!" she bucked in his hand as his middle finger slid over the wet material and grazed her clitoris.

He stripped off her jeans and panties and stared in awe at the sight of her small nude form. Turning to the wall he walked over, reached up and took a leather strap off the wall. Working quickly as she watched with a questioning look on her face, he fashioned a bridle of sorts.

"Come here."

"B-but…A bridle?"

"You said you wanted to know what a mare felt….Come here…"

Her bare feet padded over the smooth floor and she stood before him, head bowed. He fit the makeshift bridle over her head, placing a portion of the strap in her mouth as if it were a bit. Then he pulled the straps tight and felt a sense of satisfaction as he saw he could now control her completely.

"Now…Over here…"

He led her to a sawhorse used to support saddles and bent her forward, tying the bridle so that her head was down and her legs straight and her ass upturned. He could see her hair covered pussy lips peeking from between her thighs.

"Grab the bar with both hands Billi and don't let go."

"O-okay…" she mumbled through the makeshift bridle.

Again, he stroked her nipples and traced patterns over her belly until she began to buck in need. His hands stroked behind her knees and then up between her thighs until she cocked her ass up and spread her legs, revealing the slick hot pinkness of her pussy.

Stroking around the edges of her pussy, Jake lightly rubbed her clit and listened as she mewled into the leather strap between her jaws. With one slow but steady stroke, he slid his middle finger into her and buried it to the knuckle.

Her head jerked up in surprise and she squealed in delight. He couldn't help but notice that as aroused and wet as she was, her pussy was tiny…And very tight…Her small physique carried over to her pussy…Taking his cock would be an ordeal for her, but he couldn't wait to mount her.

He walked over to the small table beside the bed and opening the drawer, removed a bottle of personal lubricant he had kept there for when he needed to jack off. Moving around in front of her, he slowly unzipped his jeans, and in one motion stripped them off along with his briefs. The full nine inches of his erection sprang into view and stood rigid.

The stem was thick and heavily veined, the head shone like a freshly peeled onion, and his testicles hung like two large plums between his legs. He flexed his sphincter and the head swelled, growing angrily red...A drop of precum seeping from the slit and stood ready to drip to the floor. Wasting no time, poured his hand full of lubricant and using a motion not unlike what he used to jack off, spread it over the full length of his penis.

Billi's eyes bulged as Jake stood before her. She had no idea that he was this large and the idea of taking his massive cock into what she knew was her tiny pussy was terrifying. She pulled her head against the makeshift bridle but found she was firmly secured to the sawhorse.

Jake stepped around behind her and grasping her defenseless hips in his large hands, used his thumbs to slowly spread her asscheeks until he could see both the gaping slit of her pussy and the pucker of her tiny anus.

Again he flexed his sphincter and then milked a dollop of precum out of the stem of his penis. Catching it on his fingers, he spread it over the plum shaped bullet of his cockhead.

Pushing his legs between hers, he forced he ankles apart until her legs were sufficiently spread, then squatted and dipped his hips until the head of his penis rested between Billi's pussy lips.

Billi's head jerked up and she clenched her asscheeks and squealed in fear as she felt the massive plum-shaped cockhead begin to penetrate her body. Jake worked the head back and forth slowly, gritting his teeth at the exquisite sensation of Billi's tightness grasping his burgeoning cockhead. Eventually, he managed to get the head completely buried inside her and hesitating only for a second, gave another firm thrust forward.

"y-i-i-i-e-e-e-e!" Billi squealed around the leather bridle as she felt him stretching her hole.

"Like that little mare?" he questioned sarcastically as he drew back for another thrust.

"N-e-e-o-o-o-o-o!" she squalled shaking her head as if to shake off the pain.

"But you want to be covered by a stallion, right?" he thrust back into her, gaining another inch.

"W-a-a-a-a-a-h-h-h-h!!!" she squalled as a fine sheen of sweat began to form on her body

He drew back slowly and, as gently as he could in his state of lust, pushed in again. She stood on tiptoe and again cried out as four more thick, fleshy inches slid into her tiny body.

He stopped and held still, panting in unbridled lust. Looking down, he could now see only a third of his penis remaining outside Billi's pussy. Her pussy lips were stretched tight around his shaft and her juices gathered from the friction on his cock.

He pulled back again, this time pulling out until he could see the angry red edges of his cockhead, then grasping her hips and picking her up until her feet were off the floor he aligned her pussy with the trajectory of his penis and in one smooth thrust, penetrated her to the hairs.

"y-e-e-e-e-o-o-o-w! A-r-r-r-g-h!" Her legs kicked out straight, the muscles quivering tight with definition and her toes curled as she felt his cockhead press against her cervix.

"y-a-a-a-a-i-e-e-e-o-o-o-h!" She screeched as he pulled her pussy up tight against his groin and flexed his sphincter, causing the bulging knob of his penis to swell even more in the clinging depths of her pussy.

He held still and she quieted, panting desperately and holding on to the crossbar as he held her feet off the floor, her tiny body impaled and quivering.

"Okay little mare," he growled. "Now the fun begins."

She only shook her head side to side, desperately looking over her shoulder hoping to plead with her eyes. He ignored her.

Slowly, he withdrew his penis from her tightly clinging pussy. Pulling out until only the head remained inside, he slowly pushed back inside her. She tensed, but this time the pain wasn't as intense. Again, he pulled back and then thrust forward…And then again…And then he heard it…

"Oh! Oh god!" she whispered.

Saying nothing, he began to smoothly thrust in and out of Billi's tiny hole. Each stroke became easier, smoother, and slicker.

She began to groan in pleasure and soon her head was up and she was grunting and cursing behind the leather bridle as he rode in and out of her. With each stroke in, his balls cracked against her bulging clitoris, causing her to jerk in pleasure.

He continued thrusting in a slow, deliberate manner, every stroke pulling out to the point that only the head of his cock was inside Billi, then thrusting forward until she was fully impaled on the rigid flesh of his cock.

As she felt the bulging head of his cock burrow into her, Billi closed her eyes and threw her head back in absolute, unadulterated pleasure. Arching her torso, she bucked in one orgasm after another, desperately hanging onto the sawhorse while thrusting back onto Jake as he repeatedly pumped into her.

"Oh-god-those-balls-feel-so-good!" she panted with each slap of his cum filled orbs against her defenseless clit.

He was holding her ass in the position that gave him deepest penetration, thrusting so furiously that sweat dripped off him onto the smooth surface of her ass.

She could only gasp and groan as orgasm after orgasm washed over her until finally she was staring straight ahead but not seeing, feeling only the thick meat of Jake's massive cock pounding into her time and again. Then she noticed that his pace changed and with the change came an obvious further swelling of the head of his cock.

"Oh, god Billi! I-I'm almost t-there!" he gasped almost as if surprised.

And with those words he was pounding into her lithe frame so rapidly that her tits were swinging back and forth violently and she was squealing with every stroke. Suddenly, he slammed into her one last time, the head of his cock pressing against her now tender cervix and he began to squirt glob after glob of cum into her grasping pussy.

"Unh! Unh! Unh! Oh god Billi!" he grunted as he pressed into her, squirting his load into her tiny, tender pussy.

"O-o-o-o-o-h-h-h-h, y-e-e-e-s-s-s-s, J-a-a-a-k-e!!" she squealed as she pressed her ass back against his pelvis, wriggling against him, all the while milking his continuously squirting cock for every drop of cum, and vibrating in her own orgasmic spasms.

As their orgasms subsided, Jake leaned forward and loosened the makeshift bridle, letting it fall from Billi's slender neck. Billi had collapsed onto the sawhorse and stood bent over with Jake's penis still embedded in her pussy, panting as her heartbeat pounded in her ears.

Jake gently pulled back, groaning as her cum slickened sheath clung to his still-firm erection.

"Oh my god!" she whispered as he came free of her, his penis brushing her clit as he stepped away.

He reached and lightly grasped her shoulders, pulling her upright and back against his body. His cock, still erect, was trapped between his belly and her back.

"You okay now?" he asked as he lightly kissed the top of her head.

She sighed and nodded her head, leaning against him.

"C'mon, let's get a shower."

Again she just nodded.

He walked her to the shower and after adjusting the flow of the water, got in with her. She groaned in pleasure as his large soapy hands covered her lithe body and then stood quietly while he dried first her, then himself, with bulky towels.

Still nude, he led her to the bed, pulled back the blanket and sheet, sat down, gathered her in his arms and lay down with her small frame tucked in the protective hug of his arms.

An hour later, a somewhat confused Billi awoke to find herself alone in the bed. She groaned as she moved her legs and felt a dull ache, the remnants of what happened earlier.

Raising up on one elbow she looked across the room to see Jake, still nude, sitting in the easy chair.

"Hey Cowgirl…" he grinned.

"Hey yourself," she said blushing as her mind raced back to earlier that day.

"How you feelin'?"

"Um, a little sore I guess…"

"Did you like it?"

"Yeah, um no…Um, not at first…You're so big…It hurt like hell at first Jake!" tears brimming in her eyes.

"But …?"

"Jake, don't make me tell you…You know I liked it…You know I did."

"Well, I guess if you liked it the first time, you'll love the second time."

"Huh?"

Her eyes grew large as her reached down and raised his fully erect penis so that it was standing vertically off his lap.

"J-Jake…I don't think…"

"Hush Cowgirl…This will be fun…"

"B-but Jake…"

"Butt's a short cigarette…Come over here."

She stood gingerly, walked across the room and stood stood staring at the floor, not believing he was going to fuck her again.

Again, he stroked the lubricant onto his penis and then held it straight up so she could mount it.

"Come on Cowgirl," he encouraged gently, "Straddle your legs over the chair arms and mount up…It'll be fun…I promise."

"P-please don't make me…."

"Hush, Billi. You wanted to be covered like a mare and I covered you. Now you're going to learn how to ride like a real cowgirl. Climb on girl, I promise it will be fun."

She hesitantly moved to one side of the chair and gasping as her sore muscles stretched, lifted one leg over the arm of the chair as if getting on a bicycle. The chair was so wide that her legs were spread to the point that the large tendons stood out at the juncture of her muscular thighs…She grasped his shoulders and lifted herself…Then the head of his penis was at her widespread pussy lips.

"O-oh y-yes, p-please" she groaned at the contact, forgetting her fear.

"Go slow" he commanded between gasps of pleasure as she slowly, oh so very slowly slid down on him.

"U-u-n-n-n-g-g-h! O-oh, p-please, oh god!" she breathed as he filled her and she settled into his lap.

He wrapped his arms around her and pulled her to him, holding her still, stroking her, letting her settle, letting her breathe, reveling in sensation of the warmth of her breath on his neck. Then he turned and their lips met, tongues thrashing, and he felt her orgasm begin...

"Oh, yes. Oh, g-god y-y-y-e-e-s-s-s!" she moaned into his mouth.

Gradually, her orgasm subsided, yet he continued to cradle her in his arms, stroking her back and hips until her breathing settled...The he shifted and flexed his hips, thrusting up into her, grinding the base of his penis into her and lightly rubbing his thumb over her clit...

"U-n-n-n-u-u-g-h!" she groaned as she sat up, her eyes staring into his in surprise.

She could easily cum again, yet he didn't make the movement that will bring her to her crisis...

Slowly he stroked her face, neck and shoulders, calming yet exciting her simultaneously... Again his fingers found her nipples and began their insistent stroking and pinching...

"A-h-h-h-h, y-y-yes!" she whispered as the sensations rocket through her body.

She closed he eyes and threw her head back in ecstasy as her second orgasm crashed through her body...She ground her hips down onto his pelvis again and again, trying to get him deeper inside her.

"P-please," she gasped as the tremors in her body subside, "I need for you to fuck me...I want you moving inside me!"

The pleading in her eyes pierced his heart...He so wanted her to be happy, to have what she wanted...Yet, he shook his head side to side...

"Not yet…" he says "You're not ready yet…"

"B-but I a-am r-rea…A-h-h-h-h, my god!" she stammered as she was interrupted by another flex of his sphincter and thrust of his hips… Stretching the her tiny pussy tight around the base of his penis, his thumb again punished her clit…At the same time the fingers of his other hand lightly twisted her nipples and she fell into his arms thrashing in another orgasm…This one lasted for what seems like forever…She had trouble catching her breath and was afraid to move when he gave another thrust sent her over the edge a fourth time…

"P-please…" she plead in a whisper, her lips barely moving on his shoulder.

She felt him shift, and then stand and grasp her ass with his hands and she wrapped her legs around his back as he walked to the bed, still inside her…Each footstep caused a jolt that jounced her clitoris against the base of his penis…She was about to cum again when he bent and lowered her to the bed…Without leaving her, he got on his hands and knees and with her legs locked around his back, he moved until she was centered in the bed…Each movement caused her to gasp in pleasure and she was again on the verge of cumming…

He raised up on his hands and knees and pulled her legs around so that he held them in crook of his arms…Then the thrusting began…It was slow, yet incessant, never pausing, he pushed into her to the root of his penis then pulled out until only the head remains inside her… Looking down he could see her tiny pussy clinging to his cock like an infant's mouth as if trying to suck it deep inside her again and again…

On the fifth stroke she was cumming again, yet this time he didn't stop stroking…Soon she crying out in a combination of lust and need for respite…

His strokes slowed, then stopped…He was in her to the hilt, his balls resting on her upturned ass as she squirmed on him…He held her tight as he felt his orgasm begin to build and her eyes widened as she felt the head of his penis swell and then squirt into her…

" Oh, Jake," she whispered.

* * *

At about 10:00 PM the following Friday night, Steph walked into the den where Jake was reading, bent and kissed him on the cheek.

"I'm going to town and then I'm going to spend the night at Amanda's."

"You're going to town at ten o'clock?" Jake said as he looked at his watch.

"Yes Dad," Steph grinned. "It's not like the olden days when you were a kid and they closed town at sundown."

"Okay smartass!" he grinned back. "Be careful."

"I will…Bye!"

"Bye, baby."

Jake read a little longer, then closed his book, stood up, turned the lights off and walked into his bedroom. He looked at the room with its empty bed and knew immediately he wouldn't be able to sleep with Steph out of the house.

He turned out the rest of the lights and let himself out of the house, leaving the porch light on as a prearranged signal to Steph or any of her friends that might show up that he was sleeping in the tack room. Taking a minute to gaze at the starlit sky, he then walked across the yard, into the barn, let himself into the tack room and soon was asleep.

After what seemd like only minutes he woke with a start at what sounded like a car door slamming. Footsteps crunched as they crossed the gravel driveway, rustled through the sawdust in the barn, then lightly stepped onto the steps that led into the tack room. The sound of boots hitting the steps was followed by the door being opened.

A petite figure moved across the room and Jake squinted to see the silhouette of a shirt, then jeans being shed.

He pulled back the covers and inhaled her scent as she slid under the covers and into his arms.

"Hey Cowgirl."

"Hey Jake."

A CURE FOR STUTTERING

Mrs. Khanna ran into Mrs. Sorabji as the latter was stepping out of an exclusive shoe store at Nariman Point in Mumbai.

"Hi Yasmin," exclaimed Mrs. Khanna," haven't seen you in ages! How are you?"

"Very well, thank you. And you?"

"Oh, vadhiya ji vadhiya," said Preeti Khanna jovially, then her eyebrows knitted into a frown, "you are a clinical psychologist, right?"

"Yes, of course," said Yasmin Sorabji, wondering what was coming next from this ebullient Punjabi that she had known for years.

"Have you got some time to spare right now?"

"I start my evening counseling session at five. So I guess I have an hour or so to spare. What did you have in mind?"

"Not here. Let's go get a cold coffee at Firpo's and I will tell you. Come on, come on," said Preeti as she dragged her friend to Firpo's.

Yasmin Sorabji was an elegant, sophisticated person, someone you could easily mistake for an ultra rich socialite. In a way she was just that – she was married to an ultra rich businessman and really did not need to work at all. That she did so was because of a strong work ethic instilled in her by her father, who had been a Pediatrician. She was definitely not the kind of person you would even think of taking by the arm and bodily dragging off somewhere.

But Preeti Khanna had gone to the same school as her and was by nature the kind of person who could very easily be informal even with a queen.

"You remember Harbans Kaur?" said Preeti, once they had settled down with their cold coffees, "Oh, ho," when she encountered a blank look from Yasmin, "The one whose husband is general manager of Century Tyres, yaar."

Yasmin still had no idea.

"You were invited to their son's wedding two years ago but could not make it, because you had to rush your own son to the hospital." And he had to have his appendix removed, now Yasmin remembered! Her younger son had come home from college in the States and had promptly fallen ill.

"Aha, now you remember. Well it is about that son."

Yasmin waited, while Preeti looked at her with a meaningful expression on her face, "What?" She said in exasperation as Preeti appeared determined not to let the moment fade.

Finally, dramatically, in a whisper," His marriage crumbled."

"Well that is sad. But what has it to do with me."

"He needs help. You see his stuttering is back."

"Tried a speech therapist?"

"Oh yes. No success. I think that there is a deep psychological reason that needs to be unearthed and treated."

Oh dear here we go again, thought Yasmin. From being totally unaware or in denial a generation ago, educated Indians were now fully into Psychology.

"You see the whole thing was very messy – court shourt and all that. And suddenly the boy's stuttering was back."

Yasmin waited. It had been a while since she last met Preeti and now remembered what it was that irritated her so much about her – it was this dramatization to extract the maximum out of what could very well turn out to be a trivial issue. Typical Punjabi overacting, she thought, but then applying her professional persona to herself she calmed down and waited for Preeti to complete her story.

"You see his father arranged his marriage to this girl from a Sikh family in Delhi. Good family, very rich. Only, the girl was not educated beyond high school. As you know the boy is brilliant (and no, Yasmin Sorabji did not know this). Topper from IIT, Powai. This difference in intellectual level is what Harbans says was the problem. The girl claims otherwise – abuse from the boy and her in laws. Anyway in less than a year the girl was back in Delhi with her family. And her family went berserk. As you know because of all these dowry demanding, bride burning cases, the law these days is heavily tilted towards the bride. They used the law to extract a lot of money from the boy's father and even had the boy in jail. Not for long – just a week. But that was enough! Finally a divorce settlement was reached."

"The divorce came through last year. So Harbans and her family are finally free of the court system. But the effect on the boy has been devastating. He has lost all confidence, has withdrawn into himself and of course his stuttering is worse. He was fired by Infosys and has barely been able to stay employed. He is now working in a very inferior position for Voltas here in Mumbai."

Preeti Khanna paused with arched eyebrows, and Yasmin felt her irritation rising, because she felt once again something petty was going to issue out of her friend's mouth," It is almost as if he has suffered a significant injury. To his mind you know. When I see him now, he reminds me of Madhu Ranade's nephew after the Kargill war. And you cured him. Remember?"

Of course Yasmin remembered. PTSD. That had been Madhu Ranade's nephew's problem. It had taken concentrated counseling over four years to get him functional. To get rid of the severe trauma of seeing dismembered bodies, the smell of burning flesh and the intense sense of helplessness on losing friends.

Even now more than ten years later, she still saw him once every three or four months or so but these counseling sessions were more to allay the anxiety of everybody involved. He was fully functional – good job, excellent prospects, stable marriage, good kids. She knew intuitively that Preeti had analyzed the matter correctly. Her education may have been limited to convent school and then one year towards a bachelor of arts degree but her native intelligence and high emotional IQ allowed her to see things in clearer perspective than most other people. I guess, thought Yasmin, that is why I like her despite her irritating ways.

"So what do you think?"

"About what?" asked Yasmin.

"Oh ho baba, will you treat him or not?"

"I can certainly meet with him – if he agrees. And then we can decide if he needs to be treated or not."

So a fortnight later Balbir Singh presented himself at Yasmin's office on the fourth floor of an old colonial building in Colaba. He was slightly built, around five foot four in height, the very antithesis of the popular concept of a Sikh, though he did have thick facial hair. A large head (crowned by a neatly tied turban) with some arresting features made him marginally good looking. Yasmin, who was five foot eight, found she towered over him, more so because he stood hunched up, making himself even shorter.

There was no doubt that Balbir needed help. That he lacked

confidence was glaringly evident. Whether this was an extreme manifestation of inherent shyness, or something more pathological, needed to be determined and that thought Yasmin would direct her efforts to heal him. Balbir felt very comfortable talking to her – she was an accomplished therapist. In a few sessions she established an excellent rapport with him and ascertained that indeed mental trauma had made him regress emotionally – insecure, extremely shy and completely lacking in confidence. Stuttering, was a part of this syndrome. He had stuttered as a child, been cured by a speech therapist, then reverted as an adolescent and again been relieved of it by another speech therapist. This time around, it was the mental trauma which had prevented speech therapy from being effective. Exactly as Preeti Khanna had surmised, Yasmin ruefully acknowledged.

Exactly what the mental trauma was that had triggered this regression escaped her – for the moment. She narrowed it down to something sexual. Something had happened in the privacy of the bedroom. Through the years Yasmin had treated several married couples with sexual problems. In India where marriage was regarded as something that happened to everybody, it was not unusual to come across this problem. The usual suspects were homosexual tendencies, impotency, lack of interest in sex, or hormonal or developmental problems that resulted in abnormal anatomy. However, these usual suspects were soon ruled out.

She discovered the key to the puzzle purely by chance.

One evening they were making no headway. Balbir appeared distracted and fidgety. Finally he said, " Iii m sorry. I rrrreally hav ttto go!"

"Oh, of course," she said, relieved that the reason for his distressed behavior was so trivial, "you know where the bathroom is."

While he went to relieve himself, Yasmin stepped out on to the narrow balcony that ran the length of her office. The blast of heat and humidity that greeted her reminded her to do whatever she was going to do and quickly get back into the air conditioned comfort of her office. She had various plants in earthen ware beds firmly attached to the guard rail of the balcony, and as she had suspected, the help she shared with a few of the other offices in this building, had not done their job of watering the plants properly. There was a small extension of the balcony around the corner just outside the bathroom that housed a money plant that she was particularly fond of and which they invariably forgot to water. Picking up a pitcher of water she made her way sideways to the plant. As she started to water the plant she detected some movement out of the corner of her eye and heard the tinkling sound of water meeting water. She turned her head and found she was looking through the partially opened ventilator into the bathroom. It should have been closed to enhance the air conditioning but for some reason had been left partially open. The shaded ventilator slats were tilted vertically in such a way that the person peeing into the pot saw only the murky Mumbai sky. But the eyes of someone peering in, were directed downwards to the bowl. And what her eyes saw had Yasmin mesmerized. She saw a big cock emitting yellow stuff vigorously and noisily into the bowl.

Not just a big cock but an extraordinarily huge one! She had never seen one this big. Apart from her husband's, Yasmin had sampled a couple, one (cousin) before getting married and one (a distant cousin, during a marriage) after that. But she had seen quite a few in her line of work – on visits to prisons and mental hospitals, where deranged men would expose themselves. She always had a male escort who would quickly step in and get the loonies to cover themselves but not before she had more than a passing glance at their sexual appendage.

This thing was longer and thicker than anything she had ever seen. It was bigger in its present flaccid piss discharging state than the three cocks that had fucked her had been in their excited erect state.

She stood motionless, holding her breath till the pissing stopped, never taking her eyes off the huge piss emitter. Then Balbir swung his dong rhythmically, in the time honored way that men have of getting rid of the last pesky drops, before stuffing it back in his trousers, zipping up and leaving. Only when she heard the door to the bathroom close did Yasmin begin breathing once again. Then she quickly made her way back and stepped into her office just a few moments after Balbir had settled back on the couch.

He was more involved now and in a short while Yasmin brought up the marriage issue again. Veering from her normal practice she asked a direct question, "Was the size of your organ a problem?"

He looked at her with a shocked expression on his face. It took a few moments before he could force out a very soft," Yes."

It turned out that his wife had made it a major issue. On their wedding night they had been too exhausted to try anything. It was on the second night of their honeymoon that their first attempt at coitus took place. She simply lay passively on the bed and lifted her night garments up to expose her vagina. No attempt at intimacy, no fore play. Not really knowing what to do, he had taken off his clothes and approached the bed with a half erect cock. She had allowed him to lie on top of her but made no attempt to embrace him or make any gesture of affection or encouragement. He remembered that he had rubbed himself on her to get a full blown erection. He had then inserted his cock in her vagina. He got the head and a bit of the shaft into her cunt before she began complaining vociferously and made him take it out. She had then told him that he was too big for her and that he had to give her time to get used to his size. After that she had turned around and fallen asleep with her back to him. He remembered masturbating his frustrated cock to an orgasm later.

Subsequently he had made attempts to fuck her but had gotten nowhere. Then one night out of frustration he had gone to bed naked. She was as usual completely covered. She had looked at him sternly and asked him why he was naked and sprouting an obvious erection. Plucking up courage, the courage of the frustrated, he had told her it was time they fulfilled their marriage obligations. This sent her into orbit and she let him have it. Among the many demeaning things she said about him, he remembered in particular that she had stated that his cock was a monstrous abnormality, something no human could have possessed; he was a rakshas, a vile non human creature of the underworld and she was going to have nothing to do with him. She had made him get off the bed and sleep on the floor. And that was the end of their sleeping on a conjugal bed.

Yasmin established that his wife's demeaning comments and her despicable behavior could be traced back to a comment he made after their first and as it subsequently turned out, only attempt at copulation. He remembered that he had not felt the resistance of a hymen, something he had been told to watch out for by one of his uncles. Later, he did not find any blood on the bed sheet and mentioned this to her.

Yasmin made him think back, and slowly made him realize that unlike him, his former wife had been sexually active before marriage, and most probably had been having an affair that had been terminated by her marriage. She was unhappy because of this and more importantly she had wanted to transfer her guilt to him. To her paranoid mind his comment about the lack of blood implied that he knew she had been screwing around. She was not going to forgive him for this, even though he had not connected the dots till this moment and his comment then was one of relief that he had not injured her in any way.

Yasmin expanded on this realization and gradually Balbir came to accept the fact that his ex wife had used the size of his cock as a means to an end. She also made him realize that his former wife was not normal but a psychologically disturbed person with definite personality problems. That the onus of their failed marriage lay with her not him, and certainly not his sexual organ. As a result he began gaining confidence and went for long periods without stuttering. And this new found confidence showed at work, where he quickly advanced to higher positions.

But there remained an unresolved issue. He stone walled whenever she brought up the need to start again – get married and move on. He still thought that his cock was a disgusting piece of flesh that no normal woman would ever take into her body. Yasmin had come to genuinely care for this intelligent, introverted, gentle person. The fact that she wet her panties at the thought of his huge penis had of course nothing to do with it.

She decided on the next course of action. A completely non professional approach. Why she chose to do this, she could not have consciously explained to herself, except to tell herself it was to help a client. If she could have psychoanalyzed herself she would found the subconscious motivator – lust. Or maybe she did know but chose to continue in blithe denial.

Otherwise why did she one day in the middle of a session abruptly say," Show it to me."

He looked at her uncomprehendingly, so she pointed with a shapely, manicured finger, to his groin and said, "Your thing."

To say he was taken aback would be an understatement. He just sat there paralyzed.

"You still have this fear that it is abnormal and no woman would ever want anything to do with you once she saw it. I just want to reassure you by giving an unbiased opinion."

They sat there looking at each for what seemed like an eternity. Then he stood up and dropped his trousers and his shorts. He stood there looking down at nothing while Yasmin inspected his dong. She could no longer pretend that her interest in his cock was purely clinical. Seeing it in its naked glory made her consciously acknowledge the real reason – pure unadulterated lust.

She managed to say in a matter of fact way," Yes it is big." She saw him cringe at the word 'big', and so added quickly, " But nothing that would harm a woman."

In a flat tone he asked," How would you know?"

Taken aback, she said," I am experienced and just know."

Still in the same tone he continued," Have you directly experienced something like this? You know when it is excited it is much longer and thicker."

"No, I haven't but…. Okay let me see it in an excited state." Why on earth had she said that?! Pure unadulterated lust had made her say that. Yes, she was coming to terms with the fact that his humongous cock had triggered this reaction in her middle aged brain. She had never consciously been an overly sexual person. Yes, she loved to fuck, but what sex she had with her husband was enough. Till now that is. Even now she did not really want to fuck Balbir, but his cock – that was what she wanted. But, did she want to fuck it or just see it and maybe handle it and thus get this absurd lust for a huge cock out of her system? Let's find out thought her conscious mind.

Meanwhile Balbir mechanically reached down and began working his cock with his hand. She watched enthralled as it responded.In what she thought was a very professional tone she said," Well bring it here and let me feel it and I can then give you an informed opinion."

He stepped forward and she grasped his prick and moved her hand over it as if measuring it and comparing it to others she had handled. She was unable to get her hand around its girth. She used both her hands and looking down was struck by how small they looked on his cock.

"No," she said, fighting hard to keep her voice even, "it will definitely not harm a woman. She may take some time to get used to its size but a normal sized woman should be able to handle it." She did not remove her hands but found herself working his cock with them, stimulating it further. Her soft hands on his cock were more than he could handle, and a few strokes later he was on the brink of coming. He tried to warn her and then tried to pull away from her firm grasp on his penis but got caught up in his orgasm. With a grunt he ejaculated – all over her clothes, her hands and arms, her neck and a little on her face. She did not move till he finished coming and continued playing with his cock till he was done, only then did she let him go.

He was totally embarrassed," Sorry," he said, as he quickly pulled up and zipped his trousers.

"Nothing to be sorry about," she said in a matter of fact manner, as if this happened to her all the time, as he saw himself out of the door. Afterwards, she spent quite some time in the bathroom, washing her face, neck and arms and then sari and blouse. Luckily he had been her last client of the day, so she had the time to wait while her clothes dried under the fan. Mentally she noted to herself that from now on he would always be her last client of the day. Why? Consciously she felt it was because she was making progress in a very difficult case and having the day end in triumph was going to make her day. But subconsciously?

He was very awkward when he returned for his next session. When you have ejaculated all over your psychologist, of course you are going to be discomfited. But she continued in the same matter of fact manner, as if nothing had happened. Gradually his diffidence evaporated and they had a good session. In the weeks that followed he continued to make good progress – his confidence soared and his stuttering was almost gone. At work he reached the highest position he thought he could attain at Voltas and was actively looking around for a new job. But he still baulked at the idea of meeting another woman, of getting married, of getting on with life. And without that she knew he was not completely healed.

So, she then decided to continue her non professional approach and take it to the next level; an approach that ethically could never be justified. Consciously she convinced herself that she was doing it to help him come to terms with his disability and then move on from there to complete healing. But subconsciously, did she acknowledge the truth?

"So you really think you can injure someone with that thing?" she asked him out of the blue one day.

A surprised, "Huh?" was all he could manage.

"I mean I can prove to you that it will not cause injury."

"How?"

"By having you put it in me." Had she really said that?! That too in a matter of fact tone.

It took him a while to comprehend what she had said. Then when the realization hit him, he was stunned, and at the same time excited beyond belief. Yasmin Sorabji was a very good looking woman, tall, slim, graceful. Her chiseled features bore the few wrinkles of her passage through time very well. She had been physically active all her life – badminton champion in school and then State champion in college, finishing up as runner up at the National Championships till marriage put an end to her sports career. She still kept herself fit and supple with almost daily work outs under the guidance of her personal trainer at her exclusive neighborhood's health club. There was no sag or multiple flesh folds that were the bane of middle age of a lot of Indian women. She glowed with health and moved with the ease of a woman in her twenties.

He thought she was stunning. Had always thought so, but subconsciously. When she had handled his prick, his feelings had boiled over. He had allowed himself to fantasize about her – various scenarios where he had done very imaginative things with her body.

But subsequently common sense had prevailed. She was interested in helping him recover – clinical interest in making a client better, nothing more than that. In any case how could he even allow himself to think that anyone would be interested in fucking his beastly cock? And in their subsequent encounters she had maintained a professional distance and actually really helped him ground himself in reality.

And now this. Was she suggesting this just to prove to him that there was nothing abnormal about his cock? Or …?! Could this goddess be interested in fucking him?! It had to be the former for how could anyone, let alone this vision of loveliness, want to fuck his revolting cock?

She was looking at him and saw lust, doubt, insecurity and a host of other things flit across his face.

"So what do you think?" she asked, keeping her tone and the expression on her face neutral.

"If you are willing then I am too." Without even the hint of a stutter, that's what sexual excitement will do to you. Except how was she going to do it, he thought? Fully clothed and lift her clothes out of the way just enough for him to insert it, like his ex wife?

But it became perfectly clear that Yasmin had other ideas. She started undressing and off came the designer jacket that she had chosen to wear that day, and then the top and pants in a jiffy. When she was down to bra and panties she looked at him and said in a surprised tone, " Aren't you going to take your clothes off?"

It had not been a slow strip tease, just a routine undressing like she did everyday in the privacy of her home, but her exposed body had excited him tremendously. He could feel his cock responding to her tall, delicious curvy figure. By the time he was down to his shorts it was rock hard.

Almost in unison she took off her bra as he bent down and took off his shorts. When he looked up again he was staring at the most beautiful pair of breasts he had ever seen, not that he had seen very many. But then, what the hell, had many men seen very many, or for that matter had any man seen what he considered enough? Rhetorical questions, to which the answer truthfully was no, because men always want more without knowing why they want more and therefore never are they satisfied.

But back to her breasts. Those breasts were just the right size to hold up against the sag of middle age, and they proudly dangled from her chest.

She looked down and could not keep her eyes away from his cock even as she bent down and yanked off her panties. It jutted out like a battering ram from his mass of pubic hair, thick, strong and iron hard, ready for action.

She moved a lever and the couch leveled into a bed. She indicated that he should lie down on it, and when he did, she looked down again and marveled at the sight of that massive pillar jutting out from that small frame. The contrast made his cock even more menacing.

She shuddered. Was it fear or lust that made her do it?

She climbed up on the couch and straddled him. He looked up at the apparition of sex above him, slim stunning body with sculptured legs on either side meeting in a forest of pubic hair with the hint of fleshy lips peeking, a studious expression on that gorgeous face, as if making measurements and mapping out her next moves. It took all he had to prevent himself from reaching for her breasts. But he was petrified to break this up by making stupid moves. He just lay there, cock erect and waited with bated breath.

She looked down at him, amazed at the amount of hair covering his body. Taking hold of his cock she thought, "My God, is this really a man's penis or a horse's?" As once again she found she could not encompass its girth with her hand.

She lowered herself till the head was at her vaginal lips. She rubbed it on herself and could feel her vagina throbbing in anticipation. Gradually she impaled herself. At first all she got was the head past the labia. Then she forced herself lower till the head was snugly inside her cunt. With only the head in her cunt, she felt stretched like never before. She could stop right here and announce that she was not hurt and therefore no one could get hurt by his cock. But wouldn't that amount to cheating? She gradually sank down further taking more and more of his horse cock up her cunt. Now more than half was embedded. She could declare victory right here and triumphantly proclaim that his cock was innocuous. But to really declare victory, shouldn't she take the whole thing up her vagina? Could she? She was determined to find out. Her conscious mind tried to tell her it was a scientific endeavor but she could no longer deny what was motivating her – pure lust! Pure fucking lust!

He watched her gradually sink down on his cock. Her cunt felt like a warm tight glove. This was the first time that his prick had been this far inside a woman. It felt like heaven! He wanted to reach up and grab her breasts, to run his hands over her body, to crush his lips against hers, but he did nothing. He just lay there like a sack of potatoes, because he was too scared to destroy this sacred moment.

She moved up and down on his cock, trying yet again to convince herself that this was a clinical exercise designed to gradually impale herself further and further on this gargantuan appendage till it was all embedded in her, and prove to her client that it was all in his mind – that he was normal, and that his organ was normal; this would then modify his future behavior. But yet again she could not deny her motivation : she knew she was doing it because the sensation was out of this world. This was fucking heaven.

She felt stuffed yet craved for more, she felt nauseated yet exhilarated. She moved up and down, skewering herself on that pole, getting down further and further with each descent till finally the whole damn thing was in her. She felt triumphant and yet had broken out in a cold sweat and her stomach was actively churning. This was like child birth – with the same ecstatic feeling at the end, except this was in reverse – instead of expelling something from her body, she had taken in a huge thing.

Her pubis ground against his, their pubic hair enmeshed by the juices of their arousal and the sweat of her exertion. Now was a good moment to declare victory and withdraw. But she did not. Gone was any pretence that this was being done to help his rehabilitation. Pure lust had taken over. Pure fucking lust! She drove herself up and down that shaft even though it felt like she was being shafted by the Kutab Minar itself. She would ride up on her haunches till only the head was in and then she would clench her buttocks and drive down with the weight of her body till the whole thing was embedded in her. Slowly at first, her speed increased as her slick and more accommodating vagina grew accustomed to the size of the intrusion till she was riding him like a race horse.

Now he got into the act and his hands gripped her buttocks aiding her up till only the head was in her vagina and then abetting her downward movement so that she was slammed down unceremoniously on his cock even as he thrust upwards. She gritted her teeth against the pain but found herself floating closer and closer to orgasm from the pleasure. And then she was pounded by her climax, the best she had ever achieved in her life. It went on and on. She could not move till it passed and then felt so weak that she collapsed on him. And now it was all him, slamming her inert frame up and down on his massive erection and thrusting upwards at the same time, urgently seeking his own release till he crested the wave that led to blessed relief. First, the fierce almost maniacal feeling of intense agitation and then as his cock erupted again and again till it was spent, the feeling of peace, of fulfillment, of floating weightless on a cloud of wellbeing. This was the first time he had come inside a woman's cunt. The first time he had come so hard. It was a life changing moment and he savored the moment fully.

He could smell the sweat of her exertion in her hair – delectable! He ran his hands up and down her awesome body and finally grabbed her heavenly breasts. He fondled them to his heart's content, even pulling on her nipples still erect with excitement. Then he reached between her legs and found his cock firmly embedded in her cunt to its root. He marveled at the fact that it was still hard despite the fact that he had just come and he could feel his emission everywhere – on her thighs and seeping on to the couch. He tried to insert a cum slick finger past his cock into her vagina and found that there was no space, her cunt was fully taken. He could not help himself – he turned his head and began lightly kissing her cheeks in gratitude and then he licked them with mounting passion. He then stuck his tongue in her ear and ran it over the corrugations there before settling to chew on her earlobe.

His tongue in her ear was what brought her around. She found herself slumped against him, her nose assailed by the smell of their sweat and other body secretions, at once revolting and yet exhilarating. She gradually lifted her upper body off him, still joined together below by his steel hard prick firmly in her cunt. He smiled up at her, and she responded with a smile down at him.

Then he turned her over, with his prick still embedded, till she was below him and he was on top. " Thank you," he said, clearly and distinctly because it was important for him to let her know his gratitude. For having taken him to heaven. He lowered himself and softly kissed her lips in thankfulness and she responded by pressing her lips to his.

And then wild lust took over and he thrust his tongue into her and moved it with fervor in her mouth. She was momentarily taken aback and then her tongue responded with equal ardor. He lifted himself off her but found that her cunt was not willing to let go of his prick easily. He moaned in frustration as his hands moved all over her body – caressing her thighs, squeezing her breasts, running his fingers through her hair, all the while moving his groin against hers trying to free his cock. Gradually his penis worked itself out, till with an audible pop her clinging cunt let go of his prick. He looked down at her gaping cunt with awe. She looked down with him and then said in a voice hoarse with lust, "Put it back, now!"

And he tried to do so instantly, but found he could not get even the head in. They both worked with patience because they now knew he would be able to embed the whole damn thing in her. She reached down urgently and took hold of his prick and directed it to her cunt. She moved her legs widely apart and upwards till her knees were by her shoulders. Thrusting up she managed to spear the head in her.

It was at that moment that he realized what he had to do. He had no experience, no prior knowledge and yet he knew. Pure instinct! Pure evolutionary fucking instinct that every male of the species possesses.

He extracted the head of his penis from her cunt and then worked his way down her body. Kissing her chin, her neck, nibbling on her nipples, ravishing her abdomen and sticking his tongue in her umbilicus and loving it, over the slight swell of her abdomen, till he reached her cunt. And there he went to work with his tongue slurping at her nether lips, tickling her clitoris, till she strained to spread herself even more widely open. He stuck his tongue down her now revealed vaginal passage retracing the pioneering path of his oversized cock, retracting and piercing till she wriggled in delight and took hold of his head and used it to direct the invasion of his tongue. He moistened an index finger and strummed her clit with it. The thrusting tongue and strumming finger in unison played on her till she felt the rising cadence of another climax reaching out to her and suddenly it was upon her, washing over her in ecstatic waves pounding her till she was spent. She looked down when she was done and found her legs had closed around his head holding it prisoner as he calmly continued slurping away with his tongue. Truth be told he was really enjoying himself, he had discovered a part of him that he did not know was there – a part that felt deep satisfaction and that made him feel complete and worthwhile all because he was giving so much pleasure and joy to another human being.

But she had other plans. She lifted his head off her pubis and brought it up to her face. She kissed his lips and thrust her tongue wildly into his mouth tasting herself without any disgust but with gratitude and delight. Gently she guided him till he was on his back with his rod sticking straight up. She looked down at it with awe yet again. Then she slithered down his body and lowered her face and began worshipping that huge phallus with her tongue, licking the knob, exploring the slit, running it along the underside feeling the hardness of it. Now she opened her mouth and began the process of taking it in. No way was she going to swallow the whole thing. She had no experience whatsoever. This was the first time she had ever sucked cock. But she was determined to get him off like he had her.

He looked down and saw her beautiful face between his thighs and felt her sophisticated tongue working his cock, as her head rhythmically bobbed up and down on his groin. This was not really happening, he thought – a refined, gorgeous lady, was vulgarly slurping away at his cock as he lay there in lazy splendor and watched. Then her efforts bore fruit and he could feel the rising tide of his excitement. Now all that mattered was getting off. Gone were all thoughts of reverence of how above his station she was, of how delicate and heavenly she was, now pure fucking male lust took over, selfish, seeking only its fulfillment. He reached down and firmly took hold of her head. Then he began slamming his cock into her mouth completely oblivious to the fact that she was obviously choking and gagging and only her firm hand on his prick prevented him from ramming the whole damn thing down her throat and permanently choking her.

She was momentarily taken aback by this act of aggression from someone who till now she had perceived as being completely benign and docile. But then in a flash she realized that it was pure biology – a copulating male was also establishing his dominance. And she also realized that she was not averse to being taken forcibly – another throwback to evolutionary biology? So she let him fuck her mouth but more accurately her throat for that was where the head of his penis rested at the end of its incursion. The invasion of her throat by his cock had started an involuntary gagging reflex and she could feel her stomach contracting and pouring out it's juice in protest and she could feel the liquid rising and flowing around his cock and onto her hand with which she still clutched onto the base of his prick for safety. Her hand and face were a mess, bathed in huge amounts of saliva and now this gastric stuff.

And still he hammered his cock in and out and moved her face viciously on it. And she just patiently waited and let him have his way.

And then he was there and with a grunt came in her, his emission hitting the back of her throat in torrents. She swallowed quickly taking in as much as she could and then she gagged as the rest filled her mouth and ran out onto her hand. Gradually his orgasm abated and he returned to terra firma, along with the realization of how he had used her. Gently he lifted her off his cock, murmuring sorry over and over again. He looked at her messed up face and felt ashamed.

She moved up and rubbed her semen, saliva and gastric juice streaked face on his and kissed him softly. And now she was on fire. She shifted herself till her breasts were level with his face and got him to suckle on them. While he happily obliged she took the hand that had held his cock and was awash with fluid and introduced it to her cunt. Two fingers entered and began fucking her, as the thumb found her clitoris, exciting it. And in next to no time she was into another mind blowing orgasm. As she recovered she marveled at the amazing depths of lust her middle aged self had uncovered. She had actually masturbated in company! She, who had hardly ever masturbated, had now done so flagrantly and filthily with a younger male suckling at her breast.

Her masturbation had excited him tremendously. He had never seen a female or for that matter anybody masturbate. The fact that she had done so and so brazenly had energized his cock and it was erect and ready for action, yet again. Ah, the boundless fucking energy of youth!

He was going to fuck her now. In her cunt. He wanted to feel that tight tunnel again. He needed to feel her legs wrapping themselves around him, expressing her wanton lust in how tightly they held him.

She was ready to be penetrated again, to be taken, to feel that humungous thing fuck the shit out of her. She spread her delectable legs offering her hairy pussy to him. She took hold of his prick, yet again thrilled and intimidated by its girth, and introduced it to her cunt. Softly and slowly it worked its way past the vaginal flaps and into the soft, wet tunnel itself.

And then he took over. Unrestrained male lust took hold of him and he rammed the whole thing up her vagina in one fell swoop. It took the breath out of her so much so that she had none left to scream her protest. He paused for a moment to say, "Sorry," and then proceeded to hammer her mercilessly. He reached down and pressed on her thighs folding her sagging legs till her knees were back up near her shoulders and her feet were turned inwards resting on his back. Again, the thought struck her that this was like childbirth – the position he had made her adopt was designed to give maximum access to her reproductive channel. Now he took possession of her mouth, thrusting his tongue in and out in time with his cock, feeling the roof of her mouth, gathering his saliva and spitting it into her mouth forcing her to swallow it. At first she found this spitting repulsive and then in the next instant stimulating and she got into the act and drawing together whatever was in her mouth, she released it into his. Except at that very moment he moved his face off her and got the full force of her spit on his beard.

They found this so ridiculous that they both simultaneously burst out laughing and had to take a brief respite from their frenzied fucking. Then they were back at it and he made her lick her spit off his facial hair. And then, liking this spit play, she made him spit on her face and lick it off, and all the while he held her in that wide open position and rammed his cock in and out ruthlessly. This round of fucking went on and on. Alternating between periods of frenzied activity and periods of lesser groin action where they explored each other's bodies – tongues discovering new regions of mouth and hands spending a long time playing with their favorite parts, his being her breasts and hers his balls. She stayed in that submissive wide open position below him and had so many orgasms that they seemed to merge together putting her on a plateau of continued delight. He worked steadily to his release, till with gathering intensity it was on him and with a grunt he came, lodging his cock deep in her, wanting his semen to reach the deepest recess it could find within her.

He let her legs down and they stayed with him atop her for a long time, recovering. And then realization struck her like a splash of cold water on a cold day. It had been an hour and a half past her usual closing time! In a frenzy she got out from under him and reached for her mobile phone. She called her driver waiting in her car downstairs. Luckily, he was an incurious laid back elderly man who was only interested in doing a good job so he did not get fired. He was not surprised at all that she was so late and would take at least half an hour more before she was ready to go home. Balbir had used public transport that day. She told him how to get out of the building by exiting through the rear into a quiet back alley, thus avoiding any chance of being spotted.

Next, she called home. Luckily her husband was out of town on a business meeting, as was her elder son. The only people at home were her daughter in law (and her two month old granddaughter) and an elderly aunt visiting from Bangalore. She made sure they went ahead and had dinner and did not wait for her. Then she went to the bathroom to get herself cleaned up and ready to go. She ran the sink tap and used it to wash herself. Standing naked she splashed water on her face and body, rubbing a little soap on herself and then splashing more water to wash the soap off. Before she could reach for the towel to dry herself off, Balbir entered.

"Forgot about me?" he asked, with no hint of a stutter, " I need to get cleaned up as well, you know."

"Oh, sorry," she said, "I will be done in a moment."

But it was obvious that cleaning up was not what was foremost on his mind as he moved behind her and pressed himself against her reaching around for her breasts.

"No," she protested," Save it for another day. I am late already."

"Yes, you are right," he said, "But what do I do with this?"

'This' being his cock, which was rock hard yet again, and was being rubbed along the cleft of her delectable buttocks as he pressed himself against her, his hands continuing to play with her breasts. Was this the same guy who just a few hours ago was a timid, self effacing bundle of negativity? There was nothing timid, or self effacing, or negative about the way he was handling her tits or squeezing himself against her. Quite the opposite in fact. My god, she thought, have I created a monster? Or just awakened the sleeping hormones of a normal young man? These were rhetorical questions. Because she knew what was going to happen next in reality. She was going to get fucked. There was nothing she could do to prevent it and she truthfully acknowledged to herself that there was nothing she wanted to do to prevent it. She awaited her fate with delicious anticipation.

Sensing her compliance, he boldly spread her legs and bent her forward, her buttocks sticking out enticingly. He parted the cheeks of her ass and looked down at the furrow between, where two holes were lewdly displayed. He glanced at her asshole and briefly toyed with the idea of taking her there. But no matter what his present state of mind, or hers for that matter, he just did not have the courage to force her to accept his prick up her back hole. And in truth it was but a passing thought. His main intent was just to fuck her once again, to once again feel her cunt clasping his cock, once again feel her gorgeous body working with him to their mutual benefit.

He looked up and caught her looking at him in the mirror over the sink. He lewdly stuck his tongue out at her, and made in and out movements with it mimicking fucking. Why he did so he had no idea. It made her smile and shake her head at his foolishness, and it made it easier for her to accept his cock which had in the meantime entered her cunt and found its way into the warm and slick interior. She was stretched out holding onto the sink for support, with her legs bent to allow for their difference in heights and make it easier for him to prong her. Inexorably he thrust his cock in till once again it was fully embedded. All the while their eyes remained locked in the mirror. Now he reached for her breasts. He squeezed them to his heart's content and rubbed her nipples. Then he made her stand up, with his humungous prick lodged in her, so that he could look over her shoulders and visualize her breasts being mauled in the mirror. He sealed his viewing pleasure by kissing the back of her shoulders.

Then raw lust took over. He rudely pushed her forward and took hold of her rump with his hands. And now he let her have it. Ramming his cock in and out with so much energy that the sink threatened to come off its moorings. She took her hands off the sink and braced herself with her hands on the wall beyond the sink and thrust back wantonly at him. They both had discovered the joys of this posterior fucking position – complete and blissful penetration with the least amount of body contortion. And even though she had come so many times it was not long before she was once again transported to climax after climax, marveling how easy it had become to accommodate his cock. And so satisfying was the penetration in this position that despite the fact he had come again and again, he found the sap rising and then it was pouring into her widely accommodating tunnel of lust.

Now she firmly took charge. Uncorking herself, she quickly used a wet towel to clean him, like a mother would a small child, and then in keeping with mother theme, helped him get into his clothes and out of there. Then moving swiftly, she used the same wet towel to clean herself, got dressed, applied makeup and doused herself with perfume, before making her way down to her car.

And she carried forward this take charge spirit to their future liaisons. Allowing only so much time and only after reaching whatever it was that she had set as the goal of that session. True, she submitted to him and let him take charge of the fucking, because that was what enhanced their mutual enjoyment. But, there was a time limit to it. Once that limit was reached, she was done, no matter where they were in the scheme of things. At times he was left with a turgid cock and the resentment of unrequited lust. At times she was left frustrated and empty. But she had decided that the only way she could keep this thing under wraps was by not meeting anywhere outside her office and staying strictly within the time limit of her practice.

But within that time frame, boy oh boy, did things happen?! All out raw fucking. Hysterical fucking with her up against the wall, boom shi boom, or on her hands and knees, widely spread to accommodate his entire cock with each furious incursion, or on the couch fully clothed with only their essentials exposed and joined together, frenziedly fucking their brains out because he could not wait for them to decorously take their clothes off. What remained forever etched in her memory was him sucking her cunt. He just loved doing it. He never quite lost his awe of her and for him her cunt was perfect and meant to be worshiped (except of course when he had his cock in it and then his only thought was to demolish it). Also he had discovered this need to satisfy his partner, to really get off on getting her off. It thrilled him no end to have her come again and again with his face firmly wedged between her legs. This altruistic giving of pleasure satisfied him as much as fucking the shit out of her. A time and place for everything but on the whole it was giving pleasure that did more for him than anything else.

As for her the wonder and novelty of his big cock never quite wore off. It still thrilled her to feel its size, and it continued to bemuse her that no matter how many times she got fucked by it, the next time it still took some work dilating her cunt before it could be fully sheathed in her. She grew to really enjoying feeling it in her mouth, of running her tongue all over it and getting off on that tactile sensation. Of still gagging every time because of its sheer size and the fact that he would use her mouth as a cunt and hammer her ruthlessly, the submission to this aggression was also something that triggered a primordial need in her and really satisfied her.

In short, they became perfect fuck partners. But what of their emotions? They talked about this and were relieved when they did. He loved to fuck her but was not in love with her. He worshipped her (mainly her cunt), but did not feel the need to spend every waking moment with her or have her share his life outside her office with him. Likewise, she was very fond of him, and loved his big prick and what it did to her, but if it was not there tomorrow it would leave a void in her cunt, but not in her life. She loved her husband (and there was some guilt in that she was cheating on him, but she also knew that such was their relationship that he would understand and condone her behavior), her family was her priority and Balbir and his huge prick, a dalliance. It was strange, she thought, the popular concept was that men fuck with their cocks in isolation, whereas women fuck with their minds and bodies. In other words men were wanton lust driven fuckers, and women were reproductively driven with their lust held in check by their mind. And yet here she was totally in lust with Balbir's cock and emotionally beyond being fond of him could not give a damn about him. She spent some time analyzing herself to establish the veracity of what she felt, and then having done that, gave herself to the mindless fucking wholeheartedly. It certainly was good!

That all this fucking was good for him (along with her counseling, of course) was reflected in his professional life. He was being actively wooed by a few companies and was in the process of deciding which would be the best fit for him.

And then one day, there was what appeared to be a major setback in his progress.

The time that she had allotted for counseling had been spent well and they had actually had a great meeting. Now they were moving on to another fucking session. They were sitting side by side on the couch, thigh touching thigh. He unzipped, pulled out his cock and began fondling it. It still amazed her – this new found confidence, this lack of modesty. Her professional self had worked on his psyche and made him confident in himself. But it was her own personality that had made him so comfortable that he could just whip out his penis like this. He removed his hand from his organ and placed one of hers on it. Automatically she began massaging it marveling yet again at the fact that she found it difficult to encircle its girth with one hand. He reached over and around her neck and down under her blouse to fondle her breast.

" Ever taken it up your ass?" he asked nonchalantly.

She gasped, as the implication of what he was asking, dawned on her, " This is too big!"

"Rrrreally?" he stuttered, "why dddo you say that?" His hand lay frozen on her breast.

Oh, my god, she thought, "What have I done? His stutter is back. Just like that, months of hard work, down the drain. It must have been the 'big' allusion. Must have triggered his negative thought patterns again."

"Oh, come on Balbir," she said aloud in a very matter of fact tone, " It has nothing to do with you and everything to do with me. I am afraid. Me. Men will kill to have a weapon like yours. And I think it will kill me to have it up my ass. Ha, ha."

Nothing. The lost look was back on his face. He removed his hands from her person and held them tightly bunched up, his shoulders slumped and his head hung down. She continued playing with his cock but it refused to get excited and in fact rapidly deflated. She gave up in exasperation and placed it back inside his pants and zipped him up because he was not going to move. He just sat there every muscle frozen like an ice sculpture.

She looked at him and spoke to him. Nothing. Then she did what she felt instinctively was the only thing she could do to revive him.

She got up and took off all her clothes, slowly; doing a strip tease till she was naked. She stood in front of him provocatively, one hand playing with her pubic bush and the other squeezing her breasts – nothing, not a flicker of interest. So, she got down on her knees in front of him and once again took out his cock and began playing with it – nothing happened to it. She held the base and lowering her head began licking the top of his cock, flicking her tongue around and into the urethral opening. Every now and then she would swallow the huge head and massage it with her tongue.

This worked to a certain extent. Gradually, his prick came to life, but the rest of him remained the same. It took a long time but her patience and persistence and talented mouth finally got his cock erect. She unclenched his hands and placed them on either side of her head as she really began working on his cock with her mouth. She had never been able to swallow his cock entirely, but today she was determined to. She got it erect and then despite gagging she began moving her face on his prick grittily taking it further and further in, till at last her lips grazed his abundant pubic hair. She had swallowed that whole humongous thing!

The head felt like it was in her belly and she could feel her stomach contracting itself, protesting against the intrusion. But she was not going to stop till he came to life. Her efforts were finally rewarded. Soon he had her head in a vice grip of lust and was thrusting in and out with abandon. She passively held her mouth open and let him have his way with her oral orifice, and not just the oral orifice but depths way beyond that. She knew that it was not going to be the only orifice he would visit today.

She looked up at him and found his face expressionless even as his lower half thrust itself lustily into her mouth. Gently she extracted herself and got up. She reached for his shirt and with minimal help from him took it off and then his trousers and shorts. He just sat there naked with a glazed expression and a hugely erect enormous cock.

She opened the couch into a bed and spread a freshly laundered sheet on it (something she had been doing for some time now, along with obsessively cleaning any spot, imagined or otherwise on the couch itself) and then tenderly moved him into a supine position on it, his penis a giant perpendicular pillar. She squatted above him and lowered herself guiding his penis into her vagina. She was surprised to find herself wet with excitement and smoothly worked on him till his whole fucking organ was embedded. Then she really went to work, lifting and dropping herself vigorously on it. And yes the strategy worked. Her wildly bouncing breasts together with her warm and willing vagina finally got to him.

There was more life in his eyes now, and less of that glazed look. She would need lubrication. Where was she to find it? She thought furiously. And then she remembered the bottle of Jabakusum hair oil (ancient ayurvedic formula!) presented to her by one of her grateful Bengali clients, lying forgotten in a drawer in her desk.

Softly, she hauled herself off his prick and went looking for it. And there it was, under a bunch of papers at the back of the third drawer. She broke open the seal and the soft, earthy, herbal scent of the oil was set free. Well, she thought wryly, if I am to be buggered, at least it will smell nice. She walked back to the couch, and found him watching her with interest, the glaze had lifted, but he made no movement, just lay there with his huge pole stiffly sniffing the air. She spoke to him, but got no response. Well, at least we have made some progress, she thought.

She poured oil on to her palm and then anointed his prick with it. A chill went through her as she handled his cock, as she felt its thickness, wondering what it would do to her poor little anus. My God, she thought, I must be the epitome of a dedicated psychologist – anything to help a client, even willing to get sodomized. He watched with interest as she oiled his cock, making no move himself. Seeing that she had his attention, she sat back and spread her legs. Then she poured more oil on her hands and began lewdly playing with herself. She rubbed her oily fingers up against the lips of her vagina and then introduced a couple of fingers in and rising up on bent legs began seriously fucking herself. He was now watching her with rapt attention. Then she lay down in front of him and raised her legs up and tilted her pelvis. She spread her raised legs wide and parted her buttocks so that he could see her crinkled anus. She poured more oil on her hands and then rubbed them on her buttocks, gradually working her way to her ass hole. She teased the opening and taking more oil poured it right over her ass hole capturing the run-off on the fingers of her right hand. She then introduced one oily finger up her ass. She had never had anything shoved up her ass and it felt like she had been kicked in the guts. She quickly withdrew her finger and built up courage for another assault because she was determined to open herself up enough to take his cock.

He was absolutely interested now. No movement, but that glazed expression had definitely been replaced by an engrossed look. She then once again slid an oiled finger slowly up her ass hole. Gradually she got used to the intrusion and introduced a second finger. Her sphincter protested, it felt like when she had bad constipation and had struggled to get a hard log out. She persisted, and gradually the intensity of the sensation of dilatation subsided. Then she had a better idea.

She pulled her fingers out and moving closer to him raised him up on his knees. Then she took hold of his hands and poured the scented hair oil generously on them, getting his fingers nice and slick. Then she once again lay down in front of him and raising her legs up tilted her pelvis upwards to make her asshole more accessible. She spread her raised legs wide and parted her buttocks so that he could once again clearly see her crinkled anus, only much closer. She leaned forward and taking his hand rubbed his fingers against her anus. Then she gently pushed one of them in. He now got into the act and began sawing his finger in and out. He was clearly excited now and in next to no time had two and then three fingers up her ass. Having three fingers up her ass was made tolerable by the fact that the fingers of his other hand were strumming her clit and gently fucking her cunt. Yes, he was certainly more engaged now. Time to take it to the next level, she thought.

Tenderly, she removed his fingers from her cunt and asshole. Then she moved him till he was supine once again. She poured more oil on to her hands and worked his cock till it was steel hard and really slick. She squatted above him and getting hold of his cock, lined it up with her anus. Determined, she lowered herself till the head was at her shit hole. The moment of truth had arrived! Boldly, she skewered herself till the head was halfway in. Then she had to stop. She had broken out in a cold sweat and felt nauseated. It felt like a chili pepper had been shoved up her ass, only this was the size of giant tree trunk.

She had the urge to climb off his cock and call it quits. The man could stutter for the rest of his life for all she cared, she was not going to take it up her ass. But she stayed where she was and then began a gradual descent. She looked down and she could swear that Balbir had a satisfied look on his face, like a cat that has just swallowed a small bird. But he continued to just lie there and do nothing. This strengthened her resolve. She had to cure this client. So she continued to impale herself till that huge ass breaker was embedded to its root. Now it did not feel all that awful actually. The initial sphincter shattering sensation had subsided, to be replaced by a sensation of fullness but really not pain. Simultaneously playing with her cunt had helped to divert her mind from pain to pleasure. She rose up and descended a few times to reassure herself. Then she un-pronged herself and got on her hands and knees, next to him.

Balbir needed no further prompting. In a jiffy he was up and behind her. She was certainly not expecting this – no cajoling, no helping him up. The next moment all abstract speculation flew out of her mind as his cock was rammed up her asshole. In one fell swoop he had embedded the whole massive thing in her rectum. Involuntarily, she cried out – more in shock than in pain. But there was no stopping this suddenly energized sardar any more. He was going at it hammer and tongs, ramming her twenty two ways to Sunday. And then his hands got busy. First, mauling her breasts and then one of them finding her cunt began simultaneously playing with her vagina and clitoris till she could not give a damn about how rudely he was treating her ass.

And then she could feel that he was almost there. He removed his hands from her breasts and cunt and placed them firmly on her hips. If it was possible he began ramming her even harder. She clung to the sheet and couch for dear life to prevent being thrown off. Then with a grunt he came. In torrents up her ass. He kept hammering her ass right through his orgasm, eventually stopping only when she collapsed on the couch. He lay on top of her, kissing the side of her face, while he spread her legs and felt underneath her for his cock, still hard but softening, and then all around it for her firmly clasping anal ring as if to convince himself that he had actually buggered her. He lifted her back on her hands and knees, his prick still embedded in her ass. She understood why when he spread her buttocks – it was to feast his eyes on the sight of his cock in her asshole.

His prick softened in her ass and gradually withdrew till it plopped out of her anus. His hands still firmly held her hips and he watched as her ass hole winked shut. He reached under and found her vagina in the forest of pubic hair and then entered her with one and then two fingers and started fucking her cunt rhythmically. He moved his cock in the crease between her buttocks gradually hardening it.

She looked back at him and he smiled at her enigmatically. And that was when it struck her. He had been pretending. The bastard had feigned a stuttering relapse in order to get into her ass! And now his prick was as hard as an iron rod and he was going to do it again!

As she lay there, below him, passively on her hands and knees, feeling the giant head of his cock against her anal ring – she felt angry because he had fooled her and used her. Yet at the same time she felt proud because her therapy had obviously been so successful. And now she was filled with trepidation because he was going to bugger her again, yet she felt proud that she had taken him up her ass and knew she could do it again and again and enjoy every moment of having her guts skewered by that huge rod.

* * *

She met Preeti Khanna at an exclusive function to honor a foreign dignitary.

"Oh ho," said Preeti," Kamaal kar ditha, you are not a psychologist but a magician." Yasmin flushed in embarrassment as Preeti's loud voice had turned a number of heads towards them.

"Oh no," she said softly, "Just another day in the office, it was merely a matter of applying basic psychological principles."

"Okay, baba, whatever," said Preeti," but the result was spectacular – he was taken up by Reliance and is close to becoming a vice president. And he should shortly be getting married again. They are getting so many proposals that his mother – Harbans, has made a screening committee with me and a few others on it so that the same mistake is not made again. We thoroughly investigate each and every one of the girls and we are very close to a final decision. The boy's father has been kept out of it and rightly so considering the mess he made the first time around!"

"But," continued Preeti," We are going to need you to continue seeing him every now and then, just like Madhu Ranade's nephew, to ensure he stays healthy."

"Yes," said Yasmin softly, as lust heated her cunt," I think that will be completely satisfactory."

GHOST

The living room windows in my house are best described as odd. In the first place, they are huge, there are four of them, each one is four feet by four feet.

Nothing so unique about that except each one angles outward at the top at 45 degrees.

When I leave the doors and windows open in the warm Summer months, that makes a perfect fly trap, they move up to the top and can't figure out how to get out.

Then I smack them with my fly swatter, or I grab a squirt bottle of window cleaner and spray them. That makes then roll over and crash.

It's kinda fun, I guess.

You can already see how exciting my life is. I am 66 and retired.

The windows are also good at trapping birds, I catch Hummingbirds and the little brown ones, take them outside and turn them loose, much to the chagrin of my Cat. The Cat did try a few times to jump up on the windows to get the birds, but soon figured out there is not a heck of a lot of traction on glass.

Now it just sits there and yowls, which lets me know we have a bird.

The other close family member besides my Cat is Sam, my Dog. She has the rest of her life all figured out, she sleeps. Sometimes she gets up to go eat but then she goes right back to the exact same spot. I just leave the door open in the Summer months, otherwise the Dog wants in..or wants out..same with the Cat.

I thought about one of those doggie doors but Sam is around 90 pounds, so I gave up on that idea.

I was married once to a lively and fun woman named Sheila, but one day she came home from the Doc's office with bad news. That was a bit of a hard time, it was almost like she was there one day and gone the next.

All of my life before seems almost like a dream that happened to someone else. When I turned 62 I told the government to give me my stipend, that along with some savings and investments meant I could relax.

The trouble with relaxing is it gets boring. The great excitement in my life is smacking flies and catching birds.

At night when the Moon is out is the time I wash those four big windows. Smacking bugs makes a mess, I smack bugs a lot, too. But something about bright moonlight streaming in the windows makes every spot just stand out, I can get them perfect and streak free.

That was what I was doing when I saw the white flash of something down by my trees. It was just for a second or two, a brief shadow that darted between the huge Poplar trees that line my front yard, maybe 100 yards away.

I looked more closely, saw it again. I wasn't quite sure what it was, but it was sure as hell moving. I watched for about a half hour, nothing more moved so I went back to cleaning my windows.

The next day I was out mowing my lawn, I looked over and Kay was out there, like always. John and Kay owned the house next door, it sits back a ways from mine. Kay loved to sunbathe out there, which I wouldn't really mind except for the fact that she is about 5 feet tall and six feet around.

Well, not really that bad, her body is odd in that she doesn't have huge rolls of fat.

She is just round.

Not my thing.

She always acts surprised when I drive by close, sitting up and tugging her top back into place. Hell, I am on my riding lawnmower, so I cleverly think she knows I am coming.

That woman has a set on her that I have no idea how she holds them up. She always takes her time stuffing them back in her bikini top, too.

I waved and she waved back with one hand while she pretended to tug on one side of her top. Her giant boob hung out in space, pointed almost straight down, big black nipple the size of my palm.

I never was much into big women, though, or one that belonged to someone else. The truth is that by this point in my life I had almost forgotten what women were really like, although everyone I knew tried to help me out.

Right after Sheila passed I got introduced to every woman with white hair from fifty miles in all directions.

Hell, It was "Hey Dan, I want you to meet Martha, Geraldine, this is Dorothy.." then the big grin as they waited expectantly for me to do something.

A solid string of big'uns, a solid string of white hair. Just not my thing, I managed to stay polite but that was it. Finally everyone gave up on that.

By the time I mowed over to the other side of my yard I looked up and here came Dave. Dave lives on the other side, he likes to come up to the fence and talk to me. I can see his mouth moving so I have to shut off the damn mower to hear him.

"Hey, want a beer?" He asked.

That was different, usually he started right in complaining about his bitch ex wife. I had heard the story maybe 40 times now.

It was hot, a beer sounded good.

"Yea, thanks!" I told him, taking the can. Damn it was cold, just the way I like it.

"Say, didya see the ghost?" He asked, tipping his can back for a swig.

"Ghost?" I asked, wondering if he meant the same thing I saw.

"Yea, down by yer trees. Hadda be a ghost, it was floating and all white. Kinda spooky, huh?"

Whatever I saw didn't seem to be floating to me, it just looked like maybe somebody or something white, hard to tell in the moonlight at that distance.

Of course Dave was usually three sheets to the wind most of the time, enough so that it was a pain in the ass to talk to him.

"Well, thanks for the brew, gotta get back to mowing." I started up the machine and put it in gear. Dave's mouth was still moving as I pulled away. By the time I got over to the other side Kay had rolled over on her stomach. Her top was undone, her giant tits were pressed out each side of her upper body.

She sure as hell didn't need a pillow. I glanced at her, her behind was so big I couldn't even tell if she had on bottoms, although I knew she did.

I sighed and made the last few rounds. Kay somehow managed to be out there most of the time, I had a suspicion she was doing it deliberately.

Maybe John was getting his jollies? I looked up at his house but didn't see anybody.

Hell with it. I put the mower away, went inside to watch People's Court. Later when I woke up I caught two birds and turned them loose, then smacked a few flies.

That night I saw the Moon peek over the Poplar trees, so I got out my squeegee and started to wash them. I was just carefully buffing out the corners when I saw that motion down by my trees again.

The moon was fuller now, and a bit brighter, so I watched for a long time. It seemed to be somebody, then they stepped into view between the trees.

And started doing jumping jacks!

Honest to God.

That sure as hell was no ghost. It sure as hell wasn't floating. I turned and headed for the door, planning to go down there to see what the heck was going on. By the time I got to the porch whoever/whatever it was took off running, down into the ditch and then back up 50 feet farther away.

Hell, I am 66. No way in the world was I going to catch whoever that was.

I just went back inside.

The next day I wandered down there, to look for footprints. It had been dry and hot, even at night it was around 75 degrees. The ground was hard, there were no tracks.

But the grass was knocked down where someone had gone into the ditch, then again where they came out on the road. Not just once or twice, either, but a lot.

I knew there was a development going in perhaps a quarter mile away, but so far only three or four houses were finished so most of the spots were vacant.

I figured it was probably just kids out playing, strange to be doing that at 11 O'clock at night but kids nowadays didn't seem to have any rules like we did when I was a kid.

I saw it again the next night. This time I was on my porch, sitting there in the dark. John and Kay's house was dark so they were in bed, Dave was gone off to some bar somewhere, like always.

I quietly got up and walked over to the fenceline, which put me out of sight. I worked my way down to the trees on Dave's side, then headed back towards whoever it was.

I peeked around just in time to see the person step out and face my house. Then she did jumping jacks, I knew now it was a she because her titties were bouncing up and down.

And she was naked as a jaybird!

I was less than ten feet away before she realized.

"Hello!" I said. She froze, turned slightly towards me. She looked left and right but I was standing in the path I knew she took to escape.

"Oh!" She said, her arms coming up and over her breasts.

"I'm sorry, mister! I was just...." Her other hand came down to hide her crotch.

"Relax, miss. I am harmless, I was just curious as to what you were doing." She started moving sideways, obviously wanting to get past me.

"Hey, it's OK. I have seen pretty girls before." I told her. I gave her my very best disarming grin, which probably was a waste of time since she couldn't really see me that well in the moonlight.

"Oh. You don't..mind?"

"Not one bit, you look like you are having fun."

"Yea, I just…like being naked outside, I only do it when it is dark." She seemed to visibly relax.

"Really? That's interesting. I have heard of things like that but I never saw it before. Is it exciting?"

"Yea. It's dangerous, I could get caught."

"I guess so, I caught you!" I laughed.

"You really aren't upset?"

"No, why should I be? You are really pretty..what I can see of you."

"Nobody ever caught me before…not really." She tipped her head, now she seemed to relax even more, like everything was..normal?

"Hey, want to come up to the house and chat?"

"No, I better not. I should go get my clothes."

"Where are they?"

"Down the street, I hide them by the culvert."

I knew the culvert was about 200 yards away.

"Wow, that really takes courage to go this far with no clothes on."

"Yea, it took me a long time to get this far. Will you let me by, please?"

"Sure." I stepped several feet off the path. She walked by me, slightly wary but I didn't move.

"Hey, can I walk with you? Do you mind?" I asked, on impulse.

She stopped and looked at me, then she grinned.

"Only if you take your clothes off, too!" Then she took off running.

I stood there for awhile, then went back to my house. That was interesting as hell. She was cute, young, well built and obviously unin-hibited.

Just a kid out having fun, she looked to be around 25 or so from what I could see, way younger than me. Her hair was light, hard to say if it was brown or blonde, and she was slender, well built. Not huge in the bust but just nice. Seeing her like that was pretty amazing.

She was just doing silly risky stuff, I had heard of things like that but never really saw any of it. My wife had sometimes dressed a little bit sexy when we were on vacation, once on a beach she had even taken off her top but she spent the whole time with her front plastered to a blanket, and she could manage to put her top on without getting up.

I have no idea why she was so careful, nobody paid any attention at all. There were girls all over the beach wearing tiny patches of cloth and some string. That was as close as I ever got to getting Sheila to do anything really naughty, but even lying there with her naked back showing was kind of a turn on. We screwed like young kids that night in our hotel room.

It was several days later when I saw her again. The moon was at a different angle and it was a lot darker. I went down there half expecting her to take off but she didn't.

"Hello again." I called out from maybe 50 feet away. Can I come over there?"

"Hi, mister. Sure, it's OK."

"I suppose you want me to get naked too?" I intended that as a wisecrack.

"Sure! Go ahead, do it." Her voice sounded like she was laughing.

I hesitated.

"Come on, it will be fun!" She giggled. I could see her face now in the moonlight, she was actually kind of pretty.

What the hell.

I peeled off my shirt, undid my belt and pulled my pants and briefs down. I got the pants legs hung up in my shoes, finally got them kicked off. Then I just stood there.

It felt funny as hell. She looked me up and down, I probably looked white, too. Some would think that would give me a huge hardon but it didn't, I was just…naked?

She was about ten feet away now, there was a tiny flash of moonlight that reflected in her eyes.

"Far out!" She giggled.

"Come on, let's go!" She took off running, I took off right behind her. She ran down into the ditch and up onto the road. The damn pavement was hard on my feet and she was gaining on me, but I gritted my teeth and sped up. Finally we were trotting along side by side. We stopped by the culvert, gasping for breath. I could see her more clearly now.

She looked to be in her early twenties, slim in the waist. Her breasts weren't large, but they were high and firm. There was no sign of any pubic hair at all. She stood there breathing heavily, then she went down over the bank, coming back with a T-shirt and pair of shorts.

Just then I saw some headlights coming.

"Oh, shit!" She darted over the bank and crouched down, I was right behind her.

Dave's car went by, easy to tell since the engine had a loud knock.

"He didn't see us." I whispered.

"Nope. Now let's go back and get your clothes." She tossed her t-shirt and shorts over her shoulder and calmly walked back down the road. Nobody else came by. We went back over under my trees, I tugged my clothes back on and so did she.

"I need to get home now." She turned to leave.

"Hey, wait! What's your name?" I asked her.

"Wendy. What's yours?"

"I'm Dan."

"Nice to meet you, Dan!" She turned and started to trot away.

"That was fun!" She called back over her shoulder, then she was out of sight. This was really crazy, I couldn't believe I had just ran up and down the street stark naked with some naked girl maybe a third my age.

Several nights went by with no sign of her. I even walked down the street to the new housing project, no sign at all of her.

I had almost forgotten about that, except a couple of times I went outside and sat on my porch, not a stitch on. Of course it was dark, nobody could see me but the feeling was really..exciting? It's hard to describe the sensation, it wasn't sexual actually, it was just…free?

Well, maybe a little sexual, once I got an erection so I stood on my porch and played with myself, finally blasting off out into the yard. That was something I had never done in my entire life, not standing up anyway, and certainly not outside. It was incredible, my knees almost gave out on me.

Then several weeks later I was washing my windows. The moon wasn't up all the way yet but I could see outside barely. Suddenly she was there, right in front of my windows. I didn't have the inside lights on since it is easier to clean the windows with just the moonlight.

Wendy was just there, naked again. She waved at me to come out, then moved over towards my porch.

I went out to say hi.

"Hey, you have your clothes on." She grinned.

"Uhh. I can fix that." I quickly stripped off naked. She looked me up and down in the dim light.

"You look pretty good for an older guy!" She giggled.

"You look pretty good for a younger gal!" I answered.

"Let's go walk, want to?"

"OK. Where to?"

"Farther. Just farther. I want to see how far I can get without getting caught..again." She giggled at that.

She reached out to take my hand, we went down to the trees, then turned and headed for town. I was totally aware of how soft her hand felt. It was a cooler evening but I wasn't uncomfortable, really. The little town was nearly 6 miles away.

I was actually hoping she wasn't serious about going all the way to town, I wasn't sure my old legs would even allow that.

"Hey, I saw you!" Her voice had that laugh in it again.

"Saw me? Saw me what?"

"I was there when you…did that outside." She giggled again.

"Oh." I was glad it was dark out, I know I must have turned bright red.

"I'm sorry, I didn't see you."

"I know. It's OK, sometimes I do that too. I liked watching you do that."

Just one car went by, we hid in the grass alongside the road, then we went back out on the pavement. About a mile down the road towards town the other highway intersected, I knew there would be a lot more traffic on that one. The side road up to the subdivision and then the older homes like I lived in was still sparsely travelled.

"Do you want to cross the highway?" I asked her, not too sure of that.

"This is farther than I ever went, let's go back."

"OK." I was actually grateful for that.

We had to duck down twice as someone went by, each time she giggled hysterically. Back at my yard we crossed the grass, then sat down on my porch.

"Want a beer?" I asked her.

"No, but maybe a glass of wine would be nice if you have some." I did have some, a bottle someone had given me of some dark red stuff. I had tasted it and didn't like it. I poured her a small glass.

"This is really good!" She said after taking a sip.

"So what do you do, Dan?" Wendy asked me, leaning back looking completely relaxed. It was interesting to look at her, the way the moonlight was casting shadows across her body made it look like she had on some kind of net like outfit. I realized the chair she was in was slightly behind my Rose trellis, it had angled slats in it. The Roses had long since given up, something about water I think.

"I guess I don't do much, I am retired." I told her.

"You don't look old enough to be retired." She took another sip of the wine, made a face. I grinned to myself at that.

"Can I ask you why you like to do this?"

"I don't know, it is just..exciting? I know it's crazy but I feel so free and alive."

"Ever been caught?"

"Just by you, although once someone in a car saw me and stopped, but I hid in the brush until they left."

"That was pretty close the other night when Dave went by, wasn't it?"

"Who is Dave?"

"He lives over there." I waved my arm at the house next door.

"Oh, that guy? He was looking out the window at me a couple of weeks ago but I was too far away for him to see anything, so I kept going back and forth between the trees. Then I did some jumping jacks. Once he started down there but I took off." She giggled at that.

"He said he thought you were a ghost."

"I am a ghost! Well, I try to be anyway. Hey, the Sheriff's car parks down by the pond, I sneaked up on it and actually touched it before I ran once."

"I am curious, is it a sexual thing?"

"NO! Well…yes..oh, I don't know, it's just..exciting." Wendy stood up suddenly, set down her glass.

"I gotta go." She headed out across my lawn at a trot.

"Will you come back?" I called out.

"Maybe, look for the ghost!" Her laughter seemed to bounce off the trees back at me, then she was out of sight.

I sat there on my porch for quite a long time.

The next day I looked out, no sign of Kay or anyone, so I went and fired up my riding lawnmower. I was about halfway done when I looked over and Kay came out, this time she had on a bright yellow bikini.

Right on schedule. I did my best to ignore her, she waved at me as I went down the fenceline, I waved back. She was flopped out on her back, the color of her outfit was so bright against the green grass that it kept catching my eye.

I came back around, she sat up and waved at me again, so I stopped.

"Morning, Danny! Want a beer?" She reached in a cooler and pulled out a bottle. I took it and had a sip, as she sat there and watched me.

I was thinking that if Dave and Kay kept coming up with beer I wouldn't need to buy any of my own.

"You don't mind my sunbathing out here, do you?" She gave me a big smile.

"No, it's fine." The top of that thing she had on was maybe three inches wide, she had about eight inches of flesh hanging out both sides. She almost looked squashed.

"I normally prefer to sunbathe nude but I didn't want to upset you." She sipped her beer, then actually batted her eyes at me.

"Oh, you won't upset me, I have seen girls before." I told her, almost instantly regretting that.

"Good! This thing is killing me!" One tug and it was gone, her huge breasts flopped down, she lay back and opened her legs enough that I could see the flash of yellow at her crotch.

"Thanks for the beer!" I told her, firing up the engine and taking off. Kay still had the bottoms on when I came back by.

Thank God.

A couple of days later Dave came over, I was sitting on the porch enjoying the sunshine, watching my sprinklers spraying my lawn. It was always a complete pain in the ass, no matter how I set them up or what kind of sprinkler I used, I always had to move them to get it all.

I managed to stifle a giggle at him, he made it almost all the way when the sprinkler came around, so he sort of skipped faster but he was already on his way so he was a little unsteady. The sprinkler blasted his pant leg and went on by.

He came up on the porch, reached down and patted at his wet leg for a second, then he handed me a beer.

"Hey, I saw that ghost again!"

"No shit? Where?"

"It was down by the trees, It looks like a woman in a white dress." He looked at me for a reaction.

"I think I saw it once, it's probably just a reflection." I lied.

"Naw, it's real! I bet somebody has been murdered around here, I bet there is a body out in them woods."

"Could be." I took a swig off the beer, wishing he would buy the good stuff.

"Yea, it's like I see her out of the corner of my eye but when I look she ain't there."

I realized he was drunk as a skunk.

"Ghosts can't hurt you." I told him.

"Yea, I guess not. Say, did you see John's old lady?"

"Sure, what about her?"

"She was laying out there nekkid as a jaybird."

"Really? I see her sunbathing all the time but just with her top off."

"I saw her the other day, she was nekkid. I could see right up between her legs. She has it shaved as bare as a newborn babie's bottom." He snickered at himself.

Hell, it was 200 yards from Dave's fenceline to John and Kay's.

"How could you be sure?"

"I used my field glasses!" Then he started laughing, wiped his nose.

"Maybe she is what you have been seeing, she likes to run around half naked all the time?"

"Naw, Kay is maybe 250 pounds, that ghost is way smaller."

I was thinking closer to 300 pounds but I didn't say anything. Finally Dave got up and left, it took him two tries to get to his feet.

So Kay had gone to the next step, or at least that is what Dave had said. For whatever that was worth. I sat there and laughed at the idea of him peering at her with field glasses. Hell, why not just walk up to the fence, I doubted she would care.

Everything went back to normal around my house except for late in the evenings I went out and sat on my porch. If Dave was gone off somewhere and John and Kay's house was dark I would strip down and sit out there in the dark.

I was not even sure why, it just felt good. It became something of a habit. Nearly a Month went by with no sign of Wendy, I was beginning to wonder if I would ever see her again. My walks down to the housing development gained me nothing, I never saw any sign of her.

I now even washed my windows in the nude, in bright moonlight no one could see in unless they got real close. The weather began to cool, I still sat out on my porch, sometimes until way into the early morning hours, but I took a fuzzy warm comforter with me.

It actually felt good to be sitting out there, I could hear crickets and frogs, the sounds all around lulled me to sleep.

I had a tendency to sleep where and whenever I felt like it anyway, most of the time I tipped back the recliner with the TV on and dozed off.

I felt very warm, woke up to the Sun shining in my face. I blinked a couple of times, realized someone was standing there.

"Are you OK, Danny?" Kay asked. I looked over and there she was, wearing a tank top and shorts.

"Uhh…Yea, I'm fine."

"I saw you out here early this morning, then when I looked out and you hadn't moved…."

"I'm OK, I just dozed off."

"Well, you are getting sunburned, we better get you inside."

"Oh, I am all right." I protested.

"Come on, let me help you." She reached out and tugged on the comforter, suddenly there I was, stark naked.

She looked down, blinked.

"Oh!. I didn't...."

"Damn it, Kay!" I protested, grabbing the blanket.

"Oh, relax...I have seen men before. But, WOW!" She giggled, staring at my dick sticking out between my legs.

"It's all right." I said, getting up with the blanket tugged back up around me. I realized that making things even worse, I had a morning erection.

I turned and went inside, she was right behind me.

She was still there when I came out of the bedroom in my jeans and a levi shirt.

"You sure are a lot bigger than John is!" She actually batted her eyes at me. I didn't say anything, went to the fridge and got a glass of milk.

What the hell was she doing in my kitchen? I glanced over at her, she had one elbow on my table, those giant boobs were hanging there barely covered by the silly tank top she had on.

"I didn't mean to embarrass you, I didn't know...." She said, then she grinned.

"But I always wanted to know what that looked like..." She added.

"Kay..." I started to say.

"Don't you like me?" She asked, standing up.

"I like you just fine, but John...."

"John doesn't mind, in fact he told me I could."

"Could? Could what?" I got a sinking feeling.

Kay stood up, moved around the table towards me, I started to back up.

"Why don't you let me take care of that for you?"

"Kay, I like you just fine but I am not going to…"

I swear to God, she pouted.

"All right. But just so you know, if you ever get in the mood…for ANYTHING, just let me know." She stressed the "anything" part.

"Uhhh..ok, I will."

She mercifully headed for the front door, twitching her butt from side to side. Thank God she missed the door frame. She stopped and looked back at me for a moment, I felt a bit like a chunk of meat in front of a hungry Dog.

"I hope so, Danny." Then she was gone.

Lord.

I went into the bathroom and did my morning business, then I was upset at myself because I had a damn hardon. Why, I didn't have a clue, Kay didn't turn me on, at least I was pretty sure she didn't anyway.

Later, I had to put up with Dave coming over wanting to know all about it, how was she, all of that shit. It seemed that he was outside watching when Kay came out my front door.

Of course. Probably with his damned field glasses.

"Nothing happened, she just saw me asleep on the porch and got concerned."

"Man, I would do that in a New York minute!" He said, the ever present can of cheap beer in his hand.

"Why don't you just go ask her?" I told him. I was getting a little bit fed up with Dave.

"Maybe I will!" He said, then he turned and ambled back towards his yard. Halfway across, I reached over and hit the button on my sprinklers. He took a couple of hops, then managed to get out of range.

"Sorry!" I called out. "They are set on automatic." I lied. Snickering to myself, I went back inside.

My phone rang seconds later. I decided to ignore it, the answering machine clicked on. Then I heard Wendy's voice, damn near broke my leg getting to the phone.

"Hello!"

"Hi, Danny."

"What's up? Say, how did you get my number?"

"Phone book, you are listed and your last name is on your mailbox."

"OH. Well, what's up?"

"I want to go to town…tonight." I knew what she meant.

"Really?"

"Yea, really. Want to go with me?"

"OK. What time?"

"I will just come over when I am ready, OK?"

"OK. It's going to be a little bit cool."

"We will be warm enough."

"OK. See you tonight."

"You sure will!" She giggled and hung up.

I was excited all day. I now regularly went out and sat on my porch naked at night, but while that was fun and exciting, it wasn't the same as running around outside naked with Wendy. That was actually strange, I really knew almost nothing about her, not even where she lived or anything.

By midnight, I had just about given up, when suddenly there she was.

"Ready?" She asked.

"I guess so." She reached out and took my hand.

"All the way and back, let's do it this time!" Her voice was excited. Hell, I was feeling a bit excited myself.

It took us over two hours, there was almost no traffic. Twice we ducked into the bushes when someone went by, then we rounded the last turn before town. There were street lights there, and I got my first really good look at Wendy. She seemed to hold her shoulders back, her nice round breasts had dark nipples, they were hard as a rock. I felt myself getting an erection, Wendy glanced down at me and grinned.

"Me, too!" She giggled. We made it all the way to the chain link fence by the ball field, then we turned and headed back. The sheriff's car went by but we were well hidden in the brush by the time he reached where we were.

I was all but worn out by the time we got to my house, the night was just cool enough to cause goosebumps but the exertion kept us warm. I guessed it was close to 5 in the morning.

"Hungry?" I asked her.

"Yea, a little."

"Come on in, I can make some pancakes."

She smiled slyly and followed me inside. I left the lights off, not sure how she would react. She sat down on my couch as I went in and turned on the stove. I had a stack of pancakes whipped up in just a few minutes, took her a plate. It was just starting to get light outside, I glanced at the windows and realized she had opened all the curtains.

We sat there naked in the living room and ate. After we had finished, I took the plates and brought her a cup of coffee.

"That was sure fun, we actually did it!" She smiled.

"Yep, we did. I wasn't sure that we would make it but we did."

"Say, would you like to…look at me?" There was a catch in her voice.

"I can see you just fine." I told her.

"No, I mean more."

"More? Sure, I would love to."

Wendy leaned back on the couch, then she slowly opened her legs. Her outer lips parted slightly, she reached down and used her fingers to spread them even more.

"How's that?" She grinned, holding the pose. I could see she was damp, shiny.

"Beautiful!" I told her, feeling myself begin to erect at her blatant display.

"Come closer?" She asked.

"OK." I got up and moved over to in front of the couch, I was just inches away now.

"Your cock is hard, can I touch it? You can…touch me if you want to." I could tell she was completely excited now.

I reached out and stroked her bare sex with one hand, then I scooted up beside her on the couch. Her hand came down and wrapped around me, just held me. We sat there and touched each other for a long time. Then she rolled over and pressed against me.

"I shouldn't...but I want to!" She lifted up and straddled me, reached down and grasped my rock hard penis and set the end right against her opening. She looked me right in the eyes, then slid her hips down and over me. I lay back and let her work, marvelling at the way her breasts bounced up and down as she used her legs to pump at me. Then she pressed me down flat on my back and stretched out, breasts mashed against me, her hips working furiously.

Her body was tighter than I was used to with my late wife, and she was much more energetic.

I managed to hold back until I saw her eyelids flutter, her head went back with her mouth open. She opened her legs so my pubic bone pressed firmly against her, then she groaned. I just relaxed and let it go.

"God, you were really hard!" She said later, as we lay pressed against each other. Then she hopped up and went into the bathroom.

"Can I borrow a shirt?" She asked when she came back out.

"Sure, help yourself." She poked around in my dresser and found a T-shirt, tugged it over her head.

"My clothes are down by the culvert, it's daylight out." She grinned. She went to the door, looked back at me.

"I didn't plan that, you know. I just... It just seemed...right?"

"I didn't mind at all!" I grinned at her. I was still sitting there naked on the couch. Then she was gone.

Four months went by with no sign of her. I just mowed my lawn, slapped bugs. The weather cooled, I put my gear away for the Winter, got some firewood put in.

I needed some supplies, so I headed off to town on one of my rare shopping trips. Coming out of the grocery store I looked up and there Wendy was.

There was a young man right behind her.

"Hello, Dan, nice to see you!" She smiled.

"Well, Hi, Wendy! It's been quite awhile." She reached back and tugged on the sleeve of the young man.

"Jerry, this is Dan, he lives down the road from us. Dan, this is my husband, Jerry."

I shook his hand, managing to keep a straight face. They turned and headed on into the store. Just before the door closed, Wendy looked back at me and winked.

Man. I just don't do anybody's wife. Oh, hell, what was I thinking, I actually don't normally do anybody at all anymore.

What the hell, no use crying over spilled milk and all of that.

Besides, I had to admit that it was fun.

That night I was sitting on my porch, it was pretty cool out and I was about to get up and go back inside, since I was sitting there in the dark, naked.

"Hi!" The voice startled me, I wasn't expecting it.

"Hello, Wendy." I answered, looking over her way. She was standing by my dead Rose bushes, also naked like she always was when she appeared.

"Can I come in?" She asked.

"Sure, it's a little cool out here."

Oh well, what the hell.

Inside, I had to ask her.

"What about Jerry, your husband?"

"I told him..about the...incident, I really didn't mean for that to happen."

"OH. You mean…what did he say?"

"Nothing, he just left me. Packed his bags and got in his truck and left."

"Oh, I am sorry."

"I'm not, I had had enough of him anyway. He has more girlfriends on the side than your Tomcat does!" She grinned at me, then plopped down on my couch.

"Can I stay here with you?"

"Stay? I..sure, I guess so." I told her, she beamed at me.

"What about your house?"

"Rented."

"Clothes?"

"Down by the culvert!" She laughed.

I went into the kitchen, I had a pot of tea on the stove. I poured two cups and went back into the living room. She was sitting there on my couch. She looked so beautiful sitting there naked.

What the hell. So was I. I could already feel the beginnings of an erection when I sat down beside her. She slid one hand across my chest, tipped her head over onto my shoulder.

What the hell. I didn't mind one bit.

A GOOD WOMAN WILL FIND HIM

Brown haired and green-eyed Guy Meadows was left confused when seeking to find is the optimum age to marry because the opinions varied widely. He settled on twenty-eight and planned accordingly.

He studied hard at college and emerged with a masters in business administration and after settling into permanent employment upgraded that to an MBA.

By the time he was twenty-seven Guy was director of operations for a company that manufactured, imported and distributed LP gas and electric grills and barbecues.

He was on track to marry next year, having recently become engaged to Penny Whitehead, assistant IT manager at a bank.

Penny was rather conservative but Guy's parents thought she was lovely so he thought that was something. The months ticked by and then, without consulting Guy, Penny applied successfully for promotion in IT at a bigger branch of the bank 1700 miles away and expected Guy to resign and relocate with her.

No way.

Guy had grown up in Welling, felt it really was his home, and loved his job. So Penny was left to choose between Guy and her promotion.

She dumped Guy.

Guy's mom Mary was shocked. "The little bitch; she would have given me lovely grandchildren."

"You did the right thing letting her go," his father said. "Your career comes first."

Well his dad always had been a practical thinker.

Guy sold the engagement ring back to the jeweler who'd supplied it at 60% less than what he'd paid for it. However the jeweler said he'd give Guy a 40% discount on the next ring he sold to him and that seemed fair. Guy believed he was lucky that Penny had handed the ring back and grinned thinking she looked quite shocked when he'd taken the offered ring and said thanks, pocketing it.

During this twenty-eighth year Guy had become aware that his projected wedding might have to be put back a year or perhaps longer. Becoming engaged to a replacement babe had proven more difficult than expected. Because he had a good physique and long brown hair, and plenty of it, and brooding green to hazel eyes he thought women would line up for him. Well his mom had said they would.

Well they almost did that, the gaps between them were fairly short, but all of them wanted dates and money spent on them, good sex but as soon as Guy became serious about a relationship each date would disconnect from him. He also found some of the bitches had lied and they weren't single.

Six weeks from his 31st birthday Guy and Hazel Hunter became engaged. She appeared too wide in the ass for Guy's liking but when he'd mentioned that to his mom she'd said nonsense, Hazel had 'magnificent child-bearing hips'. A month later Guy's employer began firing workers because the company was heading for insolvency and six weeks later it closed it's doors and he was declared redundant. He'd still not found a new position a month later and at that point Hazel dumped him.

His dad said she was disloyal and anyway he hadn't wanted a daughter-in-law 'with such a fat ass'.

Fortunately Guy had two younger sisters, both of whom had married and they each had produced a grandchild so his mom was no longer too concerned about him siring grandchildren but she still remained keen to have the family name perpetuated.

Guy's longtime friend had been fired for gross negligence at his job as an insurance company claims inspector and wanted to out of their shared apartment. Guy had saved well and thought it was a good investment so purchased Gary's holding. He then advertised for a tenant for the vacated room and to share apartment facilities. Eight guys and a female applied.

Danielle Grant who's disclosed she was forty-four looked at Guy over the empty coffee cups.

"My marriage had collapsed and I'm filing for divorce. I desperately need somewhere to live and this apartment is near where I work. You are asking for $785 a month. I'll pay you one thousand a month."

"W-e-l-l I don't know, Guy said, concentrating to avoid telling this applicant she could not have the accommodation because she was female, knowing that could have her file a claim for sexual discrimination. She'd probably do that, being an attorney.

Danielle apparently mistook Guy's hesitation as a bargaining dodge. She ran her tongue along her top lip and said cutely, "Perhaps there is something else I could offer to tempt you?"

"Like what?" he frowned and only then did he realize what she might be suggesting.

"God you are a tough negotiator. To close the deal I'm suggesting I'm willing to have sex with you during my residency here."

Steady on Guy, he warned himself. If he said yes she could plead sexual extortion or whatever it was called.

"Well I don't know."

"Are you worried about possible criminal repercussions in the wake of any complaint if we do a deal based on sex?"

"It has me worried."

She smiled and said first could he answer a question, "Would you be willing to have sex with me?"

Guy used her tactic and ran his tongue over his top lip.

She giggled. "Let's do it this way. We sign the agreement for three months at a thousand dollars a month. We make no agreement about sex but you know I have made the offer. You have to decide whether or not you trust me."

"Let's sign!"

She smiled and said she believed they would get along very well. "I'll regard you as my toy boy."

* * *

Guy jerked off twice in the shower on Thursday night thinking about the excitement ahead of him next day.

Danielle had arranged for her husband's attorney to be at the marital home on Friday afternoon while she brought in a relocation crew to pack all her possessions, most of which would be taken away for long-term storage.

Just before 4:00, guys arrived with the four pieces of furniture and four paintings Guy had agreed to have in the apartment, one of the items being Danielle's heirloom dressing table with mirror. Then in came eight big cartons the guys said were filled with clothes and shoes.

They left and Danielle arrived and kissed Guy beautifully, He thought the necessities should come before sex and suggested they go and buy a two vertical racks for her shoes and two self-standing racks for her clothes because the generous sized closest in her bedroom would be totally inadequate.

Half an hour later they were back and while Guy assembled the shoe racks and clothing stands Danielle unpacked. Just over an hour later they were finished.

She placed a hand on his shoulder affectionately. "Come on, let's go our for a drink and I'll buy you dinner."

"I-I would like to lick your pussy first."

Her eyes widened and she colored and said she couldn't think of anything more she'd like better.

Without asking him where did he want her to position, Danielle hoisted herself up on to the dining table and lay back, spreading her legs.

Guy dribbled, wiped his chin and strode purposely forward and flicked her panty leg aside and crooned, "You smell lovely."

She laughed, "Liar."

Her ran his hands gently up the outside of her hold-ups thinking she had rather good legs for an elderly woman. He assumed elderly included forty-four year olds.

He reached the flesh above the stocking tops and licked some flesh.

Danielle groaned and her legs widened.

He straightened and gently tugged at the top of her high-cut panties and she lifted her ass without being asked, as if she'd don this before.

"Nice cunt," he said approving and noted Danielle now appeared to be panting for some reason.

Without warning she reached out, grabbled handfuls of his hair and yanked his face down on to her neatly trimmed bush. Her hair there was brown whereas her other hair was a dull dark-honey blonde. Ah so one of those hair colorings was artificial.

Danielle shoved down her hands and spread her outer lips for him.

Guy took a moment to study this normally concealed part of her body. It looked clean and healthy pink and was lubricating well. He reached out with his tongue and gently made connection dead center.

Danielle screamed and her whole body began jerking and she puffed, "Oh god, omigod."

Guy though obviously she wanted work done so went to work with his tongue and fingers, surprised as just how wet Danielle was so early into the act.

As they walked out of the apartment building Danielle, still breathing a little heavily, asked, "Do you know what cunnilingus is?"

"I-think so."

"Then please accept this compliment my young friend. In that department you are world class."

Guy frowned and asked how on earth would she know that and Danielle said mysteriously she'd been around.

Over the next few weeks Danielle worked on Guy's confidence and taught him things about women and updating his thinking even about life in an attempt to make him project in a more worldly manner. He cooperated fully, aware that he was a little naïve in some areas.

Danielle called one of her clients who knew someone beefing up company management and the after an extensive interview the company CEO gave Guy a 10-day contact to investigate and report on this company's administration and efficiency problems. The CEO took Guy's findings to the board and the CEO was instructed to fire the director of operations and director of sales of the hardware manufacturing and distribution company and to replace them. The CEO appointed Guy as director of operations and deputy CEO of the business that had 470 people on its payroll.

Guy was almost speechless in excitement when he rushed into Danielle's office at her law firm to give her the news of his appointment. She was delighted and took him to early lunch. That night when Danielle arrived home her sexy partner who was no longer jobless handed her a first-class return air ticket to Germany. Her daughter worked there in a laboratory of a giant international pets and livestock foods company to widen her education in development of animal nutritional supplements.

Before Danielle left for Germany Guy thought it was time to introduce her to his parents. He called his mom who was pleased he was in a relationship with a woman again and she invited them to lunch on Sunday.

* * *

Peggy was looking out the lounge window telling Daryl for the third time how she wanted the steak grilled when she stopped the nag and said, "Here they are."

"I hope this one isn't bossy, or has a fat ass over over-sized tits…"

"Don't be foul darling. The right woman will find our son eventually. Omigod."

"What?"

"He hasn't bought the girlfriend; he's arrived with her mother."

Daryl joined her at the window and said, "Judging by the way he has his arm around her and hanging on to the far-side tit I'd say this is the girlfriend, absolutely."

"Oh god, don't say that," Peggy wailed.

"Our son has begun dating grannies," Daryl said, pinching his wife's ass and having that hand smacked away.

Smiles were few in the heavy atmosphere on the porch after the introductions as Danielle and Guy waited to be invited in. Finally Daryl took the initiative and said, "Come in honey and view my collection of perfume bottles. What did Guy say what your name was?"

"Danielle but I find Honey is very acceptable. Excuse me Mrs Meadows while I go with Mr Meadows to view his collection."

"I keep the bottles to remind me where all my money has gone over the years," Daryl growled and his wife glared but Peggy's face lit up when Danielle turned and said, "Oh Mrs Meadows, I almost forgot to give you this. She thrust a hand into her shoulder bag and pulled out a perfume pack.

"Oh how lovely," Peggy said. "Estée Lauder Private Collection Tuberose Gardenia," she called, just glancing at the box and then reading the label cried, "Omigod, it's the eau de parfum spray, solid perfume!"

"Yes Guy had mentioned you were a connoisseur and he said the same for you Mr Meadows about whisky," Danielle smiled, handing across a bottle of Highland Park 12-year-old scotch. Daryl licked his lips and said, "Honey you are our very special guest."

"Yes welcome to our home," Peggy said warmly.

After that Danielle did nothing to ingratiate herself, just acting normally and leaving it to Guy's parents to accept or reject her on their own judgment.

Lunch went well and even Peggy had to admit the steaks were grilled to perfection.

At they waved the visitors off, Daryl said expansively, after a couple of wines too many, "Well that went well. She has great tits and a great ass."

"I suppose so. You know I really like her but what can I say to my friends, knowing my son's new lady friend is only ten years my junior."

"Don't mention age."

Peggy snorted and said he knew her friends, of course they would ask.

"Then be vague and lie that you don't know and say somewhere between thirty and fifty."

"Omigod you can be quite intelligent at times darling. Look leave finishing clearing away. Just deal with the scraps. I feel a little heated up and would like some attention."

"Yes dear," Daryl said, wondering if his wife had forgotten it was not the last Sunday of the month.

* * *

Ten months went by. Danielle had returned from Germany with photos of herself with her daughter and Guy had thought the daughter looked rather dishy but perhaps a little reserved. He idly wondered if she could fuck as well as her mom did.

Danielle had taken on a new client and told Guy she was rather impressed by him. A few evenings later she told Guy her new client Gus Roper had asked her to go out with him.

Guy asked what did she feel about that and she said, "A bit girly all over again."

He grinned. "Then do it. Life's too short to miss opportunities that could be taken."

Danielle said carefully, "Are you sure? He's great looking with plenty of money, divorced and about my age. It could be the end of you and me as a couple if he gets his hands on me."

"Do whatever makes you happy. Keep on fucking me until he wants in and at that stage simply advise me and move back to your room."

"Are you sure?"

"Yes."

Ten days later Danielle said, "Gus wants me to go away with him for the weekend. I told him about you and he simply said then choose and I said I'd let him know."

"Fine do it. I'll find someone else."

"You are such a gentleman about this. I feel like an ungrateful slut."

"You and I have had a great time together Danielle. You have become a big part of my life and got me back into work and I feel I'm a better person because of you. I like you very much and love fucking you but I don't love you and we both know that. It just didn't happen."

"I know and know I feel the same way. It seems we were not meant to progress our relationship further."

They talked that out and when she returned from calling Gus she said, "Do you mind if I bring April here for dinner tomorrow night?"

"April your PA?"

"Yes."

"No of course I don't mind. I've only seen her a couple of times but have talked to her a bit on the phone while waiting for you to come off your phone. She seems a very nice woman.

April was a little plump and her sexy mouth was perhaps her best physical feature and she talked too much but Guy found her okay and the three of them related well. When April rose to leave Danielle said she was off to run a bath. "Please put April into a cab Gus." She then kissed April good night.

As soon as they entered the elevator April fell against Guy, pressing him into a corner and kissed him soundly. She wasn't drunk but even so when her tongue entered his mouth he wasn't surprised. He sucked it and she groaned.

The doors opened and it was over.

Or so he thought.

As they walked to the outer doors to flag a cab she said, "You penis felt very hard against my leg."

"What penis. That was my car keys."

"Liar," she laughed just as a cab drew up outside to drop off the passenger.

Next day just before 1:00 Guy was on a bike in the company's gym when his phone went.

"Hi it's Alice. What are you doing?"

"Pumping flat out."

"Oooh," she giggled. "but you can't be. Danielle is walking away from me now."

"I'm pushing pedals on a bike in our office gym."

She giggled again. "Danielle has told me your two are redefining your relationship while she attempts to find out how compatible she and one of her clients are. What do you think of me spending Friday night and through to Sunday morning with you?"

"What for?"

She just giggled.

Guy said he would talk it over with Danielle.

"Do that but why do you think she brought me home to have dinner with you guys last night?"

"I wonder if I've guessed?"

"It was for me to look you over and to decide whether I would like doing it with you. Well after that big fat kiss in the elevator with you I informed her this morning that you may fuck me cross-eyed although I was more polite than that."

"You sound my kind of woman Alice but first I must talk to Danielle."

"Please do that. Expect me to arrive Friday about 6:30."

* * *

Alice arrived just after 6:15 and said hi and brushed by and went into the kitchen, followed by Guy eying her excessive ass sway.

She put down her overnight bag and stood, watchfully.

"Drink?"

She nodded and as he opened the fridge and pulled out a jug of vodka martinis he saw her unhurriedly lift her skirt and rip off her panties and sniff them. As he approached she held out the panties and he sniffed them and smiled, and that was about all he could do because he was carrying the jug and two cocktail glasses.

"Sexy odor,' he smiled and she smiled and sat.

"I suggest we have a couple of drinks, have some good sex and go out to dinner."

She pouted and grizzled did they have to go out.

"Alice sweetheart, I aim to perform with distinction tonight but you have to give me some breaks."

She smiled and said of course, she wouldn't want to burn him out early and took her drink.

* * *

Alice left mid morning on Sunday and although Guy kissed her goodbye warmly he wasn't pleased. She'd taken a phone call and he suspected she was having an angry conversation because after she shut the door he heard her raise her voice and that made him wonder if the 26-year old had a boyfriend.

Later when she was in the shower she'd left no instructions about her phone so when it rang Guy answered it.

"Is that Alice's phone," a woman asked sharply.

Guy reacted fast and cunningly. "I don't know. There are several phones here and I was passing and answered it."

"I'm Mrs Banks, Alice's mother. I wish to speak to Alice please. It's urgent, about her husband?"

Her husband? Well the mother ought to know. Guy felt let down by Alice and even more so by Danielle. They should have told him Alice was married, even if she was separated from him. It was only fair. As it was he'd inadvertently committed adultery. That outcome made him very cross.

"Just a moment," he said to Mrs Banks. "I'll try to find her."

He took the phone into the shower and whispered, "It's your mother. I thought it best to give the impression you were with a group of other women."

As he walked out of the bathroom Guy heard Alice say, "Hi mom. Susan has taken a bunch of us to her gym to inspect the facilities and to have breakfast there."

He muttered women and then decided to visit his own mother as soon as Alice left and to stay for lunch.

When he arrived back at the apartment Danielle was already home, acting quite perky. She looked at him and said, "Christ Alice has left you looking half dead."

Well it was the truth so he shrugged and looked sheepish.

Her next comment was nothing short of sensational. "Gus Roper proposed to me last night and I accepted. You don't mind do you?"

"No of course not," he said warmly and hugged her. "It's your big chance so take it. I wish you all the best."

"Gus wants me to move in with him now. What do you think?"

"Okay, this is just an option. I suggest you stay here till the wedding and set an early date. That way he'll remain keen to marry you to get you into bed with him every night but I'm not the right person to advise you."

"Well you have thought exactly what I think. I'll call him now."

Danielle returned fifteen minutes later, switching off her phone, and said they had set the date for six weeks from tomorrow. "The delay is to give my daughter time to make arrangements to be here for the wedding. Will you be best man for Gus and partner Montana who'll be my bridesmaid, at least I hope she well agree to that honor."

"Yes certainly. So her name is Montana. That's the first time I've heard you use the name. Montana Naples, a great name."

"If you think so. Cliff insisted she be called Montana and ignored my objections."

"I understand. Tell your daughter she can stay here when she visits and I'll stay with my parents."

"Oh that is lovely of you Guy. I have plenty of money and would be quite happy staying at a hotel."

"Happier that staying here with your daughter?"

"Well no. Thanks for your generosity. I accept the offer."

CHAPTER 2

Guy had checked the photograph Danielle kept on her dresser and fixed the image in his mind and now was waiting at the airport as the last aircraft for the evening arrived.

Ninety minutes earlier Alice had called him from his apartment to say she and Dianne, an attorney from their law firm, had brought Danielle home from her hen's party and she was out to it, drunk.

He'd been due to drive Danielle in an hour's time to the airport so rushed over to help sober her up. But it was no use. Danielle awoke when shaken but refused to drink black coffee or water and kept falling asleep.

"Oh this is so sad," Alice said. "She was having such a great time at the party that she must have lost count of how many drinks she was consuming."

Dianne went home to her family. Alice stayed with Danielle and Guy went alone to the airport.

He failed to spot a tall blonde among the arrivals who was not claimed by waiting friends or family. Finally he saw a tall woman in a light coat and white hat looking towards the entrance and guessed it was the daughter.

"Miss Naples, Montana Naples?" he asked and her aggressive reply startled him.

"Where is my mother? What have you done with her?"

"Pardon me," Guy said, his mind reeling. "What on earth are you talking about?"

"My mother is not here to meet me. I assume you are Mr Meadows."

"Yes I'm Guy Meadows but please keep calm. Your mother simply had too much to drink at her bridal shower this afternoon and is asleep. She was in no condition to be here."

"I only have your word for that."

"Do you know Alice her PA?"

"Yes and I spoke to her again only two days ago."

Guy pulled out his phone and said Alice was at the shared apartment with her mother. "Speed dial 88 to talk to Alice now."

Montana looked at the phone and then looked at Guy. "That won't be necessary Mr Meadows. Your story and offer of your phone makes your story too plausible to be unbelievable. I apologize for my sharpness. I'm tired and became stressed when finding you have arrived without my mother."

"I accept your apology and can now understand your reaction. In the months I've been living with your mother I have not seen her drink excessively. Alice said they were drinking champagne and some of the thirty women there were hitting it along and kept topping up Danielle's glass. Alice assumed your mother handled champagne well."

"No she sticks to still wine because her tolerance to sparkling wine is low."

"Well that's settled," he smiled. "Could we start again?"

She smiled and nodded.

"Hi Montana, lovely to meet you at last. Do I kiss you?"

Montana said hi Guy and offered her cheek. Guy felt like grabbing a tit to really give her something to get stirred up about.

"Come we must claim your luggage."

"I have rather a lot. I have resigned from my job and have come home for good. Some of my possession will come via sea and land including my car."

Guy said that was no problem, his work vehicle was large.

When Montana saw the latest model Cadillac Escalade she said, "This is an expensive vehicle. Mom said you work at Smith and Matheson. What do you do there?"

"I'm director of operations and deputy CEO."

"But that's a large company and you are only… um thirty?"

"Thirty-two in two months."

"God you really must have impressed them. What are your qualifications?"

"MBA and solid experience with emphasis on driving people to achieve targets and problem-solving. I started off the analytical way with a BA in computer science."

"Well in my mind I had you figured as a gigolo although mom denied that. She had told me you were jobless when you two first met."

"Yes, that was true. In fact one of her clients referred me to Smith and Matheson and obviously I impressed in the problem they tossed at me to solve. Firing the direction of operations was one of my recommendations and the company took the easy way out and engaged me as that guy's replacement."

Guy looked at the exposed inner thigh as she climbed into her seat. He looked up to find her looking at him steadily and apparently surprised her by not looking away or mumbling an apology. Instead he smiled and said, "Your mother also has lovely legs. Genetics at work I should think. Are your tired?"

"Yes we had a frustrating delay before leaving Rome and that meant I missed my connection to come on to here and that's why I had to call mom to change my arrival time till late. Had that not happened she would not have had time to drink so much and would have been here to meet me."

Guy knew to be gentle. "I apologize on her behalf but please attempt to laugh it off. She's been on a high recently and that really peaked about ten days ago when she asked me for my honest opinion about Gus."

"So you have remained living with my mother?"

"In a manner of speaking. When she told me about Gus it was agreed she should stay on but shift back to her own room."

"I bet that wasn't your idea."

Guy ignored that and said he'd had to answer the question about Gus carefully believing Danielle might be wondering about marrying for the second time. Aware Montana was eyeing him intently he said, "Danielle is a lovely woman and has been a great mentor to me so I knew this was more a plea over self-doubt than a simply probe for me to be upfront about what I thought about Gus. Strip away the emotion and nicety of language and she was asking did I think she would be happy with Gus long term. I honestly thought they would have a good chance of making a real go at it. In the last three weeks Gus had been at the apartment almost daily and we often went to dinner as a threesome or else I cooked."

"You cook? Now I understand why mom latched on to you."

Guy laughed and said that was the first nice thing she'd said to him because it was spontaneous and had humor.

"Oh god, I'm truly sorry. You must understand I was hostile about you being so young sleeping with my mother."

"Yes I understand."

"Well I think you do."

He grinned and said his mom had told him her daughter was a very lovely young woman. "How old are you?"

"Twenty-four. You were saying…?"

"I said the truth was Gus has grown on me and I believed he really had your mother's interests at heart and I admired how gentle he was with her whenever I saw them together."

"Wow that must impressed mom?"

"Well to be honest she doesn't have many truly emotional moments but that was one of them."

"Thank you for telling me that," Montana said.

As he changed on freeways for the short drive into the CBD, Guy said, "Does that mean I'm not such a bad guy, that Gus sounds like he's all right and your mom's judgment over choosing men hasn't plummeted after all?"

Montana sighed, "God do you have to be so brutal?

Alice met them at the door, rubbing her eyes.

The two women hugged, greeting one another warmly and Alice said to Guy, "Danielle hasn't moved since you left.

"Great, grab your things and I drop you home."

"Will you be okay if I leave now Montana?"

"Yes of course. And thank you for being my driver and confidant," Montana said to Guy, making no move to kiss him after she kissed Alice, on the lips.

Bitch, Guy thought. "My cell phone number is written above the cordless phone in the kitchen."

Alice kissed him in the elevator and pulled a hand on to her breast. "She didn't kiss you so that means you are the enemy."

"Perhaps she's thawing. She was alarmed at the airport when finding Danielle wasn't with me and asked almost angrily what had I done with her mother."

"Omigod," Alice laughed. "You received the full treatment. You must understand you are the young bastard who's been fucking mommy."

As they walked to Guy's vehicle Alice said, "Park over in that dark corner and I'll give you something to cheer you."

"You're married."

"Oh worked it out have you? Well I should have told you but thought it might turn you off. I'm living back with my parents during a three-month trial separation. If he does dump his girlfriend I probably will return to him."

As they set in the vehicle Guy said, "It will be uncomfortable doing it in here."

"Darling I'm highly tolerate to discomfort if I get fucked really good and you're the man for that."

Buoyed by that encouraging comment Guy grinned and moved his vehicle into the poorly lit corner of the basement.

Alice, with her knees almost against her ears fed in the seven inches of fat dick.

"Oooh you'll get it a long way up me in this position."

"I'll be careful."

"No push it up till your balls hit to prevent you going any further."

Guy licked his lips, thinking Alice was such a lovely young woman. It was good associating with a woman who knew what she wanted. He bowed his head a little in remorse, thinking he ought not be doing this because she was a married woman. Then he grinned, straightened his back and thought fuck remorse and began giving her what they both wanted.

"Bite my tits," Alice groaned.

With her doubled up like that. Guy with his long back found it too difficult to bend to back sharply to get at them so he continued by balancing himself on one hand while he squeezed a tit with his other hand and then pinched the nipple hard.

Alice began moaning, slapped her clit and then wailed "Aaaaaaar-rrrrrgh" and her eyes bulged.

He jeered, "What, finished already?"

Panting, Alice began sliding his index finger into his butt and challenge, "You just concentrate on the job in hand and say lovely things to me."

Guy toiled away happily and then had the vision of a horrified Montana opening the door and gaping at them and spitting, "You won't be doing that to me your bastard."

Guy's head shot back and he bellowed and released hugely, hearing Alice complaining that his loud bellow had scared her shitless.

Guy looked at the door and was relieved to see it was closed.

"Rest and then my ass," Alice said. "It's all ready for you."

Christ women could be so tough, Guy moaned to himself but then smiled. The ass eh? She must like him.

Driving home wearily he wondered if Montana required a rousing bout of anal to jerk her into a better mood? She needed something. He recalled the Germans were big into anal.

Late next morning he returned to bed with coffee. The house was quiet because his parents were at church.

His phone went. Fuck a crisis at one of the plants but he found the caller was Danielle.

"Good morning you lovely bride in waiting. How's the head?"

There was a pause and then a honeyed voice said, "Are you always this charming to my mother?"

Ah so Montana was using her mom's phone. He replied, "Lovely people deserve top treatment. The jury is still out in respect of you."

There was no response. He imagined Montana icing over and his phone felt cold but knew that last bit was bullshit.

"I'm sorry."

"I think the jury is returning. Oh this is promising. I don't hear them walking heavily."

"Alice is here and made breakfast. I stupidly asked them what did they really think of your and they just went on and on. I know they both like you but I was left with the distinct impression they were trying to set me up with you."

"So what do you think about that?"

"Guy you can't ask me a question like that?"

"I just did."

"Well ask me something else."

"I recall reading somewhere the Germans are big into anal sex. Is that true?"

"Christ Guy, don't ask me anything. Mom is in the shower. She wants to take us all to lunch."

"Oh that lovely for you guys."

Montana said patiently, "The invitation includes you dopey. I am to book somewhere. We will be waiting for you in the lobby at 1:00."

"Oh I get it; I have the vehicle."

"Mom said I must take you girls and that lovely, resourceful and sweet boy to lunch. She must have meant some other guy Guy."

The call was cut.

Guy grinned. Miss Frosty from Germany was thawing. That could be bullshit but he hoped not. He cringed thinking what an idiot he'd been to ask that question about anal sex. Obviously she had him primed to self-destruct.

* * *

Guy jumped out of the vehicle but before he reached the double glass doors they opened and the three females emerged, laughing. They called hi and looked at him speculatively. Although it was Sunday he'd found a woman hairdresser open, smoking and reading the Sunday paper.

"I haven't made an appointment," he'd said hopefully.

"The men's barbershop in the Mall opens at 10:30."

He smiled and said he was hoping to get a stylish cut.

She peered at him and said, "You're my husband's boss, Paul Langley.

"Paul is on the management team, yes."

"Well hop into a chair and tell me your ambition for your hair," she said, stubbing out her cigarette.

"It's this new woman, a little reserved who has just arrived back from eighteen months in Germany."

"So you wish me to give you a sexy Continental look?"

"If you can."

"The cut is easy but if you really want to lift your appearance I'll have to color the front of your hair."

"Christ no."

She cooed, "Just some highlighting halfway between brown and blonde."

"Um."

"Come on, if you're not pleased with the result you may fire my husband. I'm that confident I can please you."

"Well go to it."

Guy ended up tipping Annette thirty bucks and she smiled and said he looked uplifted. "Of you go and buy a new suit, a shirt four tones lighter and no tie. Ask for Italian cut. Good luck. I heard that your girlfriend is marrying someone else."

Guy smiled awkwardly at Danielle, Montana and Alice. The two older women were positively leering and he could almost hear Montana as she swallowed before asking, "What's the color of your suit?"

"Bronze."

"It's beautiful and makes you look very dashing. I love the change to your hair."

"Thank you."

Mother and daughter climbed into the back. As Alice sat on the front seat where she'd been the previous night she sniffed, pulled out her purse spray and applied it a little wildly, some floating into the air.

Guy thought oh crap; she could smell their spent passion from last night. He admired Alice for having the control not to look at him. He turned on the blower and asked for directions.

When they arrived back Danielle said, "Why don't you two drop off Alice and go somewhere and I'll have a nap."

Montana began, "Well I don't really..."

"The new Sinclair Gallery has opened since you left here darling."

"Oh really? I suppose we could take a look but mom I have visited some of the best galleries in the world while living in Europe."

"This is mainly local art, a different perspective," Guy offered. He expected to be asked what did he know about art but she didn't and said she'd be pleased to look over the gallery.

They had coffee at the gallery and Guy said, "Well the wedding is on Saturday, what are your plans after that?"

"I launch myself into finding suitable accommodation tomorrow."

"What something like my apartment?"

"Well yes."

"Then why don't you share with me and launch yourself tomorrow in seeking suitable employment?"

"Share with you?" she said incredulously.

"I suggest you talk that offer over with your mother."

"She'll have a fit."

Guy stood and said they should go; his parents were expecting him and his two sisters and their families for dinner.

She went ahead of him without a word and didn't speak until they were buckling up in the Cadillac.

"Your offer meant sharing the apartment and rent, nothing else."

"Yes and I keep the main bedroom."

After another minute's silence she began to discuss the gallery, saying it was impressive for a small city.

As Montana went to leave the vehicle outside the apartment building she turned back and leaned over to either kiss him or to be kissed.

He pulled away.

She frowned and said didn't he want to kiss.

"Yes but don't open your mouth."

He concentrated on kissing he lips sweetly and he felt her mouth open slowly. He was tempted to tongue thrust but managed to maintain control.

"I'm beginning to think I could get to like you," she said.

He didn't reply, thinking what a rude bitch but when she stood on the sidewalk and gave him an almost dazzling smile he grinned, winked and waved and drove off slowly, satisfied that on this occasion he'd really given her something to think about.

After the Monday morning executive meeting, Guy called the CEO's daughter Mrs Gwen Little.

"Hi Gwen it's Guy Meadows. I've met you a couple of times socially. I work with your father."

"Oh hi, of course I remember you, dad's bright young right-hand and his possible successor."

"You're too kind. Gwen what I'm calling about is I have this lady friend who has returned from 18 months in Germany studying animal nutrition after gaining her master of science degree. She is research bent and it's unlikely she will find animal research work in Welling but I suddenly thought of you and remembered you saying you had a team at the hospital studying feeding problems with infants."

"Well yes, and we have been at it for four years but the focus is on ingestion, not nutrition, although those two research fields are not all that dissimilar. Perhaps you should send your lady friend to talk to me. Because of the long-term nature of this research project we do have difficulty maintaining numbers working on such research. Younger people tend to want short projects to quickly add achievements to their CVs."

Guy called Montana who greeted him suspiciously, or so he thought. "Do you wish to speak to my mother?"

"No I have your cell phone number as well as hers."

"Well why are you calling me?"

Jesus, he thought. Why bother?

"The director of research at Welling General Hospital is interested in talking to you. I mentioned to her you have been working in animal nutrition and she agreed with me you would be unlikely to find a position in that field within several hundred miles of here. If you are interested in research into baby milk ingestion problems it's possible she could become very interested in you. I apologize in advance for not asking for your permission before I spoke to Gwen Little but your anonymity is assured because I didn't give her your name."

Sounding decidedly interested, Montana said, "That's okay. One the women I shared an apartment with in Germany was a lactation consultant and another woman who lived with us for some months was involved in research into baby milk formulas so I have developed more than a little interest in that field, knowing I'll be a nursing mother one day. Look I'm most appreciative of your initiative, a little overwhelmed in fact. May I see you tonight? Mom will be out meeting Gus' parents for the first time. Oh I know why don't your come for dinner?"

Guy accepted the dinner invitation and gave Montana Gwen's phone number and explained she was the daughter of his company's CEO.

* * *

Guy arrived fifteen minutes late, in the hope that Danielle would have left by then because he wanted to focus totally on Montana.

He rang the doorbell instead of using his own key and Montana, fully made up with her hair high and dressed in short black greeted him when opening the door, pulling him to her and kissing him.

"That's a surprise," he said mischievously, hoping to get her back up a bit and they could have it out about why was she so frigid toward him.

"That's because you are a clever, clever man," she said, standing aside for him to enter. She closed the door and asked would he like another one.

Guy nodded and licked his lips deliberately.

Her blue eyes sparkled and she came in fast, crashing against him and they kissed hard and she banged her groin against his.

Fucking hell, he gloated. Did that mean pussy was on offer?

She then bit his ear and pulled away and took the flowers he was carrying and said thanks and invited him to sit. Guy watched her walk away and thought was a neat ass and great legs. Christ her dress was short. As she lifted the arm nearest him to get a vase from a cupboard above the bench he could see in this tight dress her tits were more than a good handful. Until then he'd seen nothing of note chest high. He decided this babe was sexy or at lease she would be if she let go.

He sat behind the breakfast bar and she worked immediately in front of him. He made sure she would have seen him eyeing her breast intently.

He saw her smile appear and that delighted him.

"You effort to find me employment is looking very promising indeed."

"I'm very pleased for you," he grinned, lowering his gaze to chest high after meeting her eyes.

"I went in to talk to Mrs Little and after only five minutes she called two of her senior people in and suddenly I realized I was being seriously appraised. I had taken in a copy of my CV and documentation confirming my qualifications and limited but in my view worthy experience and handed that dossier over. Mrs Little called me an hour ago to say their decision to engage me on a year's contract into dietary intolerances of suckling babies and infants up to two years of age would go before Friday's meeting of the hospital's staffing and finance committee and if approved I could start anytime from next Monday."

"Congratulations."

"Thank you. I really owe you for this Guy."

"Would you consider rewarding me with sex, um repeatedly?"

She was cool under fine. With only a faint smile she asked when and he said why not as soon as they had a drink, if that suited her.

She said okay and then told him they were lovely flowers.

When Montana came round the bar with two martinis she carried them over to the coffee table in front of one of the sofas. Guy had followed her and watched her hitch up her skirt to her waist before sitting.

She asked, "When did you start thinking of having sex with me?"

"Yesterday when you suddenly became nice to me."

She smiled. "If you must know I'd resolved never to have sex with my mother's lover but at the airport my resolve took an instant hit and has been melting ever since. Mom won't be home before 10:30 but I would like you out of here before she arrives if we have sex. That is only to avoid any embarrassment."

"That's fine..." but then he swallowed and mentally flipped. "Look if you think this will in anyway come between you and your mother then I'd rather not have sex with you. In fact I would rather you didn't yield just to reward me. I'll wait till you WANT to have sex with me but if that time never comes then so be it."

"Those are noble sentiments," Montana said, after sipping her drink. "For your information when I made the decision to invite you to dinner I was already thinking of being cooperative if you hit on me."

"Well, in that case let's finish our drinks," Guy leered.

Montana smiled, wriggled an arm out of her dress and pushed down the bra to reveal a good-size puppy with a fresh-looking pink nipple. She said cutely, "Might you be interested in this?"

Guy thought it was polite to say yes before he dived in to on to have his hair patted and to be told in a smiley voice, "Good boy."

While he pigged out Montana thoughtfully undid the back zip of her dress and wriggled off her panties with practiced skill.

When she held his dick between two fingers and ran her tongue from his balls to the helmet of his cock Guy thought, yeah this babe was experienced. He shivered in delight and with great expectations.

Guy was not disappointed and didn't mind that Montana didn't swallow. It was every woman to her own taste.

Montana was on her back, tweaking Guy's nipples, as Guy pushed in and out of her rhythmically, with one foot on the floor and bracing himself by holding around Montana's raised thigh on that edge of the sofa. He looked down at her and she gazed back at him and eventually she asked, "Do you think there's a chance we might marry?"

"I would think so," he said, as she reached for her clit.

She said softly, "I believe my mother unknowingly found you for me."

Guy, feeling himself thickening, picked up the pace. "You fuck really well; I'd be a fool to let you go and we'll probably share other interests."

* * * A couple of weeks later when Guy's mother and Montana where stood at the kitchen bench looking out at Guy and his father standing outside over the barbecue and holding a bottle of beer. Mary said something that really delighted Montana.

"I always knew a good woman would find Guy."

THE CAR

Laura thought her world had come to an end when Josh packed his bags and moved out to live with his new secretary, who was nearly thirty years his junior.

When Josh returned to collect his property Laura was in a vindictive mood. She allowed him to collect his clothes, she had resisted the temptation to hack them into ribbons. She even let him have his collection of vinyl records of sixties and seventies Rock, and his prized Bang and Olfsen hi-fi system.

She felt physically sick as she watched as he carried them out to his Jeep. She, the other woman, was sitting at the wheel.

It was when Josh turned to go into the garage that she launched her bombshell. "The garage is locked."

"Can I have the keys – please?"

"No Josh. What is in the garage is staying. I'm keeping the car."

"Dammit Laura that's my car. I built it with my own hands."

"We built this marriage and you took it apart. You've got your records, you've got your hi-fi, and you've got all your other possessions. You've got your whore – see if she'll make you coffee all night when you're up to your elbows in grease while you build another car."

Josh raged and stormed before he eventually left. When the Jeep turned out of sight Laura opened the garage. The little car sat in the center of the garage where it had been built. Laura walked around the car, its aluminum side panels glinted invitingly in the sunlight. The long hood, the fat open wheels, and the rollover bar over the cockpit, which did not even come up to her waist, all combined to give an impression of speed, fun and power. Laura had fallen in love with the car from the minute Josh showed her the pictures in the catalogue.

Building the car had taken all one winter, during which every spare moment of their lives had revolved around the garage. It had been fall when a collection of components had arrived in shipping crates and in the spring a little European sports car had emerged. Her fingers had bled when she had sewn the roof and the seats – the car was as much her creation as his and she was not relinquishing it.

Hiking up her skirt she stepped over the side and slid down in the driver's seat. She sat for a few moments acclimatizing herself, in ten years she had not driven the car more than five or six times – the driver's seat had been Josh's seat by right. She began to put the five-point seat harness on, she recalled why she had always worn pants when she rode in this car. She lifted her butt and tugged up her skirt and pulled up the crotch belt.

When she thumbed the starter button the engine coughed then caught, it began to die away, she recalled it had a manual choke. The side muffler emitted a steady meaty beat that boomed around the garage. She dipped the clutch put the manual shifter into first gear, raised the engine revs. The little car fishtailed, its rear wheels spinning when she let out the clutch.

She scarcely lifted her foot off the gas pedal, when with the tires squealing a tortured protest, like a rocket the car shot out of the driveway onto the road. Laura roared along the Sunday quiet suburban streets, fortunately there were no cops around. By the time she had reached the freeway her anger had dissipated to some extent. As she slowed the car to the speed limit she castigated herself. Laura what the hell has got into you – you're a fifty-five year old woman and you're driving like a teenager.

Even though she had slowed down the little car still felt good. The harness straps rubbed her breasts and her nipples had hardened in response. The wind blew through her hair and she felt free. She glanced at the gauge, the gas tank was three-quarters full. She did a quick calculation there was at least six gallons in the ten gallon tank, and at twenty-five to the gallon that was a hundred and fifty miles.

She had to brake hard when a truck pulled out in front of her. The belt between her legs halted her slide forward. She felt herself become wet as the webbing ground into her crotch. This damn car is sexing me up! She thought, angry that an inanimate object could arouse her desire. Yet even as she was thinking, her hand was caressing the smooth phallic knob of the gearshift.

She had been driving for nearly an hour when she decided that it was time to return home. She was going to turn off at the next interchange, but then the black drop-head 911 roared past her. Without a second's hesitation she floored the gas pedal, the little car leapt forward responsively. As she came up along side the Porsche the driver looked across and sped up. They were running side-by-side, the cars seemed to be evenly matched and neither driver was willing to give way. Laura took a quick glance at the speedometer, one hundred and thirty-five miles an hour; she didn't think Josh had ever driven the car this fast.

As soon as night follows day, and with the certainty that water flows downhill, so speeding on the freeway for prolonged periods has a certain consequence. Sirens wailed, lights flashed, the driver of the Porsche and Laura pulled over and stopped.

Once the tickets had been issued the cops clustered around the car. The hood was raised and they all gazed with awe at the little Pinto based Ford Cosworth motor.

"Mam did ya say this little mill is only two liters?" Asked a gum-chewing cop for the third time.

When eventually they were allowed to go on their way, it was the driver of the Porsche who suggested they go for a coffee, he had nodded his head in the direction of a roadside MacDonald's.

When they were seated at a table the young Porsche driver smiled at her, "That's sure some machine and cost a heck of a lot less than my Porsche. Did you really build it yourself?"

"Josh did. I supplied coffee, sympathy and stitched the upholstery."

"Josh?"

"My husband, ex-husband." She frowned what was Josh? sketched a gesture. "I'm not sure of how to describe his status or mine?"

"Not sure?"

"Well he's moved out – traded me in for a younger model. I suppose a divorce will be the next step. I really haven't thought about what comes next."

A typical male reaction Laura thought when the young man whistled.

Although his assumption angered her she smiled when he said. "Wow and he left the car too."

"No I kept the car. It's my self respect I know without the car he'll hurt and I want him to hurt as much as I hurt."

"Maybe I can help." As if by magic he flipped a card onto the table

'Simon Lampeter Attorney at Law' it had printed on it along with an address and phone number.

"Mister Lampeter we have an attorney." Laura said abruptly, she did not trust lawyers. Was this a new twist on ambulance chasing?

"That's good because it is unethical to be involved with a client. In that case will you come with me next weekend to the Sportscar races?"

"I'm not sure. I mean I hardly know you."

"You know me well enough to get arrested with me. Read the ticket, as an attorney I'll read it for you, and without billing you but don't tell my partners. It says that we are jointly charged with racing on the highway. And if you bring your car you'll enjoy it if we stop an extra day they have a "Run-what-you-brung" you can take your car on the track."

Josh will be totally pissed, she thought. "Fine next weekend it's a date."

On Monday morning Laura picked up Simon's card and went to the phone to call him and cancel. The service man arrived to give the boiler its annual service.

On Tuesday morning, she intended to call Simon but her neighbor Marjory called for coffee and to commiserate with her.

On Wednesday, she called. "Sorry Mr. Lampeter's in a conference may I take a message," the receptionist said. Her voice sounded like Josh's secretary's voice the woman she had dubbed, 'the whore'. Laura dropped the phone.

On Thursday morning she did not call.

On Thursday evening she rang Amy, her daughter, to tell her that she would be away that weekend. Amy was preoccupied, she had only just got home with the twins from a Little League game, "That's nice mom. Have a nice time and call me when you get back." Laura put the phone down relieved that her daughter had not asked where she was going or who she was going with.

On Friday still wondering what she was doing and why she crammed some clothes into a hold-all, she put the bag on the passenger seat and drove off to meet Simon. 'A hundred miles drive, to watch motor racing with a man I've only met once, I must be crazy!'

As she was driving Simon called on his mobile to check that she was on route and to give her the details of the motel where they would be staying. She nearly turned around to drive back home, when she reflected that staying in a motel with a man she hardly knew sounded distinctly sleazy. However the idea of a weekend at the Sportscar Races and an opportunity to run her own car on the track sounded too tempting.

The Motel parking lot was like an informal sports car fest, there were some small European kit cars like her own, many other British and European sports cars; including two blood red Ferrari Testerosas, and a number of the ubiquitous Porsche 911's both drop-head and fixed-head; of course there were also a number of Thunderbirds, Corvettes and Dodge Vipers.

She only located Simon by calling him on his mobile. She was reassured about his intentions when he showed her the two-bedroom suite with a shared bathroom. Once she had freshened up they went in her car to the track.

It was practice day. Laura watched enthralled as cars, some very like her own, howled around the road track. Tires smoked when they braked hard at the end of a straightaway before taking a sharp left-hand bend that was the first of a series of bends that snaked down the hill. A Viper overcooked the bend and spun onto the bumpy grass, leaving a trail of fiberglass body parts in its wake.

"Wow," said Laura as the dust settled.

"He'll soon get that fixed."

Laura had not really believed Simon's statement but sure enough before the session ended the same Viper howled past tires and engine screaming as it slewed into the bend. "He's still got a handling problem, the rear end seems to be going light when he brakes." Simon said knowledgably.

Laura enjoyed watching the practice, she had not realized how dusty she had got until they returned to the motel. She stood in the shower stall the warm water running softly over her body, swirling away in a brown eddy. Then she turned the showerhead to its power jet setting. No sooner had the jet struck her breast than she felt the tingle, the tingle of anticipation that she had not felt since Josh had left.

When she played the jet between her legs the sensation became intense. She had to satisfy her desire and there was no one to do it. She thrust one of her fingers into the yawning chasm that her pussy had become. Once her finger had entered there was no holding back, one finger was doing nothing, she thrust in three and began to finger-fuck herself.

Standing with her legs spread, bent at the knees she pressed her back against the cool tiles of the shower stall. As she fingered herself she kept getting near to an orgasm, then something would happen and frustratingly the feeling would fleet footed disappear. With her free hand she grasped her nipple viciously twisting it, as if trying to wring from her body the orgasm that eluded her.

It was when her palm pressed against her mons veneris that the moment of euphoria eventually arrived in a series of wet abdominal muscle contractions. Wanting to capture the ecstatic moment she closed her eyes, the face that appeared was Simon's not Josh's! The image was so lifelike that for a moment she thought he was really there with her, then she opened her eyes – she was alone in the shower stall and she knew that she had locked the door, although she wished that she had not.

She wished now that Simon had not been such a gentleman. Surely he wanted her why else had he asked her to come with him, unless he was gay. She played with that thought, if he were gay it would be the ultimate cruel joke. If only he had not taken a two room suite. At this moment she wished that he would metamorphose into a monster, a Werewolf and kick the door down to take her right there in the shower stall. She pressed her body harder against the tiles as she imagined the scenario.

By the time she had dried herself she had evolved a strategy that involved a jammed zipper. As she went out of the bathroom into the small lobby that divided the two rooms she abandoned the strategy. Instead of opening the door of her room, she knocked on Simon's door.

Even as he opened the door, she could not believe that she was saying the words she was saying. "Simon let's cut the crap – do you want me? Want me sexually I mean." She let her bathrobe fall to the floor. "Do you like what you see?" She pushed him back into the room.

Simon was flabbergasted, he had planned to wine and dine her before seducing her and now she had transformed into a sexual predator. "Yes," he stammered. "Yes I like what I see."

"Well then do something. Please Simon don't make me beg."

What happened next could not be described, by any stretch of the imagination as lovemaking – it was the unleashing of two people's raw animal lust. As Simon began to undo his belt Laura dropped to her knees. She pushed his hands aside scrabbled at the buckle. She tore down the zipper.

When she pulled down his pants and shorts the object of her desire confronted her. His cock was already rampant, the network of pumped up veins stood proud from its smooth surface, the exposed head purple and proud. She wet her lips with the tip of her tongue. She bobbed her head – he tasted sweet and salty, in her greed she had not even noticed the bead of pre-cum.

He groaned as she slid her slick lips over the head of his cock. It was too soon but already he could feel his balls tightening, drawing into him. He used her hair to pull her off his cock. "No not this way." He lifted her to her feet whilst kicking off his pants and shorts.

"Pleease Simon plee …" Her pleas were terminated when Simon threw her onto the bed – she was lying crosswise her feet and legs over the edge. Simon lifted her feet, her calves rested on his shoulder. She was wide open to him. She came as his cock-head parted her swollen labia, and came for a second time as he drove the full length deep into her.

After these first two orgasms Laura could no longer identify when she was coming and when she was not. As he pounded his cock into her she was just a well-pool of wet ecstasy. This was an animal fuck, there was no technique, no practice of the arts of love, merely the act of two people relieving their lust. Laura's hands were under Simon's shirt clawing at his back, her long nails raked long grooves along his skin, spurring him to move faster and drive into her harder. No man, not even some porn star stud could keep up the furious motion and not come. Simon was no porn star and soon, too soon his body stiffened. He drove his cock into her as the sperm boiled from his pulsating balls.

She lowered her legs, wrapping them around his waist she held him inside her. Although she could feel his cock softening she still wanted, needed him to be in her, she did not want the act to end.

She felt a sense of loss, of emptiness when with a soft plop his shriveled cock slipped from her. This sense of loss was softened when he scooped her up in his arms lay her lengthwise on the bed and lay beside her, holding her in his arms.

As they lay together he began to make love to her. He snuggled up to her smelling her freshly washed hair and the scent of her shampoo. Gently he kissed her ear, his teeth nipping the lobe, she wriggled her hips in anticipation when his tongue explored her ear. Then the kisses fell on her face a gentle shower of butterfly kisses rained upon her eyelids, his lips brushed her cheeks, cooled her forehead. At last he allowed their lips to meet in a long lingering kiss, his tongue forced apart her teeth, upon entering her mouth it jousted with her tongue in a ritualistic combat.

They were breathless when their lips parted, he transferred his attentions to her neck. As his lips touched the sensitive areas of her throat she could feel herself getting wet again. I hope he finishes me off, she thought.

"This was how I intended to make love to you." He murmured as he moved his attention to her breasts.

"I was an animal – a she wolf in season – I enjoyed the rutting – at that moment I did not want love. Just to be fucked." she replied. This cannot be! She was coming again and he had not even touched her there! She had always enjoyed having her breasts played with. Even at High School she had allowed her dates to fondle her breasts. Although until she had married she had never allowed anyone to go any further – Josh had been her first lover and until today her only lover.

Surely not! She was not sure but she was almost certain she could feel Simon's flaccid cock twitching against her thigh. She reached down and her fingers encircled his cock. She gave a quiet chuckle.

"What's the joke?" Simon asked. He thought that her chuckle had sounded amazingly sexy, it tinkled musically, sounding like water swirling over pebbles in a stream.

"It's been so long, I'd forgotten how fast a young man's cock recuperates. After a session like ours Josh would have taken days to revive. I was just thinking that maybe just maybe I ought to feel just a teensy, teensy little bit, sorry for the whore."

Simon lifted his head from her breast. "The whore?"

"My name for the woman, girl really Josh has traded me in for. Simon just do what you were doing, don't talk! Keep sucking my tits." Who's the slut no? she thought. Then she stopped thinking and surrendered herself to bliss as Simon nipped her nipples in the same fashion as he had nipped her earlobe. It was a sharp nip, hard, uncomfortable, but inducing pleasure: any harder and it would have been plain pain, any gentler and it would have been meaningless. Simon was fast discovering the secrets of her body.

She bent her legs, pushed her feet down on the mattress lifting her ass up as she moved her hips. One of his hands clamped on her Mons, the palm pushing the sensitive pad against the high arch of her pubic bone; his fingers curled around it, spreading the engorged lips entering her slit where one pressured against the hard bud of her clitoris. Now by using pressure he was controlling her body, increase the pressure. He held her hips still and she was trapped on the brink of coming but unable to come.

Just when she thought that she could take no more, he eased his grip allowing her to move her body. Her hips gyrated sensuously as she ground out yet another orgasm, this on heightened by the wait and his ever-present hand. There was a delicious sense of fear, fear that he would once again stop her before she had completed. Then there was the activity of one of his fingers that tapped gently along her clitoris. She came convulsively, her abdominal muscles tensing, as she drew her knees up to her breasts.

"Oh Simon you are so good for me." She exclaimed then the moment of rapture passed and a melancholic thought entered her mind. "How old are you Simon?"

The suddenness of the question caught Simon unawares. "Twenty-eight going on twenty-nine." He responded.

"Do you realize I am twice your age?"

"No I didn't. Does it matter?"

"To me no. To you I expect that when the novelty wears off it will."

"Laura I promise you that you're not a novelty – we are here together because I am genuinely attracted to you."

"Sooner or later you will want a young woman, one of your own age. Don't worry I am not walking out I want all that I can get and I intend to enjoy every minute that I have with you."

"Laura I promise you that I am genuinely attracted …"

"Shhhhhhh say nothing and I'll say no more. Lie back, I want to try something."

Simon did as she had asked. She turned and raised herself onto all fours. Turning, she slowly slid her body down his. The touch of her nipples trailing along his body sent erotic tingles to his hardening cock. The feel of his body against her nipples increased the level of her licentious feelings. As she slithered slowly down she kept her eyes fixed upon his cock – the object of her desire.

His cock hardened the moment her warm moist mouth enveloped its head. He felt her tongue swirling over the glans, the tip exploring the ridge that marked the separation between the exposed head and the shaft. She drew back curled her tongue so that the tip was pointed and began to explore the outline of the blind oval eye. It felt as if she was entering him through the tip.

Simon wriggled and squirmed until he got his head between Laura's legs. For the first time Simon could really see her pussy. Simon had seen many women's pussies since his first sexual fumblings after a High School Prom ten years before, but Laura was the first mature woman he had ever bedded.

The pussies he had looked at before had never born children and belonged to younger slimmer women, women who were little more than teenagers. Their labia had been thin and mean, whereas Laura's were fleshy and fully developed, hanging down from her like curtains. Even their outer side glistened with hers and his juices. She responded to his touch when with two fingers he gently parted the heavy lips, exposing to his gaze her coral pink inner lips. He looked at the pulsating dark hole where only a short while ago he had buried his cock. He was intrigued by the thick untrimmed growth of her dark pubic hair; hair that he already knew grew nearly to her navel.

Laura was uncertain as to exactly what Simon was doing when he grasped her hips and pulled her down to him. She had heard of the term Sixty-Nine, she even knew in broad terms what it meant; but she had never done it before. By the time she had put a name to what was happening, Simons tongue was lashing her clitoris, flicking it one way then the other.

By way of repayment Laura bobbed her head faster than before. On each downward bob she tried to cram a little more of his iron hard cockstem into her mouth. The blunt head of his cock was blindly butting against the back off her mouth.

She took a series of deep breaths like a diver she held the last one. Just a little more, she thought, bobbing her head down with even more force. Once again the head of his cock hit the back of her mouth, then it slithered into her throat. Fighting the urge to gag she swallowed and suddenly could feel that he was lodged in her throat she gently moved. Simon gave a muffled groan of ecstatic bliss, never before had a woman deep-throated him. Her lungs were bursting when she lifted her head, taking another breath she dove down once again driving his cock down her throat.

All the time she was deep-throating him Simon's tongue was exciting her clitoris and labia. Lashing her hot inflamed organs with his active slick tongue. Then without warning he would change the tempo and delicately caress those same parts, probing and exploring every delicate fold and crease of the Lotus flower that was her sex.

With a triumphant cry of rapture jizm erupted from his rampant cock. As his cock pumped great hot globules down into her throat she felt as if she was drowning. She swallowed desperately, the more she swallowed the more that seemed to fill her gullet. This event that was in reality over in a matter of seconds, seemed to Laura to have been lasting for an eternity.

Although he pulled his softening cock out of his mouth, he did not cease lavishing attention upon her pussy. Energetically his mouth and tongue sucked and licked at her spread pussy, cajoling orgasm after orgasm from her. Laura had never in her life experienced so many nor such intense orgasms. She doubted whether even when Josh was young he had ever been capable of such a prolonged bout of almost non-stop lovemaking. What was happening to her? She thought as yet another wet geyser of joy erupted somewhere deep within her womb. She experienced momentary panic attacks – was this natural – would she ever stop? Eventually she said, "Please Simon, no more I don't think I can take any more."

In the morning when she awoke she was still in his arms, barely moved from the position in which they had been lying cuddling one another. She realized that they had drifted off to sleep holding one another.

Her first movements awoke Simon. Seeing his eyes open she kissed him before he could speak. Pressing her body against his she felt his erect cock.

"Oh my god! You're like a machine a fuck machine."

"Well I guess the machine had better perform." He laughed pushing her onto her back. "My! Oh my I think there are two fuck machines in this bed." His hand was exploring her already slick slit. Of its own accord her vagina yawned open. "This'll be a real quicky – I want to get to the track." He warned, his cock was slipping into her.

"Don't tell me. Just fuck me."

Simon needed no urging. His hands moved beneath her buttocks lifting them from the bed. He thrust his hips embedding the full length of his cock in her. She drew up her knees, wrapping her legs around his waist. She pulled herself tighter to him. Simon was true to his word, although energetic it was truly a quick fuck, but not so quick that Laura missed out on her orgasm. When they had both come they parted.

A quicky? Josh would have defined that as a full-blown orgy!

They spent the day at the track watching cars taking part in the timed practice for the big race. Then they watched a short support race. Laura watched this race intently, the cars racing were small open wheel cars of the same type as her own.

At two in the afternoon the cars taking part in the Twenty-Four Hour race lined up on the grid. Their engines roaring they made a slow circuit of the track behind the Starter's Car. Coming to a halt they took up their positions on the grid for the standing start. Even on the first Lap with twenty-fours of racing in front of them cars were jostling to overtake, pushing to get in front. On the second lap in front of where they stood, a Corvette nudged a Porsche that pirouetted along the track and off onto the grass. The Porsche's wheels spun, then with pieces of bodywork trailing behind it the car rejoined the track.

"C'mon," Simon pulled her with him like an excited schoolboy. He led the way through the spectator areas until they reached a point where they had a good view of the pits. Here they could see the mechanics making hasty repairs to the Porsche, within minutes the little car's motor was fired up and with tires smoking it headed back onto the racetrack.

"Now if my car was damaged like that the guys in the body-shop would take at least a week." Simon commented. Laura did not point out that he would not accept a car that had been repaired with Gaffer Tape. However she was impressed by the speed that the mechanics turned the cars around.

When darkness fell the cars turned on their lights, all that could be seen were the blazing pools of the cars driving lights approaching and then the red tail lights once the car passed. Only the big screens told the spectators who was in the lead, as about fifteen laps separated the leading car from the last car still running.

Laura's fingers ran with grease when they ate burgers bought from one of the trackside fast food concessions. They made their way over to the carnival, and got into a car on the Ferris Wheel. As it climbed up into the sky, Laura saw the overall layout of the track traced out by the twinkling lights of the cars.

It was not until Laura yawned that Simon said they should return to the motel. "You should have said that you were tired, I'd forgotten where we were staying." He said as they entered their suite.

"Forgotten?" Perplexed by his comment she raised an eyebrow.

"This is the first year I've not camped up by the track."

"Why didn't you camp this year?"

"Would you have accepted if I'd asked you to camp out with me?"

"Well no, I suppose not."

"When you said yes I had to make a reservation." He laughed ruefully, she liked seeing him laughing. When he laughed his eyes had crinkles around them. "It occupied an awful lot of my secretary's time last week. But it is proving to be well worthwhile."

"What? A weekend with an old lady like me?"

"A weekend with a very sexy lady. Tell me if its not an ungentlemanly question, where the hell did you learn to do a deep-throat?"

Adopting her best Southern Belle accent Laura said. "Why Sir that is ungentlemanly, but I'll answer. I have to confess that I learnt last night Sir." She reverted to her own voice. "I have never done it before, never felt the inclination to do it, and never even tried. But last night I wanted to be special. To give you something no-one else has ever had."

"So it was a first time for both of us."

"I didn't realize but I am glad. Never ever has anyone made love to me like you did last night."

As they got into bed Laura said. "Simon I feel guilty."

He was immediately attentive. "Guilty why? Are you on about our age difference again? I told you it does not ..." He stopped seeing her smile.

"No not that, I mean that I feel guilty about the money you have spent on a two bedroom suite when one bed has remained unused."

"To have you in my bed it's money well spent."

She reverted back to her Southern Belle accent. "Why Sir I do declare that is quite the most chivalrous thing that a gentleman could say."

He responded in kind. "Mam to share a bed with you is an honor. Hell that didn't come out the way I meant it to." He blushed. "I can see that I am going to have to watch Gone with the Wind a few times so I can get the words right."

"I've got the video tape."

"Well that's one way to fill our evenings together."

She kissed him. "I kinda hope against hope that there's a lot of them. Maybe they'll get to be boring after a while." She was surprised, when he returned her kiss she could feel that his cock was already hard. "My you are eager," she said as she circled her fingers around his hot cock. Last night would have had Josh protesting he was worn out for a month. In fact she thought Josh had never lasted half the time Simon had done last night and now he was ready again. After spending fourteen hours out someplace, Josh would have fallen comatose in his chair, whereas this man was obviously ready for another night of passion.

What really shocked her was her own hunger for him. The Whore's welcome to Josh she thought as she slid her lips over Simon's rampant cockhead. She was once again exploring the texture of Simon's cock when she thought of her daughter. If Amy walked in through that door and saw me with a man's cock in my mouth using my hands to play with his balls, what would she say? Laura decided that her daughter would probably call her a slut and disown her, she also decided that she really did not care.

She felt the stirring of his balls, then his hands clamped against the sides of her head. She expected him to thrust his hips toward her driving his cock into her throat. He eased her back away from him. "No not yet," he said pushing her onto her back.

With his hands against her calves he lifted her legs up high, spreading them apart then pushed them down until her feet touched the pillow by her head. He knelt between her legs. "This is the best view in the world, if I could paint I'd paint it, someday I would like to photograph what I see – to share this view with you."

Laura laughed. "Why would I want to see myself? – I know my own body."

"Do you? Think carefully. Have you ever spread yourself like this and seen yourself as I see you?"

"Of course not how could I unless I did it with a mirror or a camera?"

It was his turn to laugh. "Precisely and that my dear is why I want to photograph you."

"Have you got your camera?" She had uttered the words, before she considered what she had said.

"I'll get it." He replied as he lowered her legs.

Amy will kill me! – God she's my daughter not my mother really its nothing to do with her.

His camera was slung around his neck, when he lifted her legs again. "Relax." He said as he spread her legs.

"Promise me you will never show them to anyone else."

"I promise."

"What about when you get them developed? Someone will see them."

"It's a digital camera. Here," he said holding the camera out to her. "Look at the screen on the back and you will see the picture I have taken."

She looked, it did not feel like she was looking at an image of herself, it was too disembodied. He had framed an area that extended from just in front of her labia, a fringe of tightly curled pubic hair to just behind her anus. The way her legs had been forced over and open had flattened the tops of her thighs.

What immediately caught her eye were the beads of moisture. Diamond like and glinting. Almost as if her entire sex had been decorated with sparkling eye make-up. Her outer lips were raised, puffed up, darkened by the blood that had pumped into them. Between them peeked the coral pink inner lips that looked like a pair of delicate seashells. Her clitoris stood alone in the slit, it appeared far smaller than she had imagined it to be. Could such an important organ the bringer of such great joy really be so small?

"What do you think?" He asked.

"I don't know Simon. It is strange. I know it is me, yet it doesn't feel as if it is me. There is a sense of detachment, unreality about this picture. Can you get me a print?"

"I'll make you a print."

"Gee. You do your own processing?"

Simon laughed. "No its digital. Its an electronic image. I connect the camera to the computer and print the pictures."

"I don't understand half of that – but do me a picture. Say, can I photograph your cock?"

They spent a while taking photographs of one another from different angles. "Simon I've an idea. I want you to come over my tits and I'll press the button just as you come, capturing the sperm whilst it is in mid air." Had she really suggested that? She could hardly believe the depths her mind could sink to. What had this man unleashed when he made love to her, she was talking like a two-bit whore, without a trace of shame.

He straddled her stomach. The back of his hand brushed against her breasts as he jacked himself off. She was trying to stay concentrated on her self-assigned task as a photographer. The motion of his hand generated shards of electricity that ripped through her body terminating with a thump in her abdomen. Between his muscular thighs she writhed in torments of ecstasy. Each vicious jolt to her abdomen transformed itself into a wet jet of joy.

She had almost forgotten the photograph when he exclaimed, "Ready! I'm coming."

She tried to frame his cock and press the button as she felt the first of his hot sticky come land on her erect nipple, then her tits seemed to be overwhelmed by his gooey semen as it flowed lethargically over them. Somewhere, sometime she had read that the average male ejaculation measured a soup spoon – she was certain his ejaculation would have filled a coffee cup. He massaged the fluid into her skin causing ripples of ecstatic tremors to course through her body, soon too soon for her the fluid had cooled, drying into hard flakes.

When he had finished his cock was limp and sad looking. Laura grasped his buttocks and pulled him towards her. She crammed his cock into her mouth as if she intended to devour him. Sucking furiously she literally willed him back into hardness. "Now fuck me. Fuck me hard." She demanded.

He moved so that he was kneeling between her legs. Again he lifted them, this time none too gently. His roughness thrilled her. He plunged his cock into her open pussy and began to pound into her like a pile driver, on each inward stroke his hard pubic bone collided with her aroused clitoris.

"Oh yes honey give it to me … give it to me hard … I want, need to feel you … don't worry about hurting me just do me." She raved at him, her nails ripping grooves in his back as she spurred him on.

Eventually his body stiffened he pulled nearly out of her then slammed in as deep as he could as the sperm spurted from his cock in hot sticky globules. "I am bushed." He said as he lowered her legs.

She kissed him, when their lips parted she whispered. "Simon you are fantastic."

It was soon after that they fell asleep.

Simon was asleep on his back, snoring gently when Laura awoke. She looked at him, he looked so young, so angelic. She felt a twinge of guilt, was she as the older woman taking advantage of his youth? Then she recalled it was he who had shown her how to be adventurous in her lovemaking, not the other way around.

She lifted the sheet. His cock was hard, not iron bar hard, but definitely hard. Taking care not to disturb him she turned around and squirmed down the bed. Not touching him was difficult but eventually she had his cock in her mouth, ever so gently she moved her tongue polishing his exposed glans. His cock hardened rapidly and still he did not stir.

It was only when he was coming that he moved. She had to hold him tightly to prevent him bucking away from her as he squirted his juice down her throat. By the time he had finished he was fully awake. When he had finished coming she moved up to lie next to him. "Did you enjoy that?"

"Enjoy it! You have no idea! You have just made one of my favorite fantasies come true.

"Only one?"

"Well you had already made my deep-throat one a reality."

" Oh my poor darling. Soon I'll spoil all your dreams."

"I'm not complaining, but I will be if I don't get to see the end of the race." He said as he jumped out of bed.

They both dressed quickly and returned to the racetrack. The cars were still thundering around, the pace maintained by the lead cars was unrelenting. The first thing that Laura noticed was how many cars bore the scars of minor accidents. When she commented on this, Simon said that during the hours of darkness minor collisions and spin-offs were almost inevitable. He also pointed out that only about half of the cars that had started the race were still on the track.

Between ten and eleven the cars began to make their final pit-stops. In most cases the drivers were changed and the cars number one driver, who had been resting, got in to drive the final stint. Despite the twenty plus hours that the cars had been running almost non-stop, the lap times began to tumble as the top drivers tried to seize the lead.

Laura found that her ears were rapidly becoming attuned to the racetrack. Now as a car approached she could discern the agricultural rumble of the big V8's, the smooth roar of the V12 Ferraris, the higher pitched howl of the Porsche flat six's. The car that stood out was a lone Mazda RX that by comparison seemed to whisper as it passed.

"Why's that little car so quiet?" She asked Simon as the Mazda ghosted past where they stood.

"That's a rotary car, the engine has no piston just a turning rotor."

She did not understand what he was saying, she simply accepted his explanation.

Just after two o'clock the leading car crossed the finishing line, the chequered flag waved and the race was over. Dusty, dirty, the cars and their tired drivers completed the lap and pulled into the pits. An awesome hush fell over the track as the last of the cars turned off its motor.

It was only now that the race was over, that Laura fully appreciated how many people had been at the race. This time when they left the track they were a part of a massive seething throng. Throughout the short drive back to the motel they were in a fender-to-fender traffic jam. What had been a fifteen-minute drive took over an hour.

It was gone five when they entered their suite. They took a shower together, and got dressed. Laura resisted the urge to seize Simon and drag him into the bed. This evening they were going out for a proper meal, rather than the fast-food snacks that they had subsisted on all weekend. Laura thought, This waiting will sharpen my appetite.

The atmosphere in the restaurant was dominated by the sports car races. A number of the tables were occupied by large groups made up of the drivers, pit-crew, and the long legged, well endowed girls, who it appeared to Laura were as essential to a motor racing team as the driver himself. It was impossible not to overhear the conversation from a neighboring table that seemed to be getting increasingly acrimonious between two of the drivers. One driver accusing the other of both driving too slowly and being unable control the car. No one else seemed to agree and after a while a pretty girl persuaded the aggrieved driver to leave with her.

Simon leaned across the table. "I bet that the slow driver is either one of the sponsors or brings in a lot of personal sponsorship money."

"Well at last I know the function of the stunningly beautiful women."

Simon raised his glass. "Here's to my stunningly beautiful woman."

The meal began with a clear Mock Turtle soup. This was followed by a seafood dish. On the table where the argument had taken place they were eating oysters. Laura was relieved when Simon ordered the grilled fish dish. She had always shuddered when she'd seen people swallowing whole oysters, it seemed to be very primitive to her. The main course was filet de boeuf en croute. Although she felt full and bloated, Laura was unable to resist the elaborate chocolate confection that was the sweet. As the first mouthful melted in her mouth Laura thought I am going to have to diet for a month to loose the pounds I've put on tonight. Throughout the meal they both drank champagne. It was not until they rose to leave that Laura realized how much she had drunk.

She still felt lightheaded when they returned to their suite. Without any preamble she began to take off her clothes. "Simon I've been burning up for you all through that meal. Every-time I looked at you all that I could think of was of us making love. When you raised your food or your glass to your lips, damn zipper … that's better. Where was I? I was talking like a slut, that's your fault – your lovemaking has liberated the slut within me. Do you realize every time you put something into your mouth all that I could think of was you doing oral sex to me?" She said as her dress fell to the floor, she hooked her thumbs into the waistband of her panties wriggled her hips and the lacy briefs joined the dress. "Not a bad looking body for an old woman." She preened as she discarded her brassiere. She was naked apart from her garter belt and stockings. "Now take me any way you want me."

She could see the bulge in his pants his cock had rocketed to attention. She was sure that he wanted her, but he said. "No Laura not yet." He turned on the radio fiddled with the tuner until he found a station playing jazz. "Dance for me."

"Simon just shuck off your pants and screw me. Undressing can come later. Take me and take me hard."

He sat down on the bed. His voice was stern almost magisterial. "Laura I said dance for me."

To humor him she swayed her hips.

"Dance properly. I want to see you dance."

She felt self conscious, as if she was a hidden camera she could see the scene. A young handsome man who was fully clothed reclining on the bed; and a middle aged woman, whose only clothing was a garter belt and stockings standing swaying in the middle of the room. She began moving her body with the music, her hips and shoulders gyrating. Then as if of their own accord her feet began to move. Now the camera in her mind captured the lewdness of the situation. This is something like a scene from some French Art House film She was getting wet between her legs.

"Stop!" Simon said, when she clamped her thighs together. He jumped up grasped her shoulders, there was no gentleness in his touch. He used his feet to push her feet apart. "Stand still, I don't want you to come, not yet."

It was as he intended. His treatment of her successfully froze her orgasm. He released his hold. His voice was gentle the way it usually was. "Dance again Laura, please dance for me."

Tentatively she began to move to the music. She saw the dissatisfaction in his face, she wanted to please him she began to dance properly. Still cautious at first, then she abandoned herself to the music, dancing alone. She had switched the camera off she was oblivious to Simon's presence.

Simon watched as she swayed, shimmied, shook and whirled to the primeval rhythms. The beat driving deep into her body, the wetness returned this time, she was blatant about her orgasm her hand clutched at her pubic mound, her fingers insinuated into her slit, probing for her clit. She did not stop moving as she masturbated.

Simon lay on the bed his cock throbbing with desire as he drank the scene in. He knew that his lying on the bed not touching her, had tormented her, but now it was a torment to himself. He undid his shirt.

"Simon please honey take me. I want you. Please do it fuck me hard fuck me until I hurt. Have me any way you want to but have me now." Her words galvanized Simon into action, he leapt up from the bed.

Simon fumbled with his belt buckle – in front of him was his fantasy woman. From when he had first been aware of women as sexual beings he had fantasized about women dressed in only a garter belt and stockings. The only flaw, if there was a flaw, was that Laura had kicked off her shoes, but the shoes were not that important in his fantasies.

He kicked his pants off. He nearly crushed the breath out of Laura when, stepping clear of his pants and shorts, he scooped her up in his arms and carried her over to the bed. She lay back in his arms unresisting. The bed groaned in protest when he flung her onto it.

He pushed between her legs, she raised them and wrapped them around his waist. He had no need to arouse her, his cock glided into her moist sex. His hands clasped her buttocks pulling her towards him as with powerful thrusts of his hips he plunged into her.

There was no way that the sex act could be described as lovemaking. Both Laura and Simon were living out their own fantasies sating their own desires. If anyone had witnessed the act they would have thought they were seeing a rape. His body pounded into her as if his cock was boring its own tunnel. She kicked at his back with her heels. Scrabbled at his body with her hands. There was a ripping sound when her nails slashed through his shirt. He bit her breast when she catlike dug her fingers into his back. Blood flowed from the deep lines she scored into his flesh.

She screamed when his bite drew blood. His pubic bone continued to slam remorselessly into her mons veneris. She was nearly coming when a moment of insecurity hit her. "Don't stop Simon ... Don't stop now ... Just keep going please don't come, not yet, not until I'm ready." She arched her back, whether she willed it or not her hips moved in a circular motion, she was holding him so tight that he was unable to move independently of her and at the same time she was willing him to move.

He reached down his body, slid his hands between his waist and her legs. He forced her legs to part, lifting them high he slipped his arms around them, grasped her shoulders and returned to pounding his hard cock into her moist sex. She was so wet that there was now an audible squelching sound.

She did not stop clawing at his bloodied back. His tattered shirt was saturated in his blood. "Simon harder fucking! I need fucking harder. Hurt me! Fuck me so hard that you make me hurt! I want to feel you!" She screamed as her talons raked him once again. "No!" She cried as he pulled his cock out of her.

"Oh no ... Oh yes ... Oh Simon don't stop now, harder hurt me." She felt as if his cock was a hot knife cutting through to her vitals ripping apart, as he drove it into her asshole. He had dreamed about butt-fucking a woman, but up until this moment had never done it.

It was only when she had finished coming that she became aware of his hot sperm sloshing around in her bowel. Once or twice in the past she and Josh had tried butt-fucking, she remembered it only as a painful experience. This time despite the lack of preparation it had been delightful. She tensed her muscles unwilling to let go of his exhausted cock. "Oh honey that was the best, the very, very best. You can fuck me any way you want me any time you want me."

"Laura its I who should be thanking you, nearly every time we make love you make one of my secret fantasies come true. I've woken up with you sucking my cock. I've made love to you when you're dressed in a garter belt and stockings. And now I've butt-fucked you. You're my dream woman."

"The trouble is we all have to wake up from dreams." The cloud descended, she gripped his arms, looked him in the eyes. "Promise me Simon you won't lie to me. When it's over, when you get bored with me, tell me. Be honest with me."

"I love you Laura I'm not going to leave you."

"You do now – but will you next week?"

He held her tight to him, he could not conceive giving her up, she acted so young that he had never given their ages a second thought. In fact all weekend except when she raised the issue he had not thought about there being an age difference.

She clung to him. If I go on like this I will drive him away! "Just hold me. Don't let me go." Just after she had said these words, his limp cock slipped from her with a soft but audible plop! It seemed symbolic of the impermanence of their relationship. Feeling suddenly empty she clung to him.

Maybe it was the long day, maybe it was the Champagne they had drunk, or perhaps it was a combination of these two factors, but sleep swept over them so fast that when Laura awakened unable to breathe, aware of a pressing weight, she felt as if she was being crushed. Opening her eyes she saw that Simon was asleep still lying on top of her.

She moved as his eyes flickered, closed, and then opened again. "What time is it?" He spoke through his yawn.

"Morning I think. Simon could you get off me I feel like I've been flattened."

"What?" He was awake now taking in his surroundings. "Oh my god have we been asleep like this all night." He asked as he rolled off her. "You poor thing why didn't you wake me?"

"I was asleep too. I wanted you close to me and you were close to me."

At the track the cars were given a brief check for safety. The drivers an equally cursory talk on the track flags. Laura decided to buy herself a helmet rather than renting one.

Having paid for the track time, and belted into the car she gunned the engine. The car was sitting on a line at the pit-lane exit. The marshal dropped the flag. Laura let the clutch out, she was now used to the little car's tendency to wheel-spin the tires bit and she was pressed back into the seat as the car shot forward.

Obeying the marshal's blue flag, she checked her mirrors as she joined the track proper. Keeping the rev counter needle near to the redline she changed up through the gears.

In no time the first bend approached, she began changing down. Another car shot past her. Up through the gears again, then down one gear, another bend, she could feel that the car's back end was trying to slide. Change up, down three gears for the hairpin. The over-revving motor was screaming a protest. Change up and so on. The second lap she was as cautious as on the first lap, ignoring the cars that overtook her. On the third lap she began to test the car's limits. The fourth lap she flew. All too soon she was starting the last lap. Foot nailed to the floor she scarcely lifted off. On nearly every bend the little car was sliding. She knew now what a four-wheel slide meant, and she knew how to control one.

Then it was over, she was being flagged into the pit-lane, and her five laps were done. Dropping down to the fifty mile per hour pit-lane speed limit her pace seemed to be sedentary. She pulled up in the paddock beside Simon's Porsche. "How was it?" He asked as she removed her helmet.

"Half the time I was in a state of abject terror wondering why the heck I'd ever let you talk me into being out there and the other half was sheer unadulterated exhilaration – it was fantastic I was flying – I didn't want to stop, ever!"

"I told you that you would enjoy it. If you go over to the trailer by the side of Race Control you can get your time sheet."

Simon was talking to another man when she returned. Laura's blood ran cold when she overheard the other man say. "Your mother sure knows how to handle her little car."

Then she heard Simon reply. "That is my woman you're talking about. Not my mother." Hearing the confident way that Simon said those words gave her hope that they had a future.

She slipped her arm through Simon's arm, put her lips near Simon's ear. "Let's find somewhere quiet that driving has left me as horny as hell and I've an itch that needs immediate attention."

BOWLING NIGHT

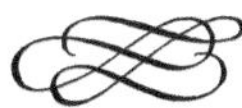

Sensual and erotic experiences I ever had occurred nearly twenty years ago now. But the memory of it remains with me to this day.

Back then I worked with a woman named Lucille. I was in my early thirty's at that time, and Lucille was some twenty or so years older than I was. But the age difference hardly mattered between us, we got along famously, and I looked forward to seeing and working with her on a daily basis. At first there was nothing at all sexual even mentioned between us, she had a very 'rigid' upbringing, and things of that nature weren't easily discussed amongst coworkers anyway, especially between us.

But as our friendship grew, I learned more and more of Lucille's personal life, and for her, it had been a very difficult one. We had worked together for several years before we'd even gotten to a 'familiar' personal working level, but as Lucille was easy to talk to, and sometimes even to confide in, we grew even closer and eventually began to share with one another things that were occurring in our lives outside of the workplace.

Our Company sponsored a weekly Bowling League, and I had signed on to bowl, as had Lucille, which surprised me a little bit. But I soon after learned from her, that it was basically her one and only night away from the 'boring' and uneventful life that she was leading at home after work. So for her, it was an outlet and gave her something to look forward to each week. As it turned out, she and I ended up on the same team so that made it equally special for both of us, it was a way to further continue our association and friendship away from work.

Lucille was a tall woman, just over six feet. And though she certainly didn't have all the curves in all the right places anymore, she was a very attractive mature looking woman, and still had (though of course I hadn't seen) fairly large full breasts. On the rare occasion she actually wore something that even hinted at a bit of cleavage, I found myself more than admiring that tantalizing sweet bit of flesh that was seen.

The place where we bowled at had an underground parking garage. Nearly everyone parked in the lot just outside the front entrance, but a few of us used the garage. I did, primarily because I had a fairly new car, and it kept down the incidental 'dings' from occurring in my doors. Lucille also preferred parking in the garage, as she didn't care to have to walk out to her car later on in the evening after it had gotten dark.

There were a few spots in the parking lot, which weren't very well lit. However, as I has teased her, there were also a few spots in the garage which had lights out that hadn't been replaced either, but she nearly always managed to park close to the door anyway, so a poorly lit basement garage didn't really bother her any.

We'd been bowling for several weeks already when on one particular night I knew by Lucille's overall attitude that something was bothering her. She wouldn't talk to me about it however, so we continued to bowl, but I knew that something was wrong, as she wasn't her same old normal self. My suspicions were confirmed when we as a group, always went into the bar for a few drinks afterwards, announced that she was going home early instead. I stayed long enough for one drink myself, but as it just didn't feel the same without Lucille there amongst us, I soon decided to make an early night of it too. I walked down the stairway to the garage and immediately noticed that Lucille's car was still there, and oddly enough that she had parked in one of the few areas where the lights hadn't been replaced, throwing a great deal of shadow over where her car was sitting. I immediately grew concerned as this was rather odd, and immediately went to her car and tapped on the passenger side window. It was obvious she had been crying, but upon seeing me, her face brightened a little and she reached over unlocking the door so I could get in.

"Lucille, what's wrong?" I asked slipping into the passenger seat, closing the door.

She just shook her head, though thankfully the tears had finally stopped. I waited patiently sitting beside her there on the front seat of her car, knowing that 'if' and when she was able to, she'd tell me what it was that was bothering her. After a considerable amount of time, she finally did.

"Brad, I really hate to burden you with my problems, but honestly, I don't have anyone I can even possibly imagine talking to about this. Certainly no one in my family would understand, and would no doubt be 'shocked' if I even told them. I'm not even sure I can honestly talk to you about any of this either without totally embarrassing myself, but if I don't talk to someone, I think I'll end up going crazy!"

She'd certainly said a mouthful, but it was evident that if it was important enough to actually sit and wait for me, which is what she'd obviously decided to do, then I was more than willing to listen, and I told her so.

"Just promise me you'll listen without saying anything, without passing judgment on me because I'm probably going to say some things that might surprise you. And worse, if you interrupt or stop me before I'm finished, I might not be able to even look at you again let alone finish what I want to say to you."

"Ok Lucille, I promise."

Lucille relaxed somewhat having heard that, and settled back in her seat though she no longer looked at me. Closing her eyes, she began.

"You already know a little bit about my 'life' at home, but what we've never discussed really is the sexual part of it as well. And this is what I guess is finally starting to get to me. I've been married now for thirty years. Our Anniversary was last weekend, and to celebrate it, I ended up cooking dinner like it was any other night of the week. My husband bought me what he thought was a sexy nightgown, but to me looked "Whorey" and completely out of character for anything I'd enjoy having or even wearing. Now don't get me wrong Brad, I consider myself to be a very sexual woman, and to be honest, I've done things I'd be too embarrassed to even admit to you that I've done. But, as hard as I have tried to be the wife, woman, lover that my husband has wanted me to be, it's the way he treats me when 'he' wants sex that I find degrading and totally unacceptable anymore. Needless to say, I refused to wear his 'fuck-gown' as he called it and we ended up fighting on our Anniversary instead of doing anything else."

I continued to sit there listening to her. I had certainly known that her marriage wasn't perfect, after all, who's was really? Even mine was on a roller coaster of good and bad days it seemed like lately, but I had no idea how difficult a time it truly had been for her either. And one 'big' thing, in all the time we'd worked together, I had never heard Lucille say anything harsher than damn or hell the whole time we'd known one another, so hearing her use the word 'fuck' even if it was in a description of something, she had always previously said "The 'F' word, and not even that unless it was absolutely necessary to whatever was being discussed. Obviously, this was another one of those very rare moments when she knew that actually saying the word would have more impact and underline the seriousness of the situation for me.

Although I remained completely silent except for the brief and occasional "Uh huhs", just to let her know I was really listening, Lucille still refused to look at me, for the most part keeping her eyes closed though she did open them on occasion staring out the front windshield of the car as though she could see whatever it was she was trying to tell me about as though it were actually happening all over again.

I knew that it was hard for her to even be sharing with me the things she was, Lucille was revealing to me a part of her that she hadn't obviously shared or discussed with anyone. So I continued to sit silently, listening and waiting for the time, if one even came, where I would or even could offer any advice, or at the very least, offer sympathy if nothing else.

Once again she 'warned' me, told me that if anything she was telling me made me uncomfortable, to just say so, and she'd stop. I of course, wasn't about to, regardless of anything she said.

"I know that this may shock you Brad, but in all the years we've been married, I've never had an orgasm with him when we've had sex. It certainly feels good yes, but 'he', 'it' doesn't last long enough for me, and frankly, he doesn't seem to care if I ever have or haven't either! The only time I've been able to is when I've touched myself."

This revelation, for that's truly what it was, didn't surprise me so much that this is what she'd been dealing with, more than I was honestly surprised, yet also flattered in a way that she could actually come right out and tell me all this as candidly as she had, though again, she still hadn't looked in my direction and I knew she was fighting off the tears which would have begun pouring down her face had she done so.

"What about oral sex?" I managed to ask just as candidly as she'd been doing. We were after all beyond the point of no return here if we were going to speak frankly and honestly about her home life situation.

"And that's another story altogether! I've 'done' him. But he's never reciprocated to me. Say's that a 'man' shouldn't have to do something like that to please a woman, and that only dykes and queer-boys would do things like that."

Even I had to laugh at that one, from what I was hearing her husband was one of the "old" boys in a very old fashioned way of thinking. But unfortunately, they did exist, and she was obviously married to one.

"I actually enjoy oral sex, I mean doing it for him. But it's something I've never personally experienced myself, and I am now getting to the point where I resent that fact, and because of it, refused to do it to him ever again unless he did. All I got from him out of that one was a total lack of interest either way. And that confused me, as well as hurt me. I began to wonder if I was even a very sexual woman, even attractive to him any more, or any other man for that matter!"

I still wasn't sure what if anything I could say or do that would help, short of telling her to get a divorce or something and find herself another husband, but she'd already indicated that divorce was out of the question because of her family and so called friends, that she'd be ostracized if she even attempted to do anything like this.

"So why don't you have an affair then?" I told her. Not fully realizing that for her, this was something someone couldn't simply run and out do.

"I've thought about that. You have no idea how often! But there isn't anyone I know, or have met who I'd even consider doing something like that with."

For the first time Lucille turned and looked directly towards me, "Until lately," She let that last comment hang there in the air for a moment, letting it sink in. "Brad," she began softly, slowly, "I've really struggled with even telling you about any of this. After all, I'm considerably older than you are, and I certainly know I'm no spring chicken either. I worried and fretted over even discussing half of this with you because you're about the only real friend I have that I could dare discuss any of this with in the first place. The more I thought about at least sharing some of this stuff with you, the more I thought about wanting to be with you as well. And so that's what's been bothering me more than anything the past few days, even more so than my feelings and situation with my own husband. Then, tonight at bowling, it all just seemed to come crashing down on me, and I decided to tell you what I was feeling and to hell with anything else. So, now that I've told you, are you shocked? Do you hate me? What?"

I answered her by sliding over to sit by her, and kissed her all in one sudden surprising motion. Lucille and I kissed and intertwined our tongues inside one another's mouths for an incredibly long period of time. I'm not even sure how long it was that we simply did this, but at one point, I felt her hand on mine, and felt it as she lifted it up to place it upon one of those marvelous full breasts of hers. I know she was nervous about sitting here in the garage in the event someone we might know would come down and find us. There were few cars however, and none that I knew of belonging to anyone we worked with. I told her to keep an eye on the door to the garage and to alert me if anyone opened it. I know she was wondering what it was I was suggesting and why, but then as I bent to undo the buttons on her blouse, she finally understood.

Though I certainly wasn't about to remove her blouse, especially under the circumstances, just seeing her bra-clad breasts showing more cleavage now than I had ever seen before had me stiffening in a hurry, though I certainly wasn't about to share that with her either. After I had finished undoing her blouse, Lucille leaned forward un-tucking it from her pants, then reached around and beneath her blouse, undoing her bra herself.

Lucille may have been in her early to mid fifty's, but the moment her bra fell away completely exposing those full mature looking breasts, all I could do was sit there and stare at them for a moment, disbelief I am sure clearly etched in my face that I was actually looking at her marvelous tits for the very first time.

"Touch me, please Brad, touch me," she whispered softly. I did.

Cupping each of them within my hands, I hefted them upwards, they were heavy and full, yet soft, pliant and warm to the touch as I continued to sit there kneading her flesh like a contented kitten. Even when I released them momentarily, I was just as content to continue to look at them, the way they rested against her chest so sensuously, the full rounded curvature of each, and though certainly not 'perky', though I couldn't imagine them ever having been so in the first place for as large as they both were, but they still maintained a gentle upwards sloping, gathering towards the still firm, very hard erect little points that became her nipples.

Even these were a simple treasure all by themselves. Lucille's nipples were a true rosy-red in color, areola no larger than dollar sized perhaps, but capped by two of the thickest, hardest little tit-nips I'd ever seen! For the briefest of moments, I could see in her face that she was becoming self-conscious about them, a slight flush spreading across her face that I could still see even in the shadowed light we were sitting in. Before she could cover them with her hands, which I realized at once that she was about to do, I leaned forward, capturing one of those delicious protrusions with my lips, my hand and fingers likewise reclaiming the other.

I heard her moan, felt her hands suddenly pressing against my head, her fingers all but digging into my scalp as I first suckled one tit, then the other, alternating back and forth between them, by hands, fingers doing the same whenever I traded off. I heard her moan even deeper then, and went from gently sucking her, to tonguing her hard little points with my tongue, flicking them rapidly back and forth, once again trading, exchanging the sensation from fast to slow and back again.

"Oh my God, your tongue," she groaned, moaning the words even as she spoke them, breathless, excited, aroused beyond imagining. "Is that…is that how you lick a woman's…a woman's…" "Cunt?" I said mouthing her nipple, sucking it even as I spoke the obscene word. And don't tell me how or why I chose to say that instead of pussy, or twat, or even vagina. She needed to hear the word, needed to hear it being used, said, lovingly, excitedly, needfully. Lucille needed to hear my own lust, my own desire for her in its use; no other word or description at that particular moment would have accomplished doing that.

"Yes. Cunt!" She gasped, hearing as she spoke, her own wanton need and desire, letting the heat of her excitement freeing herself enough to say it, and say it without self recrimination in having done so. "Cunt," she spoke saying it again, though more softly letting the word melt inside her mouth like a heavenly treat being tasted for the first time.

"Though I like saying pussy too," I told her. "I like the way it sounds, like something sweet, tasty, delicious."

"Oh yes, pussy," she said, letting the word roll off the tip of her tongue as though her nipple had suddenly become her pussy, and that I was licking it instead of her nipple.

"I wish I was doing this..." as I flicked her nipple with my tongue, "to your pussy Lucille."

Her breasts as I said, so soft, so pliant, as I now cupped one with two hands, I held, not quite pinching two tiny folds of flesh near her nipple, forcing it if anything to harden even more fully than it already was, extending itself outwards towards me. "If this was your clit," I told her, once again flicking that hard little nubbin, still firmly holding the surrounding flesh of her breast in my hands, between my fingers as though they were the very folds of her puffy swollen labia themselves. I sucked her again, softly, pulling on her tit with my mouth, holding it there, and then rolling it with my tongue as she moaned audibly, loudly into my ear as she bent her head next to mine.

Suddenly I felt her hands on me, pushing me away from her. I thought momentarily I had gone too far, said or done too much and had frightened her back into some senseless guilty reality.

"I know I told you I had never experienced that," she hesitated, her breath still raspy as she fought for control. "But I didn't mean to imply…"

"Shh," I said placing the tip of my finger to her lips. "Right now, there's nothing in the world that I want to do more," I said simply.

I looked around the garage; it would be safe enough with one or two minor adjustments. I didn't dare suggest going anyplace else. Number one, I didn't happen to know of any place at the moment that we could go. And number two, I was afraid if we postponed this moment in time, we would never gain it back again. Lucille was fragile, vulnerable, if I ruined the moment, the mood, I knew it could cause her a great deal of suffering and grief afterwards if this deteriorated into something less than magical for her. Even if we'd postponed it opting for a more comfortable setting, I somehow sensed that Lucille would convince herself it was wrong, that it was something she was asking, forcing me to do something I might otherwise not have wanted to do.

We were already taking a risk here as it was. Our mutual excitement, the element of danger that had intensified that, coupled with the sudden lack of inhibitions she was now showing wasn't something I wanted to chance losing again.

Lucille drove a fairly expensive wide-bodied car with a very large and comfy looking back seat. "Get in the back," I told her, almost demanding rather than asking her as I didn't want any fear or hesitation getting in the way. She opened her driver side door, looking quickly about as she did, then opened the door behind her slipping in quickly as the overhead light came on revealing her disheveled appearance momentarily. As she had done this, I had slid over into the driver' seat, started the car then backed it out of the parking spot she was in. Down at the far end there were few if any other cars, this particular area even darker than where we were now as the cement wall in the corner of the garage shut out any additional light from outside. Backing the car in rather than pulling it forward, gave us additional security, privacy and forewarning should anyone approach.

And though all of this took only a few precious moments, I worried that while doing so, Lucille would indeed begin to have second thoughts, reservations about what the two of us were about to do, not to mention of where we were about to do it. Satisfied how I had parked the car, I glanced into the back seat expecting to see her. Not until I actually looked over the seat itself and saw her lying there did I realize that she had completely removed her clothing, using both her blouse and skirt as a pillow now, which she had folded up and placed behind her head.

As much as I desperately wanted to, I didn't remove my own clothing as yet another precaution. If we did hear anyone, I could at least get out and delay anyone from coming any nearer, finding Lucille undressed. She could then at least get up into the front passenger seat, and quickly drive away, dressed or not dressed as she had time to do.

This I had told her as I'd moved the car, wanting to alleviate any fears she might have on being discovered, or about to be. I was surprised to see her smiling as I drove and as she obviously undressed there in the backseat, her look one of wonder, giddiness at how ridiculously daring and dangerous this all really was.

As I had been with her breasts, so was I again now as I first looked and saw her laying there, her hand coyishly covering her sex, her brief moment of embarrassment as I moved it away, forcing her to reveal herself to me fully and completely. I hadn't known what to expect of course, nor even really thought about it, she wasn't shaved, not something someone her age was doing then I suppose, but she wasn't all bushy either as I'd partially imagined. She was trimmed, her triangular patch of hair looking more neat than unruly, I actually ran my hand and fingers up through it, watching it float through the gaps of my fingers disappearing as my hand floated upwards towards her breasts once again where I caressed them momentarily, before sliding my hand once again back down over her belly, back to the tuft of soft downy like fur that greeted me, and then into the wetness that surprised me, surprised her as I gently dipped a finger, then another, lifting them to my lips, licking off the sweetness that I had found there.

For as tall as she was, Lucille had purposely positioned herself into a half-sitting, half lying position. She could if it became necessary sit up just enough to look out should we hear anyone's approach or sense movement. We also knew we could hide if necessary there in the backseat as well lowering even more into the darkness if we had to, if there were no other choice. And though we were in the back seat, it wasn't at all cramped, there was plenty of leg room for one thing, and enough space on the seat still remaining for me to comfortably lean over her as I knelt there on the floor.

She was certainly nervous, as I was. But that nervousness of excitement, desire seemed to heighten both of our senses as I finally placed the tips of my fingers on her pussy spreading her lips just as I had pretended to do while sucking her breast. Lucille knew this, felt it, and even then shuddered involuntarily as I fully exposed her hard tiny clitoris, watching it emerge from the protective sheath that until now had hidden it from my prying eyes and fingers. Even in the subdued darkness of the back seat, I could see a tiny shimmer of moisture upon the surface of her clit, which I then licked, tickling lightly, ever so softly with my tongue. More like the caress of a feather, did I allow my tongue-tip to explore her there, running it up and along side the folds of her sensitive flesh, mouthing her twin labia, gently sucking each, rolling them gently inside my mouth, then tonguing her top to bottom tasting the renewed flow of her feminely juices as they pooled comfortably within the tiny little pocket of her upturned split. From here, I returned, taking my time and enjoying the heavenly trip having bathed in that pool, taking some of her essence with me as I slid the curled pointed tip of my tongue upwards, once again seeking, finding, then pleasuring that hard little button that made her bounce, squeal and even laugh pleasurably.

I smiled, kissing her clit, and then sucking it briefly, tenderly. "Breathe," I said, kissing it, and then licking it again. "Breathe!"

She'd been holding her breath, which I'd just now noticed. "Oh God, I'm not sure I can," she said breathlessly, "I'm all tingly," she moaned emphasizing her light-headedness.

I again laughed, laughed into her cunt which made her laugh, until I licked it again sucking it a bit more firmly now, feeling that tiny little knot of pleasure harden between my lips while I stroked it, sucking it much as I had previously suckled her nipples.

Her low agonizing groan told me she was at least breathing, her hands once again digging into the top of my head as I began the assault upon her senses, flicking her clit now even more rapidly, though still lightly, one finger bathing in the pool of nectar that had again formed, then worming its way inside her where I played, feeling the heated depths of her womanly passage, stroking her, finger-fucking her there while simultaneously continuing to suck, tickle, flick and toy with her swollen hard clitoris.

I don't think she even knew she was doing it, but I began to sense her movements as she began gyrating beneath me, her mound simultaneously pressed against my face, her ass bouncing softly up and down against the seat. Finding one of her breasts with my free hand, I now began tweaking her nipples, causing her to moan even more harshly than she'd been doing, delighting myself in feeling its tautness, much like her clit which I continued to suckle, tongue-flick, or merely lick as the mood struck me to do.

I too was aroused of course, and felt the hard press of my prick digging almost uncomfortably against my pants, and then into the side of the backseat as I sat there still leaning over her. But whatever discomfort I may have felt was overwhelmed by the joyous catch in her throat as she began panting in a series of sudden intakes of air that alerted me she was nearing the edge of sweet ecstasy.

"Oh Brad, Oh Brad, Brad!" She began crying out, I felt her tense, felt her body shudder then immediately go into a series of convulsions that took her and then shook her from the inside out. Her scream I feared could have easily been heard by anyone had they been down in the garage at that very moment, and though that thought alarmed me a little, I continued to hold onto her clit, still sucking it, though I tapered off both the firmness of sucking or licking it as she slowly began easing back down from whatever heights she had gone to. Only when she became far too sensitive to continuing touching in any way, did I finally sit back up and take a nervous worried glance about our precarious surroundings. Thankfully I heard and saw nothing, turning back towards her where she now sat eyes open, and the most wondrous expression on her face.

"I never knew," she said simply, then saw tears once again forming within her eyes as she lay there still trying to collect herself.

I gathered her into my arms for a moment, holding her, but the sound of voices finally reached our ears, and we both sat up watching another couple head to their car a short distance away. We knew then that soon many others would be leaving, it was time to get dressed and leave here ourselves.

"What about you?" she asked, which surprised me.

"Don't worry about me," I told her. "I'll take care of that a bit later after I get home. And besides, this wasn't about me," I added smiling. She quickly kissed me once again, and then hurriedly began dressing as I kept watch ensuring that no one else would now come by and discover us accidentally.

* * *

The very next day at work, Lucille dropped by my office slipping me an envelope along with some files I'd been waiting for. I'd been somewhat apprehensive at seeing her, wondering how she might react towards me now having had time to think through everything that had been said, and had happened. I was relieved when she smiled, though she quickly turned heading back towards her own office having dropped off the letter. I stood up closing my own door, even as

I felt the sudden swelling of my cock begin inside my pants though I hadn't as yet even read her letter or knew of its content, but her smile and half-wink had given me some assurance that everything was fine between us.

She didn't address me in the letter, I was grateful for that, as I didn't want her to feel somehow obligated to me in any way, and then read:

"I just wanted to thank you. What I experienced last night was beyond anything I've ever felt before, and I'm not saying I am hoping for more, or expecting it. But...I also thought on the way home how I left you hanging, and it dawned on me that that was no different than what my own husband as too often done to me. And I regret we didn't have more time together to do something about that. So...I propose, if you're even still interested of course, that we park down in the garage, and rather than go to the bar, meet downstairs in the garage after-wards. If you'd like to do that, please let me know."

I wrote her back, feeling much like a teen back in High School again, and indicated to her that we should try, if at all possible to park our cars next to one another in the same dark corner where I had driven her car too. In that way we'd at least have my car to further block anyone from spying on us, or accidentally coming upon us. I managed to drop by her office then, and gave her my return letter. She looked up from her desk when I entered, pleased to see me, then actually laughed and indicated with her eyes where she was looking. I looked down at myself, knowing that I had indeed been fighting an erection, but was stunned to see the small wet spot that had appeared on the front of my beige slacks. Making a hasty retreat back to my own office, I stayed there until well after lunch not daring to embarrass myself any further.

The very next day Lucille once again came by my office even before working hours had officially begun. She again handed me another letter, though with no one else there yet to over hear anything said, told me that seeing my little wet-spot had been one of the best compliments she'd ever been given.

There was something else too. Though not totally out of character for her, she had worn a nice looking, though tight fitting sweater that showed off her ample breasts, and the fact that it was much lower cut without being too provocative, told me that she'd chosen it specifically for the most obvious reason.

"You look good," I told her. She knew what I was referring to of course, and then came over to where I was sitting and leaned over allowing me a simple peak down the front of her sweater at her magnificent breasts.

"Hope you're not wearing beige again today," she laughed straightening.

"Nope, black slacks today," I said grinning back at her.

It was like that all week long between us, flirting, though being very careful about it. Businesslike in every other respect throughout the course of the day, though we continued to toss managed smiles or a cautious wink one another's way whenever it was a hundred percent safe to be doing so.

It was like performing foreplay on one another, both of us anticipating and excited for bowling night to finally come around again.

* * *

I'd arrived a few minutes earlier than usual, and relieved when the spots I'd hoped we could park in would be vacant. They were, though there was one other car parked just one spot over from mine when I arrived. I didn't recognize the car, so didn't worry too much that it might be anyone we knew. As we didn't want to make things too obvious either, I then went upstairs to the bar and had a quick drink while waiting for the rest of our team members to arrive. Lucille arrived a short time afterwards, and we sat together putting on our shoes.

"Park next to me?" I asked nonchalantly.

She grinned nodding her head. I noticed she had already changed too, no longer wearing the skirt and blouse she had come to work in, now wearing a nice pair of jeans and another knit sweater, leaning over she pretended to be adjusting the laces on her shoe knowing full well from where I was sitting that I could see down through the opening.

"You're not wearing a bra!" I gasped in surprise. She giggled standing up straight once again.

"Surprised?"

"I am," I grinned.

"Well, we're not really at work, so I'm not too worried about not wearing one, and this is just bulky enough that you can't really tell for sure."

I was still grinning as she turned to go pick out a ball, as she didn't have one of her own.

"Oh…and I'm not wearing any panties either," she added.

By the time we finished the three games I was crawling the walls, as was she. Trying to act normal around one another all night hadn't been as easy as I thought it would be, if anything, it was far harder. We still laughed and joked along with everyone else just as we always did, but it was difficult as hell trying to maintain my ever-growing excitement as we finally finished and began straightening up the area.

Lucille didn't always stay afterwards to have a drink, only doing so on one or two previous occasions, so she immediately headed down to the parking area after having said goodnight to everyone. I stayed long enough to have one quick beer, which really was a quick one, then headed out myself.

Getting to the bottom of the stairs and looking down to the darkened area where are cars were parked gave me an instant erection as I quickly approached, seeing her sitting there in her car waiting for me.

Taking a quick look about, I then ducked inside her car on the passenger side and slid in next to her. Much to my delight and surprise, she had already lifted her sweater up and over her breasts so that they were already bare and waiting for me the moment I sat down. Without any hesitation I reached over and began playing with them, caressing and toying with those hard fat tips, soon licking them and sucking them greedily.

"I want to see you," she breathed as I sat there sucking her breast. After having driven one another crazy all week, I wasn't about to waste any time asking her if she was sure, or pretending that more than anything at this moment I wanted her to see me, see how hard I was, see how horny I was, and actually finally touch me.

I immediately unbuckled my belt, and pulled the zipper down. Lucille wasn't about to wait any longer either, the moment I had, she slipped her hand inside my pants immediately finding my hard swollen erection and began fondling it.

"Let me see it," she said once again, not even content with doing this.

It was an easy matter for me to raise my ass up off the seat, slip both my jeans and shorts down around my ankles when I did. She never took her hand off me while doing this, continuing to stroke, fondle, and then thumb my blood-engorged head for several moments, finally squeezing out a nice fat droplet of precum fuck juice which she then smeared lovingly all over my cock.

"Fuck that's nice," I moaned, not even realizing I'd used the word, though she giggled. "What?"

"Hearing you say fuck sounds so erotic," she giggled again.

"Hell Lucille, hearing you say fuck is even more erotic!" I told her moaning as she stroked my cock up and down, once again squeezing it.

"In that case…fuck!" she said, saying it again. "Fuck…fuck…fuck!"

* * *

I loved the fact that Lucille's car had a bench seat, sitting beside one another without anything getting in the way between us made it a lot easier to reach over and caress her beautiful bare breasts while she was busily stroking me. I soon slipped my hand down to her crotch however, rubbing her through the soft almost flannel like material of the pants she was wearing. "You keep doing that, I'm going to soak through them," she stated, then lifted her ass and quickly pulled them all the way off. I began fingering her as she sat jerking me, enjoying the naughtiness of so simple an act, making us both feel like teenagers at the drive-in.

"You are wet!" I grinned feeling her moisture gather and pool inside her wet split as I continued walking my fingers around inside her.

"Damn horny too!" she grinned back, and then pouted somewhat. "But I can't stay as long tonight as we did last week," she added. "He's coming home earlier tonight, and he'll still be expecting dinner."

"Shit," I allowed, "If you need to go…"

"Not yet, not until you've come for me," she said simply. "I'm not letting you go in the same condition you did last time."

Though I was disappointed we wouldn't be able to repeat some of the pleasures we'd enjoyed previously, the fact that she was stroking and playing with me while I was doing the same to her was still very erotic and very sensual sitting here in her car in the parking garage.

"Damn!"

"What?" she asked concernedly.

I felt silly telling her this. "I don't have anything."

Thankfully she knew what I meant. "Not to worry, I've actually been thinking about this all day," she told me. "When you're ready, I want you to cum on my breasts."

"Hmm," I moaned simply as her hand continued to thumb and tease the super-sensitive head of my prick.

"I'm looking forward to feeling all that hot juice running down my breasts," she added now coaxing me to do just that by the way her voice changed, the lustiness of her urgings as she spoke increasing the pleasure and bringing me ever nearer that inevitable moment.

I was still finger-fucking her as well, twiddling her twat, flicking her clit with my fingers and then slipping them deeply inside her back and forth as she continued doing similar things to me.

"Almost there," I moaned feeling that all too familiar sensation beginning to tingle deep within my heavy-laden balls.

Having heard this, Lucille drew my cock even closer to herself, placing it almost reverently between her breasts, and then teasing her own nipples with the head of my dick as she rubbed it back and forth against herself.

"Oh fuck…here it comes!" I told her, and then watched as my prick began spewing a torrent of hot creamy cum against her breasts. Almost gleefully, Lucille kept jacking me off, watching each spurt land forcefully against her breasts, careful to ensure that each one received an equal allotment of my spunk.

When I was finally drained, when she had milked out every last drop of juice from my prick, only then did she release it and begin to massage the creamy substance I'd just dumped on her into her own tits.

"That…feels nice," she almost purred, "it's so warm and creamy," she half whispered as I sat there watching her massaging in all that natural body lotion.

"Whew," I exhaled, enjoying not only the pleasure of afterglow as I sat there, but likewise enjoying the erotic view of her as she caressed and played with her breasts. Once again I moved towards her. "Lay down." There was still plenty of room, and she did so.

I quickly went back to fingering her, she was close and began that quick pant as she breathed that told me she was nearing her own sweet orgasm. Spreading her lips, I exposed her hard little clitoris even more fully, now directly teasing it with the tip of my finger.

"Fuck…yes! Yes! Yes!" she wailed, then climaxed.

We sat kissing, still touching one another intimately, though she soon broke away and again apologized for needing to go.

"Next week? Same time? Same place?" She asked being silly.

I loved it. "Wouldn't miss it for the world," I told her. Dressing hurriedly after that, I stood beside my car watching her go, already dreading another long week ahead of us, but already looking forward to it at the same time.

* * *

Once again we spent the days teasing one another with our thoughts and words, careful to not openly flirt with one another even though we were both tempted to do so. Instead we exchanged notes back and forth throughout the day like a couple of kids in school, enjoying the erotic thoughts that we shared, each one becoming more intimate, more erotic and sensual in nature.

Lucille confessed to me how she'd begun masturbating again, frequently now every night, thinking about what we'd so far done with one another there in the parking garage. I boldly asked her to tell me what she did, where she did it, to share those naughty moments with me so that I could imagine them inside my own head.

I sat reading just one such note at my desk after she's swung by dropping it off.

"Last night, as I frequently do, I went into the bathroom to run my bath before going to bed, as I lay there in the tub, once again feeling horny, aroused, I remembered something I used to do as a teenager, something I hadn't done in years, and yet remembered fondly how good it had felt back then. So I scooted myself down towards the faucet where the water splashed and pounded against my "Cunt" she underlined the word, letting me know in writing it that she'd become comfortable with using it in the context she now was. "It felt good, the force of the waters flow pounding and playing against me, just laying there feeling it, imagining it as your fingers, your mouth sucking my clit until I finally climaxed."

Just reading her short note made me horny as hell and I wrote her back.

"The image of you doing that has aroused me like you wouldn't believe. I am sitting here at my desk, my prick hard and swollen just thinking about you enjoying yourself like that. I am tempted to take it out, and secretly jerk myself off as aroused as I am."

I waited until no one was around her office, swung by and delivered my note to her before she could say anything, and returned to my office.

Brief minutes later, she came by mine, dropping off another note to me, but she had also brought along a paper cup from the drinking fountain. I took it from her, wondering curiously why she had. She merely grinned, winked and then returned to her own office.

"At lunch, close your door and jerk it off for me," she began. "Jerk off while you're thinking about what I'm going to do with your cum after you put it inside the cup. Bring it to me afterwards, I will then go into the women's bathroom and pour your cream onto my pussy and use it to masturbate myself with."

The thought of her doing that aroused me even more. I was relieved that the noon hour was only twenty minutes away, and spent it composing another note while I waited before closing my door, and then doing exactly what she'd asked me to do for her.

"I wish I was squirting it directly on you myself," I told her. "I want to squirt all over your cunt, and then watch you masturbate with it until you cum. Just thinking about doing that, seeing you and knowing that you soon will be touching yourself while using my cream to do so with has me hard as a fucking rock!"

Most everyone had gone out to lunch, as was usually the case. As I often closed and locked my door when leaving and going out to lunch myself, I wasn't at all concerned should anyone come by and find it locked and closed as I secretly sat there jacking off thinking about what Lucille would soon be doing herself. After only a few short minutes, I placed the cone-shaped cup over the head of my prick, watching as my spunk began filling it. I almost laughed afterwards as I sat there holding onto the cup, unable to sit it down really, with my prick still exposed. I finally sat it inside my coffee cup, quickly zipped myself up once again, then retrieved it and walked the short distance over to Lucille's office. She was waiting for me as I entered, smiling, and handed her the cum-filled paper cup as she came around her desk taking it from me and immediately headed off towards the bathroom.

By the time bowling night had arrived once again, I could hardly concentrate on the game, already excited and looking forward to another adventure together down stairs in the garage.

"You need to rush home tonight?" I asked worriedly.

"Not tonight," she grinned in reply. "He's working late, so we have plenty of time."

We sat there discussing our week's worth of naughty wicked thoughts, her masturbation episodes both at work and at home, as well as my own. We touched, fondled and pleasured one another the entire time until we'd both reached fever pitch.

"I want you to fuck me tonight," she said simply. "I want to feel you inside of me."

Lucille wasn't comfortable remaining in the front seat. With her car backed into the stall, the additional darkness of the broken unreplaced light to further conceal us, as well as my own car parked next to hers as a further shield from any watchful eyes, we quickly slipped over the seat rather than getting out and back in again. Hurriedly we fumbled through removing our clothes, neither one of us wanting to fuck while wearing anything. The sense of our nudity, there in the backseat, in the garage, was intoxicating as it added to the sense of excitement and danger.

I sat, Lucille climbing into my lap though facing forward so she could also see as lookout while fucking me in this position. I soon eased my hard stiff prick inside that warm soft fuck tunnel, clasping both of her firm full breasts in my hands, tweaking and toying with her nipples as she began moving, gyrating herself up and down against me. We'd hardly even begun fucking however when she stopped suddenly, only then the sound of voices reaching my own ears. Lucille quickly climbed off my lap, sitting down beside me where we both sunk down even further into the seats, prepared to hide on the floor if necessary. It was thrilling, yet nerve wracking all at the same time as the voices came closer, drawing nearer with each passing moment. We could hear them talking, a male and female but a short distance away. Then there was laughter, an obvious giggle, and together we both sat up somewhat looking forward over the seat.

In the next row across from us, though at an angle from where we were, we could see another couple standing by a car. We watched as they stood kissing for a moment, then giggled quietly as he began caressing her breast through her clothing, finally lifting the tee shirt she was wearing to better feel her, even though she was wearing a bra. Likewise, the woman lowered her hand, rubbing the front of the guy's pants, obviously teasing his cock through the material.

"Damn," I said. Even though it was somewhat interesting to watch, especially under the circumstances, the fact was they were unknowingly interrupting our own naughty little session together. We didn't dare continue doing much of anything, though Lucille did reach over and begin fondling my prick as we sat there watching the other couple teasing one another as they stood by the side of the car. Luckily, that's all that was meant to happen between them at least, as they soon parted, and the woman got in her car soon after driving away. He likewise then walked over to his, getting in and left immediately after.

"That was interesting," Lucille breathed with a sigh of relief.

And though it had been, it also made me realize that we might not be the only one's to decide to have an adventure down here in the parking lot either. We'd have to be even more cautious and careful next week, and I made a mental note to look for the woman's car before we began doing anything in the event they decided to do a lot more, just as we had been.

"Now I am really horny!" Lucille told me, and climbed back up into my lap once again where we proceeded to take up where we'd just left off.

Thankfully the lot didn't have a lot of cars remaining in it, nor especially any that were parked too closely away from us. No one else ventured down to the garage while we sat there, joyfully, pleasurably fucking away like crazy there in the back seat.

As we fucked, I touched and frigged her clit, which she enjoyed my doing, likewise continuing to fondle and play with her enormous breasts. She began humping, fucking me fast and furiously, the obvious signs of her impending climax just beginning. She began tossing her head wildly from side to side, humping me almost spastically, then climaxed, somehow managing to force herself from screaming out as she did. I had nearly cum with her, somehow managing to regain control just before I did, and just before she slipped off of me, sitting beside me now still trying to collect herself.

"I want to taste you now," she said lustily. "I want to taste your prick with my juices still coating it."

I hated to admit it even to myself, but it had been a long time since I'd even had or been given a blowjob. As Lucille placed her warm teasing mouth over the head of my prick, I knew immediately that it wouldn't last very long. I'd been too close as it was while fucking her, and now the exquisite sensation of her lips milking me renewed that inevitable pleasure.

"Fuck Lucille, I'm sorry...but,"

She never let me finish the thought, her mouth and head suddenly working me in furious abandon, coaxing the eruption of my spunk, which immediately occurred as I began filling her mouth with my semen. Each skyrocketing jettison of my spunk inside her mouth sent me to even greater heights of ecstasy and pleasure as she consumed me, gulping down the nectar that her hands and lips continued pumping out of me.

* * *

As was usually the case, the week dragged by slowly, though we continued on with our naughty notes back and forth to one another throughout the day, which helped pass the time and the monotony of an otherwise boring work day. I was of course once again looking forward to bowling night, but just before leaving to drive there, Lucille popped into my office quite unexpectedly.

"I needed to let you know before we got there," she said obvious disappointment already showing in her eyes. "I won't be able to stay tonight, not for long anyway, perhaps just a few minutes."

She didn't need to go into any further explanations, we both understood that. I was obviously disappointed myself, but it was a fact of life for us.

"Meet me down by the car afterwards?" she asked hopefully.

"I'll be there."

Luckily, we actually finished bowling fifteen minutes ahead of schedule. "I'll meet you downstairs," she said quickly walking off to replace her bowling ball, and then heading for the restrooms. I'd already informed the others on our team that I needed to make it an early night myself, and then headed down into the garage to wait for her. Glad to see no one else was down there, I stood cautiously between our cars waiting for her. When she appeared at the bottom of the steps, I was surprised to see she had changed clothes once again, now wearing an all too familiar sweater and skirt. Passing by where I stood, she immediately walked around her car over to the passenger side next to the cement wall beckoning me to follow her, which I did.

"Fuck me."

"Here?"

"Yes here, right now," she stated, then lifted her sweater up and over her breasts, revealing to me as she did that she had removed her bra. I fumbled quickly with my zipper, removing my rapidly swelling prick, and quickly discovered that she had likewise removed her panties. Standing behind her, she leaned over the hood of her car somewhat, and I slipped inside of her wet silky cunt. Watchful and nervously cautious of our surroundings, and equally grateful that I had not even spotted the other woman's car from the previous week, I stood there slowly fucking myself in and out of that heavenly quim, feeling her magnificent breasts with my hands as she fucked back in unison against me.

"Hurry…fill me," she pleaded.

"But…"

"No, don't worry about me. Just fill my cunt with your juice."

Moments later I was doing just that, spending myself deeply inside her. Lucille quickly stepped into her panties, which she'd placed just inside her handbag, kissing me quickly and once again apologizing to me for the hurried departure.

"I'll explain it all tomorrow," she said huskily, then immediately got inside her car and drove away.

I was anxious to hear from her the following day, and soon after her arrival to work, she passed by my office once again slipping me a hand written note.

"Sorry for last night," she began. "But my husband's parents are in town and he 'required' that I be there to entertain them. I almost wasn't able to even go bowling, but explained that I had to as there hadn't been time enough to locate a substitute, and I wasn't about to let my team down. Anyway, I thought you might get a kick out of knowing that I did indeed entertain his family, cooking dinner, eating, and sitting around chatting with them afterwards, all the while knowing that I could feel your cum dripping out of my pussy, soiling the very panties I had put back on. All I could think about was how you fucked me while we stood there in the parking lot together, and how wicked it felt to know that I still had your cum in me while doing all that."

Reading her letter gave me an idea, and I wrote back.

"I assume you're wearing panties today too. So, if you are, bring them to me today before lunch."

Shortly before noon, she did, handing me an interoffice envelope, which by the feel, told me immediately what was inside. She looked over towards me curiously, but then left my office without saying anything. Once again I waited until most everyone was gone, and then stood locking my door. Opening the drawer where I'd put the envelope, I removed her panties from the folder, unzipped my fly and began jerking myself off. When I came, I placed her silk-feeling panties over my prick, shooting my juice into them, then refolded them and placed them back inside the envelope.

She was obviously expecting me as she'd remained in her own office during lunch. I returned the envelope to her and smiled, and quickly headed back to my own office. Less than a half an hour later, she came back, once again handing me the same envelope along with a short note.

"I just finished using these to masturbate in the bathroom with," she explained. "If and when you think you can, fill them again and bring them back to me."

Though the lunch hour was nearly over, and though I had indeed just jacked off a load for her a short time ago, with the thought of what she had done, and would soon do again, I managed to produce another though much smaller load, spilling myself once again into her now very messy sticky panties, and stuffed them back inside the envelope, returning it to her. She seemed pleasantly surprised by this, accepting my gift, and immediately stood once again heading off in the direction of the restrooms.

* * *

The following day she was waiting for me when I came into work. Not many others had arrived as yet, so it was safe talking to her.

"Brad? I want to buy a vibrator, but I don't know where to go to get one…do you?"

I did. There was in fact one of those adult novelty stores not more than ten minutes away from the office. We decided to go there during lunch together. We'd gone out to lunch together before, so doing so again wouldn't look or appear abnormal if anyone even bothered to notice that we had, especially as we hadn't done it very often.

She was obviously nervous when we pulled around back behind the store. Somewhat worried that we might be seen going in, we quickly did so, relieved that we didn't bump into anyone else that we knew.

"Shit, I had no idea there were so many to choose from!" she stated as we walked into the back of the store where they kept all the really naughty stuff. I laughed as she browsed through a few of the toys, wondering how people could even use some of them.

"Maybe we should just get you something simple for starters," I advised her, which she seemed more than willing to go along with.

We picked out a fairly standard, though flexible realistic looking cock vibrator, and I again laughed as she blushed while we stood in front of the clerk making our purchase. She smiled at us knowingly, rang us up and told us to "have a nice day," along with a suggestive wink. In addition to the vibrator itself, I had also purchased some new batteries to go along with it. Sliding back into the car, she immediately opened the package, putting in the batteries, and turned it on. It seemed to come alive in her hand with a steady all too familiar humming sound.

"Haven't you ever used one of these before?" I asked her.

"Are you kidding? Me?" she laughed seriously. "No...never! And this certainly isn't anything my husband would care for me to be using either," she added with a distinct sense of displeasure in her tone of voice.

And as she most often did and wore to work, Lucille then quickly glanced around the small enclosed parking area. There were only two other cars, and we immediately figured they belonged to the people who worked inside as there was more than enough parking spots in front of the store that people could easily and quickly use.

"Keep an eye out," she told me. "I want to see how this feels."

Turning sideways on the seat so I could watch for any additional cars coming into the lot, Lucille placed the still vibrating toy against her clit, through the material of the panties she was wearing.

"Holy shit!" she exclaimed a second or two after that. "I think I could come rather quickly this way," she informed me.

"Then why don't you?" I told her.

She grinned. "Let me watch you while I'm doing it then," she challenged me back. So far we hadn't seen anyone else pull in, and during this time of day, the prospect of doing so wasn't very likely. I immediately unzipped my fly, removing my already hard stiff cock and began stroking it for her while she watched, and while she then slipped her panties off to one side, and slowly eased the vibrating fuck toy inside herself.

Once again like an unprepared kid, I informed her I had no place to shoot my spunk safely without making a big mess. Without any hesitation she quickly slipped her panties down her legs handing them to me.

"Seems we're making a habit of this lately," I grinned taking them from her.

"Yeah, I've got quite a collection of cum-filled panties waiting to be washed," she teased back.

Then we sat back watching one another masturbating ourselves, seeing the look of pure pleasure on her face as she experimented with the new-found toy, my hand slipping and sliding over the head of my pre-lubricating prick as the juices of my own arousal poured out in wanton expectation.

She was soon climaxing gloriously on her new toy as I covered the head of my prick with her panties and began soiling them with my semen. Handing them back to her afterwards, she grinned stuffing them back inside of her purse along with her new toy as we headed back to the office.

* * *

When bowling night finally arrived once again, we were both about as horny as we'd ever been. After another week of naughty/dirty notes telling one another how we masturbated ourselves at night, what we thought about etc, we were both at fever pitch after reaching her car down in the garage. We had again climbed into the back seat, but I had already told her in no uncertain terms that I wanted very much to go down on her again. She was obviously delighted by this, though surprising me when she sat on the top of the front seat with her legs to either side of me in back. Positioned as she was, she was the perfect height for me to lean forward and begin tonguing her, and though she was sitting this way, and somewhat exposed, we still had the advantage of my car blocking anyone from seeing us, and hopefully the advanced warning of footsteps or conversation should anyone come down into the garage.

Without any rush to be home tonight either, I took my time with her, enjoying the taste and flavor of her exposed cunt, delighting myself in pulling her rather long labia, stretching the folds and fingering her simultaneously while flicking her tender little clit with my tongue. She came twice, surprising us both as she humped herself against my face almost immediately after climaxing the first time until she had quickly done so again, and then, just as quickly, slipping down to slide over my lap, capturing my prick inside that wet, sloshy passage.

I was two seconds away from shooting my spunk inside her when we heard footsteps, and frighteningly enough, hearing them almost too close to allow us to hide without being seen. Seeing movement far too closely away from us for comfort, Lucille merely toppled sideways taking me with her as we dove into the backseat of her car. We lay there listening for long moments, hearing the sound of a door opening, closing, then the car finally driving away.

"Do you think that they saw us?" Lucille asked worriedly.

"No, I don't think so," I said hopefully, though in truth, I really didn't know for sure.

It was evident that the closeness of the call bothered her, so we quickly dressed even though I had failed to climax, though seeing her fear, it was the last thing on my mind. This time I left first, doing so in the event there was anyone we knew who might be watching, but I saw no one as I left the lot and slowly drove down the street towards home, looking back in my rearview mirror just before turning to see Lucille's car leaving the lot, heading off in the opposite direction.

I didn't worry about it until the following day at work when one of the guys we bowled with stopped by my office.

"Hey, wasn't that your car down in the garage?" he asked me pointedly. "Didn't see you in the bar anywhere though," he added.

I knew without any doubt that he knew it was my car, and that it had obviously been sitting there for a while with me no where to be found.

"Probably...dead battery," I explained. "Had to call and get a ride home," I said lamely.

"Don't you have any jumper cables?"

I did. "No, been meaning to pick some up, planning on doing that today, along with getting a new battery." I added weakly.

"Should have come and got me," he continued. "Had a pair of them in my car."

"Yeah, well I didn't really think of that, and was no big deal anyway."

Mike left shortly after that, but our talk left me nervously worried. At least he hadn't mentioned anything about seeing Lucille's car parked next to mine, so hopefully he didn't know whose it was in the first place, nor had seen either of us suddenly ducking down into the back seat. I quickly scribbled a note off to Lucille however, explaining everything that had happened and gave it to her along with a troubled look. She read it even before I had left her office.

"Meet me after work," she said simply.

I knew where she meant without having to ask. We had done so a couple of times, just quick last minute note exchanges or quick little chats before heading off to home. I pulled into the park, which was a short distance away from the office and waited for her. Minutes after arriving, she did pulling in next to me, and then quickly got out of her car slipping into mine.

"Maybe we'd better cool it for a couple of times," she suggested. "As much as I hate to admit this Brad, if either one of us gets caught, we would both be in a shit lot full of trouble."

She was certainly right about that, we both would, not only in our respective relationships, but at work as well.

"O.K.," I agreed reluctantly, "maybe we should."

I made a point of staying in the bar with the guys after bowling the following week. Lucille went home immediately after bowling with obvious sadness in her face just before doing so, and as much as I hated seeing that, I felt better and somewhat relieved sitting there with the guys having a couple of beers before heading off myself.

Even our playful naughty notes seemed to taper off the week after, though we still discussed and shared our desires for one another, there seemed to be a hesitant cautionary underlying tone to them even doing this. We had but a few weeks bowling left remaining to us as well, and we both knew what that meant. Soon, neither one of us would have a reason to be staying after work on Wednesday evenings, and unless we came up with some other idea or justification for doing so, our time together was quickly drawing to an end as well.

We had one last encounter down in the garage before bowling season ended. But even that was far less than satisfactory for either one of us. Lucille needed/wanted to suck me off, which she did, and which felt marvelous, but she'd refused to allow me to reciprocate in any way shape or form, not even allowing herself to undress even partially so that I might do so. It was quick as well...too quick, and she immediately headed off home afterwards.

As it was a main Holiday weekend ahead of us, I had long ago scheduled to be off that Thursday through Monday before returning into work. Tuesday morning as I walked by her office, I nearly tripped over myself when I did. Alarmed, I headed quickly to my own office and saw the yellow sticky note pasted on the side of my computer. CYD was all it said, which was another secret code of ours for "Check your Drawer".

Far in the back behind all my normal work files, I found the special folder we'd both been using and keeping to pass along notes and correspondence when one or the other of us wasn't around. Opening it I found a thick heavy envelope waiting for me. Inside was the very first pair of panties she'd ever used on me to catch my spunk with.

"Brad, I'm so terribly sorry to do this, this way," she began. "But after everything we'd had and shared together, it's made me realize just how unhappy I truly am. But it also made me realize that I can't jeopardize either one of us, family wise, or job wise for a few brief fleeting moments of joy and pleasure. I'm leaving my husband, which is the first thing I've been needing to do. I am going to California to stay with my brother and his wife until I can figure things out, and figure out what I want to do with my life after this. I'm sorry that I am telling you this way, but I know I couldn't have faced you directly without loosing it, and making everyone suspicious in the process. I'll be fine, as I know you will. But it is truly best for each of us that I do this, this way. I hope you will keep these as a token of my love and fondest memories of you. Love, Lucille."

It was the last time I ever heard or thought of her again, until today. I am sitting here now outside on a Sunday morning reading the paper. I didn't even really recognize her photo initially, nor the name listed as she'd obviously changed the last name I had known her by. But I now knew looking at her photo, I knew it was her.

Twenty years now and I still have that pair of panties she once gave me. They're tucked away somewhere up on the shelf in my closet now. I think I'll go find them, and spend some time remembering with fondness a very special lady.

FROM THE CAR WASH TO HEAVEN

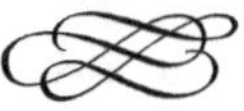

Since Dave was "in between jobs" thanks to the slow economy, he spent many of his days doing errands. He didn't particularly like fighting the moms and kids everywhere he went but it did give him a reason to get out of the house. And it kept him from spending too much money on leisure activities like golfing with none coming in right now. So the trip to the car wash with the SUV was item number one on today's to-do list and the trip outside was welcome.

Dave stopped the SUV in the entrance drive to the car wash and was met by the attendant who immediately opened all the doors and hatch and started vacuuming it. Order paperwork in hand, he walked up the stairs into the lobby and went to pay for the "Basic" as it was called. Normally he enjoyed this part of the car wash experience, as the cashier was almost always a young, attractive college girl around 20 years old and always friendly. And, since it was summer, he was guaranteed she would be wearing something sheer for a blouse and possibly no bra. Ok, he said to himself, it was a cheap thrill but it did brighten up the chore and the day. Gosh, he must be getting old if this is what he called a "thrill."

There was no line at the counter and, much to Dave's disappointment, the person behind the counter was not the anticipated college coed but a 17 year old guy. Nice fellow and competent but not worth spending too much time visiting with.

Having paid the bill, Dave went to the window to watch the SUV progress through the myriad of sprays, brushes and foam. He chuckled to himself at how fascinated he was by this process still. Boys never really do grow up, do they?

As he looked towards the entrance to the progression of cars and water, he spied something of interest out of the corner of his eye. Not wanting to be too obvious, he glanced casually around the room and then back to the wash line. Sure enough, it was a cute coed, about 5'5" tall, thin with shoulder length brown hair, short tan shorts and a loose fitting, white V-neck T-shirt with sandals, probably 23 or 24 years old. Since it was the end of Spring Break week, she had the requisite tan and no lines visible. Of course, Dave used his imagination to fill in where the lines would be, where the tan stopped and the white started. Twenty years ago, when Dave was in college, almost all the girls wore two-piece suits with bikini bottoms. Dave's cock got hard just thinking about some of his friends who had worn them out by the pool. He had even dated and fucked a couple of them. Great memories. Nowadays, though, girls wore those funny suits that looked like a boys trunks with a girls top. He failed to see the sexiness in such a combination but he was never very good with what was "in fashion" at any given time.

Dave wanted badly to give this girl a full visual inspection but knew if he did he would practically be arrested. So he continued to watch the cars as they came down the line and decided he could get away with one more look if he was careful. Then he would be content go outside and wait for the SUV to be finished and tackle the rest of the day's errands.

Before he could look, however, she walked right up beside him and joined him watching the cars progress through the line. She looked a bit nervous, like she wasn't sure how this process worked and glanced around a lot. Dave really didn't care, he was just enjoying the odor from her body. He'd swear it was some type of Hawaiian Tropic suntan lotion, his favorite. And every time she turned her head, her shoulder-length hair would move just enough to attract the eye but not look like she was flaunting her looks. His first thought was to put his arm around her waist, pull her close and bury his nose into her neck and take in the aroma.

Bad idea, he thought. Especially here in the lobby. Time to take his hardening cock and move outside, away from temptation before he acted on his imagination. He put his sunglasses on and headed out of the lobby.

No sooner had he gotten to the outdoor patio to wait for his SUV, than the coed began following him. Being a distance apart, he got to check her out a little longer without being so obvious. She had a slim figure but very nice dimensions. She wasn't very busty, maybe a 34 he guessed, but had great shapely legs that ended in a nice round ass. Her face was pretty with big blue eyes, light red, full lips, a perky nose and light makeup. She was wearing a bra but there was still a nice soft jiggle to her breasts as she walked, telling Dave they were natural. He'd swear he could see her nipples getting harder through her shirt.

"Is this where the cars end up?" She had directed the question to Dave, kind of in a general way as she put on her sunglasses. But it must've been to him, as they were the only two out on the patio.

"Yeah, they'll dry them out there and give you a wave when it's done. Then you can just hand them your receipt, and you're gone," he told her.

"Thanks," she said. "I'm from out of town and didn't quite know how they did things here. I guess it's pretty much the same everywhere."

"Pretty much. By the way, my name is Dave," he said. Dave was not going to do that anonymous conversation thing much longer.

"My name is Cheryl. Nice to meet you."

"So, where is home if you are from out of town?"

"Washington state, Seattle area," she said. "I'm just down for the night to see my boyfriend. I just got done spending the week with my folks at their condo in Las Vegas. One night here and then back home."

"End of break, huh?"

"Yeah," she said.

"Las Vegas is an interesting place. It's kind of two places in one–the Strip and then the rest of the town. Usually I'm good for about 3 days there before I get sick of it and have to come home," he said.

Dave was trying to make good, non-threatening conversation but his cock was telling him his interest was far beyond non-threatening. He was already day dreaming about Cheryl sucking his cock and then bending over so he could do her doggy style, holding on to that white ass surrounded with golden brown tan. He could even hear her moans as he fucked her, her voice asking for more. The smell of that suntan lotion didn't help matters much either. Man, did he have a great imagination!

Cheryl's voice brought him back to the moment.

"We've had a condo there for years so I'm used to it. Oh, here comes his car," she said.

"His car?"

"Yeah," Cheryl said. "My boyfriend's."

"The red car? The one with the dark tinted windows?" Dave asked.

"Yeah, he likes them that dark but it drives me crazy. I'd swear they're illegal but he hasn't gotten a ticket yet," she said. "He's in class for another couple of hours so I told him I would get the car washed. Which one is yours?"

Dave could tell Cheryl was starting to get more relaxed around him. The nervous glancing was over and now she was almost facing him to hold the conversation. He even thought he caught her giving him the once over behind her sunglasses, checking him out. He must have passed muster and not been too old or out of shape because she was still there talking to him.

"The white SUV. I never thought I would own one but it's turned out to be real practical," he said. "Good for work and dress up and also going to the hardware store."

Both the red sports car and the SUV were almost done being dried now. Dave had to make up his mind in a hurry whether he was going to try and take this farther with Cheryl or not. Otherwise they would be going their separate ways in just minutes and Dave would be left wondering what might have happened with this pretty thing. In his college days, this would have been a no-brainer, free love and all that. But times had changed and there was an age difference here that he hadn't had to deal with before.

Dave decided to see just how interested Cheryl was in him and hopefully getting fucked. He decided he would invite her for coffee but, at the same time, look her up and down with the lustiest look he could muster so she would have to know what he was really after. If she was not interested, she could politely decline and not be embarrassed. If she was interested, well he would know he wasn't wasting his time.

Dave turned to his right and saw Cheryl looking at him with a half smile, leaning on the railing. He faced her completely. He knew she could see his eyes through his sun glasses. He gave her a friendly smile, looked into her eyes for a good five seconds and then started to speak and at the same time let his eyes wander in detail down her tight, brown body.

"It sounds like you have some time to waste before returning the car?"he said. Dave began moving his eyes down from her eyes to her lips, then on to her collar bones. He loved V-neck T-shirts on girls because you could always get a hint of cleavage and anticipate what was underneath. He moved his eyes directly to her breasts, looking to see if he could turn Cheryl on more and get those nipples to be even more prominent through her shirt. Man, he wanted to get some idea if this girl was finding him desirable or not.

"The mall is across the street, you might want to go there and do some window shopping," he continued. As he had hoped, Dave could see the outline of Cheryl's nipples grow under her shirt. They were pronounced but not pointed. Dave loved nipples like this—ones that were soft, just approaching eraser size when erect. They were the best to suck.

"Or there are some restaurants up the street." Cheryl changed her posture slightly, very aware that she was being stared at in detail but the smile did not disappear from her face. Dave continued his gaze downward, across her flat stomach to the "v" made by her shorts, where those tanned legs came together. He desperately wanted to find out if she was shaved or not, and to bury his face in that young pussy.

"You could grab a cup of coffee and some danish and just hang out." Dave now returned his gaze to Cheryl's face to see what her reaction was to his visual come on. Maybe she would be too immature to know he was trying to hit on her. Or, maybe she would just be offended, having been looked over like a piece of meat. Or, maybe she was getting as wet as he was hard. Being as obvious as he was, he was sure to get his answer shortly.

Cheryl looked straight at Dave, then looked quickly at the bulge his erect cock was making in his shorts and back to his face and smiled. It was obvious she was trying to be as cool as possible about the circumstance and possibly a little unsure of committing to the rendezvous with a stranger. "Coffee sounds good but I'll probably skip the danish. Are you buying?"

"Absolutely," Dave said. "Why don't you follow me. I know several places close by. Do you prefer quiet and cozy or loud like Denny's?" Dave figured he should give Cheryl one more chance to back out if she wanted to.

"Quiet and cozy sounds good," she said. "I've had enough noise for a while. If you could find a place that gave good back massages AND had good coffee, that would be perfect!" She laughed as she said it and lightly ran her hand over his shoulder. The physical barrier had been broken finally and by her!.

"Follow me, I think I have the perfect place," he said.

Dave tipped the wash crew and watched from his SUV as Cheryl got in her car. Those legs of hers were driving him crazy and she was still smiling, though not knowing what was about to happen next.

Dave considered taking her back to his house as it wasn't far away but decided that would probably scare her off. He decided that the only thing to do was to get a hotel room at The Inn, a place about a mile from the car wash. It was nice and pretty much deserted this time of year. If Cheryl really wanted coffee, he could order it in and there would be no pressure. He was hoping she wanted more, like his cock and a room would give them the neutral, temporary but secluded playground they needed for a couple of hours.

So, he drove over to The Inn, careful to make sure Cheryl did not get lost following him. He parked near a set of rooms, just down from the registration desk. Cheryl parked right next to him. He got out of his SUV and walked over to her door.

"Their coffee is pretty good here and I'm great at back massages. Still game?"he asked. He couldn't help but stare down her blouse after asking the question, hoping to see more of those golden brown breasts.

"Sure, as long as they deliver to a room cuz I always want to take a nap after a massage, "she said, grinning. This time she answered while staring at his cock and smiling. "I'll wait here til you come back."

Dave paid for the room and came back with the key. Cheryl grabbed her purse and gym bag out of the car and followed him to the door of the room.

"Work out bag?" Dave asked.

"It has the lotion in it, silly," Cheryl said smiling.

Dave opened the door and let Cheryl walk in first. The room had one king size bed and the usual television and too small bathroom. Cheryl set her bags on the desk while Dave closed and locked the door. Cheryl then kicked off her sandals, went to the window and pulled the drapes shut. Walking over to Dave, she put her arms around his neck and just looked at him, with a smile.

"Well, we're here. Now what?"she said.

Dave could not hold back any longer. He put his arms around her waist and pulled her tight against him, so tight she could feel his hard cock against her. He placed one hand on each of her ass cheeks and grabbed them tightly. They were just as soft to the touch as he imagined them. Then he kissed her, lightly first on the lips then with his tongue, very passionately, very deeply.

"Uh,"she said, partially surprised with the sudden urgency Dave showed. As she continued to kiss him back, Cheryl began to relax and return his passion. She began rotating her hips, rubbing her pussy against his cock, while rubbing her hands through his hair. She starting moaning along with her rubbing, obviously getting more excited as they continued this embrace.

Dave let go of her ass so her could run his hands up and down her back and enjoy the firmness of her shape. He slid one of his hands up under her T-shirt so he could feel the softness of her skin, all the way up to her bra.

Her bra was silky and lacy. He moved his right hand to her left breast and felt it through the material, focusing on the nipple. It was soft and sensitive to his touch.

Cheryl broke the kiss but continued to grind her hips against his cock, just looking at Dave and smiling.

"So, Dave, is this what you had in mind at the car wash?"she asked, again teasing him with her smile.

"Well, we certainly are started in the right direction,"he said. "Are you still interested in that back massage and coffee?"

"I don't think so,"she said. "It's too hot for coffee and I think I'm more interested in this" she said, then dropped her right hand down to grab his cock through his shorts and began rubbing up and down lightly.

"You like that cock, do you?"he asked.

"Uh-huh. It feels just right. Nice and hard."

"You're not an inhibited as I thought you might be," he said.

"Well, I'm just not very inhibited with the right person," she said.

Dave knew if she kept rubbing his cock up and down through his pants that he would come before they even got their clothes off and he certainly didn't want that. He had too much exploring to do of this hot little body and too little time.

"Well,"said Dave, "since we don't have too much time, do you want to be in charge or do you want me to be in charge?"

Dave gave Cheryl one more deep kiss. Then, feeling fair is fair, Dave dropped his right hand from Cheryl's breast, down her side to her pussy and started rubbing. She was already hot and getting moister as he rubbed. Cheryl closed her eyes briefly to enjoy the sensation and then opened them again to answer him.

"Tell me what you want me to do and I'll do it all. Just no kinky shit, okay?"she said.

"No kinky shit, agreed,"Dave said, smiling. He continued by whispering in her ear. "You are so incredibly beautiful. Now stand back a bit. I want to undress you. Then have you undress me. Then I want you to get on your knees and suck my cock. Are you ready to suck my cock?"

Cheryl looked at Dave and licked her lips. "I'd love to suck your cock," then gave him another deep kiss. Cheryl's pussy was getting hotter by the minute. While she enjoyed giving head, that is not where she wanted his cock. She wanted it in her pussy, filling her with his cum.

Cheryl backed away a few inches from Dave, just enough for him to get a hold of the bottom of her t-shirt and lift it over her head. Cheryl's lacy white bra was now revealed along with the tops of her gorgeous tits. Dave was tempted to take the bra off now and dive into her tits but decided to remove her shorts first. Much as he wanted to lick her nipples which were now even more obvious to his view, he was more anxious to see her in her underwear and get a glimpse of her pussy. He loved looking at a woman in her underwear before fucking her. It was a huge turn on for him. And he wasn't even sure if she was wearing underwear but was going to find out!

Dave lowered his hands, undid the button to her shorts and with his right hand, lowered the zipper. He slid both of his hands inside her shorts and around to her ass, slowly pushing the shorts down. He dropped to his knees to get a better view of the unveiling of her pussy and panties and continued to lower the shorts.

Her panties were high cut at the thighs, almost a thong but not quite. Dave left the shorts draped around her ankles and brought his hands back up her legs, stopping when each hand was on a thigh. He could wait no longer to see where the tan ended and the white skin began. He also wanted to see her bush—if she had one.

He placed his nose up against her pussy and inhaled. He could smell her wetness and her sex! He stuck his tongue out and lapped briefly at her pussy through her panties. Cheryl reacted briefly to this licking with a moan and then by placing her hands on his head. He didn't know if she needed the support or wanted to direct the activity, and didn't care.

Meanwhile Dave had looped his hands into the side bands of the legs and began pulling her panties off. Ever so slowly he saw more of her beautiful skin. She was shaved all the way to the center of her belly, where only a small strip of pubic hair was visible, leading to her pussy. The tan ended about an inch above her pussy.

Dave brought her panties to the ground and helped her step out of both garments. He then returned to her pussy, now with both hands on her ass.

"Spread your legs a little.…I want to lick you,"he said.

Cheryl did as requested. She loved feeling Dave's hot breath and tongue on her pussy. "Oh yeah," she said. "That feels good." Cheryl encouraged his actions by leaning back a little, further exposing her pussy.

Dave continued his light licking of her pussy. She tasted just as sweet as he imagined and her ass was just as soft as he dreamed.

Dave slid one of his hands in between her cheeks to see what she would do. He expected her to jump away but she didn't. Instead, she changed position ever so slightly to give his hand more access.

"Are you an ass man, Dave?"she innocently asked looking down at him.

Dave stopped licking her pussy long enough to answer her. "Depends on what you mean by an ass man," he said, returning her gaze.

"You know, an ass man. I know you like playing with my ass. I want to know if you like to lick ass holes? And fuck ass?"she asked.

"My you have a dirty mouth for such a sweet looking young lady," Dave said.

"That's because I know it turns you on when I talk dirty, doesn't it?" She figured that out on her own, he thought. This is getting more interesting by the minute. "Now answer my question—do you like to lick and fuck ass? No more pussy until you answer my question,"she said as she moved her hips and pussy back from his face.

"In your case I'd love to lick and fuck your ass. Want me to?"he asked.

Cheryl moved her pussy back to his face so he could continue licking her. "I'd love to have you lick my ass, it makes me very wet. Fucking my ass I'm not sure about. It depends on how turned on I get and how gentle you are. We'll have to see how things go." Cheryl started grinding her hips into his mouth again. "Oooh yeah, run your tongue all along the lips, like that. Oh, that feels good on my pussy."

Dave licked her pussy for another minute then got back up to his feet. He was still fully clothed and this session could not go on forever, she had to pick up her boyfriend.

Dave undid the front clasp to her bra and moved it off her shoulders. "Have you ever been fucked in the ass before?" he asked. He may have been talking to her but his eyes went to the soft orbs he had just uncovered. They were the size of large apples with hard nipples that got bigger after her pussy licking session. He started to gently massage each breast with a hand.

"Yeah, once. It was kind of fun." Cheryl looked into his eyes, knowing she was turning him on. She dropped her hands to the belt buckle on his shorts and started undoing it. "Want me to tell you about it, huh? You'd like to hear that story wouldn't you?" She now had the zipper undone and was pushing his pants and underwear to the floor.

"Do you think you can tell me the story and suck my cock at the same time?" Dave asked. He could feel the pre-cum oozing out of his cock already.

"Uh-huh," was all she said. Cheryl dropped to her knees in front of Dave and proceeded to take his entire cock into her mouth at once. It felt like velvet to have her mouth surrounding his cock, slowly moving up and down.

Dave's cock was about average, 6 inches long and about 2 inches around, so it did not require super human skills to swallow it all. But

Cheryl knew the right way to do it and was doing it over and over again.

Cheryl loved a perfect cock and this was one of them. She loved the bulbous, pink head and long shaft. It was easy to swallow and just the right size so she could play with it in her mouth, not just try and fit it in. Dave was fairly hairy and had lots of hair on his balls as well as the base of his cock. Cheryl made a mental note to try and leave time to lick and suck his balls, too.

Not wanting to miss seeing any of the action, Dave quickly pulled off his golf shirt and tossed it on the desk chair. He then placed his hands on her head and followed her movements. Her hair was so soft and she was sucking his cock like there was no tomorrow. He would have to stop her in a minute or he would fill her mouth with cum and he desparately wanted to fuck her, even more now.

Cheryl pulled away from his cock, leaving a trail of saliva between her mouth and his groin. She continued massaging him with her hand, lightly jacking him off to keep him near the edge.

"Once," she said," I met this guy out dancing. He invited me to his place afterwards for a drink. So I went and we started making out on the couch. Well, he was afraid his roommate might walk in so we went to his room. On the way, he kept grabbing my ass so I figured he had an ass fetish."

Cheryl put Dave's cock back in her mouth, gave it two more licks and then pulled it out so she could continue with the story. She continued lightly jacking him off with her right hand and began gently massaging his balls with her left hand.

"Anyway, after a little 69 and some doggy style, he started sticking his finger in my ass. It felt weird and I told him so. But he said wait a while and I would like it. So he kept fucking me and moving his finger in my ass. Then he pulled his cock out of my pussy and put two fingers in my ass. I started digging it so he talked me into letting him fuck me. He got some Vaseline, coated his cock and my ass, slipped it in and fucked me. He didn't last long but it was kind of cool having his cum up my ass–that never happened before."

Cheryl put Dave's cock back in her mouth again and started blowing him with even more gusto. Dave by now was so turned on he could come any second. The back and forth motion of her mouth on his cock was almost more than he could take.

"Looks like you liked my story," she said, staring at his hard cock, dripping with her saliva. She started sucking him again.

Dave used both hands and pulled Cheryl's mouth off his cock with a pop. "Get on the bed, on your back, legs spread wide as you can," he told her. "I have to fuck you, now!" Dave pulled her up from the floor, pulled her close and kissed her, then released her so she could move to the bed.

Cheryl wanted Dave's cock now as badly as he wanted to give it to her. But she also knew how turned on he was by her ass. So, even though the bed was only a few steps away, she made sure she turned and walked to it with her back to him. She wanted to tease Dave with the motion of her tight, white cheeks and make him want her even more. She was glad she wore a traditional bikini when she worked on her tan–they left such great lines!

Cheryl quickly tossed the bed cover on the floor and got two pillows, one for under her head and one for under her ass. Once the pillows were adjusted, she spread her legs wide, fully exposing her pink lips surrounded by white skin and then deep tan. Her small trail of pubic hair was almost an arrow pointing Dave to his target. Using both hands she held her pussy lips open, inviting him inside her.

"Come on, Dave. Slide your hard cock in my pussy and fuck me. Fuck me nice and slow and make me cum," she said. She knew her dirty talk made his cock even harder. She liked teasing him this way.

"Man, I love it when you talk like that! Grab my cock, Cheryl, and guide me to your hot pussy," he said. She reached down with her right hand, grabbed his cock and placed it to the entrance to her pussy. Not much else needed to be said. She was so wet there would be no problem getting him inside her.

With one slow stroke, Dave was all the way inside her, up to his balls. Her pussy was so warm and tight, he just had to stop to enjoy the sensations. The look of pleasure must have shown on his face as, when he looked down at Cheryl, she was broadly smiling back at him.

"You feel so good I can't believe it," he told her. Dave leaned down and gave her a sensual, loving kiss, which she returned. Then he gradually starting fucking her, with slow strokes, bringing his cock all the way out of her pussy, then slowly pushing it back in. The feeling on the head of his cock was incredible and Cheryl must have been enjoying it, also, as she let out a small gasp each time he entered her.

After several strokes, Dave raised up slightly and grabbed both of her legs, placing one over each of his shoulders. Cheryl instinctively knew what he wanted and moved to accommodate him. This was one of her favorite positions to be fucked in, as it let her lover's cock penetrate into her deeply and she would always cum.

"You're hard cock feels so good, Dave. Are you going go fuck me harder now?" She continued the tease, smiling broadly at Dave and he loved it.

"Uh huh," he said. "But first, I want to watch my cock slide in and out of your pussy while I fuck you. You have such a pretty, wet pussy and such a gorgeous tan. I want to take it all in before I fuck you harder. You are a real tease, you know that?"

"And you love it, don't you?"she said, knowing the answer already. In response, Dave just smiled and increased both his tempo and the force of his thrusts. If she wanted to get fucked hard, then it was time to get started.

"Oh, yes, oh yes, fuck me like that!" Cheryl said, almost in a loud whisper. She was really starting to get into being fucked. Dave could see she was beginning to rub her nipples with both her hands, furthering her excitement. "Oooh, I'm getting close, getting close." Her eyes were closed as she totally immersed herself in the moment.

Dave now had moved his hands to her ass and continued to fuck her, grabbing her ass cheeks to hold on. As Cheryl got more excited she closed her legs around his neck and began to meet his thrusts with her own.

"Oh fuck, oh fuck, I'm cumming," she whispered loudly. "Ooooh, yes, grab my ass, grab my ass! Oooohhhh"

Dave slowed down his thrusting, watching and enjoying the orgasm Cheryl was having. Her breathing was heavy and head moved from side to side, enjoying the pleasure. She moved her right hand down from her breast to her pussy and began stroking her clit while Dave fucked her.

"Keep fucking, keep fucking me,"she whispered. "Ummm, keep fucking me……" Her voice trailed off.

Dave took her legs and lifted them back off his shoulders and to his sides. He leaned down and lightly kissed her and said, "Did that feel good, Cheryl?"

She looked at him with half closed eyes and said, "You know it did! Did you cum too?" Dave wasn't ready to cum yet. It was hard as hell not to a moment ago but he definitely wanted to fuck this young thing doggy style. He wanted to see and feel that cute white ass up against him as he fucked her. And he wasn't sure where he wanted to come yet. He'd love to come in her mouth and watch her swallow his cum but there was also the possibility she would let him fuck her in the ass. In that case, he would definitely cum in her ass.

"No, we have more fucking to do before I cum,"he said. He began slowly stroking his cock in and out of her pussy again. It was nice she put a pillow under herself before they got started but now even he could feel how wet it had gotten from her juices. "Did you have some special place you wanted my cum, Cheryl?"

"Uh," she said, noticing that he was still hard and starting to move again. "Your cock feels so good! Where do you want to shoot it baby? Shoot it anywhere you want!"

"How about your mouth? Would you like my load in your mouth?"

"I'd love it in my mouth,"she said with a grin. "I'll swallow it all and lick my lips afterwards!"

"Maybe you'd like a facial instead? Would you like to have my cum dripping all over your face?" Dave was now perched on his elbows above Cheryl, watching her face as they talked. He continued to increase the tempo of his cock in her pussy. He was curious as to what her response would be. He wanted to see just how turned on she was getting.

"Seems like a waste to just spray it around," Cheryl said, "but you can if you want. How about where you are now—in my pussy? Why don't you fuck me and cum in my pussy? Uh, that feels good. Fuck me a little faster now."

Dave stopped talking for a second. He took this opportunity to reach down and suck her left nipple with his mouth. He was so excited before that he hadn't taken time to explore either of these two soft mounds. He gently sucked on the nipple, then released it and ran his tongue around the edge of her breast. He then returned to the nipple, sucking hard on it and nibbling lightly, then releasing hit. Then he repeated the same actions on her right breast. Both nipples now resembled tiny erasers, turning him on even more.

"Oh, that feels good, Dave. Damn, don't stop fucking me at the same time! Let me feel your cock and you sucking my tits. Ohhhh! Fuck, I want your cum!" Cheryl was starting to respond to his fucking her now and was involuntarily moving her hips in time with his stroking.

Dave thought now is the time to test the waters. "Oh, you feel good against me, you are so soft, " he said, starting to breath more heavily. "I love the way you squeeze my cock. How about if I shoot my cum in your ass? Would you like me to fuck your ass till I cum in it?"

Cheryl knew that question was coming, especially after the story she told him. The question was, could she trust Dave to be gentle with her and was she turned on enough to let his cock in her ass. It was a good size, not too big and should be all right once the head got in.

Cheryl opened her eyes and gazed at Dave for a moment and then smiled. "You wanted to fuck my ass from the start, didn't you? I knew it, you're an ass man," she said. She paused and enjoyed a few more strokes of his cock in her pussy.

"If you promise to go slow and be gentle, you can fuck my ass. But if I tell you to stop, you have to promise to stop. Deal?" She asked.

Dave's cock got even harder now. This was a deal he had no problem making. Dave did not believe in any kind of sex two people didn't agree to, it just took the fun out of things.

"Deal. Now all we need is some lubrication," he said.

"Use my suntan oil," Cheryl said. "I'm so wet now we shouldn't need too much help getting your cock in back there. The bottle is in the top of my bag."

Dave paused and lay lightly on top of her, his cock buried in her pussy and not moving. He really appreciated her willingness to go along with being fucked in the ass. Again he gave her a light, sensual kiss on the lips to let her know how special she was.

Dave eased himself off of her, slowly pulling his cock out of her pussy.

"Oh, and I was really enjoying that in there," Cheryl said as his cock slipped out of her. She really enjoyed the site of its hardness and the glisten from all her juices.

As Dave walked over to the bag to get the oil, Cheryl asked him, "How do you want me? On my back or on my knees?

Dave looked back at her and smiled. "I prefer doggy style, but you tell me what's more comfortable for you."

"Doggy style works for me. Besides if you can't get it in my ass that way, you can always give my pussy another workout," she said with a hint of humor in her voice.

Dave returned to the bed with the oil and moved up behind Cheryl. He knew she had a nice soft ass but the visual of the tan lines just blew him away! Since it would take him a while to loosen her ass up, he decided not to waste the time. He grabbed his cock with his right hand, placed it to the entrance to her pussy and began to slowly fuck her again.

"Ooh, that's a nice surprise!" She said. "Oh, that feels good! Fuck me, baby, fuck me!" She said in a loud whisper.

Dave took the cap off the lotion. He knew if he stayed in her pussy this way much longer his load would go in there and he wanted that ass first. So, he gave her two more good strokes and pulled out to focus on preparing her ass for some fucking.

Moving off to her left side a bit, hard cock bouncing in the air, he pointed the opening of the bottle at the crack of her ass and poured a liberal amount of lotion out. It must have been cold on her pussy lips as Cheryl let out a small yelp as it dribbled down her ass crack and down her pussy lips..

"Gee, that's cold! Rub it in quick," she said.

Dave used his right hand to rub the lotion up and down the crack of her ass while holding the bottle in his left hand. Based on her motions, it appeared like Cheryl was enjoying the massage. So Dave decided to see how tight she was by slowly inserting his index finger into her ass.

The first half of the finger went in easily but then Cheryl spoke up. "Stop for a second. Let me adjust a bit."

Dave left the finger half way in and waited. He set the bottle of lotion down on the night stand and then proceeded to continue to massage her ass cheeks with his left hand, leaving his right hand to work on loosening up her hole.

"Oooh, that feels nice. Move it back and forth, just a little, ok?" She said. Dave was more than happy to start some movement there, as he could feel her grasp his finger and then let go with her asshole. She was tight as could be but doing her best to loosen up for him. As he continued to move his index finger in and out, he got up to working the whole finger in and left it there.

"Stop for a second. Leave your hands where there are but move over here a bit more", motioning Dave to move on his knees more toward the front of the bed where she was facing. He was not sure what she had in mind but he did as requested.

He was absolutely loving this experience. Here was this gorgeous coed, on her knees, with his fingers working her white ass surrounded by her bikini tan, waiting for him to fuck her in her last unused hole of the day and loving the entire experience. She even wasn't afraid to talk dirty to him. He couldn't imagine it getting any better.

But then it did! All of a sudden Dave felt a very soft, warm suction on his cock. Then a hand joined the mouth. Sure enough, Cheryl wanted Dave to move so she could suck his cock and jerk him off while he prepared her ass.

"Ummm, you taste good," Cheryl said. "Do you like this?" she asked, as she stroked his cock lightly with her fingers.

"That's a silly question!" was all the reply Dave could muster. "Just don't make me cum yet….I still want to fuck you in your ass!"

"Don't worry, baby" she said, taking a long slow lick of his cock. "I'm just about ready for you. I just didn't want you to lose any of this before I got to feel it. Give me just a little lotion, OK?"

Dave grabbed the bottle and squirted a small amount of sun tan lotion in the palm of her right hand. He figured she wanted some lubrication so she could jack him off easier.

After replacing the bottle on the table, he returned his attention to massaging her ass. Her ass had now readily accepted the in and out motions of the single finger so her prepared to insert a second one.

Just as he did, he felt Cheryl's mouth return to his cock. Man, did that feel good! After a couple of good licks, he felt something else he wasn't expecting–she had taken her right index finger and slid it up his ass! All the way!

Dave had never had a woman stick a finger up his ass before, though he had done it himself on several occasions while masturbating. He never realized how good it could feel to have his partner do it to him. It was a whole new and energizing sensation and made his cock feel even harder than before.

"Like that, Dave? Like my finger in your ass?"

Cheryl's voice all of a sudden brought him back to the situation. She wanted to know if he was enjoying her fucking his ass with her finger.

"Absolutely! Geez, where did you learn how to do that? Oh, man, keep sliding it in and out, yeah just like that, fuck me, fuck me," he said. He couldn't tell how many fingers she had in there or why he wasn't getting scratched from her nails but really didn't care—it just felt wild!

Cheryl had quit sucking his cock now to focus on moving her finger in his asshole. She enjoyed playing with his ass and watching his excited cock bob in the air in front of her face. She was even enjoying his fingers in her ass and decided that that is where his cock belonged today. She could hardly wait to feel it sliding in and out of her.

"Oh baby, I can't wait any longer, I have to fuck you in the ass." He said. Much as he hated to, Dave slowly moved away from Cheryl and sighed as she removed her finger from his ass. Positioning himself behind her, he pushed down lightly on the low end of her back. "Drop your hips just a little, baby."

Cheryl did as requested and spread her knees farther apart, moving her ass lower. She could still feel his two fingers in her, although they were not moving much now, just holding her open.

"Go slow," she said.

"Slow as you want, baby, just tell me if it gets uncomfortable," Dave said. Actually Dave knew that if she could take two fingers up her ass that he could easily slide his cock in their place and she likely would not know the change had taken place. And that's exactly what he did.

Sliding his fingers almost all the way out, he guided his cock with his left hand to her asshole and slid it in halfway. Then he stopped.

"You OK?" He asked. He was ready to start stroking his cock in and out of her but wanted to make sure Cheryl was comfortable before doing so. It had been such a wild and wonderful lovemaking session so far, he didn't want to ruin it now by being too aggressive.

"I'm fine. It always feels a bit weird at first but go ahead and start moving. Just not too fast right away," she said.

With that, Dave put a hand on each white ass cheek and slowly pulled her back until he had his cock buried all the way into her ass. Geez, there was no feel like the tightness and heat of a woman's ass! Plus he loved seeing his cock buried in that little brown hole. Dave took a moment to enjoy the view before slowing beginning to fuck her ass.

The strokes were slow on purpose. He obviously wanted Cheryl to feel comfortable but also wanted to enjoy the sensations himself to the max. Apparently, Cheryl was beginning to enjoy the action, too.

"Is it as good as you thought it would be?" she asked, looking back over her shoulder at him.

"Better than I could've imagined," he said as he continued to pick up the pace. "Although you are so tight back there I probably won't last long."

"That's ok. Just fuck me, baby and leave a nice big load of cum in my ass, please?" she said grinning at him. He could tell she was trying to tease him over the edge again with her dirty talk and he loved it. He also noticed that she had moved her right hand between her legs and was playing with her pussy.

"Oh, you'll be getting a nice big load of cum back here," he said. "It might even run down off your ass and onto that pussy of yours." Her ass was so tight he knew it wouldn't be long before he was filling her ass with cum.

"Oooooh, I like that idea," she said, starting to bounce her ass back to him, rubbing her pussy with her fingers even faster. "Fuck me good baby," she whispered.

Dave could no longer control himself. He fucked her ass hard and fast. Each time he shoved his cock in to the hilt he could feel her ass grip his cock. He couldn't last any longer.

"I'm cumming!" He said, shoving his cock into her ass to the hilt and staying there as load after load of cum erupted from his cock into her ass.

"Oh! Oh!," she said. Cheryl could feel the warmth of his cum as it entered her ass. She pushed herself up off her elbows to and upright position, hoping Dave would grab her by the breasts while he continued to cum. She wanted to feel his body close to hers now.

Dave took the hint and moved his left arm around her waist, drawing her close and making sure his cock did not leave her ass until he was ready to take it out. He could feel the last couple of loads leave his cock and knew he must have left a big load in her ass, as he could already feel some of it dripping out between them onto the sheets. Plus, this position gave him the chance to feel those soft ass cheeks against his groin again. He loved their softness against his skin.

With his other hand, Dave grabbed her left breast and began massaging it and tweaking her nipple Her nipples were still very erect and he could tell Cheryl was cumming now, too.

Now firmly in his grasp, Cheryl dropped her right hand back to her pussy and continued to work her clit to bring herself to orgasm. She was so close and wanted to cum while Dave's cock was still in her ass.

"Oh, oh, oh, fuck, fuck, fuck," she whispered as she came. She stiffened for a moment and then began to relax, still rubbing her pussy. "Don't take it out yet," she said, indicating to Dave by gently wiggling her ass to leave his cock where it was. "Leave it in just a little longer."

Dave quit massaging her breast and instead just held Cheryl. She quit playing with her pussy and brought both of her arms up to where Dave's were around her.

They both let out a large sigh, then turned to each other for a short, soft kiss. Cheryl smiled at Dave and he at her.

"Did you have fun?" She asked. She could feel his cock softening and starting to slide out of her cum filled ass. She could also feel a small stream of cum starting run down her legs. It was warm but also tickled a bit. She loved the feeling..

"More than you'll ever know. You've spoiled me for other women," Dave said, grinning. He could not remember ever having made love to a woman who was so dynamic a lover, catering to all of a man's needs and enjoyed doing so all the while cumming herself. "Thank you, that was wonderful!"

As Dave's cock finished sliding out of her ass, Cheryl let out a sigh to go along with the smile on her face. She could not believe that she had let a man, who was a total stranger until an hour or so ago, fuck her, especially in the ass. And she had enjoyed it! Was it just great sex or was there some chemistry here?

Cheryl slid out of Dave's grasp and laid down on the bed, on her back. For some reason, she left her legs wide open and her knees up. She wanted Dave to see what he had just fucked for the last two hours and to see the cum dripping from her ass and pussy. She didn't feel dirty, she was excited! She was proud that they both felt so good after their encounter. She was enjoying the stickiness of their cum on her pussy and thighs. She enjoyed the buzzing sensation still going on in her ass from its recent invasion.

Dave sat back on his haunches and took in the view being given to him. Cheryl was, indeed, a beautiful young girl. Sexy, and a wonderful lover. Sort of like that old saying, a slut in the bedroom and a lady in public. Her curves were tight and tan and her smile addictive. Mature beyond her years as a lover and so much more to get to know about her.

"I guess we should get cleaned up, huh?" Dave's voice was not very convincing but he couldn't think of anything else to say right then. Dave's cock and groin were covered in their juices and sun tan oil and his body glistening from the sweat of the workout. Still he wasn't ready to move–he wanted this experience to last, it was so good. He knew she had to go meet her boyfriend still but didn't want to speak those words for fear of ruining the moment.

Dave and Cheryl just stared at each other's eyes for a while, then each took in the sight of the other's body, mostly to relive their encounter. It had been amazing.

"I tell you what," Cheryl said. "Why don't we both go jump in the shower, together, and clean each other up. Then maybe we can do something about this appetite I have worked up. That is, if you're interested…."

"Very interested," Dave said, remembering the conversation that got them to the hotel room in the first place. " There are lots of places we can go around here and get something to eat. Did you prefer something noisy like Denny's or something quiet and cozy?"

"I think I picked quiet and cozy the last time we had this discussion," she said with that little smile on her face, " and was very happy with my choice. Maybe we should do that again?"

"I think that's a great idea, " Dave said. "Shall we hit the showers?".

A PROMISE IS A PROMISE

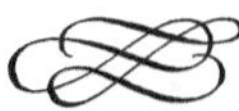

Martin sat in the dark of his bedroom and stared out the window into the night. His modest home where he and his wife June had raised their 3 children was quiet now. He could hear June breathing softly in her sleep. The dog rustled and snorted in his sleep but Martin was still awake.

He was nearing retirement and the accounting of his retirement capital wasn't looking too good. Though he had worked consistently and hard through his 40+ years of employment, the money just did not seem to stick to his savings account.

Having just past his 60th birthday, with the kids all gone, Martin was feeling glum. A clinical psychologist might even suggest that he was suffering from a mild form of depression and suggest one of several medications that might perk him up.

Despite his depression, Martin was glad that he was physically fit. The years had been good to him and the boys had always kept him busy supporting their athletic endeavors. He could still curl his arm and see muscles in his bicep, triceps and across his chest. He tensed his muscles in the light of the moon as it shown through the window.

"Martin? Are you coming to bed?" June asked.

He had just fucked her. He used to make love to her but now, he just fucks her. It is pleasant enough and enjoyable but a bit one sided.

"Just a minute, I'm thinking …" his voice trailed off.

A few years earlier, Martin had found out that June was faking orgasms. Worse yet, she had told her best friend Helen and that was how Martin had found out. He overheard the entire conversation. His wife was faking orgasms. Martin had listened as she confided in Helen that she had lost interest in sex but did not want to disappoint Martin. She often faked her orgasm. How often? She didn't know but clearly it was the vast majority of the time they had sex. Between her expectation that their sex life would wane throughout their 50's and Martin's knowledge of the faked orgasms, their sex life went down hill from those well intentioned lies.

Martin sighed as he remembered how he had been determined to confront June and then chickened out at the last minute. Instead, their love making receded and the fucking maintained. Where, in years previous, they were all over each other 5 times a week, now they had dispassionate sex twice a month. June had noticed the decline and wondered where their sex life had gone but assumed that it was just the way it was meant to be.

Martin looked out the second floor window again and. Two young lovers walked by stopping to kiss. The man grabbed the girl's ass and lifted her up into his arms. Martin's loins stirred and he felt his manhood grow even though he had just shot a load into his wife 20 minutes previous. He smiled and thought to himself "You ain't dead yet!"

He looked back to June and watched her ample bosom rise and fall in her sleep filled breathing. Pulling back the covers from his naked wife, he admired her thick nipples and her large areolas. June's breasts had always been her best attribute. After nursing their third child for 13 months, she considered having a breast reduction. Martin gently explained that they just didn't have that kind of cash in the bank and the health insurance certainly wasn't going to pay for it. Martin cupped her right breast and her nipple instinctively hardened and thickened. June had always had killer nipples. She refused to go anywhere without a thick bra to hide her nipples. It had only taken one time as a teenager for her to go without a bra. Her breasts were the desire of every guy and the envy of every girl as her nipples poked out. In their more adventurous days, Martin thought it would be fun to measure just how far they poked out. June did not find this fun or funny and refused him when he came forward with his ruler.

Looking at him with skepticism, she said "Look mister, you can measure me if I can measure you!"

She had expected him to be embarrassed but he wasn't and gladly dropped his pants. He measured 9 and ¾ inches long. It was a very big dick but since June had never seen any other dicks, she didn't know how good she had it. Martin had smiled as he measured her left and then her right nipple. His tongue licked his lips and announced "a bit more than 1 inch, dear". To that she said "So what" and marched off. She continued to be embarrassed about her breasts and her nipples and refused to wear any of the lingerie that he bought for her.

He fell asleep stroking her breast and holding her in his arms.

* * *

A promise was a promise and Sandy was holding her father to his promise. A seven day Western Caribbean cruise for Sandy and her best friend Kay on Norwegian Cruise Lines' biggest boat was hers if she could pull off straight As in her spring and summer semesters. The spring semester grades were delivered in June and were all A's. The summer grades were in and Sandy couldn't contain herself as she opened the envelope. She started screaming as she looked down the page and her father's eyes looked heavenward as he became resigned to the fact that a promise was a promise. It wasn't the money as he had plenty of that. It was the principle that he had to bribe his daughter to do well in school.

Sandy grabbed her cell and called Kay immediately. They had been friends for ever or at least since they were in first grade. While Sandy toiled at Penn State, Kay worked at Joe Jones Bar-B-Que waiting tables. Kay attended the local community college during the day as it was the best she could afford. Sandy bounded up the wide hardwood steps to her room and dove on the bed as the call connected.

"Hi! I've been thinking of you!" answered Kay.

"You have? That's soooo cool because I was thinking of you too!"

"What about?"

"I got my grades today! Allllll AAAAAAAAAAAAAAAs! We're going on a cruise! You and me!!"

"I don't believe it! Wow! Are you sure that your father is going to do this?"

"A promise is a promise, Kay and he is good for it. Don't you worry your pretty little head!!"

Everything was already picked out; the cruise line, the cabin, and the excursions. As Sandy said, the only thing left to do was to go shopping for some "cruise clothing".

* * *

June came in the door with a stack of envelops from the post box. She quickly flipped through them throwing most in the trash. The rest she tossed on the small kitchen table where Martin sat reading the newspaper. It was a typical Saturday morning. Martin looked up at his wife. He eyed her conservative outfit and imagined the buttons on her high-collared shirt dissolving in front of his eyes. He mentally pushed her shirt apart revealing her large breasts held up by a lace demi bra that gently squeezed her breasts together creating a 7 inch long cleavage. His mind had her tilting her shoulders forward seductively and sliding out of the bra, her heavy breasts hanging down, her nipples hardening before his eyes. Martin felt his cock thicken at the thought of those big tits and big areolas and especially, those long and thick nipples. His eyes blinked. That was the image that he wanted. June standing there with her shirt open and a sensual and sexy demi bra tossed to the side while her big breasts hung down tipped by long and thick brown nipples. He decided that if she were standing there like that and were to cross her arms in front of her, her breasts would hang over her arms. What a sight that would be. His cock was now a heavy bulge in his pants.

June had turned around and Martin appraised her ass. Certainly her ass was big but not wide. For a woman with such a formidable chest as June's, her ass was not quite proportional. June brought over a cup of coffee to the table and awoke Martin from his daydreaming.

"What were you staring at, honey?" She asked sweetly.

"Oh ummm your beautiful curves mesmerized me, June".

June blushed at the comment and then realized that she had kept an envelop that she should have thrown away. The outside was bright yellow and with red letters it stated: YOU MAY HAVE WON A SUPER PRIZE!"

She smiled at the term "may" and knew well that it was much more likely that she "may not" have won a super prize.

Martin had come fully out of his daydream "Why do you insist on wasting your time with those things?"

"Some I fill out and some I don't. You know I like yellow so this one I'll look at. Besides it is probably nothing but I like the suspense"

"I'll BET it is nothing."

"No" she smiled, "I'll bet it's nothing, you bet it is something. What do you want to bet?"

Martin chuckled. "Ok, if you won something more than $10, you'll sit on my lap and show me your breasts"

"Martin! How dare you!" she blushed again.

"Come on, you know that it is nothing. So, what do you want if it is nothing and it better be small as it is the most likely outcome!"

She giggled. "I'd really like to go out for an ice cream tonight. So, if it is nothing, let's go to Friendly's and get a hot fudge sundae."

Martin pretended to think it over and then laughed and nodded ascent.

June ripped open the envelop and her jaw dropped.

"What?" asked Martin.

He got silence back.

"What??" he asked more strenuously as her green eyes scanned the page.

"We ummm won a cruise to the Western Caribbean"

"You're not serious. You're just teasing me!"

"I am serious, look!"

Martin read over her shoulder. Indeed, they had won a fully paid trip on Norwegian Cruise Lines' biggest ship. They had to respond in 3 days to take advantage of the airfare. Martin read the fine print and though he was skeptical, he could find no "gotchas" within the document.

He sat down on the couch. "Hey! I won the bet! Come here sexy!"

June's heart was beating out of her chest with excitement. She had never dreamed that they would go on a cruise. "You're not really going to hold me to that silly bet, are you?"

Martin smiled "A promise is a promise and a bet is a promise to make good"

June straddled Martin's thighs on the couch and slowly unbuttoned her top buttons. Martin worked from the bottom up and they met in the middle. He sighed as he awaited his prize.

Martin was gravely disappointed when June pulled apart her shirt revealing a bra that could possibly be used as a bullet proof Kevlar vest! There was nothing to see. Then, June was kind enough to reach behind her and unclasp the bra and lift the front. Her tits popped free and Martin grabbed a handful of each tit and rubbed June's nipples and smiled like a kid in a candy store. They extended and Martin lifted the heavy tit to his mouth and sucked in her nipple. He followed suite with the other and enjoyed every second.

June stroked his face and stopped him with her hand. "Enough, honey, I have things to do today!"

Martin's disappointment was written all over his face. The kid in the candy store was just told that he'd have to buy candy on some other day.

"Honey, that bra seems awful big, is it the right size?"

"Of course it is. It fits fine"

"Well, ummm what size is it?"

"You are so silly. Why do you care? I'm a 40F and I really should have gotten that breast reduction surgery." June climbed off his lap and within seconds, her bra and shirt was returned to their previous place.

* * *

Sandy picked up Kay and drove to the mall. Kay Sandy was vivacious, outgoing and gregarious while Kay tended to be quiet and unassuming. Their first stop was at Hecht's department store. Sandy picked out several outfits to try on while Kay had only one. As they tried them on, Sandy noticed two boys leering at them from the round racks near the dressing room. Guiding Kay, she picked out several cruise wear outfits and marched to the cashier.

Kay followed but sputtered "What are you doing? I can't afford those clothes!"

"Don't worry about it, we'll try them on at your house where we can get some peace and return those that you don't want."

Kay nodded and followed Sandy out the door in a whirlwind.

On the way back to Kay's house, Sandy complained bitterly about the boys spying on them. "Ever since I broke up with Todd Jackson, boys have been hitting on me and driving me crazy. I'm tire of boys … I want a man. I want someone experienced"

The wind blew back Sandy's soft blond hair as Kay nodded in agreement.

After Sandy had pulled into Kay's driveway, Kay looked at her best friend. "What happened between you and Todd?"

It was a direct question of the kind that Sandy didn't like. Kay was her best friend but she still struggled with what to tell her. She nodded toward the house and Kay knew that the conversation had been postponed until they got inside. Gathering the packages together, they made their way into the modest, blue-collar home. It was clean and neat though none of the furniture matched any other piece of furniture in the house. Kay led the way to her bedroom and shut the door behind Sandy.

"This will be fun! It'll be like Christmas as we open the boxes and bags of clothing!" Sandy bubbled as she put the bags and boxes on the floor.

"We need to talk"

"What about?"

"You know what about!"

Sandy looked down at the floor a moment and sat on the bed. "Ok, what do you want to know?"

Kay took a deep breath and slowly sat next to her vivacious friend, wrapped an arm around her and leaned in to her ear. "I want to know what happened between you and Todd."

Tears formed at the corners of Sandy's eyes, rolled off her long dark eyelashes and fell to her cheeks. She quickly wiped them away. "He's an ass" She sputtered. "He likes to fuck me and take care of himself and then he is done with me, y'know? He's just an inconsiderate ass!"

Kay stroked Sandy's blonde hair and held her. Then she kissed her ear. "Yeah, I know, baby."

Sandy gulped some air. "I know you know so why do you make me say it? You know he's an ass. You told me when we started dating; you told me when we broke up the first time and then again when we got back together again."

"That second time, he had us both fooled sweetie." Kay spoke calmly and with careful thought.

"It's so true. We went out for 6 months but the last two months I was so horny. Hell, I hadn't had an orgasm in the last two months and was beginning to think I was frigid or something."

"Two months? But weren't you and Todd going at it just a week ago?"

"We were. But we kept on having these quickies and I wasn't getting any satisfaction."

"More than size matters, baby!" Kay laughed.

"Todd is pretty big Kay. He is big and thick but geez, you would think it would be easy to satisfy a girl with that big tool but he didn't satisfy me, that's for sure."

Kay could feel her wet pussy dripping onto her thigh.

"Well, I just like to be treated right."

"In other words, you're not a whore"

"Yeah … I'm not a whore; I'm a high priced whore!"

They both giggled and laughed. Sandy began unwrapping the clothes and organizing them by type as she talked. Kay kneeled in front of her friend and helped with the clothes. In one pile, they stacked shorts and T-shirts. In another pile were 4 tiny bathing suits. The last two piles were high heeled shoes, bras and bed time lingerie.

Sandy tossed her blond hair over her shoulder and continued. "Do you think this black negligee will look good on me?"

"I don't know. It has a nice V neck that will show off your boobs but who are you trying to impress? Me?" Kay laughed as she said it.

"Given that I'm horny as hell and would probably fuck a pencil right now, you aren't a bad one to impress!!"

Both girls laughed.

Kay picked up a dark blue, lacy demi-cup bra. "Whose is this?"

"It's ours, silly!"

"It's the wrong size, Sandy, it's a 34C"

Sandy looked at it and the other bras. They were all 34C. She smiled. "Ok, you caught me. I bought bras that were a bit too small. I just think it would be nice to have our breasts pushed up a bit and the 34 D and double D's are like ummm over the shoulder boulder holders … y'know? They weren't as sexy as the 34C's"

Kay giggled. "Well, we'd better try them on as my bras are all crap and won't work with these spaghetti-strap dresses you bought!"

Sandy stood and turned away from Kay. She took off her shirt and then her bra. Kay could see the sides of Sandy's breasts as she put on the dark blue, lacy demi-cup bra. When Sandy turned back around her tanned and taut stomach led up to her full tits bulging over the top of her bra. Her nipples were jutting out of the lace material and Kay involuntarily licked her lips.

"Is it too tight?" Sandy asked as she hefted her tits with the palms of her hands. "What do you think?"

Kay stood and looked. Smiling slightly, she replaced Sandy's hands with her own and hefted the soft and heavy globes covered by the silky lace. "Well, I think they are tight but it will do. It is very sexy. I love how your nipples stick out."

Sandy smiled. She could actually smell her friend's juices now. "Kay, you should try one on, too!" Sandy bent over and picked up a red bra and thong. "Put these on and let's see what they look like!"

Kay turned away from her friend and stripped off her pants and wet panties discreetly tossing them in her hamper. She bent slightly and Sandy giggled at her friend's crack even though much of her bottom was hidden by her oversized shirt. She pulled up the thong and took off her top. She put her arms through the bra, held the cups to her breasts and then reached around back to clasp but Sandy's hands were there to clasp the bra. Her fingers were warm on Kay's back.

Kay turned around to face her friend and Sandy gasped. "You look amazing! That bra on you is so sexy!"

Kay's body did indeed look amazing. She had thin and tight thighs and soft smooth calves. The cut on the thong made her legs look long and sexy. The bra was tight on the bust but fit around her chest. The tightness on the bust pushed her tits up and the thin material did nothing to hide her hard nipples. The crotch of the thong was already parting her wet pussy lips. The only problem was that Kay's crotch was not shaved.

"Your pubes have to go but boy, you are gorgeous!" Sandy smiled as she continued to heft her friend's tits, one and then the other. "Mmmm whatever guy gets his hands on these is one lucky guy!"

"How do you know it will be a guy?" Kay giggled.

"Would you do a woman?" asked Sandy as she squeezed Kay's tits.

"Depends on the woman. I suppose if the circumstances were right, I'd do a woman. Have you ever … you know … done a woman?"

"No but I've always been curious." Sandy smiled and leaned in closer to her friend. She reached around back with both her arms which pressed their breasts together. "I suppose we should take these bras and panties off or we'll wear them out before the cruise!"

Giggling, Kay reached around Sandy too and their breasts pressed even more together until the two young women were in an intimate hug. With the clasps undone, they both let the bras fall to the floor. Free from their confines, the breasts touched and they reveled in the feel of the warmth and the hardness of each other's nipples. Sandy kissed her friend's neck and then kissed her collar bone. Her hands roamed down Kay's back to her ass as she grasped Kay's butt cheeks. "Mmmm you have such a firm ass."

Kay said nothing but held Sandy close until Sandy's tiny kisses reached her mouth. There, she opened up and slid her tongue into Sandy's mouth with an eagerness that surprised both of them.

Their tongues played and Kay could feel her juices flowing around the thong and down her thigh to her knee.

They separated and were embarrassed by what had just happened. Kay took off her thong. "So, you uhhh think I should shave the bush?"

Sandy smiled. "Yes, definitely shave the bush. Let me see how much you have there."

Sandy kneeled by her friend and stroked the pubic hair. Without warning, she slid two fingers between Kay's legs and up her soaked pussy. "Yeah … shave this pussy but do it later."

Kay groaned and almost lost her balance. She grabbed the bureau to hold herself up and parted her legs and closed her eyes. "Why later?"

Sandy had her thumb teasing Kay's thick clit. Her thumb begged it to come out and play and it did. It elongated like a little cock. Sandy grinned. "Yeah …. Let's wait on shaving. I'm having too much fun right now."

She pushed her fingers deeper and began rhythmically fucking Kay with her fingers. Kay eased herself onto her bed and spread her legs wide. Sandy sucked Kay's nipples as her fingers continued their assault on Kay's pussy. It didn't take long before Kay was humping 3 of her friend's fingers screaming "yeah! Fuck me! Yeah! Fuck me hard!"

As Kay climaxed she sat straight up in her bed and then slammed her herself right back down again screaming "Oh god! Oh god!! This feels so gooood!"

Sandy climbed into the twin bed with her friend and held her. She kissed her neck, her cheeks and her ears before kissing her softly on the lips.

Kay smiled "I've never cum like that, Sandy! Never!" She kissed Sandy back hard on the lips. Their tongues intertwined again and Kay's hands were everywhere on Sandy. She was pinching Sandy's nipples and grabbing Sandy's ass. She pushed Sandy away and her lips dove onto Sandy's nipples sucking them in hard. Sandy groaned! Her tongue swirled around each nipple and sucked it in again. Kay's hands pried Sandy's legs apart and Kay moved into the space. She kissed down Sandy's tummy and across her hipbones. She found Sandy's pussy clean shaven except for a small vertical patch right above her clit.

Kay leaned in and loved the smell of Sandy's pussy. Her tongue flicked out and she licked her friend's clit. At first she was gentle and licked from side to side and then up and down. She watched her friend's movements and monitored which movements Sandy liked. She discovered that Sandy loved the up and down movement of Kay's tongue on both her clit and her pussy lips. Sandy's pussy lips were thick and full, much fuller than Kay's. Kay licked the full length of her lips. Then she sucked one in and Sandy shuddered. Kay knew that Sandy was on the edge of climax. She continued licking up and down and then clamped her mouth over Sandy's clit and began to suck. Kay had sucked several cocks and sucked Sandy's clit similarly. She increased the pressure on Sandy's clit and then slipped 3 fingers inside Sandy's cunt.

"ohhhh Kay … you're killing me!!"

Kay stroked the inside walls of Sandy's pussy while keeping up the pressure on her clit. In and out she pushed and then around and around soaking Sandy's pussy lips. Sandy groaned again and Kay thought how this was more fun doing it to someone else. Sandy humped Kay's fingers and then grabbed Kay's hand and began fucking her fingers. She cried out and felt her toes curl as a climax washed over her. She grunted and fell back onto the bed.

"Kay … that was fantastic … I haven't cum like that in a long long time!"

Kay smiled as she watched Sandy rub her own pussy lips. She needed something else. It was a great climax but she just wanted something else and Kay knew it.

"Kay, do you have a dildo or a vibrator?"

Kay shook her head, no.

"Your mother must have one!" Sandy sat up in the bed. "Sure, I bet she does! Every woman her age has a vibrator or a dildo!"

"Sandy, are you crazy! If she did have one, wouldn't that be gross to be fucking the same dildo that was in my mother? I can't even think of my mother having a dildo!!"

"Kay, I'd fuck a carrot or a cucumber but I need something in my pussy!"

Kay ran into her mother's room. It was immaculate. She chewed her finger for a moment as she wondered where a vibrator might be. She looked in the bedside table drawers.

There was nothing there. After a quick examination of her mother's top dresser drawer, behind some panties, she found 3 vibrating dildos in the back. There was a small cream colored one, a medium red one, and a large purple one. She carefully put back the underwear and ran back to where her friend lay with two fingers sliding in and out of her cunt.

"Holy shit, Kay, your mom must be amazing! Look at the size of that big purple one!"

They reclined across from each other on the bed with their ankles locked and their legs spread wide and the 3 vibrators between them. Sandy took the middle one and turned it on. Its hum was quiet as she put it to her clit and sighed. She worked it around spreading her swollen and engorged pussy lips until they were able to accept the head of the vibe. Leaning back, she began to slowly fuck herself with it. "Mmmm now that feels nice after that wonderful fuck you gave me!" Sandy's eyes became slits.

Kay grabbed the little vibe but Sandy moved and stopped her "Try the big one … I dare you!"

Kay smiled and grabbed the purple vibe and turned it on. It had a low, throaty hum as she pressed it against her pussy lips. Sandy watched fascinated as the head pushed past the lips. Sandy kept pumping her pussy and talking nasty to Kay and Kay loved it.

"Yeah, that's it. Push that big cock inside you."

"OHhh Sandy … it is sooooo big!! I feel like I'm going to explode!"

"Yeah, you're a dirty slut … look at you … you dirty slut fucking the biggest thing you can find. Push it in … push it all the way …" she reached forward and began fucking Kay with the vibrating dildo and Kay let go and let her. Sandy was fucking them both until she let go of her own vibrator and stuck a finger in Kay's ass.

"Ahhhhhhh!!!! OH FUCK!!" Kay was racked by a double orgasm that had her humping up in the air and gasping for breath.

When Kay caught her breath, she looked at Sandy. "You are funny doing that to me!! You're going to get it now!" Kay tackled Sandy and both girls were giggling until Sandy felt the head of the purple vibe push past her pussy lips. Within moments it was in and Kay was fucking Sandy with the vibe and writhing on two of Kay's finger buried deep in Sandy's ass.

Sandy was gasping for air when she heard the sound of the garage door opening. Peeking out of the window, Kay saw her mother's car coming up the driveway.

Kay stood next to her friend and pulled her close. She kissed her full on the lips. "I've got to get these vibes back."

It only took seconds and the girls had quickly thrown on their clothes. "I guess we should get these tried on and half of mine returned as I just can't afford them." Said Kay.

Sandy smiled, kissed her friend on the lips. "You are not buying anything. It's my treat!"

Kay sighed and thought of arguing but it never seemed to do any good.

* * *

Martin and June boarded the cruise ship and found their way to their room. It was down on a lower deck but Martin had insisted that it have a port window. He looked out onto the water as relief from the small room. June came over and sat next to him and rubbed his thigh. She showed him a paper with a list of excursions.

"We have to pick some things to do, Martin. We can't just stay in our room the whole time we're here"

He smiled. He loved her but he was missing something. He ached for more sexual contact but could not find a way to tell her without hurting her feelings. The fact was that he COULD stay in the room the entire vacation and fuck her every other hour of the day. Even right now, she was wearing a shirt that buttoned up to her neck but her breasts were so full and heavy that Martin was distracted.

"Martin? Hello?"

"Oh, I don't care, I just want to be with you!"

"OHhhhhh Martin!" she sighed and hugged him.

He could feel her heavy breasts press against his chest and he clung to her a bit longer than they normally did.

"ooo Martin!" She giggled. "Is that a banana in your pocket or are you happy to see me? I guess that means that you would like to have the couples sensual massage excursion?"

He nodded as she seductively sat on his lap. She checked off the massage as well as two other excursions and Martin boldly unbuttoned her blouse. Before she could react, he had all the buttons undone except for 2. His hand felt her soft skin on her tummy making her smile as she continued to read the excursions while tapping her pen on her full lips. June put the pen and the excursion list down on the counter and kissed Martin deeply. He felt her tongue snake into his mouth and his thick cock twitch.

She ended the kiss and stood up. Within seconds, she had her blouse buttoned up and tucked into her pants. "Let's unpack!" she announced brightly and Martin groaned with disappointment but June didn't notice. She quickly opened their suitcases and began putting pants and shirts away. Martin joined in with his clothes. Suddenly, June's flurry of activity stopped still. "Martin" she paused "Do you have my small suitcase?"

Martin looked around the small cabin. "No, I don't remember it. What did you pack in it?"

She gazed off into the distance for a moment to think. "It has all my underwear. You know, my bras and panties plus my swimsuits. Oh no! It also has my formal evening gown! I've only got the underwear I'm wearing!"

They searched frantically but could not find the small suitcase. Initially, they blamed the crew of the ship for not bringing it aboard but then as they thought about it, June had left it in her closet at home. They were just going to have to buy some new lingerie and an evening gown for June.

Soon the big cruise ship was out of port and the stores on board were open for shopping. Martin and June found a small but nice clothing store. It was amazing the number of stores they had on this ship. In the lingerie section, a nice young woman from Ukraine came to help them. They explained their situation and how the only bra and panties June had were on her body.

The young woman smiled as it was not an uncommon occurrence. "I'm sure we can help you ma'am. What size do you wear?"

June blushed a little "I'm a 40F, dear. And I'm a medium panty.

She said something in Ukrainian and began rummaging around the bras and panties. She said "Excuse me" and went into the back. When she returned, she had 3 bras and 3 panties in her hand. The bras were the only sized 40F that she had. She was surprised that she even has those. They were lacy and came in black, blue, and red. The panties matched in color as they were from the same manufacturer. Unfortunately for June, they were not her style. June normally wore panties that almost reached her belly button but these were hip huggers. Two had French cut sides while the last, the red one, was a thong.

"I can't wear those!" she exclaimed and looked to her husband for support but he just shrugged.

They were better than nothing so she grabbed them from the young woman's hands with a thank you and headed off to the evening gown area. The young woman followed as she was the only person working in the store.

"They are just all too low cut, Martin. I can't possibly wear them."

"I think they're fine" Martin stated calmly. Inside he was jumping for joy. "After all, we know no one on this cruise. There are probably plenty of women wearing gowns with similar styles and you will fit right in." He looked to the Ukrainian woman for help and she nodded.

"These are pretty popular styles, ma'am. Many people dress a little more ummm what is the word? Provocatively … yes … provocatively since they know no one on the cruise. People do things that they might not do at home ummm precisely because they are not at home."

June looked at the red dress with the plunging neckline. "Oh what the heck!"

They bought the dress and the undergarments and returned to exploring the ship.

* * *

Kay and Sandy lay on their beds with their clothes still packed in their bags. Sandy lay on her stomach reading the ship's daily news report and schedule for the next day. Their room was bigger than Martin and June's room. Indeed, Sandy's dad had kept his promise and the last minute reservation meant that they got a small sweet in an exclusive part of the "Fantasy deck."

"It says here that there are two "dress up" dinners. One is tomorrow night and the other is on Thursday." Sandy penned her picks for her excursions as she spoke.

"Let's skip them both" Kay said from the bathroom as she brushed her teeth.

"Oh come on. What an opportunity to wear some of these sexy gowns I got."

Kay leaned her head out of the bathroom. "What? Are you trying to give some poor old bastard a heart attack?"

"No, but how about some of those cute waiters? Or maybe show the Maitre D some thigh?"

And in the end, the girls decided to at least attend the first dress-up dinner.

* * *

It was the second night of the voyage and both Martin and June had gotten used to the boat's gentle movement. Never one to be late, June was ready to go 15 minutes early. Martin emerged from the bathroom in his dark gray suit and red tie to see his wife as he had never seen her before.

She smiled and it was obvious that for once she enjoyed the effect she had on her husband. She wore the red dress with the plunging neckline. Extra material gathered at the bottom of her cleavage and slightly hid her hard nipples from poking out. Underneath, she wore her new red bra and her new red thong. Her long cleavage was gently pressed together by the under wire of the bra creating 7 inches of cleavage. Light freckles sprinkled across her bare chest. Martin reached into a sleeve in his suitcase.

"Honey, I think you look wonderful but you would look much better if you had this around your neck." He produced the small black box and June opened it with glee. It was a thin gold necklace with a large single diamond in the center of a gold leaf setting. Martin had taken out a small loan from the jewelry store to buy it. "It's not very expensive but ..."

"Ohhhhhhh Martin!" she swooned hugging him tight. Martin enjoyed the press of her tits on his chest. She put the necklace on and they quickly found their way to the main dining room and their assigned table for 6 by the window.

June chattered away wondering who they might be seated with. As each couple entered the main dining room she whispered to Martin whether they were suitable company or not. Often she would comment on the woman's dress but then giggle and point out that her own dress was more revealing.

Their salads arrived and both began to think that they would be dining alone. It was then that two young women entered the main dining room. They got the attention of more than Martin and June. They got the instant attention of most of the men in the room followed by their companions!

The Maitre D greeted them politely with a smile. Kay was dressed in a dark blue dress with a flowing edge that was low on her left side at her knee and high on her right side almost to the level of her ass cheek. The dress had a blue sash belt that accentuated her tiny waist and voluptuous chest. The neck was a low scoop revealing her generous bosom and long cleavage. Her lacy matching blue bra showed at the edges giving her a wanton sex appeal. Her long hair was pulled up in a bun on the top of her head. As she walked, her 4 inch heels caused her chest to bounce and each pair of eyes only got more distracted to see Sandy walking behind her.

Sandy's black dress was tight to her hips and waist and was strapless. Her bra pushed her ample tits up, supporting them almost as if they were on a shelf. Her long legs extended from the tight bottom of the dress down to her 5 inch black pump shoes. Around her neck, she wore a simple white bow tie.

June whispered to Martin. "Look at those two young girls."

Martin smiled "I am"

She ignored his comment. "They are just sluts, I tell you, sluts! How can their parents let them out of the house like that?"

"I don't see it as a problem. It's not like you can see anything."

At that point, the girls were led right to Martin and June's table. Immediately, there was a flurry of activity around them as their orders were taken and their salads served.

Martin put his napkin on his lap and realized that his cock was at full attention. He tried to make discreet adjustments but his boxers were wrapped around it awkwardly. He was thankful that June was doing her best to be friendly to these two sluts who were going to be their dining mates for the next several days. After pretending to drop his napkin on the floor, he was able to adjust his thick cock down his pant leg.

* * *

Martin followed his wife's ass down the narrow corridor to their room. She continued to prattle on about the girl's skimpy dresses but now she was at least giving in that the girls had sweet personalities.

"I can't wait to get out of this dress! And this bra is just too tight!"

Martin smiled as he closed and locked the door behind them. From behind her, he reached out and held his wife's waist and pulled her to him. His thick cock rested on the top of her ass crack and he leaned his face over her shoulder and kissed her neck. She smelled nice and he sucked her neck as she slowly closed her eyes. His hands roamed up slightly cupping her full tits. She ground her hips back pushing her ass into his cock. He kissed up her neck and licked her earlobes as his fingers played with her already hard nipples.

She turned around out of his hands and smiled. Slowly she slid her left shoulder out of her dress and let it slide down her arm. Then the other slid down revealing her red lacy bra only barely covering her big tits. The dress dropped to the floor and Martin almost fell over with lust.

His conservative wife stood before him in a bright red lacy bra and red lacy thong.

"Honey, if you keep standing there, I'm going to be undressed and you will still be dressed!"

He smiled and began undressing. His pants were tented in front of him and his wife smiled at the sight.

"This thong has been driving me crazy all night. I don't know how people can wear these things!"

"What did it do, honey?" Martin asked.

She pulled off her thong and tossed it on the bed and then she dropped her bra and stood naked before Martin.

Martin wasn't too far behind as he quickly dropped his pants, boxers and tossed off his shirt. June lay before him on the bed on her back. Her pussy lips swollen from the evening of her new thong rubbing against her pussy lips. She touched them and felt a shiver go up her spine.

"Maybe we should not do this."

"Why not??" asked Martin quickly.

"I'm awful sore down there from the thong."

Martin thought quickly. "Let me take a look and see if I can provide some relief.

Martin kneeled between her legs and kissed her thighs. The kisses were small, soft kisses as he made his way up to her pussy. It was a sight he rarely saw. Normally, she insisted that the lights be off or only a candle or two be lit. In that light, it was hard to see a woman's dark passages. Her pussy was glistening and the smell attacked Martin's senses and it was intoxicating. Inches from her pussy, he could see nothing wrong. Her pussy lips were swollen and looked a little tender but also looked perfect for licking. He knew that she would never participate in oral sex. She neither gave nor wanted to receive but Martin was always a persistent man plus she had worn that beautiful dress! His tongue flicked out and tasted her nectar. He did it again and pushed her pussy lips apart. He licked a third time and closed his eyes. This was heaven. She tasted so sweet and his cock bobbed in approval between his legs. Her thick pussy lips moved from side to side as his urgent tongue went higher and higher to her thick clit. It was a large clit and poked out from behind its folds. Martin teased it and flicked it with his tongue.

She groaned "Oh Martin, what are you doing to me??"

He kept up his licking and held his hands firmly on her thighs. The skin was soft to his touch. He wanted her to cum from his tongue. He knew that he could make her cum if she would just continue to let him lick!

"Martin, honey, that feels nice but I'm sore down there from that thong honey."

He licked harder and his tongue parted her lips and entered her canal. More juices were flowing now and the sensation of her taste drove him crazy.

She tried to close her legs but Martin held on. "Martin, stop! Stop now!"

Martin took a deep breath and backed out from between her legs with his lips, cheeks and nose covered with her juices. His cock throbbed and bobbed in front of him. It's almost 10 inches in length and thick head was almost obscene.

"Honey, thank you for licking me but you know I don't like oral sex." She almost sounded apologetic.

He looked at her on the bed. She was a goddess. Her big breasts and huge nipples jutting out were enough to drive a man mad with desire. She was "all his" but in reality, she rarely allowed anything but missionary style. In their younger days before their marriage, with her tits, his friends envied him. The truth was that, sexually speaking, he would gladly have taken another partner to bed if she was even a bit more adventurous. He didn't find out about her prudish ways until after they were married.

"Honey, don't be so sad. Go wash your face and then you can make love to me!"

He washed his face and came out of the tiny bathroom to find her filing her nails naked on the bed.

"You were in there so long that I almost got dressed for the comedy show tonight!"

She spread her legs enough for him to kneel between them. She smiled, reached down for his cock and aimed it at her pussy. He leaned in and her wetness enveloped the head of his cock. Her pussy lips spread and received him deeper. He was so long that he couldn't push all the way in. Even so, if felt good to be inside her. Her big tits were right in front of him and despite her prudish ways, she didn't control her nipples and they hardened and thickened. They were tasty morsels at the tips of two great mountains of white, soft-skinned, flesh. He leaned in and she encouraged him. His hips pistoned quickly.

He knew that she was not going to cum so he took care of himself and pounded her pussy as best he could with about half of his cock.

Leaning further down, she put a hand around his neck and guided him to her nipple and he sucked it in and began licking. She moaned and groaned but he could tell that she was faking again. He kept his pounding up and felt his cum boil in his balls. It squirted out and deep into her pussy until it ran down her ass crack.

Martin stood up. His 60 year old frame stood strong and taut. His cock hung with its big head more than halfway down his thigh.

"That was wonderful, baby" she cooed.

He smiled knowing that she was lying but no longer caring whether she came or not. She filed her finger nails again ... she had her nail file in her hand the whole time! Martin washed his cock, got dressed and told her he'd meet her in the lounge for the comedy show. For now, he needed some time to himself.

* * *

It was Tuesday afternoon. Martin came back to the room later than he had expected. He saw a note from June stating that she was going to the spa. He quickly looked at the excursion list and saw "European Spa treatment — Enjoy the gentle hands of our master masseuse at our European Spa!" He quickly saw a 2 next to the excursion and thought he'd better get his ass up there or June would be very angry with him for missing the European Spa treatment. It cost a lot of money that wasn't included in the winning tickets. He read the note wrong as the European Spa treatment wasn't for another two days ...

Sandy sat at the reception area on the top floor at the Spa waiting for Kay to finish her pedicure. She had scheduled a massage but the masseuse was sick. She saw the buxom woman from their table the night before come in the foyer and Sandy remembered her name was June. She was wearing an oversized T-shirt with one of those big, thick bras and black spandex pants. Wow, Sandy thought those were big tits! She overheard the woman ask for a manicure and watched as the receptionist check her reservation list and then guided her to a private room where Kay had just started her pedicure a few minutes earlier. A few minutes later, the husband entered and walked right to her.

"Did you see my wife? I think we are supposed to be here for a European Massage. I hope I'm not late."

Sandy stood up and looked around. "You just missed her. She just went in for a ummm" she knew what June went in for but thought of something better. "Yes, you're late. Let me take you to the massage room."

Sandy guided him around the corner right past the open door where his wife and the receptionist were chatting next to Kay. She found the massage room easily enough and was happy to see that the door was unlocked. She wasn't sure where she was going to go with this. Maybe just goof on the guy a little. Get him to strip down and laugh at him secretly for a while. It could be fun. She'd tease him, give him a look down her shirt and rub her tits on his back and get him hard. That's what she'd do … get him hard and take his clothes and leave!! No, that would be too mean. Leave his clothes with him but get him rip-roaring hard first!

Once inside he looked at her carefully. She looked young. Her face was silky smooth with no wrinkles or smile lines. Her blonde hair flowed down onto her shoulders. Her eyes were sharp and sparkled. Her lips were full, smooth and had a slight trace of pink lipstick.

Martin's eyes ventured south. Her breasts were large and full. She had a slight bulge at her tummy and her hips barely flared out at all. Her tan legs seemed longer than her height should allow. She was like a gazelle with long thin legs. She wore a pink top with a low slung V neck. The spaghetti straps and the V neck hid little of her lacy dark pink bra. The top stopped short of her belly and a small hoop was in her belly button. She wore gym shorts that were rolled up at the waist hiking the legs high on her thighs right to her crotch.

"Where's my wife?" he asked innocently enough.

"She's getting her European Massage in the other room!"

"Weren't you at our table last night? I didn't know they let employees dine with passengers."

"You are right but we won a prize and got to eat with the passengers last night. I'm sorry, we should have told you. It's kind of like being a princess for a night for those of us working on the ship! Ok, may I call you Martin?"

"Yes, that's fine."

"Ok, Martin, please strip down to your underwear and lie on the table face down."

Martin stripped down and Sandy reviewed the massage oils. She had many massages at her father's club before and these oils, mud packs, and rinses were of very good quality. When she turned around, Martin was on his stomach on the table wearing only white briefs.

"Oh, Martin, we're going to have to take those briefs off. They'll restrict the blood flow in your skin."

Martin was about to object when she put a towel over his butt and instructed him to remove his briefs.

She left the towel there with the full intent of taking it off and running out the door at sometime but she hadn't teased him enough. She stood in front of him where he could see her and reached around behind her back and unfastened her bra strap.

"This bra just gets in the way. You are my first customer today and I forgot to take it off earlier. I hope you don't mind".

"No, no, I don't mind. Whatever makes you comfortable."

She was able to remove the bra without lifting her shirt. Her nipples hardened and poked out of the soft cotton material. Martin just stared. She put oil on her hands and leaned forward to work his shoulders and upper body. With each stroke of her hands into his shoulders, he watched her breasts wobble and move. They were tanned and fantastic. As they moved under her top, he could see her brown and hard nipples. His erection began to grow.

She moved to the side and began to work the rest of his back. From the height of the table, her breasts rested on the back of his arm and with each movement her nipples scraped his skin the cotton material of her top. She rubbed the oil into the small of his back and slid the towel further down his butt. She edged the towel further and further down. She giggled to herself as she thought of the poor man's small penis getting hard under there.

Switching modes, Sandy worked on Martin's legs. She worked up from his calves and as she did, she caught a glimpse of his ball sack. It was bigger than she expected. With her hands on both sides of his thighs, she worked his thigh muscles back and forth. As she did, she bunched this end of the towel right up to the edge of his butt crack. She let her fingernails drag across his balls and heard him gasp and then he adjusted his position. The old guy was getting quite a thrill. She realized as she took a quick break that this was hard work. Martin seemed to have more muscles than she thought a guy his age should have.

Sandy instructed Martin to turn over and she held the towel so that she couldn't see his private parts. As she laid the towel back down she realized that it hadn't laid flat. There was a lump and it moved as Martin watched her big tits wobble. It couldn't be his cock, it was too big.

She rubbed his chest with an apricot spread with her eyes glancing back down to the towel every few seconds. The lump seemed to have grown. She worked the front of his legs getting a much better view of his ball sack. It wasn't an illusion, it was a very big ball sack.

"What are you doing?" Martin asked as she pushed the towel higher and higher.

Sandy smiled. "This IS a European massage … "

Her hands rubbed his stomach finding that it wasn't as flabby as she had expected. She edged the towel down further and reached under it to find a thick and throbbing cock. She moved the cloth back in shock to reveal its length. Martin looked away in embarrassment. She stroked it from the bottom up and her other hand joined the first and still the big thick head poked out. Neither hand could complete the circumference of his hardening meat. The veins were large and made their long crooked journey down to the base. The head was much thicker than the rest and looked purple, the size of a plum.

Sandy leaned over him but she could not reach it with her mouth. She climbed up next to him on the table and got between his legs never letting go of his cock. She looked him in the eye and opened her mouth to take in his cock head. It was big. She stretched her mouth wide and was able to get the top just passed her teeth. She licked and sucked the head as best she could. She put more oil in her hands and began a reverent pounding of his meat. Using both hands on his shaft while licking and sucking of the head, she gave Martin the view of her big tits bounding up and down with each thrust. It didn't take too long.

The hot sticky cum spewed into her mouth and she sucked it in swallowing as quickly as possible. Martin cried out with each jet that jumped from his cock. Some dribbled down her hands as she pumped every ounce that she could get from his cock.

After the last swallow, Sandy was giddy with excitement. This was the biggest cock she had ever seen and he came so hard it excited her. Her pussy was soaked right through he gym shorts. Without even looking, she knew that her clit was engorged more than ever and her pussy lips were slick with her juices.

She sighed and continued to stroke his cock.

"I doubt my wife is getting THIS European Massage" Martin said with a smile.

"No, you're right. She's getting a manicure."

Waves of guilt washed over Martin. He had just been seduced by this vivacious and beautiful young woman sitting on the table next to him. What if June found out? That would be the end of their marriage. That would be the end of his life!

Sandy could see the change in him. She misunderstood and thought it was happening again. Another guy had gotten satisfied and didn't give a shit about her satisfaction. But, she noticed that he wasn't exactly like the others. There was something different about Martin and it was more than his big dick.

He looked at her. She had given him great pleasure. He'd never been worked like she had. She had excited him, brought him to a mountain of excitement and pleasured him like no woman had ever done before.

He moved aside and gently pushed her onto her back. She had a confused look on her face. She hadn't expected this. He got between her legs and she eased them wide apart for him. Pulling aside her gym shorts, he found she wore no panties and Martin saw his first hairless pussy. It was beautiful! Her lips were full and her clit was barely hidden by the hood. His kisses were soft on her thighs and moved carefully up toward her pussy. He was nervous that she would tell him to stop. Instead, as his tongue reached her nectar, she moaned and groaned. He licked her lips left and right and up and down and was thrilled to see her grab her tits and squeeze her nipples. He kept licking, getting his tongue deeper and deeper into her slit. Then he pulled out and licked her clit softly at first and then increasing his vigor. She didn't tell him to stop. She begged him to keep going.

Sandy reached down and spread her lips with her fingers. "Suck it! Suck it, please!!"

Martin obliged and sucked her clit into his lips and flicked it with his tongue.

Her first climax started in her toes and they curled. Her legs stretched and flexed and stretched again as Martin clung on and kept licking and sucking. The grunt and groan escaped from her lips sounded like a lion, deep and throaty. "Ohhhhh Martin!!"

Her juices ran out her cunt and Martin lapped them up as fast as he could. They flowed down over her asshole and tickled her.

Sandy breathed a large sigh and collapsed on the table exhausted.

Martin smiled and thought "So, this is what a woman looks like after she climaxes."

Sandy kissed him on the lips. It was the first time they had kissed. Her tongue slipped into his mouth and she tasted herself. She didn't care that her juices were all over his face. They stood up beside the table and kissed for a long time. Her hand instinctively wrapped around his cock feeling it growing again. She smiled. No, this was not a young man but his recovery time was quick enough for her.

Martin backed away but Sandy held on to his cock. "No, I think we should stop" he said quietly.

Sandy whimpered a little. "Please? Just a little more. Please?"

"I really have to get back to my wife and I feel terribly guilty about this"

Sandy's mind whirred into motion. She wanted that cock between her legs. She just wanted to feel its size press on her pussy walls. She pushed him back onto the table.

"Your secret is safe with me. You don't have to worry about anything" she cooed. "Just let me have this one little or should I say big experience and I'll keep quiet and won't bother you again!"

Martin could see the veiled threat. He had to give her what she wanted.

She crawled up on top of him and straddled his hips. She pulled off her top and held his cock up to her tits and rubbed his cock all over her tits and nipples. It felt great! She leaned over more and sucked the head in.

"ohhhhh" Martin groaned. "I don't get to do this often."

"What? Sex? With her body, you'd think she does this all the time!"

"oh no. I mean we don't have oral sex and she rarely gets on top."

She sucked his head in again. She stroked his shaft and was deliberately being rough with him. Martin loved it.

"Honey, with a cock like this, I'm surprised she isn't chasing you around the house all the time!"

The next words came out of Martin's mouth without any thought. It was a rarity for Martin. "She fakes orgasms …"

Sandy looked at Martin and didn't believe him at first. She got on all fours and reached between her legs to put his cock head between her pussy lips. Her nipples dragged across Martin's chest and he thought he would cum again right there. She slowly lowered herself onto the head. It felt like it was ripping her apart but she pushed more. She gritted her teeth and pushed and felt the head pass her lips with a pop. A shiver rolled up her spine and her toes curled again.

Looking down into Martin's face she spoke quietly as she continued to work his cock inside her. "Honey, why fake an orgasm when you can have a real one? She just needs some training. OHhhh your cock is soooooo big!"

"It's too big, isn't it. That is what she always has said."

Sandy ignored him. Her mind was losing control. Her body was taking over. The sensations spreading from her hot cunt traveled throughout her body. It started with a small tremor and was building as she pushed further and further down his pole. Her pussy lips engorged and gripped Martin's cock. She had taken more inside her than Martin had ever put inside his wife, June. And she kept going deeper. Finally, the base of his cock began to bend and Sandy knew that he was pressing hard against her cervix. She lifted up and slammed down hard. She did it again and cried out with each slam. Her head began to shake back and forth. Her hair flying around her as her fingernails dug into the sheets beside his head.

Arching her back to get as much cock in her as possible, her big tits were practically smothering Martin. He loved it. He sucked her nipples in as she pressed again and again against his cock. He was trying to think of anything nonsexual so that he wouldn't cum too soon but this vixen was deeper on his cock than anyone had ever been and she kept on going.

Suddenly she stopped on the upstroke and gasped. Her eyes were wide and then she squeezed them tight. She rocked slowly back and a smile crossed her face as inch by inch re-entered her pussy. She was on the edge of her climax. She was making it last. She lifted up slightly and slammed down for the last time screaming. She felt her cunt juices fly out of her pussy dribbling down to his balls and asshole. She grunted and screamed and then punched him on the chest and his cum erupted into her full pussy.

Spurt after spurt poured out of Martin's cock. His hips fucked up at her as her second and third climaxes blasted through her body. Suddenly, she had become a rag doll and collapsed on her chest. She was tired and limp and curled her hands together and lay on his chest with his big but deflating cock still firmly inside her.

He held her for a few minutes.

"I can't believe that I cheated on her" he said quietly.

"You need to train her." Sandy said with her chin on his chest.

"What do you mean?"

"She's just gotten into a rut. I bet she just doesn't know how to enjoy her body or yours! She needs to be trained to enjoy her body and to enjoy this cock"

He looked at her. "No, you're crazy. First of all, you trick me into this and second, you talk crazy talk like teaching my wife how to enjoy her body. You're crazy!"

She smiled. "Yes, I'm crazy. And you know what's worse?

"What?"

"I only want to train her so that I can have this cock of yours a couple more times on this trip. If I train her, will you give me your cock some more?"

"What do you mean 'train her'?"

"When I'm done, she's going to be a great lay for you. She is going to want your cock as much as I know you want to suck her big tits. If we're lucky, we might be able to change the way she dresses so that she doesn't always look like a Victorian school master. I know that dinner was not her usual attire!"

Sandy got down and using her tongue cleaned up Martin's cock. It got semi hard but Sandy needed a break.

"There's one other thing."

"What's that?" asked Martin.

"I have a friend and you need to fuck her too."

Martin just sighed.

"And another thing … you need to participate in the training."

"Promise you won't tell her I cheated on her?"

"I promise and a promise is a promise … But, if things go right, you'll probably tell her yourself!"

Martin doubted that and wondered what he had gotten into and what he had just agreed to.

* * *

The next day, June dressed in her usual large and thick bra, an oversized T-shirt and black stretch shorts. Each morning of the trip, she had gone for a walk on the top deck and today was no different. As she walked, she noticed the two girls from the formal dinner and waived. They waived back very friendly and began to walk with her.

The three lovely women walked the track 4 more times and the two girls invited June to see their suite. June said she could visit another time when she wasn't so sweaty. Sandy was persuasive and said that they had some ice cold water waiting for them.

June entered the suite after Kay. It was a large suite with sitting areas, a refrigerator, a fully stocked bar, a dining area and another room with two couches and a coffee table.

"Wow, this is a huge suite! How on earth did you girls afford it?"

Sandy giggled and said one word "Daddy"

"Daddy?"

"Yes, my daddy promised me a cruise if I got straight A's and I did. A promise is a promise!"

Sandy handed June bottled water and she drank it gladly. A few minutes later and June was asleep on the couch from the sleep-aid Sandy had put in her water bottle.

"I cannot believe that you talked me into this! This is kidnapping!" Kay whispered.

"Why are you whispering, no one can hear you. We are on the top floor and it's the only suite up here!"

"It just makes me nervous. Doing this"

"When you feel his cock spreading your pussy lips, you will thank me!"

Sandy and Kay stripped June of her clothes. They had to work quickly as they were not sure how long the sleeping pill would last.

* * *

June awoke to blackness. Her eyes were covered by a soft cloth tied around her head. She tried to move but couldn't. "Help me" she said softly.

"That's right, honey. We're here to help you." The voice said. It was one of the girls. It was coming back to June. She was walking and stopped at the girls' suite and drank some water. Did she fall?

"Where am I? Why can't I move? Did I fall and break something?" And then she realized that she was naked. Her hands were tied above and aside of her head. Her knees were trussed up to her arms and open wide. Her ankles were pulled out. Thankfully the ties didn't hurt but she was frightened and began to cry.

"You will be fine as long as you do as we say"

"Sandy, please let me go. I'll tell no one. Trust me. I won't tell a soul!"

"There are some things that you need to learn. I'm here to teach you. That is all this is. This is a classroom where you are going to learn how to behave. Participate and you will get an A and get to leave early. Struggle and fight and you will get an F and have to stay after class."

June began to struggle. She tried rolling from side to side and could hear the bed creak as she did it. "Look young ladies! You let me go now, right now!"

Thwack! It was the sound of a ruler on her ass and it stung.

"You are not starting out well." Sandy said calmly and nodded to Kay who swatted her two more times.

"OK, OK!!"

June felt a warm washcloth between her legs soaking her pussy hair. She heard the sound of shaving cream and felt it applied to her pussy. Then the feel of the razor on her skin and she held very still. "Why are you doing this?" she said as a tear of fear rolled down her cheek onto the bed sheet.

The blade continued its work and the question went unanswered. When they were done and washed away the shaving cream, her pussy was completely bare except for a small thin strip above her clit area.

"You have beautiful, big tits, June". She could tell that it was Kay and her hands began a massage of her tits. Oil was added and they became slippery. June's nipples expanded and grew to their full size. "ohhhh, you have huge nipples! They're beautiful! Why do you hide them behind that hideous bra?"

"They are not beautiful! They are too big. They get the wrong kind of attention."

"They are very big and long now … are you getting excited?"

"No, this is humiliating, illegal and immoral!"

Thwack! Thwack! Two quick spanks and immediate lips sucking her nipples. The tit sucking felt nice, soft and warm but the spanks stung this time. June decided she should just try and endure this humiliation and not fight back. It was useless anyway. As soon as she caught a break, she'd run for it but for now, she had no choice.

"Say that you're sorry … say it or get another spanking."

"I'm sorry."

"Mean it!"

"Ok, OK, I am sorry"

The lips were back on her tits and she could feel fingers roaming her inner thighs. She again tried to close her legs and the ties held firm. Her heart began to race from the insistent sucking and fondling of her tits.

Suddenly, they stopped sucking her tits. She was just getting used to it and they stopped. Someone was between her legs. She could tell from the shifting of the bed. June felt something warm and wet on her pussy lips. It was a tongue. The back of the tongue was rougher than the front and whoever was doing it was using all parts of their tongue. She sucked air into her lungs as she tried to control her temper. This had gone too far and then she felt a finger slide between her pussy lips and the tongue continued licking her lips. Now lips were on each of her nipples again. How many of them were there? Her pussy was getting licked and both her nipples were getting sucked. She could feel a surge of heat emanating from between her legs rising up her body. Her breathing became rapid. The fingers, now there were two of them, were very slowly exploring her hot love canal. She was soaked down there. It must have been from the shaving but it was more slippery than water.

The fingers stroked and pressed her pussy open on all sides.

"Do you like men?" asked Sandy.

"Yes, I love my husband" June was surprised at how raspy her voice sounded. Was she getting turned on by this? No, absolutely not.

"You love your husband. Hmmmm. Do you fuck him?"

"We have intercourse."

"Do you fuck him or make love to him?"

"We uhhh ... " she hesitated.

"Don't lie or you'll feel the ruler!"

The fingers kept prodding deeper and the lips on her clit and tit was confusing her.

"We just fuck! It gets him off and keeps him happy"

"What about you? Do you get off? OR do you fake it to also make him happy?"

"I ummm" that tongue on her clit was really feeling good. "I fake it to make him happy. He wants me to climax but a woman my age just doesn't climax or have the sexual libido that you young girls do!"

The fingers in her cunt curled up and found the soft mound of tissue known as the g-spot. Their first touch brought a loud groan from June's lips. She was breathing hard. Her big tits bounded up and down on her chest. Her nipples still long and hard as Martin continued to suck them. Sandy kept up her play with June's pussy while Kay sucked her clit.

"ohhh what are you doing to me? You need to stop that! It's not right …"

"Who says so? You like it, don't you? Yeah … do you want me to stop?"

"yes …stop now … " she murmured without conviction.

The fingers continued to stroke her g-spot and the lips and tongue on her nipples wouldn't slow down. The tongue was on again, off again sucking of her clit and it was driving her wild. She began to shake her head as the first wave of orgasm swept up her body.

Sandy's fingers increased their pace. She was frigging the pretty older woman as fast as her fingers could take her. Suddenly, it happened. June squirted with a scream. Three jets of her pussy juice shot out of her cunt just missing Kay's face and landing 6 inches between her legs soaking the sheet. The rest dribbled down her pussy lips and across her asshole. Kay urgently licked up June's juices from her pussy lips. She sucked and licked and another orgasm rocked June. She screamed again and sucked a big gulp of air into her lungs. Her big tits fell to the side of her chest as she arched her back.

Martin's cock was rock hard as he watched his wife squirt onto the sheet. It throbbed and needed relief. Watching these beautiful young women sexually attack his wife was more than he could stand. Now, with his wife's cum shooting out like that … his cock just continued to throb and was about to explode.

June cried out a third time and tears fell down her cheeks "YOU SEE! YOU SEE!!" She sobbed. "I climax and it's embarrassing. You're laughing aren't you!"

She felt Sandy's lips on her ear whispering. "I wish I could cum like that! I mean it. It was beautiful!"

"There's not a man in the world that would put up with a woman doing that! It's disgusting!"

"Well, we have a man in the room and for your sake, I'm sorry to say that he is not disgusted. As a matter of fact, he is very turned on. His cock is huge and your display has just made him even bigger!"

June groaned but Martin smiled as he moved between his wife's legs.

"No, please. I can't be unfaithful to my husband!" She felt the head of the cock part her pussy lips. "ohhhh what are you doing to me?!"

Sandy kissed Junes tear stained cheek. When we're done, you're going to appreciate your husband even more. Aren't you?"

"Yes, yes … I already do! You don't have to do this!"

Sandy kissed her lips softly and whispered again. "You need to have this big cock so you can truly love your husband."

The pressure was intense on her pussy lips as they parted and widened. The head slid in slowly and she grunted. More of Martin's shaft entered her. Martin pumped his wife like he always did. He had

4 inches in her and kept pumping in and out as the girls sucked his wife's tits.

Sandy whispered "Beg him!"

"Beg him what??" gasped June.

"Beg him to put it all in!"

"No!"

"Do it!!"

"Ok. Please put it in deeper!"

Martin shook his head and kept up the four inches.

Sandy said quietly "Not fucking good enough!"

June licked her lips. Her tits were bouncing back and forth under Martin's fucking.

"I need it."

"Tell him that you want it!"

"I need it and I uhhhhh ohhhhh I want it! Yes … I want it! Fuck me with it!"

Martin drove deeper pushing another 2 inches into virgin territory never stopping with his pumping. He drove deeper still until he was hitting her cervix with each and every stroke.

June was meeting every thrust and hadn't stopped talking. "Yeah … that's it! Fuck me!! … Do it … fuck me HARD!!!"

"Do you like his hard cock in you?" Sandy asked softly

"Yeah … I love his hard cock!"

"You love it?"

"ohhhh shit … it feels soooooooooooo fucking good!!"

The waves washed over her in rapid succession. The first was a tidal wave that shook her whole body for 2 to 3 minutes. Martin didn't stop. The second ripped through her starting with her toes and ending with a tingling in her neck. The third climax was less than a minute later as Martin still hadn't stopped. Tears streamed down her face. These were tears of joy and not fear. Sandy and Kay hugged her and kissed her. Martin kept fucking her. He pushed deep inside her for the last time and June could feel his cum shooting deep inside her. "Yeah ... Yeah!!! Give me that cum ... give it to me!!"

They all relaxed for a few minutes. Sandy had her own pussy juices flowing down her legs. She was hot and wanted Martin fucking her soon but the job wasn't over.

"We're almost done June. You have to clean him"

"But I'm so tired!"

"I know" said Kay. "But I'm going help you in your learning. Suck a man to get him hard. Make love to him to make him climax. Never fake an orgasm. Clean a man off when he is done. If you do those things and he'll lick your pussy and make you cum and cum and cum!"

The big cock was at her lips and June licked it tentatively at first. Within moments, her prudish senses finally broken down, she was sucking the tasty juices from his cock and liking it.

A tongue licked June's ear and she knew it was Sandy again. "Honey. I want you to get rid of your bras. Throw them away. You are now going to dress more stylish. You are going to make men look at you. Men are going to want you. They are going to desire you. Women will be jealous. Your husband will love you for it and you will be faithful to your husband. Do you hear me?"

June nodded. "But I was faithful to my husband up until tonight! You made me unfaithful!"

Sandy smiled. "You're lying again. Do you want to be spanked?"

"No … I'm not lying. I've never had sex with anyone but my husband!"

"That's not faithful, my dear! Have you sucked his cock? Have you cleaned him after he was done? Have you allowed him to suck your pussy? Have you teased him and made him want you with those big tits of yours?"

"No but is that what you think men want?"

Thwack!

"It is as I suspected the first night I met you. If you aren't doing those things then you are not being faithful. You are being stingy with yourself. You MUST give yourself to him so that he can give himself to you!!"

"Ok. I understand. I don't know how I will do it but I will try."

Kay got close to June's ear. "June, if you don't or even if we suspect that you aren't being a good and faithful wife to your husband, we'll post this video on the internet and send a copy to your husband."

"What video???"

"The one we just created of you having sex with a big, hard cock and two very cute girls."

June was silent. She felt the ties on her arms and legs loosen. Pulling off the blindfold, she looked back and forth to Kay and Sandy. She stood on shaky legs and slowly got dressed. She opened the door to leave and looked back at the two naked girls.

"Remember" Sandy said. "Dress sexy for your husband and be faithful to him. We'll be watching".

Kay locked the door behind June and turned to see Martin back in the room with Sandy on her knees sucking his soft cock.

"I don't think I can get it up again, girls. I'm sorry" Martin said with a wry smile.

Sandy smiled back. "Sure you can … why don't you just rest for a moment and watch?"

Kay giggled and kissed her friend full on the lips. They both looked at Martin making sure that he knew that their performance was for him. Kay fondled Sandy's big tits and brought her nipples up to her lips and began sucking and licking.

"Mmmm, Kay, didn't you think that June's tits were the sexiest tits you've ever sucked?" Sandy knew talking about Martin's wife would get him excited.

"Ohhhh yes. Her tits were gorgeous" she said through a mouthful of gorgeous tit. "And I love her pussy. Such sweet pussy juice!"

Martin stroked his cock absent mindedly and it quickly hardened.

Kay stood next to the table and bent at the hips and spread her legs. "Umm Martin? Could you take care of me?" she asked in a little girl voice. Martin was surprised to find that his cock was hard again. With a big grin, he positioned himself behind Kay and Sandy guided his cock into her best friend's wet pussy.

Martin pushed the head in. It was not easy going.

"My God, this is big … shit … " and Kay smiled as Sandy spread her pussy lips to help Martin's entry. Martin kept up his pace forcing more and more of his cock deeper into her.

"ohhh I don't think I can do this! It's too big!" Kay cried out.

Martin started to apologize and take it out when Sandy stopped him. Her face twisted in anger. "Look Martin. We took a big risk fixing your wife and you can't blow it. Do you understand?"

"What do you mean?" he asked innocently enough.

"I mean that you are as much of a problem as your wife!! If you let Kay up now, you're admitting that she can't take it. She CAN take it. You tell her to shut up because you are going to fuck her and fuck her until she puts a puddle of cum on the floor! You have a fucking fantastic cock. Act like it!"

Kay smiled. It had all been planned. Part of the training that she and Sandy had worked out the night before. "Martin ... oooh ... it hurts!"

Martin looked at Sandy. "No baby, it's going to be just fine!" and he pushed his cock another two inches deeper into Kay's pussy. Kay grunted from the thrust and smiled.

"Ohhhh Martin, you're so big and thick! I just have a small pussy and big tits!!"

Martin increased his tempo and was pushing his rod all the way up and crashing at her cervix. He slapped her ass and she winced.

Sandy climbed up on the table and spread her legs before Kay's face. "Eat my pussy, bitch!"

Kay gladly dove in to Sandy's pussy while Martin's cock continued its assault.

Martin looked into Sandy's eyes and smiled. She smiled back. He mouthed the words "Thank you" and she seductively licked her lips and fell back on the table as an orgasm raced through her body. When she was aware of her surroundings again, she saw Kay sitting astride Martin's cock. She had just lowered herself onto him.

Sandy raced over and caught Kay's eyes.

"Kay ... ummm Martin likes big tits like yours and mine ... "

Sandy giggled and they both leaned forward forcing their big tits into his face. With all that tit staring at him, Martin lost control and squirted deep inside Kay's pussy. As Martin lay there, the ever insatiable Sandy scrambled between Kay's thighs to gobble up Martin's cum.

"Martin, you have the sweetest cum" she said as she swallowed. "If you wife doesn't change her ways, call me!"

* * *

It took a while for Martin to regain composure so he walked around the ship. He stopped for a drink at a ship's bar. With all the fucking he had done in the last 2 days, he doubted he'd be able to get hard again for a month! He laughed at the thought of what had happened. It seemed unreal, like he had fallen asleep and had one of those half asleep and half awake dreams where you don't know what is real and what is dream. He sucked down his drink and when he looked up, he saw a beautiful and sexy woman coming toward him.

It was 4:00 in the afternoon and the sun was behind her blinding much of his sight. She wore a sheer white, button down shirt open and tied in the front below her tits. Around her waist was a white wrap that tied at her hips. Under the skirt was an orange bathing suit bottom with French cut hips. She wore nothing under the shirt and her long and thick dark brown nipples were easily visible to all around her.

As she walked, her giant tits gently swayed from side to side playing peek-a-boo with the open front of her shirt.

"I've been looking everywhere for you, Martin" she said with a smile. "Don't you know that it's happy hour which means its time for you to make me happy?"

She climbed up onto the stool next to Martin. There were four other men at the bar and their eyes were glued to her tits. She ordered a drink and she and Martin conversed as if nothing had changed. She slugged down all of her drink as she needed courage for what she was going to do next.

Standing up, she backed away from the bar and the men glanced at her while trying not to look. "It's ok, boys. You can look. C'mon, it's alright. Feast your eyes on my big tits. I know you want to."

Martin stood up.

June untied her shirt and slowly opened it up. First her left nipple came into view and someone whistled. Then her entire right tit was exposed and one of the guys bravely stood and walked to her to feel her.

"That's right. C'mon … come and feel how real they are. No silicone here boys. Each of you gets a nice feel." Then she pointed at Martin. "But only he gets to fuck me!"

All of them took turns feeling her tits. Martin watched and his cock became engorged spreading down his leg. One of the guys began to feel her from behind while another was in front. The guy behind her cupped her tits while the guy in front sucked her nipples.

The guy in back kissed her neck and she leaned her head back onto his shoulder and almost forgot what she was doing. It felt so nice to have all that attention. The girls were right.

She stopped them and smiled politely. "It's happy hour gentlemen and his big dick is going to make me happy!" With that, Martin and June left and went to their tiny cabin.

He shut the door and she pinned him back against the door kissing his lips. "Did you like that baby? Did you? All those men feeling and sucking my big tits? They all wanted to fuck my cunt but only you get that pleasure, baby. Do you like it when I talk dirty?"

Martin nodded with a faint smile.

She kissed him again and pushed herself away. "Like how I look?" She twirled.

Martin nodded and pulled down his pants to release his cock. She smiled and kneeled before him. She took his cock head in her mouth and sucked and licked. Martin thought he would explode. She bobbed up and down on his prick stroking his shaft until she could wait no longer. It was thick and purple with that plum of a head.

She lay on the bed and mouthed "fuck me?"

He climbed up next to her. Her hand wrapped around his shaft and began stroking. He kissed her lips and slipped his tongue inside her mouth. She returned his kiss with fervor, licking and sucking his tongue. He kissed down her neck and nibbled at her earlobes. His kisses continued to her big tits. He kissed them all over and hefted one to his lips to draw in her dark and long nipple. His mouth felt wonderful on her tits and he kept going. His hand crept between her open thighs and found her soaking pussy open and waiting. She gasped as his fingers slipped in and found her g-spot. She was so excited at showing the men her tits that Martin's fingers put her over the edge. She started cumming and cumming hard.

"Ohh God Martin!! Ohhhh shit!! I'm cumming again!! Ohhh Martin!! Don't stop, don't stop!!" She squirted 3 times from her hot pussy.

Martin kept playing with her all through her climax until she reached down and stopped his hand from moving. It was the most beautiful sight for Martin. His lovely wife cumming and crying out his name and he hadn't even fucked her yet.

He began kissing her again as her breathing almost returned to normal. He kissed down her belly to her crotch and playing his part stared at her pussy for a few minutes.

"You shaved?"

"Yes, honey. I thought you would like it." She smiled.

He kissed her pussy lips and she stopped him. "Get on your back. I want to ride you!"

Martin eagerly got on his back. It was his favorite position because it put her big 40F tits right in his face. She straddled him and reached down between her legs to push his purple cock head between her lips. Once properly aimed, she worked her way back. Slowly, she worked him into her sore pussy. After several strokes she was consistently taking 8 inches of his thick meat inside her. It was tight and she was sore.

She fed him her tits. Teasing him as she pumped on his cock and wiggling her tits in his face. First she would smother him with them and then back off and let him suck them. Martin was loving every moment of it. His cock was pulsating inside her. She was so tight because he was so deep inside her.

"Martin?" she kept up her pace.

"Yes love?" he replied through her tits as they hit his chin.

"Where were you today?" she dug her fingernails into his chest a little.

"Around the boat. Watching the ship and how it works" he replied nervously. "Where were you today?"

She smiled and slammed hard down on his cock and it surprised him. "Oh here and there but I think you know exactly where I was."

"You do?" he said with a jump as she slammed down on him again and again.

"Yes. Did you enjoy watching?"

Martin didn't know if she knew or not. Did she know that he had been watching the girls "train" her or was she talking about him watching the ship operate?

"Oh yes. I enjoyed it very much. There was so much going on." He replied vaguely.

She smiled and kissed his lips squishing her tits into his chest. As she leaned forward, only the head of his cock was in her pussy and it teetered on falling out.

"Mmmmm I bet there was. I bet that you went to the engine room where those pistons go up and down and in and out … didn't you …" She sucked his lower lip into her mouth and rode her ass up and down just on the head teasing his cock right on the sensitive underside.

"ohhhh that feels good" he groaned.

"Yes, I'm sure it does. I just want you to feel as good as I felt this morning …" She smiled and he looked at her blankly.

"Tell me the truth and I'll let that big cock cum, baby. All you have to do is tell me the truth … where you in the room?"

He nodded and her hips went a little lower pushing his cock in deeper on every thrust.

"Did you like watching?"

He nodded again and she rewarded him by sliding her cunt all the way down and then back up again and he grunted.

"Did you like fucking me while I was all tied up?"

He smiled and kissed her quickly on the lips.

"But is it as good as what you are getting now, baby?"

Martin shook his head and she slid down onto his cock three times. He was so close to cumming if she had gone down a fourth time, it would have been all over.

Her hips kept pumping on his head. It was driving him crazy. He had never felt this good in his entire life.

"Who do you love?" She asked. "Me or those two little girls?"

"You" he croaked out. "You".

She smiled and licked her lips. "Do you want to fuck them again, honey?"

He said nothing but remembered his bargain with Sandy. She had said she wanted his cock later in the week.

June kept pumping on the head and teasing him with her tits. "It's ok with me as long as I'm there. Maybe we could tie Sandy up next time …"

She slid down his pole hard and pumped him as fast as she could. Her tits were flying below her, smashing his chest and his face. Martin cried out with a guttural scream as his cum erupted from his cock like a dam bursting. June sat back on his cock and shoved as much as she could get in her hot cunt and rocked back and forth as another orgasm swept over her as well.

When they were done and their breathing returned to normal. She kissed him on the lips. Her tongue snaked out to his.

"June?"

"Yes?"

"You knew?"

"Yes, I knew it was you. But I'm glad that it happened."

"Me too."

"Will we make love like this again?"

June smiled. "Yes, as often as I can… this feels too good to give up!"

"Promise?"

"Yes, I promise … Martin … and a promise is a promise. Suck my cunt out and I'll clean off your cock … we're late for dinner!"

This story has been buried deep inside of me for a long time. I remember all of it very well, almost like it was last week. I've reminisced and re-lived it all many times over the years. Much of it is quite fun to remember. Some of it is bittersweet. Some of it is painful still.

When I was out of college and in my early twenties I got a job selling radio advertising in a suburban/rural area, and although new to the region, I became successful in a fairly short time.

After a couple of years I left the radio station and started my own business by acquiring a licensing agreement from a national company to sell direct marketing products. As this was an outlying area and not heavily populated, the company looked at it as an area with limited profit potential and whatever I produced would just be a bonus to them. They had never planned to develop the area anyway until I approached them so they pretty much left me alone.

But within a year I had the area thriving. I was working hard and enjoying the fruits of my labor. Soon the regional manager was after me to expand the area. I told him I was maxed out as it was and I couldn't cover much more ground. 'So hire somebody' he hollered. 'Why, so I can give my profits away to somebody else'?" I countered. But we hammered out an adjacent area and worked out a plan where I would hire a salesperson and then get bonuses on their sales and price breaks on the production costs. I ran the numbers a hundred different ways and didn't see how I could lose. So I advertised for a salesperson. It was summer and I hoped that I could get a sales rep up and running by the fall, our busiest time.

Most of the responses I received were not too impressive, and the interviews didn't go that well. The people were either not qualified, didn't understand the business, didn't have car insurance, or didn't have a clue. But one looked pretty good. In more ways than one.

Her name was Denise. We met at a small coffee shop in the midst of what would be the new territory. After introductions we sat down and faced each other from across a small table. She said to call her Dee. My name is Rob.

She had dark brown hair, cut neat and short, big green eyes and wore a sharp blue pantsuit with a white blouse. She was maybe 5'-7", thin with a nice ass and her firm, abundant tits pushed at the cloth of her attire. Her face was thin with sultry lips and just a touch of gloss. We held eye contact and I felt a sizzle in her glare. She gave a demure smile and her tongue flicked out just a sliver between her lips as she handed me her resume. She seemed a little nervous. I was too.

I took a quick glance at her resume and saw that she was thirty-six years old and married. In those days that kind of information was commonly found on resumes. As I sat across from her and pretended to study her resume I tried to hide my uneasiness.

Here I was: a twenty-five year old newly-single guy, blond hair, blue eyes, tall with a thin, runner's build; and I was interviewing this older, mature, married woman with much more experience than I. Her resume told me she had had several media sales jobs and was more than qualified.

As the interview went on we relaxed and it not only went very well, we shared some laughs and became more comfortable. And those eyes! She always looked me right in the eye and hardly blinked. I could tell she was a no-bullshit person who probably knew how to get things done.

She told me a little about herself. She had gone to France to study, met the man who was now her husband, got pregnant, had a daughter and they moved back to the U.S. Her daughter was now twelve. I asked her about her last job, almost four years at a newspaper, and why she had left. She said she'd left the job to go to work for her husband at his small construction company and to try to straighten out the business end of things. Her husband was good at building things, just not very good with the office and the paperwork and the rest of it. But now that was straightened out and she wanted to get back to what she did best, and the position I was trying to fill looked like a perfect fit. We discussed the compensation and commissions and she was agreeable. After about 75 minutes we ended. She thanked me for the interview, we shook hands and parted, and my eyes followed her ass all the way to the door.

The interview had gone well in every respect. Dee was qualified, knowledgeable, made a great impression and would represent the company and its products well. We said we'd be in touch. But I knew there was no way I could hire her.

—

Two days later I received a very professional thank-you letter in the mail from Dee, but I hadn't spoken to her since the interview. When I had placed the ad for a salesperson I had scheduled it to run for several weeks and it ran again the next day. Soon I was getting follow-up calls from her and she left multiple messages with my answering service. I knew I was putting off dealing with the inevitable. When the next ad ran my phone rang first thing in the morning and I picked up.

"Hi Rob, this is Dee _____, how are you?" she said.

"I'm doing well, Dee, thank you. How are you?"

"Oh, I'm fine, thank you. I'm calling about the sales position. I saw the ad is still running. Have you hired anyone yet?"

"No, I haven't," I replied. I explained about the ad and its scheduled flight to run for several weeks.

"I can start tomorrow!" she said enthusiastically.

I chuckled and hemmed and hawed. I said I was narrowing it down to two or three and she was definitely in the mix. She reiterated that she was perfect for the job, she was flexible, would work hard, do whatever it takes, she needed the job, etc. So we set up a second interview at the same place.

—

My problem was this: At just about every job I'd ever had, I'd ended up fucking somebody. And it always ended up making things awkward or unpleasant or worse. It's hard to work closely with people of the opposite sex because if you click, the sparks are going to fly. Throughout college I worked at the campus library and ended up fucking a couple of co-workers and the relationships didn't end well. My summer jobs, same thing, I always ended up putting my dick into some chick, making things weird at work. Even at my last job before starting my business I had fucked four different women: two cute female deejays at the FM station, a secretary at the AM, and our black receptionist's cousin who had a thing for white guys.

Now I had a dilemma: I wanted to expand my new business but I didn't want to screw things up. Dee might have been older, but she was attractive and sexy and confident. I was afraid that if we worked together the sparks would fly and then I might end up opening my fly and then it would ruin everything. And she was married to boot; I couldn't risk fucking up somebody else's marriage!

But I couldn't get around one fact, and that was that she was an ideal candidate for the job. She had all of the qualifications and lived only about fifteen minutes away, which would make it convenient for both of us. And no doubt she looked good and would make a positive impression on customers. So, to be fair to the business and to her, we should have another interview.

So… We had another interview and it was a slam dunk. I hired her and never even told her about my fears. I knew she was right for the job and trusted it would work out.

—

We worked closely and spent a lot of time together the first few weeks as I trained her in the different facets of the job and the system. We went on sales calls together, we spent a lot of time side-by-side at my desk in my home office learning the paperwork and had informal meetings to plan our promotions. We worked very well together. And there was definitely a natural chemistry between us.

After about three weeks we were sitting elbow to elbow in my office working on some copy when she mentioned that she was moving that weekend. I was shocked; my mind started wandering, here I thought I'd found the ideal salesperson and she's moving away already…? I asked her where she was moving to and she told me the location, which was the perfect location: right in the center of her territory.

"I didn't know you were planning to move," I said. "When did you decide that?"

She looked straight at me with her big green eyes and said, "About two days before I answered your ad. That's when I decided I was leaving my husband. That's why I needed this job so badly."

I must have inadvertently peeked at her left hand, I couldn't recall if she'd had a ring on before.

"It's gone," she said. "I threw it at him the night you offered me the job. He's cheated on me for the last time!"

"I'm sorry…" I started to say."

"Oh, don't be," she said, "it's for the best, believe me. I did everything for him, even quit a good job to run his business for him, and he still managed to find a new bimbo to boink!"

We both chuckled at her use of words. She laughed and cried at the same time.

"So I found a nice little apartment for us. It is right in the middle of my territory, and my daughter won't have to change schools."

It all sounded like great news. She was moving right into her territory and would be more motivated than ever.

—

Over the next few months we became more and more comfortable with each other. Even though she was a little farther away, we found convenient places to meet when she needed to drop off her paper-work or if we needed to have a brief meeting. Things became more casual between us too. We had lunch a couple of times. She would occasionally touch my arm when she spoke. Sometimes she would come by the house in the evening to drop something off, and if I wasn't home she'd leave it in the box. One Friday evening around 6:30 she stopped by and I had just gotten back from a long run. It was a hot, humid evening and I was shirtless and my sweaty running shorts clung to my body and I know she stole a couple looks at the bulge between my legs. I looked up and noticed a young girl sitting in the passenger seat of her car.

"Looks like you have a passenger," I said.

"That's Lynn, my daughter."

I started walking toward the car and introduced myself. "Hello Lynn, I'm Rob," I said. "I've heard a lot about you."

"Hi. I've heard about you too."

"How do you like your new apartment?"

"It's okay."

Dee came up from behind and said, "We're heading to a big party. Her best friend turns 13!"

"Oh wow, the big one-three!" I said, looking at Lynn. That ought to be fun!" Then I turned to Dee and thanked her for dropping off the work and said drive safely and I'd talk to her on Monday. Then she gave me her green eye burn and held it and I swear I felt my dick grow a little from her stare. I watched them back out and drive off. I walked back into the house and the cool air hit me. As I peeled off my shorts I could see that the drenched synthetic fabric had adhered and molded to my cock and balls and was sucked into the crack of my ass. I realized then that she must have seen it too.

–

As fall approached we worked hard and spent a lot of time together. This was typically the busiest time of year in our business as we had promotions for back-to-school, Halloween and then the end-of-year holidays. Throughout those months we worked closely and were constantly in contact, in person and talking on the phone. There was definitely a strong attraction between us, we both could sense it, and you could feel it in the air around us and almost cut it with a knife. There were a number of times when I felt we were very, very close to one of us saying something that would cross that line between business and personal and would take us from being colleagues to being lovers. It was that close.

The ice was cracked in early December when we went together on a Friday afternoon to the annual Christmas party for our region of the company. It was held at the home of one of the company bigshots and it was about an hour's drive away. She drove to my house and then we got into my car and I drove us to the party. We had a lot of time in the car together and we were relaxed and we talked easily about a number of things. She told me about her college days, going overseas and meeting her husband and how he was older and swept her off her feet.

And how he was always a cheat and always wanted them to be swingers from the time they first met. At the party we mingled some and we met a lot of people that we'd spoken to on the phone many times but had never met. We had a couple of drinks and relaxed even more. On the ride back we opened up further and talked about some of crazy things we did in college, the courses we took and the drugs we took. I told her about the on-again off-again blues band I played in and told her about a gig I had coming up the next weekend and suggested she come hear us if she could. She said she might do that because Lynn was scheduled to be with her dad next weekend. We were both feeling a new level of comfort together.

When we got back to my house I didn't know what to do. It almost felt like I was dropping her off after a first date. It was a little awkward but we both did the professional thing. We wouldn't cross that line today, but part of me had wanted to drag her into my house and rip her clothes off. I changed clothes and went for a run. I thought about her the whole five miles and I swear I had half a chubby.

—

The following Thursday we met at a clients' business where we had bartered for holiday gifts for our customers. We assorted nice gifts such as champagne, gift baskets, and sweets which we would deliver to our various customers over the following days. We loaded our cars with the gifts for the customers. Then I handed her a small wrapped gift which included a gift certificate to a nice boutique and a Christmas bonus.

"And this is for you," I said.

She gave me the green eye burn. Her big eyes were moist and I thought she might start to cry. I could tell a million thoughts were rushing through her head. She looked like she wanted to speak but she didn't, she just burned her liquid eyes into mine.

"Thank you," she said in a shallow, half-broken voice.

Then she leaned up to me and kissed me, half on the cheek and half on the corner of my mouth. Then she spun around, walked to her car, got in and drove off.

She had done it. Now it was just a matter of time.

—

The following Saturday night we were playing our occasional gig at Slackers, a local restaurant and bar. We were midway through our first set and I was blowing a solo on my saxophone and hit a couple of clams when I saw Dee walk in. She was with another foxy chick and they did not go unnoticed by some of the customers as they strode to the back and took stools at the bar. The place wasn't that big and we made eye contact almost immediately. She smiled and I felt the burn from across the room.

When the band took a break I walked over and stood in front of them at the bar and ordered a beer as we greeted. She introduced me to her friend Sharon, who looked fine. She was long and lean with long dark hair and black jeans that looked they were painted on. Dee looked great in blue jeans and a tight red sweater that hugged her curves. I thanked them for coming and Dee grabbed my arm firmly with both hands when she told me how good the band sounded.

"I didn't know you were so talented!" she said. "What other talents do you have that I don't know about?"

"Oh, I don't know," I blushed. "I make a mean omelet! I'll have to have you over for brunch sometime."

Dee and Sharon shared a sly glance and Dee said that she thought that was a great idea.

Before we knew it the break was up and it was time to return to the bandstand.

"Work, work, work," I said to them. "Can you stay another set?" They said they would.

"Great," I said, gripping her hand in mine. "I'll be back in forty minutes!" Then I ordered a beer to take to the stage, which I almost never do.

—

The set flew by and I rejoined Dee and Sharon at the bar. Sharon was talking to some folks at a nearby table so I had Dee to myself.

"I'm glad you hung around," I said. "I was looking forward to talking some more."

"Me too," she said, her big green eyes looking right through me.

"I wanted to ask you something."

"Really? What?"

"Let's go outside for a minute," I said. I took her hand and led her out the side door to the parking lot. It was a mild December so we were okay without jackets. We walked toward the back of the lot where it was more private and we faced each other.

"What did you want to ask me?" she said.

I licked my lips and took a deep breath. "I wanted to know," I began, "The other day, when we were picking up the presents for our customers…"

"Yes…"

"You kissed me. And I wanted to know what kind of kiss that was."

"What do you mean?"

"I mean: Was it a 'thank you' kiss, was it a 'you're a really nice guy kiss', or was it a 'I want to fuck you' kiss?"

She pursed her lips and then cracked a subtle smile. "What kind of kiss do you think it was?" she said, playing with me.

"Well," I said. "First, I gave you the gift, so 'thank you' would have been appropriate. And second, I know that I'm a nice guy, so that would make sense. But to be honest, I was hoping it was number three."

She shook her head and burst out laughing. "Rob, you are too much! Tell you what, Sherlock, let's start over so that you completely understand what's going on here. First, I'm going to give you a 'thank you' kiss."

Then she leaned up and kissed me on the exact spot she had kissed before, on the corner of my lip.

She then said, "Okay. Now I'm going to give you your 'nice guy' kiss."

She then grabbed my shoulder with one hand and kissed me full on the mouth.

Then she stepped back, looked in my eyes and said. "Now our next kiss will be the 'fuck me' kiss and it will be waiting for you whenever you are ready to come and get it!"

I was on her like a tomcat on a tuna truck. My arms went around her and our mouths met and my tongue entered her mouth and I tasted her for the first time. I inhaled her sweet scent and sucked in her tongue and her essence. Her hand was in my hair pulling my head to hers, my hands roamed her back and neck and shoulders. I backed her up against the wall of the building and we made out like a couple of tenth graders. In between the kisses and gropes, we babbled.

"Oh God, what took you so long?"

"I've wanted to kiss you since the day we met."

"Why didn't you?"

"You were married, I wanted to be professional…"

"I wanted you to be unprofessional…"

"You're so fucking hot…"

"The way you teased me, standing in front of me in your tight, sweaty shorts with your…"

I was pressed against her and I knew she could feel my stiff cock.

We gradually slowed and I peppered her with gentle kisses, my hand made it down to her firm ass. I wanted to take her home right then but I had another set to play.

"We better get back in," she said after we broke a long, soft kiss. She was right, the time was up.

We reentered the bar and the band was already in place onstage.

"Gotta go," I said as I gripped her hand. "Are you hanging around?"

She said they'd probably leave in a few minutes. I said goodbye, we'll talk tomorrow and I kissed her lips. Halfway through the second tune they got up to leave. Dee waved goodbye with a smile and mimed 'Call me' with her lips. I missed those lips already.

–

I called Dee in the morning and we talked about how relieved we were that we would no longer have to hide our feelings and tried to figure out when we would be able to see each other. With her responsibilities as a mom and her need to be discreet while going through her divorce, there would only be certain times we could get together. She said that Lynn stayed with her Sunday through Thursday morning, then after school on Thursday she would go to her Dad's till Sunday. Plus Dee would have her on a day every other weekend. So Thursday nights would be when we knew we could meet, and weekends would be hit or miss.

The holidays were coming to boot which would mean more commitments for both of us to juggle. But our work was slow that time of year and we wouldn't get busy again until after January first. So we decided that we would blow off Tuesday and spend the day together, and then we would have Thursday night. On Tuesday morning she would get Lynn off to school and then come to my place and we would have all day until Lynn came home from school. She said she would be over around nine.

"Good," I said. "And at 9:01 I'll be tearing your pants off."

Then she said something like, Oh I don't know, we should go slow, take our time, and some other such baloney.

"Oh, no," I replied. "Forget that, we're not playing that game. If that's the way you want it don't even bother to come. We've been holding back for months, dancing around it, and last night we pretty near swallowed each other's tongues. We are ready and we both know it. And it's going to be the best we ever had!"

She said she'd see me Tuesday at around nine.

—

It was an icy cold, windy Tuesday morning and Dee wore a heavy coat when she arrived. She walked through the door and into my arms. We kissed deep and long and our tongues slow-danced as we gripped each other tight. When we broke the kiss I helped her off with her coat and was stunned at what was underneath.

She was hot as a firecracker! She wore a snug, low-cut, light green top, that made her tits look ready and her eyes like ripe melons, tucked into super-tight designer jeans that hugged her ass and crotch and every inch of her long, thin legs, and red pumps. Decorated for Christmas.

"My God," I said, "You look remarkable!" I said.

She blushed and said thanks. "Not too much?"

"Hell no," I said, "You look sensational. Come to the kitchen. I made Bloody Marys!"

She followed me and I poured us two drinks from the pitcher I had prepared. I handed one to her and she took a sniff and then a sip, and then a larger drink. I had made them strong and spicy.

"How did you know I love Bloody Marys?" she asked as she took another swig.

"I took a chance," I said. "I figured if you didn't I would just pour it all over your body and lick it off."

She took another gulp, then struck a pose and said, "So, do you like my outfit?" and wiggled her butt.

"Oh, absolutely!" I said. "Like I said, you look fabulous. Good enough to eat!"

She put down her drink and moved in close. She put her hands on my hips and looked up at me, her eyes sending me the green burn. "Good," she said. "Because I haven't worn these pants for a long time. These are my 'fuck me' jeans." I put my hand behind her head and pulled her lips to mine.

"Make love to me," she whispered.

—

"Take off your shirt," she said. "I want to massage you."

We were in my bedroom. I whipped off my shirt in one quick motion. She asked me to lie face down on the bed. Then she knelt beside me and I felt her hands begin to explore my neck, my head and my back, high and low. Her sturdy, supple fingers caressed my flesh and over the next few minutes my muscles eased into submission.

"It's so nice to finally be able to touch you," she whispered, and spread kisses on the nape of my neck.

I groaned in agreement. Her lovely hands worked their magic to my lower back and underneath the fabric of my jeans.

I soon sat up and said, "It's time for your top to come off! I need to touch you, too."

As we sat facing one another kissing, I pulled her shirt off and kissed her breasts as I removed her skimpy bra. I then eased her onto her back and lay beside her. I kissed her head, her hair, her ears. Her forehead, her eyes, her nose. And of course her lips. We lingered on the lips.

I caressed and kissed and tongued her upper body and when her nipples were stiff hard rubber I put my mouth on them and didn't stop for twenty minutes.

Her hands were in constant flux, in my hair, on my back, around my neck, into my pants, seeking.

She was a loud lover. There were moans, groans, growls, howls, occasional dirty words and many other guttural utterances. She never shut up. I was taking my time. She exhaled a breathy murmur when I slipped my right hand inside her jeans.

"Time to pull down your pants," I said.

I opened her jeans and kissed her lightly on the fabric of her damp panties. I smelled her finger-licking love funk for the first time. But as I started to undress her bottom half I found that her skin-tight jeans didn't want to cooperate. I yanked on them and it was slow going, and then I gripped my fingers in the belt loops and tried to peel them off.

"Jesus Christ, girl," I exclaimed. "What the hell did you do, glue these fuckers on?"

Dee giggled like a schoolgirl. "If it's too much work Romeo, just let me know."

I kissed her lips and asked for a little help.

"Oh-kay, I guess so," she said, in mock annoyance. "Men nowadays…"

She lifted her ass and pushed her pants down as I pulled on them. Finally they were off.

"Damn, pulling off your pants is like shucking an ear of corn!" I hissed.

She laughed again. "You shuck, we fuck!"

I laughed at that and tossed her pants on the floor. "Not quite yet," I said. "But, we'll get there."

I covered every inch of her lower body with my mouth. Licking and kissing her toes, her ankles, the tops of her feet, her soles, her ankles and shins, her calves, her knees. My tongue touched all of it. And Dee moaned and groaned and yelped and scratched the whole way. When my mouth reached her thighs my hands went round to her ass and I squeezed her taut cheeks. She squeaked when I did that.

By this time her clit looked like a ripe okra. So I wrapped my lips around it and she let out with a shrill gasp I'd never heard before. And I didn't let go.

–

One time when I was in college, age nineteen or twenty, I was in a bar and I met a divorcee in her mid-thirties and went home with her. Her kids were with her ex-husband that weekend and she was horny. We got back to her place and she took me to bed. She made it clear that the night meant nothing but she needed to get off. She told me to eat her pussy, and she taught me how. She said to wrap my lips around her clit and never let go, forget all that tongue flying licking shit you see in the porn flicks. Stay on it, don't breathe on it and don't let air hit it. Keep your mouth on it, keep it covered, and keep it warm: Suck, kiss, lick, whatever, but don't let go. She held my head in place with her hands. And her pussy exploded into my face. That's been my approach ever since with my women and I've yet to have a complaint.

I dove down on Dee and I stayed down there for quite a while.

"Oh my, God!" she hissed. "Oh, shit. Oh, fuck." I grabbed her ass cheeks with an iron grip and tried to squeeze the cum out of her. "Eat my pussy baby," she went on, "I can't believe the way you're eating my pussy!" I hummed a tune into her clit like I was playing a kazoo. She screamed like a cougar.

Her whole body quivered and quaked and wiggled and writhed in constant locomotion, but her hands were locked like a stationary vise on the back of my head. My lips and tongue continued their assault on her hard, swollen clit. When she came her love gates opened and months of her pent-up cum flooded my face.

"Oh fuck..." she shrieked. "Oh my fucking God...Oh fucking shit...Ughhh..."

When her spasms receded she tried to pull my head up toward hers but I stayed put. I wasn't done. I was staying down there until she came again. I started humming a new tune and she shook so hard she almost fell off the bed. Her hands retightened around my head and my hands spread her butt cheeks wide and I slipped part of a finger into her ass. That elicited from her another gasp of surprise and pleasure. My sax-playing skills were paying off as my strong mouth and lips stayed clutched around her hard rod and I blew a love song into her snatch.

Dee quickly figured out we weren't stopping yet and started swinging her groin up and down and grinding my face. She squawked with every sway and my bed squeaked in harmony.

"Oh Rob...Oh God..." she moaned. "I love your mouth...ugh. Eat me... ugh...Fucking your mouth...ugh. I love your mouth! Oh shit..."

We rocked in rhythm for a few minutes more. Then I could feel another orgasm coming. She closed her legs tightly around my head.

"Oh Christ, I've never been eaten like this!" she wheezed. "I'm gonna come again...ugh. Ugh. Oh Ssshhhhiiiiitttt..."

Her love levee overflowed again and my face was the delta. It wasn't as forceful as the first but it was still a whole lotta love and I tasted her stewed tang for the second time.

When I finally started to move my head away from her crotch she pulled my head toward hers and we began a long, wet, sloppy, cum-filled kiss. Her hands roamed my upper body and slid into my pants.

Her fingers reached the tip of my rock-hard dick as we were breaking our kiss. Her eyes drilled me and glowed green and hot.

"Fuck me..." Dee rasped excitedly.

I stood up before her at the side of the bed. I wore nothing but my beltless jeans so when I unzipped them my hard eight inch cock popped right out and was pointing at the ceiling. Her eyes grew into saucers at the sight. Now her green eye burn was directed at my swollen, purple pole.

I wiggled out of my pants and she reached over and pulled me closer. She held my cock in her hands and ran her fingers along its long edge and down to my balls. She softly kissed its glistening head.

"What a beautiful cock," she said, and looked up. "Fuck me."

I got on the bed and she guided my steely member right into her hungry cockpit. It was wild and wide and wet and warm and I slid right in. I didn't waste any time, I started stabbing it into her pretty good.

"Squeeze me, Dee," I said. "Let me feel your sexy walls. Pinch me... yeah, that's it." With each poke I felt her sweet pussy pressure surround my cock. "Ah, that's it baby, suck it out of me!"

Her moans grew louder with each push and her nails dug into my back. She sucked my tongue into her mouth and I wiggled my finger back into her ass as I pounded away. All her holes were filled. We grunted in a syncopated rut, and as the minutes elapsed I held back my load.

When our mouths parted I asked her if she could come again. She nodded her head four or five times in quick succession. We fucked even harder. She stroked her juicy okra in perfect tempo as I stuffed her with raw cucumber.

When I was ready to come she knew it, which triggered her third ejaculation. I let out a loud, dissonant grunt like a bull gator in mating season. I vibrated in spasms while spewing strings of my love syrup into Dee's heavenly honey pot. As I was ejecting my seed into her I felt a fresh warmth surround my cock and ooze out to my balls and I knew she had come again.

—

Our aftermath was sublime. Sweaty lovers, side by side, enwrapped. I had my arm around her, her head was on my shoulder and our naked bodies were molded into one. There was total peace and a comfortable silence for a few minutes before Dee spoke.

"Wow," she said. "Wow."

I kissed her. "My sentiments exactly," I replied.

"I mean it, really. I have never had climaxes like that, ever! And your mouth… I never knew I could come like that."

I maneuvered my arm more snugly around her so I could take her breast in my hand. Her hand went to my penis. After another quiet interlude she said, "I sure wish you hadn't waited so long to be unprofessional!"

I chuckled and gave her tit a little squeeze. She did the same to my reawakening dick.

"Really, Rob," she said. "I've had sex many, many times but I have never in my life felt so completely, totally, thoroughly, absolutely, utterly, perfectly fucked! I feel like I'm high or something."

I put my mouth to hers and we shared a fresh, deep kiss. She stroked me, bringing my one-eyed monster back to full attention.

"It takes two to tango," I said. "And I knew it would be great."

After another prolonged silence, she softly said, "I love the feeling of your cock in my hand."

"Not as much as I do…"

"You know, I knew you'd be big, I just knew it. But when I first saw it pop out of your jeans, I believe my eyes about popped out of my head. And two thoughts popped into my mind."

"What were they?"

"First, I thought 'wow'; that thing is BIG! And second, I thought how jealous my husband would be!"

She giggled and gripped me tightly around my fully-loaded grenade. I had nothing to say to that.

Dee pivoted around slightly so we were closely face-to-face. Those eyes sizzled. "I want to suck your cock," she said, and kissed me. "I want to feel it in my mouth. I want to taste it. I want you to come in my mouth."

She lowered herself into position and took my cockhead between her lips. Her fingers massaged my titillated chestnuts as she took me into her mouth, little by little, adjusting her position for her best angle of acceptance. I ran my fingers through her hair as I watched, mesmerized by her movements, so smooth and easy, and the sexy sight of my inflamed shaft sliding in and out of her dexterous mouth.

And so it went for a time as I watched the show and enjoyed the pleasure of Dee, the skillful cocksucker. But of course before long my little cobra was fixing to spit and wouldn't be able to hold back much longer. I gripped Dee's shoulders strongly and started pumping. She knew the drill. She grabbed my ass and sucked, sucked, sucked. I groaned and she knew it was on the way, and with eight inches of cock in her mouth she stayed on it through my spasms, and when I shot my load into her, four, five, six times, she moaned with each spray, once again two lovers in perfect sync.

She came up for air swallowing, and kissed my mouth with her cummy lips. It was my turn to say 'wow!'.

—

We soon noticed the time. It was early afternoon and we were hungry. Dee offered to take me out for lunch but I shot that idea right down, I was going to keep her naked and in my house as long as possible. I told her there was no way she was putting those jeans on again because I may exhaust myself tearing them back off, and we weren't finished for the day. I pulled a sweatshirt out of my drawer and gave it to her to wear.

We went to my kitchen, Dee dressed in only a sweatshirt and me in only my jeans, and whipped up lunch. We didn't do too badly either. We baked up a frozen pizza and somehow in my fridge found the makings for a pretty good salad. As Dee was finishing her second slice of pizza she said she wanted to suck my cock again. We went back to bed.

I told her that the pizza must have made her horny. She said she was horny for my pepperoni. From that day forward the word 'pizza' would always be our euphemism for sex.

The next hour was spent in 69 position, each of us sucking out whatever was left from the other, then we topped it off with another racy fuck. But by then it was getting late.

Dee had to get home; her daughter would be getting home from school soon and she had to be there to greet her. So we showered together. And damn, somehow my cock became slick and soapy and erect again. And damn if it didn't end up in back in her pussy.

When she was dressed and her pants were glued back on, I admired her figure in her tight clothing.

"Does Lynn know those are your 'fuck me' jeans?" I asked.

"I don't know, she might."

I told her to get on home and change before the school bus arrived.

–

We had started into the most intense period of wild fucking any couple could have. Because of our limited times together, we made the most of them. We grabbed a quickie on Tuesday morning when she dropped over to pick up some sales materials. She came over that Thursday night for a four hour romp. Then again the following Thursday.

On New Year's Eve she spent the night, the first time we would actually sleep together. We had gone to a club and met a couple she knew, I don't remember their names, and we danced and had a decent time but we both just wanted to get back to my house and screw. Dee took me by the hand at five minutes before twelve and led me to my car, it was time to go. She gave me a slow, masterful blowjob as I drove us home.

Once naked in bed I got busy eating pussy. Her first orgasm was almost immediate, but as usual I stayed with it until she unleashed her second coming, and I felt her swamp water flow. Then I mounted her sleek, fine frame and slipped my bat into her cave, and I pounded her until my rocket lifted off inside.

We held each other for what seemed like a long time. At first nothing needed to be said. But soon we were talking intimately and she opened up about her marriage and her husband. She said he had swept her off her feet in Paris and she'd ended up pregnant, but found out soon enough that he was cheating on her from the start and he would fuck anything that moved. She actually tried to come back to the U.S. with only her child, but he complained that she couldn't take her away, she's my child too, etc. So they came to the U.S., were married, she took care of their child and he had his affairs. He would always try to force her to swing and fuck other couples, which she went along with a few times but was never comfortable with. So she settled into a life of knowing her husband was usually fucking around on her. And this last affair was the final affair as far she was concerned.

"What was the final straw?" I asked.

"He knocked up an eighteen year old girl."

"I guess that would do it," I said.

After a few moments of silence she took my penis in her hand and began stroking it, and eventually said, "I have a New Year's gift for you."

She rolled over and reached into her purse on the table and turned back to me.

"Rob, you have stuck your love muscle inside me many wonderful times. I love it in my snatch and I love it in my mouth. But there's one place you haven't stuck it yet."

She opened her hand and placed a small tube of k-y jelly on my stomach.

"Happy New Year!" she said.

I stared at the container for a moment then looked at her.

"It's not going to bite you," she said, picking up the tube. She opened it and squeezed some lube into her hand, then slathered it all over my now-hard cock. Then she handed it to me and said, "You can do the honors on me!" She rolled over ass-up. I greased my fingers and lubricated her asshole.

Her bunghole opened wide, then closed, then reopened, two or three times. Like it was winking at me. This was no virgin ass. I placed the head of my dick to her o-ring and she opened for me. And I pushed.

I was not the most experienced assfucker at that point in my life but I didn't let that stop me. She moaned at first, but with gentle swings I eased it in, an inch at a time. When I was halfway home I started fucking that sweet ass with solid thrusts and soon my balls were slapping her ass. Dee was shrieking in tongues and letting out what sounded like painful groans. I was hoping it was a good pain.

"Oh yes...fuck my ass, boy! Fuck that fucking ass!"

I was driving her like a semi-automatic nail gun. Harder, harder..."

"Oh shit...what the fuck! Such a big fucking cock in my ass. Shoot your cum up my fucking ass..."

That's just what I did. It flew out of me, into Dee, and I held her tight with my cock still assbound as I quivered through my aftershocks. When I pulled out I watched my jizz seep out of her asshole and onto the sheet.

I spooned Dee's body with mine and held her. "Are you alright?" I asked.

"I'm wonderful, I feel terrific," she said. "How 'bout you?"

"Never better," I said, and I meant it. After that, anal sex was regular part of our repertoire.

I made us breakfast at four a.m. She said she loved my omelet.

—

The mad fucking continued. Over the next couple of months we had our usual Thursday nights and every other Saturday night. In between we'd have "sales meetings". That was when she'd come over to drop something off or pick something up and we'd get naked and see how many times we could get off. A couple of times she came over my house for some work-related purpose and had her daughter wait in the car and we still found some time for fucking and sucking.

One Thursday night I was over at Dee's apartment and her older sister called. We were seated on the sofa in her living room and Dee handed me the phone and started taking off my pants. Soon she was sucking my cock while I was talking to her sister on the phone.

"I hear you're turning my sister in a nymphomaniac," her sister said, as Dee licked my balls and stroked my dick.

"I think she's turned me into one," I grunted, as Dee took my swollen cock back into her mouth.

"Well, she says you've done some amazing things to her. Says you make her spurt like a monsoon," she said as Dee throated all of me.

"Ugh…ugh…"

"What did you say?…"

"Oh my God…" I blurted. I dropped the phone, held Dee's head and ejaculated into the back of her throat. She only gagged once.

After that Dee spoke to her sister briefly while I pulled her pants down. I went down on her and she howled and yelped for several minutes until she came all over me and the couch. I didn't find out till later that the phone was off the hook and her sister listened to the whole thing.

Another Thursday night I was over at her place and Dee cooked us a nice dinner. We ate delicious lasagna and salad, and I had her pussy for dessert. After she'd come twice and I'd dumped a hefty load of my lemon juice into her thirsty throat, we were lying together in our lambent flush and, as we usually would, talked. And when our bodies were naked, our thoughts usually were too.

I told her my band had an early gig at Slackers on Saturday, and asked if she would like to come. Then she started to hem and haw, saying that it's not much fun sitting around for forty minutes of every hour to spend twenty minutes together. She was right of course, and I suggested that maybe she could coax a friend to go along.

"Who? Maybe Sharon?" she asked.

I said Sharon would be fine.

"You like her, don't you?" she said.

"Of course I like her, she's your friend," I babbled.

"You want to fuck her, don't you?" she said.

I started to blather some mumbo jumbo but she cut me off.

"Oh, relax Loverboy, we both know she's hot!" Then she reached over to her nightstand and picked up the phone.

"Hey, honey," Dee said, when Sharon answered. I only heard one side of the conversation, but it went something like this: "Rob and I were lying here, resting in between orgasms, and your name came up… Yeah…And he thinks you're hot and he wants to fuck both of us…No, together…Can you get away Saturday night?…Rob has a gig…Afterward at his place…"

She looked at me and asked what time was the gig. I told her three to seven. She went back to her conversation with Sharon.

"Three to seven, what do you say?…Really?…Great, I can't wait… Okay, perfect…Sure, I'll tell him. Bye."

"It's all set," she said with a satisfied smile. "You're gonna have two fine women in your bed Saturday night! There's just one small condition though."

"Uh oh, here we go. And what would that be?" I asked.

"She wants you to cook her up one of your mean omelets!"

"Okay," I said. "I'll pick up some eggs." I kissed her. Her phone call had aroused me again and I was ready to pick up where we'd left off.

"Rob," she said, when we broke our kiss. "Remember when we talked about my marriage and I told you about all of my husband's affairs?"

"Yes."

"Well, I had one too. It was with Sharon."

Our sex was sweet, and I couldn't help thinking how it might be sweeter still come Saturday.

—

On Saturday, we were just finishing up the second set when they walked in, and just about every eye in the house followed them to their table. They both wore their 'fuck me' jeans, Dee in blue and Sharon in black, with heels and tight tops. They looked sensational. I sat down between them and thanked them both for coming.

"Oh, no problem," Sharon said softly, her mouth close to my ear. "It's not every day I get to fuck a handsome man and a pretty woman at the same time!" She squeezed my hand.

Dee asked me for my house key and said that they would be leaving before the end of the gig to go to my house and set up. I handed her the key and asked what they had to set up.

"You won't be disappointed," was all she said.

–

The lower level of my house was a large, carpeted family room, and was where I did most of my entertaining and where my TV and stereo were located. And when I walked in I was not disappointed.

There was a fire burning in the fireplace and soft jazz music playing. Scented candles burned in various locations around the room, giving a soft glow to what lay before me. On the floor they had created our love nest: a king-sized lair of cushions, pillows, and a mass of layered quilts and comforters. A stainless steel wine bucket with two bottles in it was sitting on the floor reflecting the flicker of the fireplace.

At the sight of the women entering the room, my dick was already on high alert. They held hands and both wore short, sheer negligees and thongs, and nothing else. Dee's thong was red, Sharon's was black, and their four nipples were plain to see through the gauzy fabrics.

"Hello, Handsome," Dee said. "Are you ready?" I nodded. "Let's start with a kiss."

She pressed her lips to mine and we embraced, and we kissed long and deep. As soon as we parted Sharon took over, kissing me hard, groping me, tasting my mouth and tongue. When we separated, she wrapped her arms around Dee and they kissed like lovers right before one of them went off to war. This was a hard rock turn on.

"I think we should help Rob get a little more comfortable, don't you, Dee?" Sharon said.

"Absolutely," Dee replied.

Sharon stood facing me, kissed me again and started slowly unbuttoning my shirt. Dee stood behind me and pressed her pussy to my ass, kissed my neck and reached her arms around my waist and started unsnapping my jeans.

My shirt came off and Sharon's lips tickled my shoulders. My pants dropped to the floor and Dee dropped to her knees and I felt her tongue enter my ass. Sharon's tongue slipped into my mouth and her right hand fondled my dick in my boxers.

"We're going to have fun tonight," Sharon murmured. I didn't have to tell her I was having fun already.

Now that I had a raging hard-on and was stripped to my boxers, they told me to have a seat on the chair they placed in position. Dee handed me a glass of wine and said that they were going to do a striptease for me. I sat down and sipped my wine.

They started with a slow, silky dance, holding one another close and French kissing to the jazz samba background music, a few minutes of lezzy love. Sharon's hand slid under Dee's thong, then she slowly opened Dee's wrap, pulled it over her shoulders and it fell to the floor. Dee's nipples were rigid like crabapples. Then Sharon knelt, slid the thong aside and put her mouth on that glorious gash. My dick was at full staff, jutting through the slit in my shorts. I slurped the rest of the wine in my glass.

Soon Sharon rose and Dee undressed her while they kissed. Dee removed Sharon's thong and replaced it with her mouth. Sharon whimpered with delight and grinded into her face. Sharon's left hand was on the back of Dee's head, but her eyes were on me, beckoning. I rose, tossed my shorts aside and walked over to her, put my tongue in her mouth and we kissed with a savage lust.

"I want to fuck you," she rasped.

"I'm going to eat you first," I said.

"Yes…"

Dee rose to her feet and kissed me, then kissed Sharon. "Lie down," she said. "I've fantasized about watching Rob fuck you."

We lowered onto our love nest and Sharon and I shared another bionic kiss. Then my lips and tongue traveled southward bit by bit, to her neck, her shoulders, her luscious tits. I sucked those tits, I licked her navel, and I kissed her thighs, circling around her seductive slit. She was squirming with anticipation. I got in position for my attack and I felt Dee's hands between my legs.

Sharon's pussy was clean shaven, the first shaved pussy I'd ever seen. In those days women would trim and wax their pubes, but I'd never seen one shaved. But if one thing could possibly have turned me on more than I already was, that was it.

I was on my knees between Sharon's legs and she let out a loud cry when I put my mouth on her love knob. I must have hit the right button because she started squealing and wouldn't stop.

Dee was behind me with her hands on my cock. One hand stroked my shaft, one hand massaged my balls and her tongue caressed the crack of my ass.

"Yes!" Sharon squawked, "Eat my goddamn pussy!" My hair was squeezed in bunches in her fists as her body thrashed. "Goddamn, Dee, where did you find this guy? Yes, that's it!"

Dee pulled my cock back through my legs and began sucking my cock from behind. Another first: not only eating a bald pussy but getting a backward blowjob at the same time! She pulled it back as far as it would go without breaking it. I could feel her face on my balls and ass so I know she must have had most of it in her mouth.

"Oh, fuck…" Sharon screamed. She came in a mad rush and her body throbbed like a wounded duck.

Sharon expected me to come up for air, but of course I didn't. Besides, Dee had my dick in her mouth. I just kept munching on her honeysuckle and she kept wriggling like a hooked eel. I gripped her buttocks to help squeeze out another frenzy from within. She yowled when I rammed a couple of fingers in her ass.

"Oh my god…" she wailed, "I'm going to come again…Oh shit…"

That's when I came. It was intense too, my body was quaking like a willow tree as I tried to shoot my wad into Dee's mouth and keep my lips on Sharon's walnut at the same time. She came soon after and as I rolled over to her side, Dee moved her cum-filled mouth to Sharon's open lips and they shared a long, greasy kiss while lying in a puddle of Sharon's jungle juice.

The rest of that night went pretty much like that, one sex act after another, and with many interesting combinations. I fucked and went down on two glorious twats, fucked two magnificent asses, had my cock sucked three times, sucked four killer tits and had my ass licked. But I think the hottest of it all was watching those two fine women eat pussy. What a turn-on! The highlight for me was fucking Sharon's ass while she was eating Dee's pussy; and Dee was smiling shyly and staring straight at me the whole time. Ooh, that green eye burn.

—

My relationship with Dee continued on very well for a while, and the sex remained great, but after about three months things started getting weird. Her behavior became erratic. She would occasionally miss appointments for no good reason or forget to do something that was rather important. Also, I started receiving bizarre phone calls at all hours, some odd, some cranks, some threatening. Dee was pretty sure her husband was behind it.

It looked like the stress of her dealing with her divorce, a child, her work and our relationship was getting the best of her. We broke up. But then of course that made working together awkward and after a few weeks she found another job. I always felt bad about the way we ended.

I didn't see her after that for a long time. About a year later, I was leaving a meeting at a radio station and I saw her entering the building. It was uncomfortable to say the least, but we chatted for a couple of minutes. She said she was now working there as a sales rep.

Over the following year or so I saw her at the station perhaps three times and it was always cordial but uneasy. As the months elapsed I continued to feel more and more remorseful about the way our good thing had ended so abruptly, and thought perhaps I should make some kind of effort to smooth things over a bit, and remove the thorniness. So, I called her at the radio station. They told me that Dee didn't work there anymore.

About three hours later I was sitting at my desk when she called me back. I explained my feelings about finding a comfort zone between us. She thought it was a good idea and we arranged to meet for lunch a couple of days later.

We met at a seafood restaurant right on the river, and got a table in the corner by ourselves. We made small talk: how's business?, Lynn is growing up, the ugly divorce is final, things like that. We were uptight at first but it didn't take long before we relaxed and our playfulness returned. I truly had intentions of us just finding some kind of level of friendship, but it soon went past that. She told she had never had climaxes like she had with me, before or since. I told her about the many times I'd missed eating her sweet pussy. We laughed about our first kisses and the first time I fucked her ass. We both were turned on and when we left the restaurant she was wet and I was hard. She followed me home.

We spent the rest of the afternoon fucking and sucking and I came in all her holes. It was just as good as we remembered. It wasn't until she was getting dressed to leave at around four thirty that she told me she had blown off a doctor's appointment. I found out later the doctor was her psychiatrist.

Then things got weird again and I slowly started to realize what a mistake it had been to hook up again. She began stalking me. I'd come home from work and there would be notes and gifts left on my porch. She would call me at all hours, early morning, late at night. If I didn't answer she would leave long, rambling messages while she masturbated. She said she loved me, she wanted me to fuck her brains out, she wanted to have my baby.

This went on for several weeks. I stayed away from my house as much as I could to avoid her, but eventually she caught me at home one evening. She wanted to fuck. I tried to reason with her about how unhealthy our alliance had become but she wasn't processing the information. She just offered to suck my cock. Finally, I just told her she was nuts and to get the fuck out. When she left I had gooseflesh up and down my arms thinking about her next phone call.

About an hour later the phone rang, and I said, "Oh, shit," out loud. I let the machine pick up and listened to a female voice begin to leave a message.

"Hello, Bill," the message began. "This is Lynn _____, Dee's daughter. I hate to bother you, but…" I picked up the phone.

Lynn had called to warn me. She said that her mother may come by to see me, and if she did please call her right away and keep her mother there until she could come get her. She told me her mother had been diagnosed with a serious mental illness and had gone missing. As soon as they found her, her doctor was going to have her committed to a psychiatric hospital. I felt terrible having to tell her that Dee had already been here and I had told her to fuck off.

–

A few years later I read in the newspaper that Dee had passed away due to an undisclosed illness. I didn't really know her family but I felt a need to go to the memorial service. I didn't know anyone and certainly didn't want to make anyone uncomfortable, so my plan was to slip in at the last second, sit in the back and leave right before the end.

I sat in the back row just as the service was beginning. It was not a large church and I could see some familiar faces as I looked around. I recognized Lynn in the first row, now a young woman in her early twenties. And I saw Sharon too, seated near the front with a man I guessed was her husband.

I didn't get out of there quite fast enough because soon Lynn was tracking me down in the parking lot. Someone must have told her I was there. She called my name and I turned toward her voice. She ran up to me and surprisingly gave me a hug.

She was a smaller version of her mom. She was perhaps two inches shorter, but just as slim and shapely. Nice perky breasts, brown hair cut neat and the same big green eyes. She was an attractive young woman.

"Thank you so much for coming, Rob," she said. "It means a lot. But weren't you even going to say hello and let us know you came?"

I told her I didn't want to make anyone uncomfortable and offered my condolences.

She said she was happy I'd made it and had hoped that I would. She asked if I had any free time over the following couple of days. She wanted to talk. She said she would be home for several more days before heading back to school for the end of her senior year and graduation. I didn't feel I could say no.

—

It was a pleasant afternoon and we met at a park along the river and sat at a picnic table facing one another. We sipped iced teas through straws. She was dressed in snug blue jeans and a tan sweater. I could appreciate her body; it was much like her mother's.

"Thank you, Rob, for meeting me," she began. "I've wanted to talk to you forever. Mom and I were very close, especially as I got older. We didn't have any secrets. She told me so much about you that I feel like I know you really well even though I hardly know you at all."

She looked me in the eyes. Her eyes were moist and had the same green glow as Dee's.

"You were good for her. You made her happy." Tears snuck out of her eyes.

I reached over and held her hands in mine. I didn't know what to say but mumbled something about what a good woman her mother was.

"I remember the first time I saw you," she continued. "Mom was dropping off something at your house and you came out onto your front porch. I told her I thought you were handsome." She wiped her eye with her thumb. "I think she loved you," she said with a teary chuckle. "She said you were 'good sperm'!"

"Good sperm?" I replied. "What the hell does that mean?"

She smiled and said, "That was Mom's term for a guy that would make the ideal life and soul mate. Good looks, good genes, intelligent. A guy that would be good to create a heritage with. You know, good sperm."

She talked at length about her parents' divorce, her mother's depression and illness, the difficult family issues. I could feel her catharsis as she unloaded and enlightened me on so many things I'd missed. But after a while she returned to reminiscing about the good days of her mother and me.

"You know, I've seen you naked," she said, out of the blue. I almost fell off my bench.

"Yeah, right," I said.

"No, really," she said matter-of-factly. "And I know you have a big cock. I saw Mom sucking it."

The hard drive in my brain froze up and crashed as I attempted to google my memory. I tried to recall when and how the hell that could have happened and how that might have affected a twelve year old girl.

She noticed my unease. "Oh, it's okay," she said. "I wasn't damaged by it or anything."

I asked her on what occasion she had observed this. She said she was waiting in the car out in front of my house when her mom had come over to drop off some papers. She grew tired of waiting and got out of the car and walked around. She found a window at the back of the house.

"You fucked her too," Lynn said. "She was up against the back of a sofa. And the sounds she made, oh my god... I was pretty young but I knew they were good sounds. They were sounds of joy. Sounds of ecstacy. I could smell your sex when she got back in the car."

"Lynn, I'm so sorry you had to see that..."

"Oh, it's okay. Rob, it was beautiful. My mom was going through hell at the time and she found bliss. With you. And looking back, I truly appreciate that." She rose up off her bench, spanned her sleek body across the table and kissed me on the lips. "Thank you."

We walked around the park and she told me more of her memories. She held my arm much of the time as we walked. We ate slices of pizza at a shop near the park. When we left the shop and started our walk back Lynn again grabbed my arm.

She thanked me for the late lunch, then sighed and said, "Pizza makes me horny."

That stopped me in our tracks. She spun around and green eye burned me.

There was a brief, edgy silence, and then with a coy smile she said, "You know, Mom told me everything."

"I can see that…"

Then she kissed me. I was hesitant at first, but soon our lips parted and I savored the power of her tongue in my mouth. Wrapped in her arms, the kiss lasted and lingered.

We parted and she held my right hand in her left. She gently caressed my face with her right.

"That was not a 'thank you' kiss," she said. "And it wasn't a 'nice guy' kiss either. She squeezed my hand like a vise.

"Take me home with you," she said.

—

I tried to tell her how wrong it was in so many ways but I wasn't very convincing. I said I was too old for her but she shot that right down by saying that that an age difference hadn't stopped her mother when I came along. She had me there. The truth was that after all the verbal intimacy I wanted to please her. And I wanted her too.

She followed me to my house and we were no sooner inside the front door and we attacked each other. I told her I needed to use the bathroom and when I came out a minute later she was naked on my bed. I pulled off my clothes and got into bed with her. We kissed with fierce abandon and I sucked her nubile nipples and covered her body with kisses. Then I put my mouth on her young pussy for the first time.

Lynn was not a loud lover like her mother. She just repeated "uh…

uh…uh…uh…" over and over in a breathy, staccato cadence as she rhythmically pushed her groin toward the source of her pleasure. She came in a rush and I tasted her fresh spunk. She pulled my head to hers and our mouths meshed and our tongues danced. She touched my cock for the first time and pulled it toward her soaked pink sinkhole. That snatch was snug, and it hugged me tight. But she was good and wet and we soon fell into a sexy sync as I pushed my package into her. I slipped a finger into her asshole: it was small and super tight. I didn't think I would be buttfucking this gal.

We fucked with fierce abandon as we rocked, and her sweet pussy sucked my cock as my mouth sucked her tongue. I came with a groan and shot sticky strings of semen deep inside of her. I rolled off and lay beside her and she instantly curled up in my arms and kissed me. We basked in our own silent glimmer for a couple of minutes before she spoke.

"That was unbelievable!" she said. "You really know how to fuck a girl! No wonder you drove my mother wild!"

"Yeah, well, pizza makes me horny," I said.

She laughed, kissed me and said, "Let's do it again!"

I fucked her lovely pussy twice more that night before we fell off to sleep. In the early morning she sucked me awake and soon I was pounding her tasty pickle jar again. It was a beautiful eye opener: coming together as daylight began peeping through the curtains.

We fell back to sleep and woke a couple hours later. As usual, I woke up with a hard-on, so of course something had to be done about that. Lynn took immediate action and put it to good use by sitting on it and feeding it into her slimy slot. We rolled over and this time we fucked slow and easy, lips to lips, for some time until we both had achieved our release.

I told her I would cook us breakfast, so I threw on some shorts and

Lynn put on a t-shirt. I had to work in the kitchen while she shuffled around bare-assed. She did have a nice behind.

After we'd eaten and cleared the dishes she thanked me for a delicious breakfast and kissed me. We kissed again.

"Omelets make me horny," she said, unzipping my fly.

"Holy shit, girl, I think you're going to kill me!" I joked.

"Aw, come on Rob. I have to leave in a little while. How about one more for the road?" My shorts were at my ankles and my dick was already armed and ready. I put my hands under her ass and lifted her up onto the kitchen table. The angle worked just fine. I slammed my cock into her right on the edge of the table and I fucked her with her shirt on. When I shot my seed into her I shivered and shuddered convulsively and briefly lost my balance. I swear it must have been her pussy's grip around my cock that kept me from falling over. We kissed until I went limp inside her.

She jumped in the shower because she had to get going back to school and had a three hour drive. Soon she was dressed again in those skin-tight jeans that showed off her firm ass so well. I felt another tingle down south.

When we kissed goodbye she told me what a fabulous time she had had and how good it was to finally talk and get to know one another. I didn't disagree. She then put her hand behind my head and kissed me hard and her tongue dive-bombed into my mouth. After the kiss she put her other hand on the crotch and felt my growing member.

"And take care of this bad boy," she said with a little smile, as she rubbed it. "I may have to come back for more one of these days.

She drove off and I didn't talk to her again for quite a while.

– – – –

About seven months later I went out to dinner with Robin, a woman I had recently met. It was Christmastime and the place was decorated for the holidays and yuletide melodies were playing nonstop. As we were entering the restaurant I saw a familiar face walking out. It was Lynn, and she was holding hands with an attractive blond woman. And Lynn was very obviously pregnant.

We said our hellos and she introduced us to her companion Irene, and I introduced Robin. We chatted a little, avoiding the obvious elephant in her womb. Then Robin broached the subject.

"When are you due, Honey?" she asked.

"In early February," Lynn said. "I can't wait."

"Well, you look radiant!" Robin said.

"Thank you," Lynn responded. "I lucked out and found some 'good sperm.'"

Lynn's big green eyes moved from Robin's to mine, then to Irene's, then back to mine. I was burned again.

We said our goodbyes and Irene slipped me a subtle wink. She lipped 'thank you' to me right before they turned and walked off hand-in-hand.

"What the hell was that all about?" Robin asked, just as the hostess greeted us.

As we were walking to our table, I knew I'd better think up something pretty damn quick.

TEACHING THE YOUNG

I enjoy young women; not that an older woman can't do things that are fantastic, but I just prefer them young. Matter of fact, the younger the better. Nothing under 18 mind you, but still 18 to 25 is my preference. Look at me and you might say, "Sure Pops, guess you would like something you can't get". Agreed, I am past my 45th birthday, but I still get my share. Sometimes it is the age that works the magic for the young ones. True, stamina is not my forte' and washboard abs are not mine to display.

But I do have a distinguished look about me, dark brown hair with slight graying at the temples, over 6 foot tall and under 225 pounds, a strong athletic type build and from what most ladies say, piercing blue eyes and an ear for hearing things that can be used to my advantage. In other words I rely on what I have and not what I have not. And some, but not all ladies like it that way.

Lacking a better term I'll start by saying I stalk my prey at the normal areas, the Mall (careful not to go for those who say they are old enough, but aren't, the grocery store, and the quaint little hang-outs where a lot of lovers quarrels and just flat 'didn't show-up for a date' happens. My most recent lady came from just such an encounter.

I had gone to a small club close to my house and was sitting near the back of the room, watching all the young men and women jockey for position. You learn more from just watching from a distance than if you are in the middle of the activity. It was not long before the true jocks had taken the floor and you could watch the testosterone levels climbing. Some of the ladies loved it and those were not for me. Simple hormones for simple minds are not my idea of a long sensual encounter. Rather I prefer the type woman that will watch and then back away from such men. Several ladies call me for months and years after our encounters. Some to just talk while others would like to remember what it is like to be made love to. I am more than willing to work a damsel in distress into my bed, for her sake of course.

This particular night I watched as four young women in their early 20 came into the club. From their attire I would say entry-level executives or secretaries, but it mattered not. All were attractive and were as distinctive from each other as you can be. A blonde that was tall with legs that went on forever (she would not be the one for me, too many alpha males to wade through), while another was a gorgeous brunette with a killer body. The two remaining were similar in height, about 5 foot 6 or so and both were about 115 to 120 pounds. But one was of a darker completion and had nearly jet-black hair and the final one was a smartly dressed redhead with hair that was on the lighter shade of the red scale.

I watched intently as the men in the group eyed and then moved over almost in mass. Sure enough the blond took the lion's share (or should I say Lioness's share), with the busty brunette coming in a close second. The remaining had little to pick from and you could tell that the redhead seemed happy about it. She sort of backed away and left the rest of the men to her friend. I watched intently as they filed past and each was given a simple no thank you from her and some got a headshake was all. Seems she did not wish to be bothered tonight – maybe she was the designated driver. Regardless, as the line grew thinner and the offers to dance diminished I figured it was time for me to either get shot down as well or have a shot at a pleasant conversation with a lady with taste.

I rose slowly and made my way over toward the table and stood along side for a few seconds before she finally looked up into my eyes. The look she had in her face almost made me want to leave and not say a word. She was tired of the same old lines and the dating scene in general if I caught her drift. Still she looked up and my entire approach changed.

I looked straight at her and opened my mouth and then said, "Never mind, you've heard it all by now, sorry to have bothered you."

I was completely turned away before I heard any sound from her, a slight exaggerated swallow. I paused and turned my head back toward her and said, "You know the best way to avoid being ask by every guy in the joint, right?"

She gazed up at me an ever so slight sparkle came from her eye, "No, apparently I don't."

I turned back toward her, "The best two ways to avoid being asked by every guy is first, be very unattractive, something you can't do, and second and almost as good as the first, is be in the place with an older guy that everyone thinks is your dad. Care to try it?"

She pondered for a moment and then said, "Well, I think I have already told every guy here no, so I don't think I'll have any trouble. But thanks anyway."

It was an answer I had anticipated because of hearing it for years before. I looked around and said, "You're most likely right, but the evening shift gets off from the hospital in about 10 minutes and this place will be really crawling with 'us guys'. Tell you what, if you change your mind, I am sitting right over there and if you want a change of tempo, pick your drink up with your left hand and I'll be right back over to help move them along – deal?"

"Deal", she smiled and deliberately picked up her drink with her right hand. I smiled as I caught the intention and moved back to my chair. It was the best I effort I was willing to put into this tonight. If I got lucky, then great, if not, well there is always other nights.

There was a small band and when they started playing it was almost on cue for the room to fill up again with the disproportionate number of men to women. I watched as the young red head started her dutiful shaking of the head and politely saying no. Then as the door opened to yet another gaggle of men she glanced my way and I held up my glass in my left hand. I could see the gears working in her mind as she toyed with the idea. Just the men surveyed the area and saw only a couple of available ladies they were heading right toward her. I smiled inwardly as she grasp her glass in her left hand and brought it to her lips.

I stood and moved as quickly as I could to be beside her just as a guy was leaning in to ask the important questions.

"Hey honey, sorry I didn't see you come in. Guess I was in the little boys room."

The guys there looked at me and then at her and I calmed them quickly, "Sorry guys, but my daughter is taken tonight. She promised to help me celebrate my birthday."

I leaned in and gave her an innocent peck on the cheek. "Hope you haven't been waiting too long."

"Just got here dad", she said not too all convincingly. Still it worked as they began to back off.

"Care to join me at my table, a little off the beaten path, but sill you can see your friends when they are ready to leave."

"What makes you so sure I want to know when they leave?"

"Well, you are the only one that refused all the massive male humanity in here and you are drinking plain coke, generally a good sign that the person is a driver for the group. Am I right by chance?"

"Yes. I am the driver, but if the girls are like normal, the only one I have to get home will be myself. They always seem to end up with someone for the night."

"But not you. I figure you are just being nice to your friends. You most likely don't even enjoy this sort of place."

"You are right again, but hey, it's either this of a night in front of the tube. I may not enjoy it too much, but it is better than that."

"By the way daughter, my name is Richard. Mind if I ask you yours?"

"Samantha, Sam for short."

"And which do you prefer to be called?"

"Well 'dad', you can call me anything you like."

She gave me a big beautiful smile and then said, "I prefer Sam."

"Sam it is. Glad you decided to try my anti-guy therapy." I stretched out my hand and she took it in hers and again the smile, "I am too."

We continued to chat for some time and when her first friend left, the blond, I figured my time was drawing near. But I did not pursue, just enjoyed the company. Then eventually I excused myself to go to the little boys room and when I came back I had three women at the table – Sam and her two friends. As I approached the conversation at the table stopped and all three women looked at me. Soon as I sat down the conversation began again but it was strained. I sat for a moment and then offered to introduce myself. The brunette quickly cut me off as she glared at me.

"Pardon me, but just what did I do wrong here?"

"You trying to pick our little Sam up and she isn't ready for that."

"First off, I thought I was doing her a favor by keeping the dogs at bay and even introduced myself as her dad so she wouldn't have to worry about comments being made. Second, she is a grown woman and if I did want to pick her up, she would most likely say no for fear of killing me."

I paused for that to sink in and then even the brunette began to laugh. The ice was broken and we soon returned to our respective activities. The brunette, Laura, was dancing with a guy who was on the drunk side and was trying to get her clothing off on the dance floor, and Tina, the last one was being led outside by her date. I held on to the idea that I might get lucky tonight for another 15 seconds or so and then decided it was better to try a different angle. I could tell Sam was to the point of not knowing what to do with me. Laura was leaving with her 'date' and the others were already gone. Plenty of guys still around, but most were well past too much to drink.

"Think it is about time for us to call it a night. Mind if I walk you out?"

"I would like that."

I paid our tab, all $19.00 of it, including tip, and we made our way outside. Once in the night air I reached an arm out and she glided up close to me. I gently left it on her should and arm and we walked to her car. Once there she beeped the thing (I hate those things) and I opened the door for her. She hesitated for an instant and looked at me with the most inquisitive look I can ever remember seeing. Almost like she were trying to figure me out. The time was right and I took it. I gasp her hand and brought it to my lips for a soft kiss.

"You know, while I really enjoyed your company tonight and you may still not know what to think of me, I would be honored and pleased if you would have dinner with me Friday night."

Sam gave me that smile again, "I would like that."

"If you like Italian, maybe we can meet at Lucianno's about 8. That be OK?"

"I love Italian and that would be great."

She started her car and drove into the night. Would I see her again or not? Who knew? But about 80 percent of the time, I do.

Friday night came and I found myself at the restaurant at 745. I waited and at 8 she was not there. 810 came and still no Sam. The time hit 815 and I was about to call it a "no show" when she hurried around the corner.

"I am so sorry, time slipped away from me and then the traffic. I thought you might not even be here."

"Are you kidding? I have my tent stashed in the back and was going to wait you out. No matter how long it took."

"You probably do, don't you?"

"Not really, but hey, it makes for a great story."

We ordered appetizers, and some of their special dishes, they had the violinist walking through the area and when he got to us he paused for a little longer than normal and then moved on. I was dressed as youngish as I could get and Sam was stunning in her mid length black dress with pearls. Fitting in the right spots with a fairly deep plunge at the neck to highlight the pearls and split to an area that was both concealing as well as revealing she was a vision to behold. A young goddess with an older man – me.

I ordered wine and we drank, nothing too serious, but enough to get a good feel for the night. Dessert came and went and before we knew it the hour was approaching 1030. Too early to call it a night and yet getting late as well. Eventually we went outside and walked over to her car. As we stood chatting away the air was filled with the wonderful sound of live jazz. Across the parking area was a jazz club. I must admit jazz does things to me and makes me want to dance.

"I don't suppose you care for jazz?"

"I love jazz."

"Really now. Not a lot of ladies like it, least those that are younger. They prefer the harder driving sounds of a harder sound of music."

"Give me a little Tom Scott, or a little of the older Herbie Hancock any day over what they call music today."

"Are you game for a dance or two?"

"Sure. Let's do it."

To the club and when we came out later we were both hot and sweaty from all the dancing (slow numbers were awesome I might add) as well as needing a drink of something other than alcohol. The moment of truth was upon me and it was time to see how she would react.

"I do not know how to tell you this without it sounding like a lone wolf but I do want you to understand. I figured the chances of you showing up tonight, based on what all my friends tell me, at about 10 percent. It was for that reason I selected this restaurant. Nothing against you, just figuring you would be apprehensive at best about meeting me for dinner after our beginning. Anyway, I did not drive tonight – because I live one the next street over. Your call, we can call it a night, or if you would like I can go get my car and we can go somewhere else or you can trust me to come to my place?"

Sam looked a little hurt to start with and then surprised me with "Your place it is. By the way, if I showed and then elected to go to your place, did you clean it up just for me?"

"No, same as always, dirty socks hanging from the light switches, dishes in the sink and most likely all the bottles in the frig have been opened. Still want to go?"

"I think so. Can tell a lot about a man by the way he keeps his property."

We arrived at my house in short order, she drove us, and her immediate reaction was "WOW".

"Combination of earning and having a great-aunt that I did not know existed, pass on and leave me a little money."

We walked inside and I turned on some of the lights. I have collected local artists for years and was fortunate to collect some of an artist that had hit it fairly big. One was an original oil that was purchased for under $1,000 and was now appraised at nearly $100K, so it looked impressive. We went through toward the back to the den and I hit a couple of switches. The curtains opened and the lights came on outside at the pool and the Jacuzzi.

Sam stared out at the water and commented, "Gee, a person could get real used to something like this."

"So what would you like to drink?"

"Surprise me – you are doing very well so far."

I picked up a glass of delicate wine and brought it to her.

"Here's to a wonderful evening. May it continue until we are ready to start another."

Sam took a sip from her glass and commented, "I bet that water sure feels good. Especially after all the dancing."

"Yes it does. Care to take a plunge?"

I don't think so, but maybe just dangling my feet in, if that would be ok."

"Sure, lets go."

We went outside back into the night air and walked over to the swirling waters of the tub. Sam began to sit on the edge of the hot tub but before she could I dropped a thick towel down so as not to have the material of her dress catch and get ruined. She sat on the edge and was reaching for her shoe, but I beat her to it. Gently drawing the foot from the covering and then placing it down on the edge. I reached for the other and picked it up and did the same thing. Her smile was intoxicating and the sparkles in her eyes were unmistakable. Still I did not press. Instead I sat and began to take my own shoes and socks off. She whirled and dipped her feet into the water. As soon as she was set I grabbed the remote and hit the Jacuzzi switch. Jets of water began to caress the parts of her legs that were close. I looked at her face and knew she wanted more, but did not want to ask. Then using the remote the lights were dimmed with only one small bulb still being illuminated.

"Goodness. It is almost pitch dark like that."

"Yes it is."

With that I stood, undid my slacks and drew them and my shorts off. Followed quickly by my shirt. Then I eased into the water and let the jets do their thing. Sam's eyes adjusted to the near dark conditions and she knew I was in the tub.

"Richard, did you plan to do this so you were wearing a suit, or?" she trailed off.

"Well since you can't see, does it matter?"

"I guess not. Not really."

"You know Samantha, you can join me if you would like. I promise not to bite or do anything else you do not ask me to do. The decisions are all yours from here on out. Do you understand me?"

"Yes, I think so Richard."

I sat with the sounds of the jets going in my ears. I strained to hear something, anything that would tell me which way she was going. Then I knew. I felt her leg as it slid into the water next to mine, softly touching me a couple of times and then she moved a little away from me to enjoy the water jets as I was doing. Times like this I wish I had gotten a smaller tub, but when you have 10 people in one tub, you have to have a bigger one.

I then began to hear a muffled sound, like a cry but not quite. It was Sam as the waters were sweeping her into a world that was safe and warm. We sat for what seemed an eternity, but most likely just 10 minutes or so, before she spoke.

"Richard."

"Yes."

"If I come over to where you are, will you kiss me?"

"Like I said if that is what you would like, yes. It that what you want?"

She did not reply. Instead I felt her move against me. First her toe and foot followed by her leg and torso, then finally her arm. I moved my arm around and over her shoulder and she came into my safe zone without any hesitation. I held her tightly, but with being too firm. The there was the unmistakable sound of her beginning to softly cry. I was not prepared for that. Instead I held her a little tighter and she continued to softly sob. Finally, she stopped and when she did she raised her lips and lightly kissed me on the neck. I continued to hold her even when she kissed me again. Her lips lingered on my flesh, causing electricity to surge through me, straight to my cock. I turned my face toward her and even in the near darkness I could see her eyes brimming with tears. I brought my free hand to her face, stroking softly, brushing hair from her face and remained steady as she strained to rise up to my lips. After she had gone as far as she could I lowered my lips to hers. I was surprised by the intensity of her kiss. She was so full of passion and yes, even lust. I adjusted to her lips on mine and was shocked when her hand began moving on my arm and chest. My hand moved to her thigh and I knew there was little distance from where my hand rested to the dew covered honey pot nestled between her legs. Once contact was made Sam began to squirm, her legs moving apart.

I moved my fingers slowly along her silky skin from her thigh to her knee and back up. Finger nails trailing, goose bumps rising to greet a passing traveler. Each time I moved my fingers on her leg she'd shift slightly, until her inner thigh was available. She was uncertain, my hand movement slowed to allow her to back out. Ultimately my hand stopped within centimeters of her prize. I could feel heat rising from her and it was all I could do to resist plunging a finger into her womanhood, making her scream aloud with passion. I remained in control for what seemed hours. Sam then increased the intensity of her kiss while her hand moved down to my lap. She moved her hand along my shaft as it rose to the occasion. Using her fingers she climbed to the top. It was now obvious she was more than willing.

My hand still moved on her creamy thigh and trailed along the surface of her skin. Moving up to her swollen breast she took in a large amount of air and caught it in her lungs. My hand didn't stop until it touched her chin softly.

She paused and I ask the question, "What do you want me to do?"

Sam looked at me with lustful passion and I knew her answer before she spoke, Make love to me Richard. I want you so bad. I want you to fuck me. Fuck me now."

An inner smile came to me as I pressed my lips to hers. Our tongues were in a battle with no chance of victory or loss as they lashed back and forth, each trying to gain the upper ground, retreating and then advancing. Even as our tongue war continued her hand began a quest for the fountain of youth sprouting from my hip area. She wrestled with it trying to move it toward her area of need.

I timed my approach perfectly. As her hand went to grab me, my fingers hovered high on her thigh. Just as her fingers encircled my shaft, I touched her smooth pussy. Her sharp intake of breath indicated our mutual contact. Her hand marveled at my still rising shaft as my fingers began to explore. Tracing the outer edges of her pussy lips, then pushing the material into her vulva and rubbing. Her clit stood proud and erect, craving more attention. I wanted to give but I have always desired a woman's breast, but only the proper proportion. From what I had seen earlier and my hand action earlier I knew Sam met the qualifications. Her flesh was smooth and yielding, the kind made for worship and praise. She seemed flawless and from her touch, I wanted to see, smell and taste all of her. My fingers ran along the inner edge of her thigh to the smooth surface of her back. After a couple of minutes of this Sam released my cock, broke our kiss looked into my eyes and rose from the tub. She moved from me and I knew it was over as soon as it began. But instead, she surprised me again.

"Can we go inside so I can see what I doing?"

I rose from the waters and told her that her wish was mine to grant. As I stood I felt the water dripping from my erect cock and running down my legs. I hit the remote and a couple of smallish lights came on to light the path. We made our way inside and she followed me without question or hesitation. Finally we reached the master suite. I turned on a couple of effect lights and turned to see one of the most beautiful bodies I had ever seen in my life.

My eyes traveled over her body spying a near flawlessly shaved mound of Venus. I looked upward and found a slim waist and a flat tummy that spoke of youth and exercise. Higher still to the twin breasts perched on her chest with the rose colored nipples that so many red heads have. A soft well defined neck and lips that begged to be kissed over and over again. Then I reached her eyes. What could I say the best part was the eyes of a woman bearing her soul? They were beautiful just beautiful. Her hand made an involuntary pass against her nipple causing the flesh to grow even more rigid. Back her nail went, flicking at the tip of her breast, elevating it as if on a small silver platter, being served to the hungry man in front of her. Then her thumb came to play also as she caught the tender morsel, pinching between the two as she rolled it back and forth.

If her intention was to make me more excited she had succeeded. My cock was sticking straight up into the air. Her eyes were riveted to my cock. The purplish head was staring back at her. An eerie silence hung in the room. I waited, but she was still transfixed by my cock. My hand went to her but she didn't respond. I leaned forward and took her hand. Tugging gently, I pulled her toward me while at the same time spreading my legs so she could get a good look at what I was offering to her. Gradually she sank to her knees, eyes glazed over, and looking straight ahead. She was unable to move so I brought her hand to my thigh and left it there. Then I reached behind her head, pulling her gently toward my shaft. My remaining hand went to my shaft and encircled it. Lazily beginning an up and down motion, while not using much pressure. I knew I'd pop my cork with too much stimulation. Her resistance was minor as her hand moved toward my shaft. Finally making contact, her fingers stretched to make it around. Her touch was soft, yet determined. Languidly her hand rose, changed direction and return to the base. Again and again, never using much pressure, yet so stimulating. Each time applying the same pressure, like she had never seen a cock before.

Finally words came to her – "I've never seen such a beautiful cock. I don't think I can take all of this."

I smiled knowing she must not have seen many men since I know I m not the big cock in the barn. As she spoke, her mouth came to my steel hard cock and her tongue wormed out, touching the engorged head, pressing into the fleshy tip. Just then a small eruption of pre-come ran from the end. Sam pulled back for moment to watch as the liquid trickled down the shaft. With a quick stroke she captured the lead edge and ran her tongue back to the top of the shaft, collecting it all. Her tongue was like velvet as she played with the hole in the tip causing yet another spilling of precious fluid. I reached down and found her breasts. They were standing proud, indicating her increased level of excitement. Nipples were taut, rising with each breath only to sink backs down with each exhale of air. My fingers touched those marvelous melons as Sam played tongue tag with my cock head. Her level of excitement grew from the contact and caused her mouth to open wider still.

Slowly she took my soon to be erupting love stick into her mouth. I could feel every thing she did to my cock. Her teeth were playing on the top of the shaft while her tongue was working the underside from mid length to head. I told her I would come soon and her eyes met mine to she was proud of herself and she had no intention of letting me come anywhere but her mouth. Realizing this and wanting to lick her pussy before I fucked her, I no longer tried to hold back my seed. The feeling built in my nuts and worked from there.

In less than two minutes I spoke the words "I'm coming."

Sam opened her eyes wide and took me deep into her throat. Her lips touched my sack and triggered my first eruption. As if rehearsed, she pulled back just in time to take my full load into her mouth, not her throat. Her faced showed the signs of struggle to contain the volume, but also showed bliss and pride. My orgasm was one of the most intense I could remember in some time with my balls flexing up only to fall back and flex again.

Finally, the eruptions ended and Sam pulled off with nary a single drop being lost. She smiled triumphantly. Victory was hers, but the pleasure was shared. Her face took on a distinctively different look, one of lust and carnal anticipation. Slowly I drew myself up, my strength returning, until I could sit on the edge of the bed and begin to move her onto the surface also.

Gently and gracefully she reclined onto her bed, her eyes sparkling in the light. Even as she did so her hand began to trail downward past her enlarged breasts, past her flat abdomen, over the smoothness leading to her love hole. Pausing at the edge of her labia, her fingers gingerly played along the edges. Sam eased her full pussy lips apart, while the unmistakable sounds of her juices ebbed and flowed within her. Testing the inner chamber with just the tip of her finger, she sighed softly before withdrawing the finger. She dragged it forward leaving a slim trail of coital fluid behind. As she drew near her naval the trail ended for she had extracted only a small portion.

She had laid a trap for an unsuspecting fly. A fine trail of honey leading toward the hive and I was a willing fly. I lay next to her and then moved slightly over her to kiss her. Her lips were full and her tongue active with my own. From a check of the back of my throat all the way to the surrounding lips she covered all the area, lashing my tongue with hers. But it was time to move south, so I went. I moved from her warm and receptive mouth to the hollow of her neck, only to rise and take an ear lobe into my mouth to suck gently. Going back to her neck I nuzzled into the folds for no other reason then to delay my approach to her glory spot. Moving back onto the main highway to paradise, I went between her breasts into the valley and wandered to both sides of the road. My hands encircled each of her globes as they spread out on her chest. Pulling them both toward the center so that I might lap at her nipples and gently persuaded them to give forth the milk that they did not contain. Lavishing both nipples with my tongue and paying humble obeisance to each in my own way. They rose and fell, from soft and pliable to erect and stiff to near pulsing with a life of their own. My own saliva was keeping them wet and the coolness of the room caused them to grow even stiffer. But as much as I enjoyed playing with her twin peaks, I knew even more fertile ground lay ahead and so my journey continued.

Using my fingers I lightly traced each rib as my tongue traveled southward. The rise and fall of her chest and stomach indicated her excitement for she knew where I was going. My cock was hard once more, but it would have to wait for I could smell her nectar and I was not about to mix it with my seed.

I reached the end of the road to heaven. Breaking my trail of fluid and homage, I slid off the bed and came back up between her outstretched legs. But instead of diving right into the nectar nest, I returned to where I was before. Resuming my path along her abdomen, I moved again, reaching her navel. Her sharp intake of breath told me she either liked attention being lavished there, or it was something that was seldom done. I traced the outer perimeter making smaller and smaller circles as I went. Then when it was obvious the area had been sufficiently covered, I moved in for the kill. Stabbing straight into the heart of her navel with my tongue, only to tease and retreat. Even as I pulled back, her stomach lurched upward trying to recapture my invading instrument. But my tongue was too quick. Back to circling and then stabbing once more. I repeated the exercise over and over as her breaths became more pronounced. My hand moved back to her breasts, tweaking her nipples even harder, causing her voice to elevate her desires. Finally my tongue stayed in her navel, splitting the tiny folds of flesh, trying to root out some hidden enemy or morsel of food. Sam grabbed my head and pulled me even tighter against her abdomen. Only a short distance to travel, the aroma was becoming intense, matching my desire. I pulled from her navel and started south again. She seemed disappointed until my nose began playing on Venus mound. My breath continued along her thighs while my tongue was still searching for whatever it could find. Her leg brushed my arm and I allowed it to continue until it rested gently on my shoulder, followed by her other leg. When settled, she had a leg on either side of my head, the backs of her knees resting on my shoulders that would allow for maximum penetration.

Finally I pulled back, her legs sliding along my shoulders; I gazed at the form spread before me. Her juices were literally dripping from her cunt, running down the crack of her beautiful ass and pooling on the bed. The amount of liquid was impressive and I knew as hungry as I was, it was time to "wet the appetite" so to speak. Using my tongue once more I traveled along the outer perimeter, causing her to shift as she tried to make me slip off the ridge and fall into her waiting chasm. But I was careful. Finally with strength I didn't know she possessed, she took hold of my hair and at the same time used her legs and feet to pull me into her waiting orifice as her first orgasms struck. Just as I thought, hers was the nectar of a goddess, sweet and plentiful and my entire face was coated.

When her tremors ceased I glanced toward her face and couldn't see it. Her breasts had risen, trying to touch the ceiling. They throbbed with a life all their own. As much as I wanted to suck them in, I knew there was something else I had to do first. I rose and my cock popped up from between my legs. I was ready to fill her cunt with my fluid to replace that which I had just lapped out. Sam rose on her elbows and her eyes grew wider from and anticipation once more. My cock had swollen to an even larger proportion than before. The large purple head was bobbing back and forth as I rose to my feet between her thighs. Her legs remained over my shoulders until she was bent into an "L" shape. The position elevated her pussy off the bed and was at the right position for me to assault her. I approached her love hole as Sam reached down to spread her pussy lips apart to help me inside. I approached her channel until the head of my cock touched her. Her sharp intake of breath told me she was ready. Grasping my cock I moved until the head eased into her love channel. It was so smooth as I began to move back and forth, never going too far in or pulling out. Sam began to rock with me as I sawed in and out, building speed. Her steamy cunt had gapped open, and when the time was right, I saw her face, a veil of unbridled lust, distorted in her excitement. Her eyes were tightly shut and her teeth clinched into a frown of determination as I shoved. My cock sailed past areas untouched by anyone until now. I struck bottom and my nuts ended against her up turned ass. I held it there as a shriek came from her indicating how she enjoyed being impaled by my iron rod.

Nesting in her hole, I withdrew only to charge again. Increasing speed with each thrust, hammering away, my sack crashing against her ass cheeks until contractions indicated an impending explosion once more. I concentrated on my own pleasures, but became aware of her body beginning to tremble as an overwhelming spasm overtook her body. Still I rammed in and out and when the time arrived for me to dump my seed, I grasp Sam's hips and pulled her forward while driving forward. The impact was loud but drowned out by her cries of pleasure. Spurt after spurt shot from me into her reservoir until I slowed in speed, letting the last couple of spasms jettison out. My seed was depleted and my cock shrinking as a fierce battle had been waged, but well worth the losses.

As I released her legs and moved away from the bed I noticed her form was not at rest. Instead she was still experiencing the last throngs of an orgasm. Not being able to tell if she had made it at this point and was coming down or if she was still climbing, I took a deep breath for energy and dove into the wetness we had created. Soon as my tongue crossed her clit she nearly screamed and locked her legs around my head, pulling my face deep into her come soaked snatch. The aroma was musty, but the flavor was sweet and I lapped it up with increased fervor. When Sam reached her last plateau, I felt her thighs begin to tremble against my ears and her breath became even more labored. All was music to my ears, metaphorically speaking of course. Finally, she released me from her death grip. I crawled back up on the bed, resting beside her. I was spent, as was she. I had not come so much since my early twenties. Later we rose and took a shower together. After failed attempts at resisting each other, we ended up making love again. In total we made love seven times that night and it was only the beginning.

Younger women are indeed a wonderful thing and when you can find one as unique as Sam you should hold on. I did not. We both realized that we could not have a sustained relationship, as she wanted children and a father for them that was not 50 or so when they were born. That does not mean we have not had a wonderful time on numerous occasions since our first time. She is now married to what seems to be a nice guy and we have decided to not do anything to jeopardize her marriage, but who knows.

PHARAOH'S LOUNGE

"I'll take a deluxe bacon cheeseburger with fries and a double Stoli martini on the rocks."

The corner of my mouth curled in a smile as I listened to Jack's order. Some things never change. I turned to the waitress.

"I'll have the Chef's Salad, please, and a sparkling water with lime," I said.

Jack leveled his gaze at me and smirked.

"I don't know about your generation, son. Your father never would have ordered rabbit food and water for lunch. What's the world coming to?"

My yearly lunch with Jack always started this way: bemoaning the good old days. Our family printing business had been buying paper from Jack for several decades now and he insisted on taking me out to lunch once a year, as he had done with my now-deceased father for years. He was usually sloshed by the time our lunch ended, but he was always good for some juicy gossip.

His territory was all of New England so he had a pretty good feel for what was going on in the region and never ceased to amuse me with the his tales from the road. He was well into his second martini when he imparted some information that certainly set my course for the following week.

"Oh, I almost forgot to tell you. Remember that young lady, Amber, that worked for you several summers ago? That cute one with the incredible ass?"

Yes, I certainly remembered Amber. She had only worked for one summer before going off to college. She was a gorgeous young lady and had turned quite a few heads that summer, including mine.

"Of course I remember her. She went off to URI and I haven't heard from her since. Why do you ask?"

Jack leaned in as he always did when he had a juicy tidbit to impart.

"Well I saw her last week in a strip club in downtown Providence. She didn't remember me, but I never forget an ass. She goes by the name of Angel and she gave me one of the most incredible lap dances I've ever had. And I've had a few."

At close to 250 pounds it was hard to believe a stripper would even be able to find Jack's lap, but I had no doubt his voracious appetite for life included sex. I was intrigued by this information, however, and wanted to learn more without looking overly interested. I didn't have to worry. The alcohol had Jack's tongue flapping and he continued on his diatribe.

"Ronnie, that girl has the most incredible body and face, but her ass, holy shit, her ass is perfection. She's still in school and stripping to pay tuition. Thankfully, for schmoes like me, she needs dough. I think I paid for a couple expensive textbooks the other night. "

"Where'd you see her?" I asked innocently.

"Pharaoh's Lounge. Great club downtown. Good food, very sexy dancers, and a VIP lounge where the girls get pretty frisky. Jesus, to touch that sweet ass was like heaven, I'm telling you. I used to check her out that summer she worked for you. What a treat to find her there. I gotta get back to Rhode Island again soon."

He looked off wistfully as he took a huge swig, finishing off his second martini in one huge gulp. I might have to find an excuse to visit Providence myself, I thought, but I didn't share that information with Jack. His mouth was much too big.

Amber. We hire summer kids every year to help us run errands and do odd jobs. I knew her parents casually and her father had inquired one spring as to whether his daughter might be able to earn some money that summer for her impending first year of college. I knew the answer to that question as soon as she walked through the door for the interview.

Amber was eighteen at the time, but had the demeanor of a young lady that wasn't too innocent. She had one of those body types I love: slender, but curvy; the curves coming from her bone structure as opposed to body tissue. Her heritage was Mexican Indian and German, which gave her an exotic look with smooth brown skin and dark expressive eyes.

She had an amazing body and she knew it. Her breasts weren't large, but were beautifully proportioned to her slender body. Her graceful neck, slender arms and long lean legs all added up to an incredible package for a young lady just finishing high school.

But it was her ass that was the crowning touch. I wouldn't be exaggerating to say that Amber had a perfect ass. And her ass in motion, walking across a room say, was a sight to behold. She loved to wear tight jeans to show off her butt and she knew how good she looked in them.

Now I love women. I love their body shapes and sizes, their variety and their movements. Name a body part, I love it. Nice breasts, long legs, slender necks and taut stomachs – I love it all. But if there is one part of a woman that is always the first thing I look at, it's the ass. In my book if a woman has a beautiful rear end, then all the rest is good. Her tits can be big, small or medium-sized; her hair can be black, brown, or blond; her skin can be white, black or anything in between. But as long as she's got a nice ass, then I'm attracted.

It's not just the ass that I find attractive. It's the way the ass moves when a woman walks or the way it protrudes when she stands a certain way. To me the ass is the center of the womanly universe and the rest of her body radiates from there. Okay, call me obsessed, but that's the way it's always been for me.

And Amber? Well she had one of the best asses I had ever seen – anywhere. She drove us all wild that summer, well, at least me. She'd wear these skin-tight, low-riding jeans that hugged every curve, accentuated her sultry shape and exposed a sexy hint of smooth flesh. Some days she'd wear short skirts or mini-dresses to show off her slender bronze legs. When she walked her hips swayed and her ass cheeks did a little swiveling dance that I could never get enough of. I used to fantasize what it would be like to see her walk naked; to watch her pert little butt bounce as she sashayed before me; to fuck her from behind as her tight ass bounced with each thrust.

And, as I said, her ass just led to all the other exquisite parts of her body. Her toned thighs, her flat stomach, her pert little pussy, were all one with her ass. To say I was obsessed might be too strong a term. But finding out Amber was working in a strip club certainly got my attention.

I did my research that night on the computer. I found Pharaoh's Lounge had a website that listed their dancers. Sure enough, Amber, or Angel as she was known there, worked three nights a week including Sundays. I travel to Providence occasionally so I found an excuse to go the following Sunday. I made reservations at the Biltmore Hotel, an upscale downtown hotel and an easy walk to the club. I was taking a chance that this was all a wild goose chase, but I figured I didn't have anything to lose. Worst case is I'd spend an evening hanging out in a strip club.

I headed down the next Sunday afternoon, checked into my hotel and double-checked the club's website. By all accounts, Angel would be working the early shift – noon to 8pm. I had a light snack and headed over to the club around 6:30. I wanted to give myself some time to get acclimated and figure out my approach for greeting Amber.

Pharaoh's Lounge is a typical strip club. It looked a little seedy on the outside, but the parking lot was full this particular evening and the bright neon lights advertised the allure of what went on inside the windowless box of a building. I walked inside, paid a ten-dollar entry fee and headed through a beaded curtain into a dark room. It took my eyes a few minutes to adjust as I slowly circled the central stage and found a seat a few rows back.

There was a dancer onstage strutting her stuff and half-naked waitresses running around serving drinks. The music was loud, punctuated by an obnoxious DJ announcing who was onstage and who was next. His rap between songs was lame, but I didn't care. I was on a mission and I sat down, ordered a beer and surveyed the crowd. It wasn't too crowded after all and only a few of the patrons sat up close to the stage.

To the back of the club was a neon sign denoting the "VIP Lounge". Several dancers circulated the club, leaning down to speak to the customers and trying to lure them into the back for a lap dance. Pharaoh's was supposed to have excellent lap dances, according to Jack, and I was looking forward to doing a little research of my own.

"And now ladies and gentlemen, put your hands together for the lovely Angel!"

My eyes were now riveted front and center as a diminutive figure climbed up on the stage. Her 5'-3" frame was elongated by a pair of 4 inch stiletto heels with straps that wrapped seductively around her slender ankles. Her bronze skin shone golden in the spotlight and her long wavy brown hair glistened as she flipped it over her shoulder.

She was wearing what I guess could be called a mini-dress. It was skin tight, royal blue and fit her like a second skin. Her smallish breasts strained against the silky material and the bottom of the dress barely covered her pert ass. That incredible ass was now on the stage, twitching as she walked to the brass pole and swung around in one of those one-handed moves that showed she was no newcomer to this stage.

I was riveted to her performance, as was everyone else in the room. She moved in sync to the electronic beat, her body at one with the rhythm and pulse of the music. She never lost eye contact with the crowd, showing off her body while looking in earnest at her likely suitors. She'd lock in a patron's stuperous gaze and smile with a subtle hint of seduction. I was far enough back to be out of her range, but I was drawn in, nevertheless. I knew that once her stage show was over there would be guys crawling all over themselves to be with her. I knew I would have to act quickly.

She turned her back to the crowd, grabbed the pole and stuck her ass back toward her drooling admirers. As she arched her back, her sweet little buns slowly emerged from the tight short dress that wrapped her hips. Suddenly her beautiful ass was protruding and bouncing to the beat pulsating from the speakers. A slim strip of fabric bisected her buttocks and showed that she wore a thong for modesty sake. It cupped her mons and bulged with the sweet flesh barely hidden beneath. It tucked tightly into the deep round crevice of her ass and emerged at the top of her buttocks as it stretched thinly over her curvy hips.

Then she got on her knees, the dress rode up past her waist and she lifted her sweet butt cheeks into the air as she leaned forward and rested her head and arms on the floor. She reached between her legs, pulled the thong to one side and, for the first time, exposed her sweet wet pussy to the selected few that had the appropriate vantage point. She bobbled her butt in the air, a blatant call for attention to anyone that wanted to pursue this fantasy once she'd left the stage. There wasn't a guy in the place that wasn't thinking what it would be like to plow their dicks into her from behind. A crude thought, yes, but very true.

She moved with an assuredness and grace that exuded confidence. She knew she looked good and she obviously enjoyed showing off her body. She turned and lay on her back, dug her heels in and lifted her butt off the floor. She spread her legs slightly and reached down to cup her pussy with her hand, rubbing it very lightly while she humped her pelvis to the music. Then she pulled her thong to the side again and displayed her glistening pussy to the lucky souls who happened to be in the right spot. She lowered herself to the stage and continued to gyrate to the music as she looked from one patron to the next.

The music ended, she gathered up her tiny panties and the many dollar bills scattering the stage and made way for the next dancer. All eyes followed her, including mine. She left the stage and headed through a door to the rear. I watched the door like a hawk, knowing she'd soon emerge and begin to circulate through the crowd.

I saw her come through the door five minutes later and head toward the nearest seated patron, leaning over to invite him to explore her sweet body further in the VIP Lounge. I knew it was my time to move. I hopped up and headed around the stage, hoping this first fool was too drunk or too stupid to take her up on her offer. I tapped her shoulder and told her I'd like a private dance. She didn't look at me closely enough to recognize me, but grabbed my hand and lead me toward the back.

We entered the so-called "VIP Lounge", Amber leading the way. She brought me down an aisle of red curtains to an open booth and pulled me in, shutting the curtain. I sat down on a wooden chair and looked up into her eyes with a wan smile. It was then that recognition set in.

"Mr. B? Holy shit! What are you doing here?"

She put her hand to her mouth in a moment of realization and embarrassment.

"Oh my God. I'm so embarrassed."

"Amber, I mean Angel, don't be embarrassed. I'm the one who should be embarrassed. I'm the one that drove 70 miles to see you. I'm the older guy that shouldn't be here. You're just doing your thing. Please don't be embarrassed."

I did my best to put her at ease. I looked into her eyes and tried to reinforce my words with an understanding look. She stared back with a quizzical gaze.

"What do you mean you drove a 70 miles to see me?"

"Well, I heard through someone that you were dancing here in Providence and I, well, I had always been very attracted to you and I couldn't pass up the opportunity to see you in the flesh, so to speak."

"Really? Oh, that's so sweet. Thank you. But I still can't believe you're here. I rarely run into anyone I know here. I guess I've always thought I was sort of anonymous here."

She looked at me with a strange look on her face.

"But not anymore," she stated matter-of-factly

"Well, I didn't come here to make you feel bad or embarrass you. I just, I just need to see you, I guess. I can't explain it."

Amber suddenly turned into Angel again. I was on her turf, after all, and she found strength in the familiar surroundings of this private niche. She did her best to hide her embarrassment, placed her hands on my thighs and leaned down to speak.

"So what can I do for you, Mr. B.?"

I reached into my breast pocket, pulled out a one hundred dollar bill and placed it on the table.

"You can start by dancing for me, Angel. Or may I call you Amber?" I smiled.

She leaned in closer and whispered in my ear.

"No one knows my real name here. Except you. So you can call me anything you want."

I looked her straight into her eyes.

"Then I'm going to call you Amber, if you don't mind. And I want you to call me Ronnie."

She may have been embarrassed initially, but now, being on familiar turf, she took the upper hand and used her wiles and experience in such a venue to put me a bit on the defensive. I was seated on an armless chair, my legs spread and my cock beginning to rise to the occasion. She leaned into me, her soft brown hair cascading over my head, and put her sweet wet lips next to my ear.

"Well, welcome to Pharaoh's Lounge, then…Ronnie."

Her leg came up between my thighs and the front of her shin began to stroke up and down against my groin. I had come to attention very quickly, under the circumstances, and she knew how to apply enough pressure to bring me to full hardness in a matter of seconds. She lifted her tight dress up and over her head and stood before me in only a thong and heels. She breathed heavy into my ear, pressed her body forward between my legs as my hands reached up and back to encircle the sweet roundness of her exquisite buttocks.

I gasped as I held her ass cheeks in my hand for the first time. Her skin was like silk and the flesh of her ass was compact, but very squeezable. I massaged her buttocks, then let my hands drop slowly down the back of her thighs, feeling the strange sensation of taut muscles under silky smooth skin.

"Oh shit, Amber. I've wanted to touch your body for so long."

"Really? I never knew. I always thought of you as a sort of old…"

She caught herself and tried to recoup.

"I know, Amber. Don't be embarrassed. I'm old enough to be your father. I know that. But even a man my age finds it hard to resist the beauty of a young woman. Especially a young woman as incredibly attractive as you."

At fifty I was certainly her elder. But I'm six feet tall, have a trim athletic figure, a full head of graying hair and I've never been ashamed of my body. In fact I've always found that young women seem to be attracted to a well-groomed, experienced older man. I was hoping Amber wouldn't be an exception.

She looked deep into my eyes, trying to understand where I was coming from. I knew I was throwing her for a loop. She'd been expecting her usual old man grope: five minutes, maybe a quick hand job and onto the next victim.

"Sit down on my lap, baby," I said daringly,

She looked at me a little funny, then spun around on her high strappy heels and deposited her exquisite ass directly on the huge bulge in my pants. She leaned back into my chest and I breathed directly into her right ear. I grabbed the sweet flesh of her supple hips and began to rock her back and forth, while my still-clothed cock slid into the groove of her butt cheeks. I felt her bend forward and hiss ever so quietly as she felt the first physical expression of my desire for her.

She began to rock back and forth in a nice rhythmic motion, one meant to get me off. I let her go for a minute or two, but I had other ideas. I pulled her shoulders back and put my panting lips to her ear again.

"I'll tell you the reason I'm here, Amber. I have a proposition for you."

I hesitated before going on, knowing this was the moment of truth.

"Listen, we both need something. You need money for school, and lots of it. I know how expensive college is right now, especially if you're paying for it yourself."

I could tell from her body language that she both understood and agreed to this statement.

"And me, well I have money, but I need something too. I need companionship. I need to make a serious connection with a young female." I hesitated. "I need you," I stated bluntly.

I could feel Amber slow in her movements, sort of waiting for the punch line.

"So here's the deal. In the inside breast pocket of my sport coat is an envelope with $2,000 in it. Twenty crisp new one hundred dollar bills. It's yours for the taking. All you have to do is spend the night with me."

I'd said it. I awaited her response. I could tell that she was thinking. I tried to add to my case.

"I'm staying over at the Biltmore. I've got a beautiful corner suite. I know that you get off in the next half hour. I'm going to leave at the end of this song. If you're willing, I'd like for you to meet me in the dining room in an hour or so. We'll have a nice dinner, some good wine, then retire to my suite. When you leave early tomorrow morning, I'll be a happy man. And you'll be two grand richer."

I could almost hear her brain whirring.

"So I'm going to open my sport coat and if this offer interests you, all you have to do is reach in and take the envelope," I whispered into her ear.

I hesitated slightly.

"And the two K doesn't include a generous tip for good service," I added.

She stood up. I missed the pressure and warmth of her body already. She turned to look me in the eye. I was either going to get hit, or I was going to hit one out of the ball park. The left side of my jacket was open; the envelope protruded from the inside pocket for her taking.

She hesitated for just a moment, the reached in and took the envelope. She grinned at me, I grinned back. I was the happiest fucker alive.

"I don't really have clothes for a fancy dinner," she said.

"No problem. We'll eat in the bar. It's dark and, believe me, whatever you wear, or don't wear, will be fine."

She lifted up one corner of her cute mouth in a smile, leaned down and gave me a soft warm kiss directly on the lips. Hers were wet, warm and inviting. Her tongue darted into my mouth for a moment, giving me a tease of things to come. She pulled back and leaned down to whisper in my ear. I cupped and squeezed her soft natural breasts.

"Well then. I guess I'll see you within the hour," she said demurely.

I stood, reached into my pocket and gave her another hundred dollar bill. I had come prepared and I wanted to make sure money wasn't an issue. I thanked her for the dance and she smiled, I gathered myself together, folded my sport coat over my erection, headed out of the club, and into the cool Providence night air.

I floated back to the hotel, flushed with the fullness of the night that lay before me. I sauntered into the hotel lobby and headed for the bar. I had a double and bided my time. At a quarter past eight I found a nice little table toward the back of the bar, a spot where a gentleman might entertain a lady in some privacy. I kept my eyes peeled on the entrance and a few minutes later Amber entered the bar.

She was wearing tight jeans, high heels and a short top that left several inches of smooth flesh exposed at her tummy. Her hair was piled high on her head in a loose, unkempt sort of way and a large bag was slung over her slender shoulder. She strode with confidence on her high heels, stopped to survey the scene and saw me wave nonchalantly from a dark corner of the bar. Several men interrupted their conversations to watch her weave between the tables and make her way to me.

I stood, kissed both her cheeks and waved her to the chair next to me.

She sat, we ordered a Pinot Noir for her, another drink for me, and we began to talk. Our conversation was initially tainted by the former relationship of boss versus summer intern. But as we talked and I made her feel at ease, we began to explore new territory. She was now a junior and had a few years of college under her belt. She was still living on campus and was majoring in business.

We sat at ninety degrees to one another and as we talked my hand rested softly on her denim-clad thigh. I squeezed the taut muscles of her lean leg and she rested her hand upon mine. As we talked about my office, her school, and the club, I let my hand wander gently up and down her thigh. There could be no mistake that she had thought through my offer, had been given the opportunity to back out or not show, but was now ready to complete her end of the bargain. As much as I was enjoying our conversation the sight and smell of this gorgeous girl sitting next to me was soon overwhelming. I asked if she was ready to go to my VIP Room and she laughed.

"I'm ready when you are," she said with a devilish smile. I left a couple twenties on the table and we stood up to leave. I could feel the eyes of others on us. What was an older geezer doing with a hot young chick like Amber? But those questions were followed by sighs of envy. We snaked our way out of the bar, across the hotel lobby and onto an open elevator. I rested my hand gently on her waist as the elevator rose to the tenth floor.

My key card slid into the slot, the green light signaled our entrance and I threw open the door. I flicked on a few lights and Amber gave her seal of approval with a low whistle. Our room looked out on the lights of downtown and we made our way over to the window to survey the view. I rested my hand on the top of her hips, touching bare skin, and felt myself thicken with thoughts of what lay ahead. I opened a bottle of cold burgundy that I'd left in an ice bucket, poured two glasses and sat down on the bed. Amber looked at me over the rim of the glass as she took a sip.

"So Mr. B., I mean Ronnie. How do you want me?" She smiled coquettishly.

I sat on the bed, put my wine glass on the side table and held out my hands. She glided toward my open arms.

"I just want to watch you get undressed," I stated quite simply. "Very slowly," I added.

She stood between my spread thighs and I reached out to touch her. My hands roamed lightly over her curves. She crossed her arms, grabbed the bottom of her skimpy top and pulled it over her head. She wore a simple white bra. Her breasts were not large, nice B cups, but sat so nicely on her slim shape. I softly caressed her nipples through the thin silky material and felt them stiffen. I slid the straps down over her shoulder as she unclasped her bra. It fell into my lap and there, inches from my face, were her beautiful brown-tipped breasts.

They were perfectly formed; their sweet conical shape punctuated by perfectly smooth nipples that tilted up and seemed to call out for sucking. My hands wandered lightly over their roundness and gently massaged and kneaded them. Amber let out an almost inaudible sigh as I licked my fingertips and rubbed her nipples.

Her face was beautiful. Her wavy brown hair cascaded over her shoulders and her large brown eyes watched me with intense interest. I spread the fingers of each hand and touched her taut stomach. A small cross dangled from a piercing in her belly button. She placed her hands on the back of my head and pulled me toward her torso. I kissed her belly and my hands reached to cup the beautiful round cheeks of her denim-clad ass. It was finally time for them to be exposed to my touch.

I used both hands to unclasp her jeans. I lowered the zipper and began to unpeel the jeans off her buff frame. She took over, shed her heels and jeans and was left standing in a tiny black thong. She put her heels back on and I again cupped her ass, now touching flesh. It was smooth, soft and silky to the touch. I gently kneaded her butt cheeks and kissed her stomach. She sighed and pulled me toward her. I hooked my fingers on the slender straps of her thong. I dislodged it from between her legs and pulled it down over her slender thighs, grazing her legs with my thumbs as I pulled her panties free. I could barely perceive the musky aroma of her sex.

She stepped out of the thong and now only her strappy high heels remained. I was still seated on the edge of the bed as I palmed her body with my hands: her stomach, her breasts, her ass, her thighs. Her pussy was shaved except for a small landing strip of downy hair which sat directly above the pert vee of her sex.

She spread her legs slightly and my hand finally found its way between her legs, cupping her moist mons in the palm of my hand. She caught her breath and leaned down to stroke my cock through my pants. I needed to get out of my clothes. I stripped quickly and stood up. We embraced and I pulled her body against mine. My erection stood up hard, fast and long between our bodies. She cupped my ass and pulled me against her. We kissed deeply.

She tasted wonderful. She opened her mouth to me and our tongues gently explored each other's mouth. She sucked my tongue as I reached down between her legs. She spread them slightly to give my fingers access. My middle finger slipped into her slick groove and it felt like her body pulled my digit into her wetness. She was soaked and the flesh of her pussy was pulsing with excitement. I slowly inserted my middle finger to the hilt. Amber moaned and reached down to grab my dick. We stood touching, rubbing and stroking each other, getting more and more excited with each passing second.

I needed to absorb this at a much slower pace. At the rate we were going I would explode within minutes. I told Amber I needed her to slow down; that I wanted to look at her and explore her body. I wanted her to show me her body.

I lay back along one edge of the king-size bed and gave Amber room to move. I lightly stroked my cock as I watched her. She began to give me a private show, up close and personal. She moved slowly and seductively with feline precision. She maintained eye contact as she moved and rolled and crawled, using the entire bed as her stage. She showed off one part of her body after another: the exquisite form of her breasts, the graceful arch of her back, the long smooth lines of her legs, the slenderness of her ankles and tiny feet and, of course, the perfectly formed ass that held it all together and was her crowning glory.

She leaned this way, spread that way, her arms, legs and torso moving in a wonderful ballet on the bed. My cock stood hard and strong and when Amber wasn't looking me in the eyes, she was gazing hungrily at my bobbing erection. She'd occasionally sweep in low, maybe drape her hair across my lap, or lean into to give the tip of my glans a soft lippy kiss. She was teasing me unmercifully and pulling out every move she'd ever seen or done. I was in heaven.

She lay down diagonally on the bed, her legs straight and her feet on my lap. The sweet pout of her pussy lay hidden in the triangle of her thighs and lower belly. She lifted her legs straight up and together into the air and reached her hands down to cup her ass. The folds of her outer labia peaked round and full from between her upper thighs. Ever so slowly she spread her legs and as she did, her pussy opened up like a flower, the delicate ridges of her minor labia unfurling from their hidden place. She placed a hand on each side and pulled her pussy open further, exposing pink wet flesh. Her fingers pulled up her hood to expose her clit. She tapped it ever so gently with her fingertip and smiled knowingly at me. I needed to touch her now.

I moved between her spread, slender thighs as she touched herself. I encouraged her with words and showed my appreciation for her show as I gently stroked my cock hovering above her.

"You are so fucking sexy, Amber. I need to touch you, baby," I croaked, barely able to speak.

She closed her eyes and used both hands to massage her moist labia and spread her lips for my perusal. She reached underneath with one hand and gently inserted her middle finger into her ass, already moist and slickened from the expert maneuvering of her fingers. Her other hand worked her pussy and eventually two fingers found their way into her groove and she began to stroke herself. I could hear the wet sticky sounds of her juices intermingling with her frantic stroking. I could smell her desire and see the results glistening on her open flesh.

I encouraged her with my words and told her how fucking hot she was and how much she was turning me on. She opened her eyes long enough to see me stroking my member as it hovered in a stiff cantilever over her face. She disengaged her fingers from her ass and cunt and reached up to gently squeeze my balls. She opened her mouth and I gently descended into her hungry mouth. She took me inch by inch, absorbing my length deep into her throat. I felt like she wanted to suck me dry; she wanted me to come in her mouth.

And I could have. I wanted to come right there and came very close to unloading in her eager mouth. But I also wanted to please her, to make her lose herself in pleasure, to make her come hard. So after a few minutes I disengaged from her hungry sucking and kissed her deeply on the mouth. Her tongue searched for mine in a frantic and desperate search for pleasure. I kissed my way down to her ear and told her what I wanted to do to her. I told her how bad I needed her pussy in my mouth; how bad I needed her to come for me.

I kissed my way down her neck, taking my time, teasing her with innocent kisses after our flirtation with my orgasm. I worked my way to her waiting nipples. Shit, they were so stiff and succulent – long and hard. Amber moaned from a deep place as I kissed her breasts. Her head was tilted back in a sign of acceptance as I licked and sucked her nipples, gently at first and then with increasing fervor as her body language told me to suck harder.

I reached down with my middle finger as I sucked and felt her sopping wet pussy. As I inserted my finger I felt her acknowledge the multiple assault on her sexual senses. I pushed in two fingers, sucked on her nipples and snuck my left hand down behind her ass to explore her backside. Her anus was wet with pussy juice and open for my exploration.

My tongue continued its journey, licking her stomach as I headed south, my fingers working furiously, her body arching to accept my manual manipulation. She was on her back and I hovered above her. I swung my leg across her face and set up in a 69 position. I put my hands under her ass to bring her sweet pubis up to my mouth. I could feel her lick and suck my balls as I descended on the wettest pussy I had ever eaten. I licked up and down her wide open, soaking wet slit, and then settled into a rhythmic sucking of her clit. She moaned her approval and her hips arched up to meet my slurping tongue and mouth.

Her long lean legs were spread wide for me and I had full access to her open sex. She bucked her pelvis into my mouth as I ate her in a full and open-mouthed assault on her wet treasure. I burrowed my hands down under her ass and pulled her cheeks up and spread her pussy to my mouth, tongue and lips. Meanwhile she licked and sucked my balls, moaning her approval of my actions and spurring me on to deeper penetration. I zeroed in on her clit and could tell from her response that I was applying just enough pressure.

I hummed and moaned my appreciation as I licked and sucked her supple lips. The moisture of her desire covered my face. My nose delved into her pussy as my tongue flicked her clit and my lips sucked in her liquid. The aroma of her cunt and the silky wet texture of her lips were driving me wild. I could feel her edging toward the brink of an orgasm. I didn't let up, but doubled my efforts and moved my head up and down and in and out to maximize the effect. I felt her mouth pull away from me and could feel her heated and erratic breath on my asshole.

"Oh, God! I'm gonna come!"

Suddenly she stiffened, quiet pervaded for a few seconds as her pussy convulsed and sent spasms of pleasure through her body, soaking my face with her pulsing moisture. She groaned loudly and bit my thigh. I eased back and licked gently, kissing my way out of her depths in slow languid slurps. Her breathing returned to normal over a minute or two.

"Welcome to my VIP Room," I joked.

She didn't respond. I rolled off her and twisted around to face her directly. I reached to hug her and she folded into my arms.

"Oh my God, Mr. B. That was so intense," she said with a big smile on her face.

"Glad you liked it, baby. I've wanted to do that for so long, you can't imagine."

"If I'd only known."

We kissed deeply. She may have come hard, but she was ready for more, and so was I. She pushed me onto my back and straddled my thighs. I could tell she was ready to return the favor, and who was I to argue? My cock was at full mast and she licked her way down from my mouth to my neck, on to my nipples and then a long, slow steady kissing assault on my stomach as she headed south to my stiffness.

She grabbed two pillows, inserted them under my ass to bring my pelvis up at a sharp angle and resumed working me with her mouth. Her lips felt warm and wet and I could only imagine how they would feel wrapped around my cock. I didn't have long to wait. She reached my dick and lowered her mouth slowly and wetly down my erect flesh. Not the slightest feeling of teeth; only wet warm sucking and full lips absorbed my most sensitive part.

She went deep, gagging just slightly as my cock hit the back of her throat. She pulled off, licked me up and down and moaned her approval. She ducked down low and pulled my shaved balls into her mouth. It felt so fucking good, her furious licking and sucking. She delved down even lower and licked my ass, probing my bottom with her pointed tongue, then pulling back to suck my sac into her open mouth. I couldn't believe the sensations racing through my lower body. I put my hand on her head to encourage her explorations.

I had no doubt that she would have hungrily accepted my coming in her mouth. She seemed to yearn for it. But I needed her and told her so.

"I need to fuck you, Amber. Right now."

She pulled back, perhaps a little disappointed that I wasn't going to unload deep into her mouth. But she shifted gears quickly and pulled back to accommodate.

"How do you want me, baby? How do you want to fuck me?"

I bounced up onto my knees, pushed her onto her back, spread her sweet thighs wide and leaned down to kiss her deeply. She reached down for my cock and groaned, pulling me down and eagerly guiding me toward her wet juncture. The head of my cock grazed her swollen lips and I heard her gasp.

"I need you so bad! Fuck me!"

I slid in. I probably could have bottomed out on the first stroke, she was so wet. But I wanted to engage slowly. I began to pump, back and forth, a little deeper with each inward thrust. She grunted and grabbed my ass to pull me into her. I pushed up on my arms so I could look at her beautiful face. Then I began to fuck her with long steady strokes, deeper and deeper until I was sunk to the hilt.

I began a furious physical assault, fucking her with long, deep strokes. I slowly increased the pace and intensity. At some point, it seemed like forever, but was surely just a minute or two, I began to fuck her with all the speed and intensity that I could muster. She was moaning loudly now, urging me on with her vocal assent. I shifted my angle slightly to maximize the depth of my plunges.

I could hear the wet slurpy sounds of my cock and her pussy. Each plunge elicited some sort of vocal response. She talked dirty to me, telling me to fuck her harder, deeper, faster. Our lovemaking was punctuated by the loud slap of wet skin on wet skin; of a hard cock slamming into a soaking wet pussy. I felt a swell of fluid ready to launch from deep in my groin.

"Oh shit. I'm going to come!" I shouted.

"Fuck me, baby. Fuckin' fuck me!" she screamed.

And as I pounded my cock into her with all my strength, I felt the unleashing of an incredibly powerful orgasm. I unloaded one spurt after another deep into her body, plowing into her with all the intensity I could muster. And as I came, I could feel her pussy spasm and grip my cock as she came again and milked my cock for every ounce of cum.

We collapsed in a sweaty, heaving mess; breathing heavy from the incredible exertion, but feeling fully satisfied in a mutual orgasm unlike anything either of us had ever experienced before.

We were both speechless. There was nothing to say. We both knew what had just happened and we kissed softly and cuddled up against one another, blocking out the world and absorbing ourselves in one another's body. A short nap might have been in order if it were up to me, however, I didn't want my own stamina to dictate the pace of lovemaking required by a young twenty-one year-old. Even she needed a little recuperation time, so we cuddled and talked while gently touching and stroking one another's body.

She eventually rolled onto her stomach, put her arms under her head and pushed her sweet ass into the air.

"I need a massage," she stated rather assertively. Who am I to turn down such an offer; and one I had fantasized about on more than one occasion?

I sat up, straddled her protruding bubble butt, let my semi-limp cock settle into the groove of her sweet ass and began to knead her shoulders and upper back. I took my time and concentrated on giving her pleasure, finding the deep muscle tissue that would benefit the most from my manipulation. She groaned under her breath with eyes closed, giving herself up to my hands.

I worked my way around her shoulders, up onto her neck, then began to slide down the middle of her back, using both hands and fingers to reach deep into her tissue. Slowly, I made my way down to her glorious butt. I scooted back to expose it in all its glory. It was soft and supple; perfectly round and silky to the touch. The succulent swells of her cheeks narrowed and sloped wonderfully into a deep recess at the small of her back. On the bottom her cheeks tucked in tightly to her upper thighs and it all tapered into the dark inviting crack of her ass. Perfection was at my fingertips and my cock began to come back to life.

I moved to kneel between her legs, forcing her to spread them to accommodate me. Now I could see the sweet succulence of her labia, still moist from our fucking and further enhanced by the massage. I kneaded her buttocks with a deep powerful grip and could hear wet sticky sounds emanating from her pussy as my massage pulled her ass cheeks back and forth, revealing the hidden treasure of her exquisite ass and equally alluring pussy.

My fingers did the walking, and eventually found their way to the edge of her labia, swollen with desire and wet with anticipation. I teased her lips and put my middle finger into my mouth to moisten it. Her inner lips were slightly protruding from her pussy and I gently ran my finger along the delicate folds. I reached down and barely touched her clit. She acknowledged my arrival by lifting her hips off the bed to allow me full and direct access. I began to twiddle her clit with the tip of my finger and she gyrated her hips to meet my rhythm.

I climbed from between her legs and kneeled to the side. Her face and chest stayed prone on the bed, but she arched her back up and pushed her ass into the air. What an exquisite sight. My right hand continued its party with her open pussy. I licked my left middle finger and began to explore the sweet pucker of her anus. It felt well lubricated and I gently probed and prodded. Hearing no hesitation I slowly inserted my finger into her ass. She groaned deeply as I pushed it in to the first knuckle.

All these years I had fantasized about the feel and grip of her beautiful ass. Now my fingers were giving her pleasure and she was completely giving herself to me. Her eyes were closed, her mouth was open and sounds of delight emanated from somewhere deep in her being. I inserted two fingers into her cunt, deep as I could push them, and then leaned down to her sweet round ass and replaced my finger with my tongue. She hissed in pleasure and bucked her bottom to meet my oral invasion. The smell of her sex overwhelmed my nostrils as my tongue explored her asshole and my nose nestled into the wet nectar of her pussy.

Suddenly she turned her head to me and ordered me to fuck her.

"Oh, fuck, Ronnie. I need you. I need you to fuck me, now. Hurry up and get that big cock inside me."

I kneeled again between her legs and put my hands on the beautiful curve of her hips. Her pussy protruded forth from between her legs: open, wet and inviting. She pushed up onto her knees as I guided the head of my cock to her gaping opening. I teased her with the tip of my cock, sliding it up and down the gaping slit of her soaking wet pussy.

"Oh, fuck, Ronnie! Stop teasing me and fuck me!"

She was in the very position she'd been in on the stage earlier in the evening. I slid in. I could feel her well-lubricated pussy grab at my dick. I pushed in deeper with each thrust, working up slowly to a rhythm and sliding in a little further each time. Within a minute I was sliding in and out, my hands grabbing her hips and pulling her back hard each time I exited. I was in deep and fully hard.

The view was incredible and a fantasy come true. Her sweet ass was spread for me. I could clearly see the starfish of her anus and the lips of her pussy grabbing and sliding on my fully engorged cock. Her ass cheeks bounced tightly with each thrust and she began to groan in rhythm to my thrusts.

"I love fucking you, Amber. I love sliding my cock deep into your pussy. I dreamed of doing this for years. Fuck!"

"Fuck me harder, Ronnie. Come on, fuck me with that big dick. Faster!"

And so I began to fuck her hard, real hard. I pounded my cock into her like there was no tomorrow. Our bodies were slapping together and the sounds of sex, the groans, the pounding of flesh, the heavy breathing, the shaking of the bed, all combined into a cacophony of sexual music. This girl loved to fuck and she liked it hard and she liked it fast.

I pulled her toward the edge of the bed so I could stand rather than kneel. Now I really got up a head of steam. Amber climbed up on all fours as I worked her as hard and fast as I could go. Our bodies became a blur. Her hair was flying every which way, her ass cheeks were bouncing from the fury of our motions and she pushed her ass back to meet each thrust. I began to slap her ass hard, first one side, then the other.

She loved it and told me to slap her harder. But I went back to fucking furiously. Sweat was pouring off me and I began to feel that familiar feeling welling up deep in my groin. Amber was moaning loudly.

"I'm going to come, Amber. I'm going to come in your pussy. Oh, fuck!"

"Yes!" Amber screamed.

I cried out as the first spurt of semen shot deep into her body, followed by another and another. I could feel Amber's pussy contracting strongly from her own orgasm as her spasms clenched my cock in a rhythmic display of sexual crescendo. We slowed down from our hectic pace, I pulled out of her soaked pussy and we both collapsed on the bed laughing.

"Oh my God, Ron. Fuck."

"Amber. Sweet Amber," I whispered in her ear. "Thank you, baby. That was unbelievable."

We cuddled together, spooned our bodies so her wonderful ass was pressed against my belly. I fondled her sweet breasts and kissed her delicate neck as we collected ourselves and laughed about the lunacy of the last hour. There was no place I would rather be at that moment.

We fucked twice more that night, and once more in the morning, before Amber headed back to school. We shared a naked room-service breakfast before she left and made plans to get together again in a few months.

And to think that I would never have known about her whereabouts if it hadn't been for my lunch with Jack. Just goes to show that tradition comes in handy sometimes. I drove back to Connecticut floating on a cloud and already planning my return to Providence.